ASSASSIN'S HOOD

Garrett Hutson

This book is a work of fiction. Aside from historical figures, names, characters, events, and places are the works of the author's imagination. Any resemblance to actual events, places, or persons living or dead is entirely coincidental.

Warfleigh Publishing first edition July 2019

Cover design by Steven Novak

For more information, or to book an event, please contact the author at www.garretthutson.com

ISBN 978-0-9982813-7-7 (paperback)
ISBN 978-0-9982813-6-0 (eBook)

For my father-in-law, Earl Lee, a bibliophile among bibliophiles. May the largest library in the universe show you all the books you'll ever want.

Hutson

1

Saturday, November 9, 1935

Douglas Bainbridge both loved and dreaded the arrival of a mail shipment from the United States. This morning's visit to the Shanghai Municipal Post Office provided two letters that had come on the steamship from San Francisco yesterday.

Sitting at a corner table at the Cantonese teahouse he frequented a few blocks from his apartment, Doug re-read the letter from his girlfriend, Lucy Kinzler, to reinforce his good mood before taking in the much briefer letter from his mother.

It was a beautiful fall day in Shanghai—November having finally brought an end to summer-like weather—and a fresh breeze blew through the large open windows that ran the length of two walls in the teahouse. It was in the upper sixties on the Fahrenheit scale, a relief after the stifling heat and humidity he had experienced for most of his first five and a half months in Shanghai. Plus, the pervasive sour stench that enveloped the city like a blanket diminished somewhat as the temperature moderated.

The letter from Lucy put a smile on his face, even with a second reading. The first had been before he left the post office, and was rushed. This time, he read slowly, savoring her words to him.

Before she'd left in August after a summer tour of Asia with her mother, Doug and Lucy promised to write to one another every other week, and they had kept that promise. It usually took three or four weeks for their letters to travel between Vassar in upstate New York,

1

and Shanghai, so she was always answering questions he'd asked her two letters ago, and vice versa.

He didn't mind a bit.

Finishing the letter, he didn't care that he had a big goofy grin on his face as he folded it and put it back in the envelope. He kept a stack of Lucy's letters in a dresser drawer in his bedroom.

"Good morning, Mr. Bainbridge!" a familiar friendly voice said to him in English, with a Chinese accent.

Doug looked up to see Li Baosheng—one of his next-door neighbors—coming into the teahouse. He waved to Doug, and Doug returned the wave.

"Good morning, Bao. How are you and Charlie this morning?"

"Charlie caught a sniffle yesterday, drank all the tea. I come to get more."

"I'm sorry to hear that," Doug said. "Tell him I hope he feels better soon."

"He's OK," Bao said with a laugh. "Just a little sniffle. He went to work little bit ago."

Charlie Ford, Doug's other next-door neighbor—Bao's lover—worked as a handyman at a Chinese theater downtown. He was English, forty-three years old, and one of the most genuinely nice people Doug had ever met. He hated hearing Charlie caught a cold, even a minor one.

He hoped he didn't catch it. He took a long drink of his Oolong tea. He shared the Chinese belief that tea was the best prevention, if not also the best cure.

Then he looked down at the envelope addressed to his full name—Douglas Preston Bainbridge—in his mother's stilted script, and decided to take another drink of tea for fortitude. He took a deep breath and tore open the seal.

It was brief—one page, front and back—and consisted of the barest details of news regarding family and old friends, followed by one of his mother's signature scoldings.

"In the most recent letter I received from Rev. Allen in Shanghai, he mentioned that he saw you 'on a few occasions.' This was after multiple inquiries to him, which he failed to answer in any but the vaguest of ways. It is clear to me that you have abandoned regular attendance at Sunday services, which causes me great consternation."

She continued on for a couple more sentences, mentioned that she would write again before Christmas, and signed "Cordially, Mother."

Doug sighed as he refolded the letter and put it back in the envelope. He was twenty-five years old, and capable of ignoring her admonitions—but it still got into his craw in a way that he couldn't stop.

He finished his tea, and contemplated where he might go for lunch.

Then the peace of a late Saturday morning was shattered by the loud crack of gunfire nearby, followed by screams.

Doug jumped from his chair, and put his head through the open window to look down the street in the direction the sound had come. It had seemed to come from the east—from Japantown.

The bustle of mid-day activity came to an eerie standstill, people standing in place and looking around. Shouts of confusion and concern on the street, mixed with nervous murmurs from the other patrons inside the teahouse, replaced the initial screams from a few blocks away.

"What do you see, Mr. Bainbridge?" Bao asked from behind him.

Doug pulled his head back inside, and turned to face his neighbor. The young man's eyes were wide, and Doug patted his shoulder to reassure him.

"Nothing within sight," Doug said. "I'd stay inside for a little while, though, just to be safe."

Rumors flew in multiple languages through the crowds on the street. Doug listened for snippets in Shanghainese or Mandarin.

"They're saying someone shot a Japanese man," Doug murmured to Bao, and kept listening. "Some say he was in a Japanese navy

3

uniform. And others are saying a store has been attacked on Wusong Road." He turned back to Bao and shook his head. "I don't think anyone really knows what's going on—some are saying there was one assassin, and others are saying a group of masked bandits sacked a Japanese store."

Shrill police whistles tore through the noise, and a pair of officers—one Chinese, one Indian in a bright red turban—went hurrying down the street, shoving crowds of pedestrians out of their way as they went. Doug heard other police whistles from the direction of Haining Road, a block to the north.

"I suppose it's safe to go home now," he said to Bao, and laid a few coins on the table next to his empty teacup. "I'll walk with you, if you'd like."

But Bao shook his head. "I have to go to the fish market in Yangtzepoo, get some to make *Geng* for dinner. You come for dinner tonight, Mr. Bainbridge?"

"Thanks Bao, but I have dinner plans with friends tonight. I hope the stew helps Charlie's sniffle."

"He be OK," Bao said with a grin.

"I'll walk with you as far as Wusong," Doug offered. Now that the police were there to take charge, he wanted to look around and satisfy his curiosity.

It was two blocks east to Wusong Road—until recently, the western boundary of Japantown, though of late the growing Japanese colony in Shanghai had spread to the west side of the road. This was a source of tension with the Chinese residents of the neighborhood west of Wusong.

As Doug and Bao drew close to the intersection with Wusong, angry shouts in Japanese rose above the noise of the crowd, and mixed with screams and shouts of protest in Chinese.

Doug put a protective arm across Bao's chest. "Wait here," he said, and hurried ahead to get a look.

Dozens of uniformed Japanese marines moved north up Wusong, swinging the butts of their rifles at Chinese pedestrians and clearing the road.

Doug stood on the sidewalk and craned his neck toward the north, where he could see several police officers keeping a tight perimeter a block away, at the busy intersection of Wusong and Haining Road. As the Japanese marines cleared the street, he got a better view, saw a pool of blood on the pavement, and glimpses of a body lying in the street.

Then he was startled by a loud shout in his ear, in Japanese. He jumped, and looked at the Japanese marine standing barely two feet in front of him, jabbing a finger toward his chest and shouting incomprehensible words.

"I don't understand," Doug said, first in Shanghainese, and then in English.

The Japanese marine shoved Doug's shoulder, glaring. Then he repeated whatever it was he had shouted a moment before.

Doug held up his hands. "Alright, alright," he said, backing away. The Japanese marine continued shouting at him, and gesturing angrily, until Doug was far enough away that he felt safe turning his back to him and hurrying back to where Bao waited.

"You're not going to the fish market today," Doug said, taking Bao by the arm and turning him back toward their neighborhood.

"What about the *Geng*? What will I do about dinner?"

"Try one of the grocers on Nanking Road," Doug suggested. "You can't cross Japantown right now, trust me."

An hour later, Doug answered a knock on his door, and was greeted by a young man in an American Express uniform.

"Telegram for Mr. Douglas Bainbridge," the young man said in English, with a Chinese accent.

5

"I'm Mr. Bainbridge," Doug said, and signed for the telegram. He gave the young man a dime, which elicited enthusiastic thanks.

Doug took pride in being a good tipper.

He closed his door and tore open the telegram.

VISITING SHANGHAI MONDAY, STOP
MEET FOR LUNCH NOON CATHAY, STOP
YOUR FRIEND, BOB

Doug was only mildly surprised to get the invitation. His next quarterly meeting with Commander Hilliard wasn't due for another two weeks, but he suspected today's shooting—and the Japanese reaction—might have something to do with the early visit.

**

He arrived at Velardi's Italian Restaurant at seven-thirty, and found his friends Kenneth and Abigail Traywick already waiting for him. He kissed Abbie on the cheek, then he and Kenny shook hands and patted each other's shoulder with their other hands.

"We hear there was some real excitement over 'round your neighborhood today, eh? A*boat* noon, was it?" Kenny said, his accent Canadian.

"That's one way to put it," Doug said. "As it happens, I was at the teahouse around the corner from my place when it happened, and the murder was only two blocks from there. I got a front-row seat to the panic in the street."

"It must have been terrifying!" Abbie said, fingering the pearl necklace around her neck, and looking at Doug with wide eyes. She was an attractive woman with wavy black hair cut just above the shoulders, and dark brown eyes, that both contrasted nicely with her pale white skin. She wore a burnt orange dress that hugged her curves.

Doug shook his head. "Not really. Not at first, anyway—I walked over to Wusong Road to get a better look, and Japanese marines were

6

clearing the street. One got in my face and started shouting at me in Japanese."

"Good lord!" Kenny said, mouth staying open. He was a very tall young man, six-foot-four, and thin like a bean-pole, with light brown hair cut short and parted on the right without brilliantine, and pale green eyes. His white dress shirt was baggy, and his black necktie was knotted high so that it hung low enough that it didn't look unnaturally short—which meant the back was too short to tuck into the band. "What did you do?"

"I left," Doug replied with a shrug.

"I'm glad you're safe," Abbie said, and stood on her toes to kiss his cheek. "You should be more careful."

Just then a portly middle-aged Italian man with bushy eyebrows and sideburns approached the host stand, and greeted them with a broad smile.

"Ah! Mr. and Mrs. Traywick, Mr. Bainbridge—so lovely to see you tonight. Your usual table? I'll have Gino bring you some Chianti, on the house, huh?"

"Thanks, Luigi," Kenny said, reaching out to shake the owner's hand. "That sounds marvelous."

Kenny and Abbie lived a block around the corner, on Soochow Road South, in a building that faced north overlooking Soochow Creek— which was actually a small river more than a hundred feet wide, lined with houseboats. They were regulars at Velardi's, on Honan Road just south of the bridge, and Luigi Velardi always made a point of taking good care of them.

"Did you get a good look at the victim?" Kenny asked after they'd been seated at a table by the window. "I mean, before the Jap marines shooed you away."

"Not really," Doug said. "I couldn't get close enough to see much. The police had formed a circle around him by then."

"The evening paper says the victim was in the Japanese Navy," Kenny said, a gossipy sort of smile curling up one corner of his mouth. "A Seaman First Class named Naka—Nakayama."

Doug let out a low whistle. "That explains the response from the Japanese marines."

"Two hundred of them!" Abbie said. "That's what Kenny read me from the paper."

"They were from the same ship as that Nakayama fellow," Kenny explained.

Doug shook his head. "It's awfully gutsy to attack a sailor from the Japanese Navy, right on the edge of Japantown. Foolhardy, even."

"This is our second year here, and I don't think there's been a single day since we arrived that there hasn't been a Japanese Navy ship of some sort docked in port," Abbie said.

"And usually more than one. Foolhardy is right, Doug." Kenny grinned and patted the side of Doug's arm.

"No matter what they took from that store, it wasn't worth the retaliation they'll get for shooting a Japanese sailor," Abbie said, shaking her head in wonder.

Doug somehow doubted that robbery was the motive, but he just nodded in agreement.

"I got a letter from Lucy today," he said, changing to a happier subject.

"That's wonderful," Abbie said, briefly touching Doug's hand on the tabletop. "I got a letter from her about three weeks ago, I think. How is she?"

Doug filled them in on everything Lucy had written. Almost everything, that is. He kept the more intimate romantic notions to himself.

"I'm so glad she's coming back," Abbie said as the waiter set a giant wooden bowl of antipasto salad in front of them, and began tossing it.

"The four of us had such fun while she was here this summer. And the two of you are really adorable together."

Doug felt himself blush, and he covered it by taking a drink of wine.

Doug had first met Kenny and Abbie Traywick at a swanky cocktail party at the Sassoon House in June. It was not a particularly fun evening for Doug—he'd nearly been shot by their host, whom he learned had murdered his friend Tim McIntyre the week before—so he barely remembered Kenny when he ran into him on a street corner downtown a couple of weeks later.

But Kenny remembered him—enthusiastically, in fact—and invited Doug to dine with them at Velardi's. Doug thought, 'why not?' and accepted the invitation. He ended up hitting it off with both of them, and the three of them spent hours talking and laughing over multiple carafes of Chianti, until they were the last patrons in the restaurant.

By the time Lucy returned to Shanghai at the beginning of August from her travels around East Asia, Doug was excited to introduce her to his new best friends, and thrilled that she and Abbie hit it off so well. The four of them went out dancing almost every other night for the next two weeks, before Lucy had to return to the States with her mother.

"This probably sounds silly, but sometimes it's hard to believe it's only been three months since she left," Abbie continued. "Or that we only knew her for a couple of weeks before then."

Doug smiled. "I know what you mean. Not silly at all." He hadn't really known Lucy much longer than that himself. And yet it sometimes felt like she'd been part of his life forever.

It was after nine-thirty when they left the restaurant, and parted company at the corner. Doug kissed Abbie's cheeks and shook Kenny's hand, then crossed the bridge out of downtown and into the Hongkou district. It was only a half-mile walk home from Velardi's, so he ignored the street car as it went past, clanging up Honan Road.

On the other side of Soochow Creek, the Temple of the Queen of Heaven was dark and silent on his right, but there were plenty of people on the sidewalks along Honan Road, mostly westerners returning home. The side streets were quiet as he approached his building, with only the hint of conversations in Shanghainese coming from the open windows above him.

He spotted a police constable strolling down Huang Lei Road, and caught up with him just before reaching his building.

"Good evening, Billy," he greeted, and fell into step beside him for the rest of the short distance to his door.

"Oh! Good evening, Mr. Bainbridge, sir," Constable Billy Dickinson said in his thick working-class English accent, touching the rim of his police hat.

"Are things tense at your precinct tonight, after the shooting in Japantown today?"

"Yes, a bit," the young constable said with a nod. "Very nice of you to ask, sir."

"Have they caught the killers?" Doug asked.

"Not yet, but they will," Billy said. "The Japanese consul insisted only Japanese detectives work the case. Our captain didn't like that bit of interference at all."

"I can imagine not." Doug stopped at the front door of his building.

"Don't worry, Mr. Bainbridge, sir," Billy said with a grin as he kept walking. "Me and Constable Patel are on patrol tonight, and we'll keep the neighborhood safe. Those killers won't stay at large for long, in any case. Good night, sir."

"Good night, Billy." Doug unlocked the front door and headed up the stairs.

Monday, November 11

The English maître'd at the Cathay Hotel downtown informed Doug that Mr. Hilliard had already arrived, and led him to a booth in the back corner, partially hidden by a potted palm.

"Sorry for the short notice," Hilliard said as Doug shook his hand.

Commander Robert Hilliard was an Assistant Naval Attaché at the U.S. Embassy in Nanking, but when he came to meet with Doug every three months, he wore a civilian suit, and shook hands rather than accept a salute.

"I don't mind," Doug said, taking a seat. "I assume this has something to do with the shooting of that Japanese sailor on Saturday."

"That's correct," Hilliard said. He paused as the Chinese waiter approached their table and bowed. They ordered lunch in Shanghainese, and the waiter bowed before departing.

"I also assume the shooting had nothing to do with robbery," Doug said after the waiter left. "That sailor was assassinated, wasn't he?"

"We believe so," Hilliard said, nodding. "Do you remember the August First Declaration?"

Doug was surprised. "The communists?"

Hilliard nodded, his expression grave.

On August 1 of that year, at the Seventh World Congress of the Comintern in Moscow, the Chinese Communist Party Central Committee issued a declaration calling for a "National United Front" for resistance against the Japanese in China. It called on the ruling *Kuomintang*—the Chinese Nationalist Party—to end the civil war and unite with them against the Japanese.

"So you think Nakayama was assassinated by the communists, as part of their 'national resistance' to the Japanese?"

"That's what we're hearing," Hilliard said.

"From government officials?"

Hilliard nodded.

Doug took a second to ponder that. "But why attack a Seaman First Class? Why not an officer?"

"Testing the waters, perhaps."

A puzzle piece seemed to fall into place as Doug thought of the two hundred Japanese Marines who had secured Japantown within fifteen minutes of the shooting. "An experiment, to test the Japanese reaction."

Hilliard nodded. "And they got what they wanted. The Japanese reaction was swift, strong, and readily observable—and yet, the assassins got away."

"So a pretty successful experiment," Doug said.

Hilliard fell silent, and leaned back as the Chinese waiter returned with their bowls of soup and cups of tea. Hilliard thanked him in Shanghainese, and the waiter bowed and backed away.

"When we met in August, and you filled me in on your first three months here," Hilliard said, and blew on a spoonful of steaming soup. "You mentioned that the shop girl who works in Mr. Hwang's store— Wong Mei-ling—is part of a communist cell that meets at a Sichuan restaurant in your neighborhood."

Doug was surprised at the specificity of Hilliard's recall. "Yes, that's right."

"How well do you know her?"

Doug shrugged. "A little bit. Not very well, really. We chat sometimes when I drop off or pick up laundry."

"But you're friendly with her," Hilliard said. It wasn't posed as a question.

"Yes."

"You think it's possible you might befriend her?"

Doug shrugged again, thinking of that day in June when she'd walked him home from the Old City, and the hostile things she'd had to say. "I'm not really sure she'd be open to a real friendship with a westerner."

"Give it a try, she might surprise you," Hilliard said, and then chuckled. "You're a good-looking fellow, Bainbridge, and you're blond— use your charms."

Doug had to resist rolling his eyes at the suggestion. Though, if he were being honest, he had actually tried that his first week in Shanghai, before he and Lucy got serious. And Mei Ling had shown him nothing but reticence.

"I'll see what I can do, sir."

"Good. Once you two have gotten friendlier, she might open up about what she knows of her party's plans for 'National Resistance.' And then you pass that information on to me."

The very idea made Doug uncomfortable—not to mention how laughably unlikely the whole scenario was.

"I didn't think ONI engaged in cloak-and-dagger tactics."

"Not what I meant at all," Hilliard said, a brief scowl crossing his face. "But we do sometimes use information gleaned from local sources."

"Local *naval* sources," Doug said. He realized he was arguing with a superior officer, and hastily added, "Sir."

Hilliard scowled again, and this time it stayed on his face longer. "Yes, naval sources, primarily—but also manufacturing sources. And sometimes others. This is just a slight expansion of that."

But this would be more clandestine, and that's new, Doug thought. "And I should keep this just between us, of course."

"Of course."

Hilliard's expression grew very serious, and he leaned as far forward as the table would allow. He continued quietly, "You should know that this is the future of our operations in East Asia. This is highly classified, understand—but for the last two months a Marine Corps major has been in Shanghai, posing as a retired officer, recruiting a network of Chinese agents in the International Settlement who can travel in and out of Japan and report back on the movements of the Japanese fleet.

"I can't tell you the identity of the Major. I want you to know of his existence, though, so you can understand that what I'm asking you to do with Miss Wong is no different on a tactical level than what we recently started doing here."

Doug felt his heart skip a beat, and his stomach flutter. "I understand, sir. Thank you for your confidence in me."

They spent the rest of lunch talking in general about Doug's experiences in Shanghai since their last meeting in late August. Hilliard was pleased with the way Doug's immersion was going, and told him he was doing a fine job.

When they left a while later, Hilliard stopped to shake his hand by the elevator. "As usual, if you have anything you need to discuss—or any new information for me—just call the embassy and leave me a message. Otherwise, I'll set up another lunch in three months."

As Doug walked through the cavernous lobby of the Cathay Hotel toward the front door, a deep voice called his name from behind, in a flat Midwestern accent.

"Doug Bainbridge! I thought that was you."

Doug turned around to see a stocky man in his early forties approaching from the bar, bowler hat in his hand. He had neatly combed brown hair, and a thick brown mustache. His round cheeks were dimpled with a hint of a smile.

"Been a little while since I've seen you here," the man said.

"How are you, Jonesy," Doug said, shaking the man's hand.

"Can't complain. The weather's finally turned, plus I've been getting some good stories lately."

Art Jones—known as Jonesy to almost everyone—was a reporter for the Associated Press, and had been best friends with Tim McIntyre. Doug had disliked him at first, but Jonesy was with Doug that fateful night at the Sassoon House in June, and killed Tim's murderer in a shoot-out.

That earned him Doug's respect, and perhaps even a bit of admiration. Now they were friendly whenever they saw one another. That was not as often as one might expect, given that the bar at the Cathay was Jonesy's usual lunchtime haunt.

"Meeting with Commander Hilliard?" Jonesy asked, his voice quieter.

"That's right." Doug was still uncomfortable that Jonesy knew his connection with ONI—Office of Naval Intelligence—but it had been more than five months, and nothing bad had come of that.

"I'll bet he wanted to talk about the murder of that Japanese sailor over the weekend," Jonesy said, keeping his voice low. "That was over by your place, I understand—get a good look?"

Doug tried to act nonchalant. "Not really. The police got the scene under control pretty quickly, and then those Japanese marines kept everyone else from getting close."

"Yeah, how about that?" Jonesy said, with a curious gleam in his green eyes. "Unusual reaction, wouldn't you say?"

Doug shrugged. "The victim was one of their ship's men."

"But they stayed onshore for most of the weekend, keeping Japantown locked down tight."

Doug didn't say anything.

"I won't pry," Jonesy said with a wink. "I know your conversations are secret. Just maybe throw me a bone every now and again? For old times' sake?"

Doug allowed himself a friendly smile. "We'll see. Nice to see you again, Jonesy." He shook the reporter's hand.

"Always a pleasure to see you, Mr. Bainbridge," Jonesy said with a twinkle in his eye. Then he winked as he turned away.

Doug hated when Jonesy did things like that.

Hutson

2

Thursday, November 14

It was several days before Doug had a reason to enter Mr. Hwang's shop and drop off some laundry. Wong Mei-ling was sweeping the floor when he entered with his basket heaped with clothes. She gave him a polite bow of her head, set the broom against the wall, and walked behind the counter.

"Good afternoon, Miss Wong," he said in Shanghainese, giving her a bigger grin than he actually felt.

"Mr. Bainbridge. How many today?"

He itemized the laundry, and she jotted it on the sales slip. When she had finished, she gathered it in her arms and dropped it in an empty hamper.

"It will be ready tomorrow, around noon."

"Thank you," Doug said with a bow of his head. Then he lingered, and she stared at him dispassionately, waiting. "How are you?"

A curious look crossed her dark eyes for a second, and then her expression went blank again. "I am well."

He noticed she didn't ask how he was. "I know my actions caused you difficulty some months ago," he began, and paused to gauge her reaction. Seeing none at all, he proceeded. "I can't apologize enough, and I know I can't undo any scrutiny that I brought on you because of it—but I hope you'll let me try to make it up to you somehow."

"That is unnecessary."

He forced a smile, and leaned against the counter in a friendly, casual sort of way. "I appreciate your graciousness. I would like an opportunity to get to know you personally. We see each other several times a week, and yet we hardly know each other. I wonder if we might even become friends. That would be nice, wouldn't it?"

Seeing no reaction, he flashed his baby brown eyes at her in the flirty sort of way he'd seen American girls do countless times. He felt a little silly.

"I have friends already," she said, but he detected a touch of hesitation in her gaze, and the bravado in her tone might have been forced.

"That's good," Doug said, making his smile as broad as possible. "But one can never have too many friends."

He thought of Lucy, and for a second he felt a pang of guilt. Then he scolded himself for that—this was just flirting, after all; and for a good reason at that. Lucy would understand.

Mei-ling watched him for a few seconds with an odd look in her eyes, as if she were searching him for sincerity, and not finding confirmation either way.

"I could not be friends with an American capitalist," she whispered, then turned toward the laundry hampers behind the counter, and carried one into the back.

For a second, Doug wondered if he might pretend to be a secret socialist. But he dismissed the thought; he didn't know how to play that role convincingly. If he needed to observe a mentor, the only one he could think of was Jonesy.

No, thank you. I'll come up with something else.

Doug sighed, and went back upstairs. He climbed slowly, turning the conversation over in his mind, trying to find something he could have said or done differently—or some hint of an opening that he could exploit next time.

Nothing came to him.

His first instinct had been correct—she would never trust him enough to let him in on any secrets. She would never trust him enough to even let him get close. There was no hope that he could persuade her to tell him anything at all about the workings of the Communist Party in Shanghai.

He let himself back into his apartment, and started boiling water for tea. As he worked, a thought jumped into his head.

Jonesy had covered the labor movement in Detroit for sixteen years, had said he knew plenty of Socialists and Communists over the years. Could *he* get the information Doug needed for Hilliard?

Doug groaned, already knowing the answer.

Friday, November 15

Doug found Jonesy sitting at the bar in the Cathay Hotel the next day at noon, as expected, his hat on the bar next to a half-full martini glass.

Doug took the seat next to him. "Hi, Jonesy."

"Well, look what the cat dragged in," Jonesy said with a surprised half-smile. "Second time in a week. What brings this good luck my way?"

Doug couldn't help a small chuckle at Jonesy's jocular tone. "I'm looking for some information, and thought you might be able to help me get it."

Jonesy grunted. "Ah, I see. Yeah, I probably can. I'll tell you what— buy my lunch, and I'll listen to your proposition."

Doug was uncomfortable hearing the word 'proposition' come from Jonesy's mouth, though he knew he shouldn't be. It was a gut reaction. He took a deep breath and focused on the purpose of the impromptu meeting.

"You've probably guessed this is about that assassination on Saturday—Seaman First Class Hideo Nakayama."

"I wasn't born yesterday."

Doug suppressed his annoyance. He glanced around to make sure no one was close, and continued in a low voice. "We have reason to believe Chinese communists are behind the attack. The first exercise under their August First Declaration. But we don't know for certain."

Jonesy stroked his chin, looking up in thought. "Interesting," he murmured. "Entirely plausible, too. Truth is, I'd wondered the same thing—and you'll be happy to know I have some information that you probably don't."

Of course Jonesy would've already started asking questions. It's the first thing a reporter would do. The question was the quality of Jonesy's sources. "What did you learn?"

"Let's order food first, then we'll talk." Jonesy raised his hand, and the young Chinese bartender came over right away.

"Another martini, Mista Jonesy?"

"Yes, and a chicken salad on wheat. This guy's paying for both of us." He pointed his thumb at Doug.

"Same sandwich, but with tea." After the bartender departed, he looked at Jonesy with a scowl. "*Two* martinis? In the middle of the day?"

Jonesy shrugged. "Ordinarily I'd only have one at lunch—but this is a special occasion."

Yeah, because I'm paying. "OK, food's ordered, let's talk. What have you learned?"

Jonesy drained the last of his first martini, and shoved the glass aside. "First off, my sources wouldn't tell me anything at all about Nakayama, which is telling. Very tight-lipped, and after all these months they trust me about as much as they'd trust any outsider."

This caught Doug by surprise. "You've had sources inside a communist cell for *months*?" he whispered.

Jonesy gave him an annoyed side-glance as his second martini arrived.

"Yes—ever since we saw them in that Szechuan restaurant the night of Tim's funeral."

Doug's gut clenched. That had been his fault. He dined with Jonesy and Gladys Sherman, the secretary at the Associated Press Shanghai office, after Tim McIntyre's funeral on June 1, when Wong Mei-Ling entered and joined a group of gray-clad university students at a back table; it was the same scenario Doug had witnessed the week before, on his first night in Shanghai, and so he said something out loud. Jonesy made the connection that they were a communist cell, having seen that before from his work covering labor unions.

"Is Wong Mei-Ling one of your sources?" Doug hadn't meant his tone to sound so sharp, but it slipped out that way.

Jonesy snorted. "You know I can't reveal my sources. I've gone to jail for that before, you think I'm going to cave for you? I don't think so. You're not *that* pretty."

Doug ignored the jab, with effort. *You doth protest too much, Jonesy.* The thought popped into his mind unbidden before he could slam the door on it.

"But you think your sources were tight-lipped because they weren't saying what they knew, and not that they just didn't know anything?"

"That's right," Jonesy said, and paused while the bartender brought their sandwiches on porcelain plates. "I know how to read people pretty well, you know. Inevitable when you've been in this business as long as I have. They knew something, and they weren't telling, not for anything. Which means what they know is big—plenty big enough to be scared to reveal it, even to a sympathetic guy like me."

"They seemed scared?"

Jonesy shrugged. "Yeah, but also resolute. They're a pretty disciplined bunch, the Reds. I'd be lying if I said there wasn't fear underneath their resolution, though."

Doug took a moment to digest that. "If you're right, that all but confirms the communists were behind the attack."

"Yeah, probably. Now eat your sandwich; you're too skinny to skip lunch."

Doug ignored him. Something was bothering him—when Jonesy had referred to himself as a 'sympathetic guy.' Just how sympathetic?

"Just between you and me—are you a communist, Jonesy?"

Jonesy snorted again, loudly this time. He shook his head and wiped his mouth with his napkin. "No, I've never been a commie. I was a member of the American Socialist Party for almost twenty years, though—and as far as these sources know, I still am—but I switched to the Democrats about three years ago. I voted for Roosevelt, and I'll vote for him again next year."

"I had to be sure."

Jonesy fixed him with an icy stare. "Why? Would my information be less credible if I was? So then, how about the credibility of my sources, since they're reds? What's the point of asking my help if you're going to question my reliability?"

Doug put his hands up. "Calm down, that's not what I meant at all. It's just that I have to pass along to my superiors at Nanjing what I learn, so you can understand I'll be asked to vouch for my source—you."

"And you couldn't vouch for a commie," Jonesy said, bitterly, and popped the last of his sandwich in his mouth. "Trust me—I'm no fan of the Soviets. Not that it makes any difference. The only thing you Republican types hate more than a socialist is a communist."

That stung, though Doug wasn't sure why. "I'm not a Republican," he protested, sounding more defensive than he would have liked.

Jonesy gave him an incredulous look. "Don't tell me you didn't vote for Hoover in '32."

"I didn't vote for Hoover."

"Oh come on—you expect me to believe *you* voted for Roosevelt? You, a rich boy?"

It had been a long time since Jonesy had insulted him by calling him a 'rich boy,' and Doug didn't expect the hurt feelings that conjured.

"I lived in the District of Columbia in '32—so I didn't get to vote for president."

"That's convenient," Jonesy said with a frown, and took a swig of his martini.

"For the record, I wouldn't have voted for Hoover in any case, even if I'd lived in California," Doug said, not sure why he was defending himself. "Not that it's any of your business how I vote."

"Uh huh." Jonesy swallowed the last of his martini and picked up his brown bowler hat from the bar. "You know how much I love our little tête-à-têtes, Douglas, but I have an appointment with a source for another story. Thanks for lunch." He shoved his hat on his head and turned away.

"Will you let me know if you learn anything useful?" Doug asked, louder than he would have liked, but necessary to get Jonesy's attention as he started to leave.

Jonesy stared at him for several seconds, his green eyes narrowed. "We'll see."

Thursday, November 28

Doug looked at his watch in irritation as he waited outside the doors of the American Club on Foo Chow Road downtown. Almost ten minutes past two o'clock. He had forgotten that Jonesy was always late.

He'd received a telegram from Jonesy yesterday afternoon, asking him to call his home phone. Doug didn't have a telephone in his apartment, so he went downstairs to Mr. Hwang's store, and paid him a nickel to use his office phone.

"I got some information for you," Jonesy said. "You're going to owe me big for this."

"What is it?"

"Not over the phone line—let's meet in person. Are you getting Thanksgiving dinner somewhere tomorrow?"

"Yes."

"Where?"

Doug took a deep breath, trying not to get irritated. "Downtown—at the American Club."

"The American Club, huh? Fancy. Can't say I've ever been. Not surprised you sprang for a membership, though."

"You want to meet me downtown before dinner?" Doug asked.

"No, you're taking me as your guest," Jonesy said. "What time is dinner?"

Doug felt his gut tighten at the presumptuousness. For a second, he considered refusing—but, he had gotten nowhere trying to get anything out of Wong Mei-Ling. He needed Jonesy's information, no matter how big or small it might be.

And he'd implied it was big. *It had better be, if I'm buying him Thanksgiving dinner.*

"Two o'clock, sharp," Doug said at last.

"I'll be there."

But he wasn't. Doug resisted the urge to pace the sidewalk in front of the building, but his breath came shallow and fast as his irritation rose.

Then he spotted Jonesy's stocky figure coming down the sidewalk from the direction of Thibet Road, with the familiar swaggering step. Not even hurrying.

"I said two o'clock *sharp*," Doug said as Jonesy approached.

"Relax, don't be so uptight. I'm sure they haven't run out of turkey. Can they even get turkey in China?"

Doug felt his face flush. He was *not* uptight, damn it. "Yes, they have turkey. They're serving a traditional American Thanksgiving feast, with all of the usual dishes."

"Swell, then! I haven't had a good turkey dinner in years." He followed Doug inside the building.

Doug stopped at the concierge stand. "Douglas Bainbridge and one guest, here for the Thanksgiving dinner."

"Sixth floor sir, right that way," said the concierge, a thin white-haired American man of about sixty. "It's just off the elevator."

"This is fancy, just like I thought," Jonesy muttered as they crossed the marble floor toward the brass door of the elevator. He looked around at the mahogany paneling on the walls, and nodded appreciatively. "Was it hard to become a member?" he asked as Doug pushed the elevator call button.

"I had a sponsor," Doug said. His friends Peter Tolbert and George Howerton, whom he met last summer through Kenny and Abbie Traywick, were members of the American Club, and offered to sponsor him.

"Ah, a friend of yours? Will we see him here?"

Doug shook his head. "No, I assumed you wanted to meet privately, and speak confidentially."

He didn't admit that Pete's wife Julia had organized a fancy dinner party of her own for Thanksgiving—but it was "just for couples, Douglas." Her words.

"I didn't tell you to break plans with anyone else," Jonesy said. "We only need to speak privately for a little while."

Doug found that he couldn't argue with Jonesy's assertion. He in fact had not specifically said to break plans.

Not that Doug would admit to Jonesy that he hadn't had any plans to break.

The elevator arrived, mercifully, and they stopped talking as they stepped into the car. A middle-aged Chinese elevator operator bowed his head as Doug requested the sixth floor.

The grand dining room was packed with Americans of both sexes enjoying Thanksgiving dinner. Ordinarily, the American Club of Shanghai was a men-only establishment, but on a few occasions—such as Thanksgiving and Christmas—they allowed members to bring their wives or fiancées to dinner.

Doug wished Lucy were here with him. Instead, he was dining with Jonesy.

"I have a reservation for two, please," Doug told the maître'd. "Douglas Bainbridge."

"Yes, Mr. Bainbridge, we had begun to wonder if you were still coming," the maître'd said, his accent a posh New York lockjaw. "Fortunately, we haven't yet given away the table. This way, please."

Doug flashed a scowl Jonesy's way as they followed the tuxedo-clad maître'd to a small table along the wall.

"This is good," Jonesy said as they sat and put their napkins in their laps. "Crowded and loud—no one will hear a word we're saying."

"So what's your information?" Doug asked.

"Straight to business, huh? Alright, have it your way. I've placed some inquiries in many places. None of the communists I know here in Shanghai are saying a word—and in fact, they've stopped talking to me now, thank you very much."

"Sorry," Doug muttered.

Jonesy waved it off. "Don't worry about it. I'll get back in their good graces eventually. They know the value of having a friendly liaison in the press. Anyway, next I went to my friends at the embassy in Nanking—I mentioned last summer that a friend of mine in the embassy provided some of the information about those *Juntong* fellas you saw killed, and about their boss, Wu Shan. You remember."

Doug nodded. He remembered well. He had gotten himself entangled with a beautiful and refined Chinese woman named Ming Lin-Wen, only to learn from Jonesy that she was married to a captain of the Chinese secret police—the *Juntong*—named Wu Shan.

Jonesy continued without seeming to notice Doug's discomfort. "My friends also confirmed that the communists are keeping total silence on the subject of Seaman First Class Nakayama—which we all agree is proof they're responsible. They'd have *something* to say, otherwise. Needless to say, none of them were surprised that no killer has been found, after more than three weeks. We take *that* as a sign the Reds did it too—no one else would be so careful. Well, almost no one."

Doug scowled. "Please tell me that's not all you've got."

Jonesy chuckled. "Don't be sour, I'm getting to it. While I was at it, asking them about the Reds and the Nakayama assassination, I decided to ask them about some rumors I've heard." He stared at Doug hard, his green eyes unblinking.

Doug stared back for several seconds, but then looked away, uncomfortable.

"Do you want to come clean, or do I have to ask you about Nagasaki?"

Doug looked back at Jonesy, confused. "I've never been to Nagasaki." He'd never even been to Japan.

Jonesy chortled, but fell silent as a young Chinese man filled their water glasses, bowed, and departed.

"No, you haven't—but I heard through the grapevine that an American is recruiting Chinese nationals to take trips to Nagasaki, and watch the Japanese navy there. Then when they return to Shanghai, they conveniently pass along everything they saw to this American. Relax—I know you're not him; they said he's older, retired military. Ha, 'retired' my foot. But you know all about it."

Doug looked around. In fact, he knew little. For all he knew, ONI's new man in Shanghai could be dining in this very club, at this very moment.

"Alright—off the record, if you'd prefer." Jonesy said.

Doug scowled at him. "I thought this meeting was for you to give *me* information, not the other way around."

"It is, but you've got to earn it."

"I'm buying you your damned Thanksgiving dinner."

Jonesy chuckled. "That's true. Fine, have it your way. I thought we could scratch each other's backs, as they say, but we'll play by your rules. I learned from my friends at the Embassy that this new ONI operative in Shanghai—and don't worry, they don't know who it is, or at least they say they don't, and I believe them—this fella met with Dai Li himself in Nanking a couple of months back. And apparently, the dreaded Dai Li has visited your man here in Shanghai on at least one occasion."

Dai Li was one of the most feared men in China—the head of the dreaded Commission of Clandestine Investigation, the parent organization that included the *Juntong*. His name—a *nom de guerre* he had chosen himself, actually—meant a black assassin's hood in Mandarin.

And it was said he had earned that moniker.

Jonesy leaned back in his chair and searched Doug's face. "You didn't know any of that, did you?"

Doug's mouth had gone dry. He shook his head and swallowed hard. "No."

Jonesy tapped his chin with his finger, but stayed silent.

"So why have you told me this, Jonesy? What is your point?"

Jonesy took a long, deep breath, and released it slowly, audibly. He looked up as if in thought for a moment. "I don't know—but I suspect your people at Naval Intelligence are playing both ends against the middle here."

"What do you mean?"

Jonesy shrugged. "Not entirely sure—but isn't it interesting that your boss asked you to check up on the communists, while someone else in your organization, right here in the same damn city, is chummy with the head of Nationalist government security?"

"I never said I was asked to check up on the communists," Doug said.

Jonesy chuckled again. "Fine, deny it. But for what other reason would your boss have come into town right after Nakayama's assassination to meet with you; and right after that you come find me to ask about the Reds? I ain't stupid, you know."

"I'm not denying anything," Doug said.

The waiter came by then, a young American with thick brown hair and dark, bushy eyebrows, carrying two plates piled with sliced turkey, dressing, mashed potatoes and gravy, green beans, candied yams, and cranberry sauce.

Jonesy rubbed his hands together, an eager grin on his face. "Enough business, let's eat."

Wednesday, December 25

"Here, let me show you, Douglas," Charlie Ford said, taking the tube of brightly colored paper and twisting the ends. There was a pop, and he opened it into a paper crown, while a small strip of paper and a tiny toy fell out onto the table. "Happy Christmas!" His accent was working class English, with heavily bent vowels.

He put the paper crown over his thinning and graying light brown hair, as Li Baosheng did the same, grinning.

Doug pulled the ends of his paper tube, and after the pop a little toy compass fell onto the table beside his plate. He picked up the slip of paper, read the words on it, and groaned at the corny joke.

"No, you have to read it out loud," Charlie said, a crooked smile on his lips. "But here, you have to wear your crown first." He put the crown onto Doug's head and nodded in satisfaction.

Doug felt a touch silly with the thin paper crown on his head, but his hosts were wearing theirs, so he put it out of his mind and read the awful joke out loud. Bao laughed, Charlie laughed at Bao, and Doug found himself laughing at both of them. Charlie and Bao each read the jokes on their slips, and by the time they finished they were all laughing.

"Now we can eat," Charlie said. He stood, carving knife in hand, and began slicing the breast of the roasted goose on a silver platter. "You don't know how difficult it is to find a goose in Shanghai for

Christmas dinner, Douglas—and completely impossible to find a turkey, so I hope you don't mind a more traditional English Christmas."

"I look forward to it, and thank you again for including me."

"Don't mention it, glad to have you, mate."

The holiday season had an almost surreal feel to Doug this year, his first in China. In San Francisco and Washington D.C., he'd been accustomed to seeing elaborate Christmas displays in store windows, and decorations on every building and many houses. Here, only a few stores downtown that catered to a western clientele had Christmas displays, and these were modest. The Chinese neighborhoods and shops went on with day-to-day business as usual. And while church bells had pealed on Christmas Eve—Doug had attended candlelight service at the Presbyterian Church at eleven PM—it hadn't seemed that the city rang with their music. And this morning, out his window the neighborhood activity continued as if it were an ordinary Wednesday—which it was to most of Shanghai's residents.

At least it didn't feel as strange as Thanksgiving had, with only the American community observing a holiday while their fellow westerners went about their daily routines. But he'd at least expected that. He wasn't sure why he hadn't anticipated the muted response to Christmas, given that more than three quarters of the people living in the International Settlement and French Concession were Chinese.

"There you are," Charlie said as he put a thick slice of goose meat onto Doug's plate. "I wish we had mashed potatoes to go with it, but you can't find a potato in a Shanghai grocery. So we've got rice instead. You'll get used to that after a few years. At least I'm always able to find cranberries downtown, and Bao made the sauce."

"Everything looks wonderful," Doug said, dishing up the roasted vegetables—carrots, turnips and parsnips.

Charlie gave the spread an appreciative nod as he retook his seat and tucked his napkin under his chin. "Not one hundred percent traditional, but a close enough facsimile, I think." He raised his glass of red wine, and toasted, "Happy Christmas to one and all, and a very happy new year to come."

"Cheers!" Doug said, tapping his wine glass against Charlie's, and then Bao's.

"What's on the horizon for you in the new year, Douglas?" Charlie asked as he cut up his meat.

Doug looked up in thought as he chewed his meat, not sure what he could say. "I'm sure I'll have projects to work on at the office, but I can't say what at this point. The one thing I'm looking forward to the most is my girlfriend Lucy returning from the States at the beginning of the summer—for good this time."

"How lovely," Charlie said. "I'd begun to wonder if that was still on."

Doug cocked his head in surprise. "Oh? Why did you wonder that?"

Charlie looked embarrassed, and a sheepish half-smile crossed his lips as he blushed. "Well, you hadn't mentioned her in a while, and I couldn't help but notice you started spending a lot of time chatting with Miss Wong in the laundry shop downstairs." He shrugged, looking uncomfortable.

"There's nothing between me and Miss Wong."

Doug noticed a strange look cross Bao's face.

Charlie turned beet red. "Oh! I didn't mean to imply that you were doing anything *wrong*. Not at all, believe me. I just wondered if your plans with Miss Kinzler had fallen through, and that's why you were spending time getting to know Miss Wong. Oh dear, I'm putting this badly, aren't I? I didn't mean anything, really I didn't."

Doug couldn't help but smile at Charlie's awkward apology. Of course they'd noticed—in retrospect he'd been pretty obvious. But he'd had to be, or it wouldn't have been believable.

"Don't mention it. It's quite alright."

Charlie looked relieved. "Most kind of you, Douglas."

31

Bao looked confused. Charlie asked him if everything was alright. "Yes, I'm sorry. I thought what you thought, that all."

Doug faked a big grin. "Well! I guess I'd better be more careful with appearances. I wouldn't want the whole neighborhood thinking there was anything untoward going on."

Charlie nodded. "One does have to be mindful of appearances, even in Shanghai." He glanced at Bao, and Doug thought he detected a hint of sadness in his eyes.

Doug wondered, not for the first time, how safe Charlie and Bao actually felt, living together in a one-bedroom apartment. Not that they ever said anything to anyone about being a couple, of course, and never showed any affection in front of anyone—but it still wasn't difficult to put two and two together and come up with four.

Charlie owned a gun—he'd had to use it one night when the three of them were in an alley behind some sailors' taverns in Yangtzepoo, interviewing some boys who met with Tim McIntyre before he was killed. He said then that someone in their position couldn't be too cautious.

And it was worth noting that they didn't have any other friends over for Christmas dinner.

What a lonely life it must be. They sacrificed everything to be together. He scolded himself for thinking the obstacles he and Lucy had to overcome were high, given the distance and the ocean between them.

"It will be very busy when Lucy arrives," he said, changing the subject. "I'll have to help her find an apartment, a job—she's not familiar enough with the city yet, having only been here twice. But we're very excited for it."

"Ah, to be young and starting a new life!" Charlie said, a wistful look in his gray-blue eyes. "I was nearly forty when I came to live here in Shanghai, and it was very exciting—but I remember how thrilling it was when I was seventeen and ran off to sea, starting a whole new life for meself, whatever I wanted. And how fortunate for Miss Kinzler that she doesn't have to do it alone."

Doug couldn't agree more. It had been lonely when he moved to Washington D.C. after college, not knowing anyone there. And not fitting in well with his colleagues, either.

"Lucy likes my best friends, too, and that helps a lot," Doug said. "They're looking forward to seeing her back here."

"That's wonderful, Douglas." A genuine gleam of pleasure lit up Charlie's eyes. "We'd love to get to know her, if that's a right with you, that is."

"Of course."

"Did you get each other anything for Christmas?" Charlie asked. "I know that's probably difficult, being halfway around the world from each other."

Doug lit up. "Yes, actually—she sent me a thick wool scarf and a nice pair of gloves. The package arrived a week ago, but I waited until this morning to open it. It's a shame—I could have used them last weekend when we had that sleet."

"It'll get cold yet," Charlie said.

"It always snow in January," Bao added.

"And what did you get Miss Kinzler for Christmas?"

"I got her a couple of books," Doug said. He hesitated to admit that one of them was a mystery, but Lucy enjoyed those. "Both British books, actually—*National Velvet* by Enid Bagnold, and *Gaudy Night* by Dorothy Sayers."

Charlie's face lit up. "Ah, Peter Wimsey! I've read a few of her Wimsey mysteries, and I enjoy them very much. Are you a fan of Lord Peter Wimsey? Or do you prefer Mrs. Christie's Inspector Hercule Poirot?"

"I actually prefer Hemingway, Fitzgerald, or Steinbeck," Doug said. A mischievous smile crossed his lips. "I considered sending her *Green Hills of Africa*, Hemingway's latest—she detests Hemingway, and it would have been something of a joke—but I thought better of it and instead sent her books I knew she'd enjoy."

"Wise choice I think," Charlie said with a wink. "She might not have seen the humor in your jest."

Doug wondered—Lucy had an excellent sense of humor, and they'd always joked with each other during the weeks they'd spent together last summer—but Christmas hardly seemed the time to test the limits of her good humor.

Especially with an ocean between them and no way to readily explain himself.

Doug was stuffed by the time they finished dinner, and could feel himself growing drowsy—either from the full stomach, or the two glasses of wine. When Charlie brought out a large bowl of raisin pudding, Doug raised his hands in protest.

"Oh, please, I couldn't eat another bite of anything."

"Oh, but you must," Charlie said. "It's bad luck to skip dessert on Christmas."

Doug suspected Charlie had made up that superstition on the spot, but he relented and accepted a large scoop of the raisin pudding in a porcelain bowl. Charlie offered cream, and he accepted, inwardly groaning as Charlie poured a generous portion over the pudding.

He ate about half of it before he had to push the bowl away. But after a moment, he pulled it back and took another bite. He repeated this little ritual for the next ten minutes, until the bowl was empty.

He rose from the table. "Thank you for a lovely dinner. I should get home and rest up a bit before I have to meet my friends at the Park Hotel later. Merry Christmas to both of you."

"Wait just a moment, Douglas," Charlie said, and motioned to Bao. The young man disappeared in the back, and emerged a moment later with a box wrapped in silver paper and tied with a red bow. "Just a little something from Bao and me, to thank you for your friendship these past months."

Doug was stunned. He hadn't expected a gift from his neighbors, and was embarrassed that he hadn't thought to get them a gift.

"This is unexpected. You didn't have to get me anything for Christmas."

"Nonsense," Charlie said, waving a hand dismissively. "We're happy to. Bao and me, we like you very much, and we're most thankful to have you as our neighbor. Good neighbors are hard to come by, you see, and good friends even harder to come by."

"But I didn't get anything for you."

"Of course you did, you brought the wine for dinner."

Doug was about to protest that a bottle of wine was not a Christmas gift, but kept his mouth closed and accepted the wrapped box. He opened it carefully, and inside was a porcelain tea set.

"We know you like tea very much," Bao said. "So you can have nice tea cup to drink now."

Doug felt his heart melt. The tea set had probably been expensive, and he had no doubt Bao had picked it out himself.

"Thank you," he said, his voice unexpectedly croaky.

Charlie nodded and looked away. Bao just beamed. "You like?"

"Yes, very much."

"Good! You make us tea tomorrow, then."

Doug had to laugh. "It's a deal. Tomorrow at four o'clock—you and Charlie come for high tea."

Charlie sat up straight and waved his hand in a display of exaggerated refinery. "Oh, my! *High* tea! Well, well, how fancy!" His working class accent made the statement comical, and Doug burst out laughing.

"Well, maybe not *high* tea—but I'll have little English finger sandwiches and tea cakes. Four o'clock."

"We'll be there. A Boxing Day tea party. Happy Christmas, Douglas."

3

Tuesday, January 21, 1936

Doug met Kenny for breakfast at a tea house downtown. A fresh inch of snow had fallen overnight, and he huddled his chin down inside the upturned collar of his overcoat as he trudged through the cold, pale January dawn, his gloved hands stuffed inside his pockets as he tried to hurry without slipping.

The inside of the tea house was warm, and the glass was fogged so that he couldn't see through. He spotted Kenny already sitting at a corner table, reading the local English-language newspaper.

Kenny grinned and stood as Doug approached.

"Nasty little cold snap, isn't it?"

Doug shook his head as he pulled off his gloves. "I'll admit I never expected it to get this cold here. We're on the same latitude as Savannah, Georgia, for heaven's sake."

"I read once that the way the prevailing winds blow, most of Asia is colder than North America at the same latitudes, but North America is colder than Europe at the same latitudes," Kenny said, retaking his seat. "So we lost the winter weather lottery, I'm afraid."

"It's as hot as Georgia in the summer," Doug grumbled.

Kenny laughed. "Ha! It is at that."

A young Chinese waiter stopped by, and Doug ordered in Shanghainese, a pot of tea and *bo luo bao*—a pineapple bun with red bean paste.

"Chinese New Year is on Friday," Doug said, nodding at the red lanterns that were already strung from the ceiling.

"Speaking of that," Kenny said, sipping his tea. "Pete and Julia are organizing a last-minute trip to Hong Kong for the holiday weekend. They called last night. Peter asked me to invite you along. I assume your office is closed on Friday, like everything else. You should join us! It will be nice and warm down there."

It was a tempting offer, and Doug nearly accepted on the spot. He had discussed tentative plans with his neighbors, though; plus, he hoped to take the opportunity to spend time chatting up Wong Mei-Ling during the festivities in the neighborhood, when her guard might be down.

Still, he might be able to slip away for a bit...

"When do you leave?"

"Thursday afternoon, the four o'clock train. We'll be back Sunday night."

By which time the festivities would be winding down. The celebration was technically a week long, but the first few days were always the most festive. After Sunday, most of the on-going celebrations would be private, at home.

"I'm not sure I can swing that," Doug said with an apologetic shrug. "Thanks for the offer, though."

"If you can't close your office early on Thursday, just take the later train," Kenny said. "We might be a few drinks ahead of you by the time you get there Friday, but you can catch up, eh? It's hardly the end of the world if you miss a few hours."

Doug couldn't come up with an immediate excuse, so he shrugged again and said, "Thanks, I'll think about it."

"Would you let me know by tomorrow? Pete's going to ask me."

"Sure. Where are you staying?"

"The Peninsula Hotel, in Kowloon," Kenny said. "I hear it's very fancy—but that's Pete and Julia for you."

Doug agreed. Their friend Peter Tolbert, an American from Cincinnati in his late twenties, was some type of investment banker. He and his wife Julia, an heiress from one of the Queen City's oldest families, often rented a penthouse suite at the top of the Palace Hotel on the Bund, just to throw giant parties. That they would rent a suite—or suites—in a fancy Hong Kong hotel for Chinese New Year, did not surprise Doug in the slightest.

And if he was being honest with himself, he was enticed by the idea of spending a holiday surrounded by friends and friendly acquaintances—after three years of spending holidays alone in Washington, where he had no real friends, or friendly acquaintances.

"I'll see if I can make it work," Doug said. "I did say that I would celebrate with my neighbors—one of whom is Chinese—but I'm not committed for the entire weekend. We'll see."

"It *is* last minute," Kenny said. "I'm sure Pete will understand if you can't make it."

Julia already thinks I'm a stick in the mud. And he was probably foolish to think Wong Mei-Ling would open up to him, even loosened by the biggest festival of the year. But part of him still nagged that he had to try.

"I'll find out for certain and let you know by tomorrow evening."

They walked together to their office building a half-hour later. Pale winter morning sunlight from behind the long shadows of the skyscrapers on the Bund cast the city in a silvery hue. They hurried to get out of the cold, while simultaneously taking small steps to avoid slipping in the snow, in a sort of quick shuffle.

As they approached the corner of Honan Road and Peking Road, crowds gathered around newsboys hocking a special late edition of the Shanghai Times.

"King dies! New king in England!" the newsboys shouted.

A look of concern came to Kenny's face, and he rushed toward the nearest newsboy, his big feet sliding a few times along the way. He fished a coin from this pocket and handed it over, grabbing a paper and hurrying back from the crowd. He stopped and opened it.

Doug came up beside him and looked at the paper in Kenny's hand.

BRITAIN'S KING GEORGE V DIES AT SANDRINGHAM

Doug's heart broke for his friend. Kenny and Abbie had made passing references to the king and royal family over the several months that he'd known them, often in reference to Kenny's work at the British Supreme Court for China.

"*'King George, seventy, passes just before midnight, surrounded by members of the Royal family,'*" Kenny read aloud.

"I'm so sorry, Kenny."

"Thanks, old chum," Kenny said, almost absently. He swallowed hard. "He was the only king Abbie and I have ever known. I was an infant when he ascended. Abbie was born after."

Doug let him have silence for a moment.

Kenny straightened and cleared his throat. "Well, long live the new king, I suppose." He raised his hat. "To His Majesty, King Edward VIII. Long may he reign."

They started back toward their office building, down the next block. Their gait was slower now.

"Are they going to close your court today?"

Kenny nodded. "I'm sure. I'll go down there in a bit, just until we get the official word. We may be closed until after the funeral."

"Then you'll have a whole week for vacation," Doug said, trying to lighten the mood.

Kenny gave him a weak half-smile. "I suppose that's true."

When they got to the second floor, Kenny paused before walking down the corridor toward his office. "I probably won't be here long. Send me a note at home about Hong Kong, will you?"

"Absolutely."

Thursday, January 23

The temperature had returned to the low forties Fahrenheit by Thursday afternoon, and Doug walked home from downtown at five o'clock instead of taking the trolley. It took about thirty minutes, and darkness was falling by the time he reached his building. The occasional blast of wind took on a cold bite.

He stepped inside the shop to pick up his weekly laundry and rubbed his hands together, relishing the warmth of the room.

Wong Mei-Ling came from the back a few seconds later, and she bowed her head in polite deference. "Good evening, Mr. Bainbridge. You're here to pick up?" she said in Shanghainese.

He bowed his head and answered in the same language. "Yes, to pick up. It's considered good fortune to wear clean laundry on the day of the lunar New Year, is it not?"

She gave him the sort of condescending look that one might give to a child, or to a stupid foreigner. "One must wear only clean clothes on the New Year. Everyone knows that."

He tried a broad smile. "Then I suppose it's a good thing Thursday is my regular laundry day, isn't it? Since the lunar New Year is Friday this year."

She made a little grunt as her only response to his attempt at jocularity. "The charge is four dollars, Mr. Bainbridge."

He handed over the four dollars, plus a half-dollar as a tip, rather than the usual quarter. "A prosperous New Year to you, Miss Wong," he said with a big smile. "Will you celebrate the festival here in the neighborhood tomorrow? I believe there is a parade on Honan Road—perhaps we could watch it together."

A brief scowl crossed her face, but her expression quickly became passive again. "I will watch the parade with friends." She hesitated, seeming unsure for a moment, and then added, "We cannot stop you from watching it near us, but do not think you would be made welcome."

He wondered if that meant she wouldn't mind, but her friends would.

He bowed his head again. "I understand. Thank you, Miss Wong. To see you tomorrow would still be most welcome, and I would see it as a sign of good fortune in the coming year. Now would you please bring up my laundry, so that I can wear clean clothes to start the New Year?"

She went into the back, and returned a moment later hauling a wooden hamper. She removed a large stack of pressed and neatly folded shirts and pants, tied with twine, and handed them across the counter to him. She bowed when he took the stack, and disappeared behind the door.

Friday, January 24

Doug yawned as he straightened his tie in the mirror. The firecrackers that went off at midnight last night—just after he got to sleep—had continued for forty-five minutes, accompanied by squeals of delight from the neighborhood children. It never completely quieted down all night, so he slept lightly.

Charlie and Bao's door was framed with a dozen red paper cut-outs of rats, and the door itself bore two red paper cut-outs of fish.

Charlie answered the door, and grinned from ear to ear. His gray suit was brightened with a crimson red necktie.

"Welcome, Douglas! Do come in. *Gōng xǐ fā cái.*"

Doug bowed and thanked him, and wished him a prosperous New Year as well. He pointed to the decorations on the door. "These are new since I came home last night."

"Yes, Bao put those up before midnight last night. Supposed to bring in good luck for the new year. The rats are for the Year of the Rat, and the fish are meant to bring us more than we need in the coming year."

"Ah, I wasn't familiar with the fish symbols."

"Hello, Mr. Bainbridge! *Gōng xǐfā cái!*" Bao said with a grin and a bow. He wore a shiny red shirt fastened down the front with bamboo sticks, and crisply-pressed black pants.

Doug returned his greeting, and complimented his bright new clothes.

"Always wear new clothes for New Year," Bao said. "You wearing new clothes, Mr. Bainbridge?"

"New shirt," Doug said, aware of the tradition, though his was a plain white dress shirt. Still new, though.

"Before we leave," Charlie said, and handed Doug a bright red envelope with gold embossing on the edges. "It's called *angpow*. I know these are traditionally meant for children, but Bao still qualifies since he doesn't turn twenty for a couple more weeks; and since I was giving him one, I made one for you, too. You *are* younger than I am, at least."

Doug laughed as he opened the envelope and let the two gold coins fall into his palm. They were Chinese currency instead of Shanghai money, with a square hole in the middle.

"Put them in your pocket, for good luck," Charlie said.

The street was crowded with Chinese revelers shaking noise-makers or waving smoking bamboo sticks. Everyone wore red, some with elaborate gold or silver embroidery. And though the Chinese rarely smiled in public, almost everyone was laughing and smiling today.

A crowd lined Honan Road, but it was early enough that the three of them were able to get close to the street. Numerous westerners were scattered amongst the Chinese residents of the district, so he and Charlie didn't stick out too much.

Doug searched the throng for Wong Mei-ling, but the only familiar faces were Mr. Hwang and some of the other residents of his building.

Then he spotted her, a block down the road toward downtown.

"I think I see Miss Wong, down that way," Doug said to Charlie and Bao, pointing south. "Want to join her?"

A brief look passed between Charlie and Bao, but then Charlie smiled and shrugged. "Why not?"

Doug greeted her by name in Shanghainese, and wished her a prosperous New Year. She turned in surprise, and three girls around her turned and gave Doug suspicious stares.

It took him a moment to place them—they were the three girls from the student group he sometimes saw her with at the Sichuan restaurant up the street. He hardly recognized them out of the drab gray clothing they always wore; but today they were in bright red shirts—plain and simple—and black trousers.

Mei-ling was dressed the same way. Doug did notice the contrast with the other Chinese women around them, who all wore red dresses; these girls were dressed in the same style as the men.

"May we watch the parade with you?" Doug asked in Shanghainese.

Mei-ling shrugged. "You may, if you want to." She turned back to her friends and resumed their conversation, but Doug noticed their voices were quieter now.

From the corner of his left eye, Doug saw a Duesenberg limousine come across the Honan Road bridge from downtown, and it stopped in front of the Temple of the Queen of Heaven a block down. He watched the Chinese chauffeur—dressed in the typical black uniform, but with a bright red necktie today—open a backdoor, and a woman's leg in silk stockings and red pumps slid out, followed by the woman herself in a long red sequined dress with a slit up ore leg.

Doug stared at Ming Lin-wen for a moment too long, and her eye caught his. A faint smile curved her lips, and she turned to the man getting out of the car behind her.

Not her husband, Doug noticed. Her husband, Wu Shan, was a big man many years older than her. And a captain in the *Juntong*, the Chinese secret police.

This man was young, probably about Doug's age, and as he turned to look over the crowd, Doug couldn't help but notice the striking resemblance between the two.

This must be Ming Lin-wen's brother, Colonel Ming Zhonghu. Doug remembered that he was rumored to be a member of the Blue Shirts Society—a secret fascist organization within the Nationalist Party, a sort of unofficial military secret police, far more fanatical and secretive than the *Juntong*.

A younger woman in a red dress got out behind Colonel Ming, and took his arm. His wife, Doug assumed.

For the first time, Doug noticed that a long podium with chairs stood along the side of the road in front of the temple. Several chairs were occupied, and the men stood as Ming Lin-wen took her brother's other arm and stepped up onto the podium.

"The local Chinese dignitaries," Charlie observed next to him, nodding toward the podium. "The two Chinese members of the municipal council, plus a few other business leaders."

Doug nodded, embarrassed that Charlie had noticed him watching the scene at the temple. "I believe I know the young woman who just arrived." He didn't elaborate.

"If you want to go say hello and wish her a happy New Year, Bao and I will hold space for you here."

"Thank you, but that won't be necessary. She's the only one I know there, and it would be awkward if I inserted myself on their eminences."

That wasn't the main reason it would be awkward, but he left that unsaid.

The noise level ratcheted up considerably, accompanied by the steady *dong* of a bell. Everyone looked toward the north, where a pair of men dressed all in red rang a large brass bell on a wagon, while two wooden dragons manned by a half-dozen operators apiece wove around them. Several people in the crowd began to ring little silver bells they had brought. The wagon bearing the bell made its way down the street as far as the Temple of the Queen of Heaven, and then turned into the temple compound.

As Doug watched, Ming Lin-wen turned her head, and he inadvertently caught her eye again. She held his gaze for a moment, and he couldn't make himself look away. A hint of smile curved up the corners of her mouth.

For the next twenty minutes, a parade of dancing dragons, plus dancers in big-headed lion costumes, made their way down Honan Road to the temple while the crowd rang their little bells and cheered. A powerful smell of incense filled the air.

"The dragon and lion dancers are said to bring good luck," Charlie explained.

Doug didn't mention that he already knew that.

"Later today, families with means will pay the lion dancers to come into their homes, bringing an extra dose of good fortune for the coming year," Charlie added.

Doug nodded appreciatively, having not known that detail.

Doug turned toward where Wong Mei-ling stood a few feet away. He leaned toward her and said in Shanghainese, just loudly enough to be heard over the din. "You and your friends should have a lion troupe come to your home. Maybe it will bring good fortune to your cause."

She looked at him with eyes widened by surprise. She wouldn't have expected a 'bourgeois capitalist American pig' to wish good fortune on their cause.

Then her expression went passive. She nodded her head in polite acknowledgment, and then eviscerated him by saying, "The lion dancers cost money that could be better spent on practical matters, instead of superstition."

Ouch, Doug thought. But he allowed a self-deprecating half-smile and a shallow bow. "I'm sure you are right. It is very wise to focus on practical things." Then he leaned closer to her ear, and said just above a whisper, "Perhaps I can offer practical assistance sometime in the coming year."

Her head snapped his direction, and cocked to the side while she studied his face for several seconds, her eyes seeming to search his.

In truth, he had no idea what he'd really meant by that; it had seemed a good thing to say to build some trust. Follow-through could be tricky. He'd worry about that later.

"We are very capable, Bainbridge Douglas," she said with an enigmatic look on her face. She held his gaze for several seconds before looking back toward the street, and he felt his heart flutter.

He looked around, and he caught Ming Lin-wen staring at him. Her gaze had grown cold.

He took a step away from Wong Mei-ling without thinking, and then scolded himself for it. He glanced back at Ming Lin-wen, who still looked his way, though not directly; he thought he detected a look of satisfaction on her face.

Doug turned back to the parade, which was drawing to a close. A company of Chinese police constables took up the rear; they wore the standard uniform of the SMP, but with red arm-bands around their sleeves in a nod to the lunar New Year.

From the corner of his eye, he saw Wong Mei-ling and her three girlfriends slip away into the background and disappear.

Damn. He wasn't sure how much more he'd hoped for from their conversation, but he had a vague sense that there was more he might have gleaned.

"It is nice to see you again, Mr. Bainbridge," a bell-like voice said behind him in Mandarin. He turned, and Ming Lin-wen stood before him, a hint of smile on her lips. "It has been quite a while."

He bowed his head to her. "Yes, it has." *Because you lied to me.* He wished her a happy New Year.

"You should come for tea one afternoon. I would enjoy having you for tea again."

I'll bet you would. "I don't think that would be a good idea," he said, and hesitated. "I have a girlfriend, you see."

An icy look flashed across her eyes, but then she gave him a polite nod, the corners of her mouth turned up in a hint of smile. "I saw her. I confess, I am surprised by this news. I would not have pictured you being interested in someone so—plain."

She thought he meant Wong Mei-ling. He opted not to correct her, but a flash of irritation swept through him at her judgment of Mei-ling's looks. "I think she's pretty." It was the truth. He had always thought her round face and bright eyes were pretty, in a simple sort of way.

Ming Lin-wen nodded in deference. "Of course." Her tone was formal, polite. Then she allowed herself a hint of smile again. "Nevertheless, it would be most pleasant to spend time with you again, Mr. Bainbridge. You remember my address—send me a note."

She gave him a smoldering look as she turned away, like a panther eyeing her lunch.

She walked toward the limousine, smoothing the dress over the back of her hip. As she took her brother's hand to step into the vehicle, she hiked the skirt a bit higher than necessary, showing the curve of her calves in sheer silk stockings.

Doug shook his head as he turned toward home. She was good, alright. He'd give her that.

Back at home, Doug removed his tie and loosened his collar on the way to his bedroom, when he was interrupted by a knock on his door.

48

As he walked to the door, several thoughts tumbled through his brain. Was it Ming Lin-wen coming to call on him? Would she be that bold? Perhaps he had been right about what he'd seen in her eyes this afternoon.

And what on earth would he do if he did see her standing at his door?

An image of Lucy flashed across his mind as he turned the door knob.

The figure on the other side of the door was far less welcome than Ming Lin-wen, and he shoved his way inside before Doug had the chance to open it all the way.

"I would like a word with you, Bainbridge Douglas," the thin Chinese man said in Shanghainese, putting a hand on Doug's chest and pushing him backward. "Close the door and sit down."

Doug took a second to glance around the hallway to be sure the communist cell leader was alone; as he closed the door, he was a bit shocked that he was.

He couldn't have come all alone, though. He would never. No doubt someone was watching from across the street, but Doug wasn't about to go to the window and check.

"What is this about?" he asked in Shanghainese, trying to sound confident, commanding.

"Sit down." The leader's voice wasn't harsh, but it carried a quiet command that demanded obedience.

Doug sat in an armchair, and tried to relax—or at least look relaxed. The leader took the other armchair and faced him, sitting straight-backed, staring at him with intense, dark eyes.

"You have been making great efforts to be friendly the last two months, Bainbridge Douglas," the leader said, speaking slowly and deliberately. "We have chosen to ignore you, even if you are obviously after something. We believe you are of little concern, a gnat who buzzes around one's ear without landing."

49

Doug said nothing in response, and the two men stared at each other in silence for more than a minute. Doug grew increasingly uncomfortable, but refused to fidget or even shift his weight in his chair—if the head comrade could sit perfectly still, so would he.

The comrade's stare was steady, unblinking and unshifting, but Doug imagined he could see a buzz of activity behind those dark eyes. He was certain there was.

"I believe you can be useful to us, Bainbridge Douglas," the comrade said at last.

This surprised Doug, and he couldn't help but raise an eyebrow. "Oh? How so?"

A hint of smile crossed the leader's mouth. "You were invited to Hong Kong, but you did not go."

Doug's surprise grew, along with a touch of alarm. "No, I didn't."

The leader's closed-mouth smile grew slightly. "Yes, we know many things about you, Bainbridge Douglas. Did you really think that we would not learn everything about you, after your little interference last summer?"

Doug scolded himself for being caught off guard; *of course* they were still watching him, and of course they had asked questions about him. He forced himself to stay calm.

"What do you want from me?"

The leader chuckled. "You will take the overnight train to Hong Kong. You should hurry—it leaves in forty minutes. You will join your friends at the bourgeois hotel—but Saturday afternoon at three o'clock you will go to the spa, where you will be given a message; and you are to take it immediately to the place that you will be instructed, and give it to the man who is described to you. Then you will return to your fancy bourgeois hotel, and prepare for dinner as if nothing out of the ordinary had happened."

Doug took a few seconds to digest this information. "Why me? Surely you have many others who could deliver a message for you."

The leader's smile grew, and began to look sinister. "But none are as above suspicion as you, Bainbridge Douglas."

'...above suspicion...' From whom? He had an idea.

"The *Juntong* are watching you, because of your role in the Nakayama assassination," Doug said.

"None of that is any concern of yours, Bainbridge Douglas. You have been given a task, and you will carry it out tomorrow, and then forget it ever happened. Do you understand?"

Doug nodded. "Just one question, though—will anyone die because of the 'task' I'm being given tomorrow?"

The leader's smile grew, and he chuckled again. "Do not worry, Bainbridge Douglas—we do not kill innocent people."

Doug found that hardly reassuring.

The leader got up from his chair and strode to the door in a swift, smooth motion. He stopped and turned with his hand on the door knob, and looked Doug hard in the eyes again.

"If you fail to complete your task, Bainbridge Douglas, I will know it within an hour." He turned and opened the door.

"And then?" Doug asked, but the man had already disappeared into the dark hall. Doug hurried to the door and looked toward the stairs, but they were empty. The man had vanished.

Hutson

4

Doug sprinted down the platform, valise in hand, as the six o'clock train's whistle blasts pierced the cold air. Steam released from the wheels as they crept down the track.

A Chinese porter at the entrance of a passenger car some thirty yards ahead waved his hand and reached out. The train was picking up speed, but Doug's run was still slightly faster as he reached the porter's outstretched hand and grabbed it. He felt the man pulling him in and he leapt onto the step and nearly tumbled inside, but the porter caught him by the shoulders.

"Almost late, sir," the porter said in accented English, a big grin on his face. "New Year very lucky for you, so far."

"Yes, indeed," Doug muttered, not bothering to switch to Shanghainese or Mandarin. "Thank you."

He walked down the aisle of the half-empty car, and picked a window seat midway down, setting his valise on the empty seat beside him rather than stowing it on the rack above. He wasn't sure he would stay here, but he needed to catch his breath.

He'd been rushing for the last forty minutes. He'd thrown some clothes and personal grooming items into his valise, hurried down the stairs, and half-run through the still-crowded streets. It was about a mile via Haining Road to the Shanghai Railway Station, just outside the boundary of the International Settlement, in the Chapei District of the Chinese Municipality—and normally he could walk it in twenty-five minutes, but with the dense crowds it took him thirty, even trying his best to hurry. Once there, he ran to the ticket counter, bribed several Chinese people to let him cut the line, and then sprinted to the platform to find the train starting to depart.

But he'd made it. He took a deep breath and blew it out hard. It was a nineteen-hour ride to Hong Kong—plenty of time to relax, he told himself. Then he wondered if he could possibly relax, knowing what he had to do tomorrow.

Or rather, *not* knowing exactly what it was he was going to be doing tomorrow.

The train would arrive just before one o'clock in the afternoon—he would have two hours to get from the station to the Peninsula Hotel, check in, and get to the spa before three o'clock. This was the first he'd thought about the timeline he would have to keep. It would be tight, but it was doable.

If he wasn't delayed much by running into his friends, that is. He debated whether he should call their rooms upon arrival, to let them know he was there and make plans to meet them later. That carried the risk that they would insist on meeting up right away, and he would be hard-pressed to make excuses to meet later.

Not calling them also carried risk; he might run into them in the hall, or at the spa, and they could be put out that he hadn't told them he was coming.

He decided he would figure that out later. It was a nineteen-hour train ride, after all, so why not make use of all that time?

His stomach grumbled, and he realized he had relaxed enough to become hungry. That was something, anyway.

He got up and carried his valise down the aisle toward the back of the car. He asked a Chinese porter there in Mandarin where he could find the club car, and the porter grinned at his use of the Chinese language, pointing him in the right direction with a deep bow.

Saturday, January 25

His sleeping berth was dark and comfortable, and he usually slept well on trains, with the gentle rocking motion soothing him; but he slept fitfully on this ride. At one point a vivid dream disturbed him—he arrived in Hong Kong, realizing he had forgotten his passport, and police constables with bad British accents dragged him away to jail.

He awoke with his heart racing, covered in sweat that soaked through the back of his pajama top.

It took a moment to return his mind to reality, and assure himself that he did in fact have his passport in his suit jacket; as a foreigner in China, he always carried it with him, even in the International Settlement.

He reminded himself over and over that it was just a dream, likely an expression of his unease. The word 'imposter' sprang to mind unbidden, and he seemed to recall one of the constables in his dream calling him that. It was a bit hazy now, but he thought that had happened.

He dozed after that, but never fell deeply asleep.

The sounds of activity in the aisle of the sleeping car, and whispered conversations in English and Cantonese, awoke him some time before morning light began to creep around the edges of the berth curtain. He lay still on his back, listening to the sounds of the train, trying not to think too much about the coming day.

After a while, as the light grew stronger and the activity more constant, he sat up and reached for his clothes hanging from the hooks above his feet. The first thing he did was feel his suit jacket, making sure that his passport still sat in the inside pocket.

He dressed quietly—an awkward thing in a train's sleeping berth— folded and repacked his pajamas, and then took his shaving kit to one of the two bathrooms that bookended the sleeping car. He waited in line behind three other men, shaved quickly, and returned to his berth to fasten his necktie and put on his jacket.

He checked the inside pocket one more time, removed his passport and gave it a quick glance to assure that no one had nefariously replaced it in the night with a fake, and made his way to the dining car for breakfast. He carried his valise with him—an unusual precaution, to be sure, but a feeling in his gut wouldn't let him leave it unattended in his berth, as customary as that may be.

The train stopped at Guangzhou—Canton, in English—as Doug finished breakfast, and about half of the passengers disembarked, all of them Chinese. The club car was now occupied mostly by white passengers, most speaking English with refined British accents. A few Chinese passengers got on at the Guangzhou East train station, most dressed in western-style business suits, but the train was less crowded for the last leg of the journey.

Doug watched out the windows as the train pulled slowly through the gritty industrial city, with massive dockyards visible in the distance on the Pearl River estuary.

His grandfather Bainbridge had spent his childhood here some sixty years earlier, before being sent back to California for boarding school. Doug thought the city of Guangzhou looked very much like Yangtzepoo in Shanghai.

The scenery returned to rice fields as the train passed out the east side of the city, picked up speed, and turned south along the east bank of the wide, muddy Pearl River. Unlike the rice fields outside of Shanghai, these were still green and growing in January, and stooping workers in plain tunics and conical hats dotted the landscape.

Three hours later, the train came to a stop at a check-point. Out the window, Doug could see a painted white sign with black letters announcing the border of Hong Kong. Conversations in the club car continued, until a middle-aged white man in the uniform of a British Customs inspector came through with the conductor, asking to see passports. A black mourning band circled his right arm, in honor of the late King George.

The International Settlement in Shanghai might be quasi-colonial, but Hong Kong was the real thing.

Doug handed over his passport, barely containing his growing sense of nervousness. The Customs Inspector perused it, stamped the visa, and handed it back. "Welcome to Hong Kong, Mr. Bainbridge," he said in a working-class English accent, and moved on.

The train began to move again less than fifteen minutes later, passing through an open red and white striped border gate next to a guard shack flying the Union Jack at half-staff. Doug supposed a Customs officer had boarded each car, to speed up the entry.

The tracks continued through green rice fields for twenty minutes, before the landscape became industrial urban again, and soon the train slowed as the scenery transitioned into brick high-rise buildings of a modern downtown. As they pulled into the station, the sign above the platform said "Kowloon." The large clock on the wall showed a few minutes until one o'clock.

Doug took his valise and rose from his seat while the train was still moving, reaching the exit before they came to a stop. He leapt off onto the platform the moment the porter allowed him through, and hurried toward the doors to the station.

Now he was racing the clock.

Hutson

5

Doug grabbed the first rickshaw in front of Kowloon Station to take him down Salisbury Road, along the waterfront of Victoria Harbor, to the Peninsula Hotel—so named because it sat at the southern end of Kowloon Peninsula, opposite the quays where the ocean liners docked. He arrived at the hotel fifteen minutes later.

It was cooler than he'd expected for the tropics—a large mercury thermometer on the wall at the train platform had said it was fifty-seven degrees—but it was still pleasant compared to the chill in Shanghai, and the sky was less cloudy. He told himself to enjoy that, but he couldn't get his mind off his apprehensions about the coming afternoon.

A circular drive occupied a courtyard between the east and west wings of the seven-story U-shaped hotel, the brick façade gleaming white; the rickshaw deposited him at the brass-handled plate glass doors. A white doorman in a crimson uniform opened the door for him, wishing him "Good afternoon, sir," in a crisp British accent.

An Indian desk clerk in a crisply-pressed suit greeted him in a near-perfect British accent, with just a hint of Indian lilt to the vowels. "Good afternoon, sir. May I help you?"

"I'd like a room for one night please," Doug said. "Do you by any chance have a vacancy near the rooms where Mr. Peter Tolbert and his guests are staying?"

The desk clerk perused the registry book for a moment. "Unfortunately, I do not have anything on the same floor as Mr. and Mrs. Tolbert. Apologies, sir, but I can put you on the floor below them. It's a very nice room, sir, on the fourth floor, with a view over the harbor."

"That will be perfectly acceptable, thank you." He paid for his room, and the clerk handed him a brass key.

"Would you like for me to send a note to Mr. Tolbert telling him you are here, sir?"

Doug hesitated, thinking that over. He decided he didn't want to have to explain his absence this afternoon. "No, thank you—I'd like to surprise them myself."

"Very well, sir. I'll get a bellboy to take your luggage."

"No, thank you—I only have the one suit case, I'd prefer to carry it myself."

The clerk looked stunned. "As you wish, sir. The elevator is that way, just over there."

As he walked to the elevator, Doug wondered if he should have allowed the clerk to call a bellboy to carry his valise. He might have made himself more memorable by refusing the offer—and given the questionable nature of the task he had to undertake this afternoon, he didn't want to be memorable.

He was alone with the Chinese elevator operator at first, until the car stopped one floor up. Several guests got on at the mezzanine, where the dining room was located.

Doug's heart skipped a beat when Abbie Traywick stepped onto the elevator with Julia Tolbert. Abbie's face lit up.

"Doug, you made it! What a surprise." She stood on her toes and leaned up to kiss his cheek. "Why didn't you tell us you were coming after all? We would have saved you a seat at lunch."

Doug smiled at her enthusiasm, and also to hide his discomfort at being found out so soon. "Thanks, but I had lunch on the train. It was a last minute decision to come down."

Julia had been watching him with a tiny enigmatic smile, reminiscent of the Mona Lisa's. "Hello, Douglas. How thoughtful of you to join us. Abbie and I were just on our way upstairs to freshen up a bit, but then we'll rejoin the men in the dining room. You should come have a drink with us."

"Oh yes, do," Abbie echoed.

Doug felt his stomach drop. This was exactly what he needed to avoid.

"Thank you, really—but I'd like to rest up a bit from the train ride. I'll meet you all for dinner? What time?"

Julia's lips tightened ever so slightly. "Don't be rude, Douglas. Come be social and have a drink with us. You can rest after. Then we have a harbor cruise scheduled at four o'clock, followed by dinner over in Victoria."

Her tone said that she expected no further discussion. Doug knew that tone well—his mother used it almost constantly.

"Where are you staying?" Abbie asked, still excited at his unexpected presence. "We have a block of rooms together on the fifth floor—which is really the sixth floor. Are you up there with us?"

The floors were numbered in the European fashion—Ground Floor, First Floor Mezzanine, Second Floor, etc.—so the 'Fifth Floor' would actually be the sixth floor to a North American.

Julia seemed momentarily uncomfortable. "We couldn't get the penthouses, unfortunately," she explained, sounding almost apologetic. "We didn't plan enough in advance, you see, so they were already reserved. We're one floor below them, which is the next best thing."

"I'm on the fourth floor," Doug said to Abbie, ignoring Julia. "In fact, here's my stop."

"We'll see you in the dining room in ten or fifteen minutes," Julia said behind him as he stepped off the elevator. He barely glanced back as he nodded and hurried down the hall.

It was a surprisingly large room, with big plate glass windows overlooking the harbor. Hong Kong Island rose like a crown across the half-mile stretch of deep blue water, with verdant green mountains rising toward the nearly cloudless sky behind the granite and limestone high-rises of Victoria, the capital city of Hong Kong.

The busy harbor was crowded with small boats, iconic Chinese junks, and giant steamships, along with the occasional British warship. Doug allowed himself a moment to study the British naval vessels, reciting from memory their various features as a test for himself. He nodded in satisfaction as he recalled every significant detail.

He wondered what kind of 'harbor cruise' Julia had booked, and then realized there was a good probability he wouldn't be able get back by four o'clock. He had no idea where he would be sent to deliver the message.

Or to whom.

He cringed as he stepped into the hall and locked his room, thinking about Julia's reaction later to his absence on the boat. He would have to say he took a nap and overslept.

He found his friends at a long table beside the bay windows overlooking the courtyard and quay, and there were happy shouts of surprise when they saw him approaching.

"We thought you weren't coming, old chum!" Kenny said, rising to shake Doug's hand and clap him warmly on the shoulder.

"Last minute change of plans," Doug explained. "So I thought, 'what the hell,' and I came down. I ran into Abbie and Julia on the elevator a little while ago, and they told me you fellows were down here."

Their friends Pete, Fred, Stuart, and George all took turns shaking Doug's hand and welcoming him with enthusiasm that was genuine, if clearly aided by a few cocktails. George's wife Betty remained in her seat, but smiled at him from across the table and murmured "Glad to see you."

"Pull up a chair, order a drink," Pete said, gesturing at an empty seat.

Abbie and Julia arrived a moment later, and Pete raised his hand and snapped his fingers for the waiter. Abbie beamed at Doug and took the empty seat next to his, patting his knee.

"I'm so glad you changed your mind."

"I'll say!" Kenny echoed.

Doug couldn't help but smile at their enthusiasm. "Me too," he agreed, and meant it.

The thin young Chinese waiter arrived and bowed. "You called, sir?"

"Yes, another round of drinks for everyone," Pete commanded, then pointed at Doug. "And this fellow over here, if I know him, will want a gin and tonic."

Doug shook his hand at the waiter. He needed to keep a clear head. "No gin yet, not this early—I'll take a beer instead. Do you have Bass on tap, by any chance?"

"We do, sir."

"I'll take a pint of Bass, please."

"*Beer*, Douglas?" Julia said with an amused smile and an arched eyebrow. "How very droll of you. So bourgeois."

Doug noted the red wine glass in front of Julia. He couldn't help himself. "You know, in many ancient civilizations, beer was drunk exclusively by the wealthy, while wine was considered base and low class."

"Really?" Abbie said, intrigued.

"You don't say?" Kenny said. "I never knew that."

"Oh, poppycock," Julia said, waving a dismissive hand in the air, and then an indulgent smile spread across her lips. "He's pulling our legs. So very droll, Douglas."

"It's absolutely true," Doug said, sitting up tall in his chair. "I learned this at Stanford. Beer is made from grain, which was a precious commodity in early civilizations like ancient Egypt and Mesopotamia. It was a sign of great wealth that you could afford to spare grain to brew beer, and didn't need it all to make bread to feed your family. Huge vats of beer were entombed with the pharaohs, even.

"Grape vines, on the other hand, were considered not much more than an obnoxious weed—they grew wild, and anyone could collect grapes to press into wine. Wealthy farmers hired laborers to keep the vines away from their fields. Peasants drank wine, because that was the only spirits they could afford. It wasn't until the Romans came along millennia later that they elevated viticulture to an art form."

"Well, how about that," Pete said, sounding impressed.

His wife gave a little shrug and sniffed. "How times have changed."

Doug enjoyed her show of indifference.

The waiter brought out a round of drinks, and the conversation shifted to more amusing topics. It was clear to Doug that everyone was slightly inebriated, but not completely drunk, which made them enjoyable to be around. Almost before he knew it, it was two-thirty, and his stomach tumbled with butterflies.

He got up from his seat and nodded to the table. "I apologize, but I'm afraid I'm awfully tired from traveling. I'm going to go upstairs and rest a bit before we board the boat. Please excuse me."

"Stay and have one more drink," Pete said. "We're having such a good time."

Doug smiled and thanked him, but said he really did need to rest.

"Don't be such a stick in the mud, Douglas," Julia said with a condescending sort of smile.

Doug was about to make a passive-aggressive retort, when Pete touched his wife's arm. "It's alright, dear, let him rest. He'll better enjoy the evening's festivities that way."

Julia's eyes flashed, but then she smiled indulgently at Doug. "Meet us in the lobby at five minutes to four."

Doug nodded at her, and walked back to the elevator.

He found the spa in the basement, hidden away from windows and prying eyes. A young Chinese woman sat at the reception desk, and greeted him in English. "Good afternoon, sir. How may we help?"

He replied in Cantonese. "Good afternoon. What services do you offer?"

She smiled when she heard him speak in her own language, and she rattled off the services in an almost excited tone. He was about ten minutes early, and he assumed his contact would find him somewhere inside. Doug wasn't actually sure where he would be contacted, so he reluctantly purchased the full package.

The receptionist directed him into the men's spa, where a Chinese attendant bowed and handed him a towel that Doug found uncomfortably small; it barely wrapped around his waist, and only hung to mid-thigh. The attendant gave him a pin with the number of his locker, and he fastened the towel with it.

He walked into the Warm Room, and took a seat on a couch. A handful of other men relaxed on the comfortable furnishings, most with their eyes closed and their heads back. Doug noticed that all but one of them were white. The air was warm and humid, and within minutes Doug was glistening with sweat. He waited for a while, opening and closing his eyes to see if anyone approached him, but when no one did he proceeded into the next station, the Hot Room.

The air in this room was visibly steamy, and it took his eyes a few seconds to adjust enough to see the figures of a few other men scattered about the room. He took a seat on the wooden benches that lined the wall, and took deep breaths of the steamy air. He waited here for as long as he could stand it, observing the comings and goings, but no one approached him. When he could not take the heat any longer, he got up and hurried through the exit to the bathing room.

The only other occupant was drying off by the exit when Doug entered. He unfastened his towel and hung it on a hook along the wall, then stepped into the small, shallow pool. The water was cool and salty, and he crouched down and submerged to his shoulders to cool himself off, before rising to stand in the waist-deep pool and splash water on his torso, arms, neck and face.

He stepped out of the pool a couple of minutes later when a young Chinese man entered, one that Doug had not seen before, wearing the white uniform of an attendant. He locked the door. Doug wondered immediately if this was his rendezvous, since the young man didn't look a day older than twenty.

Doug nodded and said "Good afternoon" in Cantonese. One did not normally speak with others in these rooms, but he assumed he needed to say something if this were the person he was supposed to meet.

"Keep quiet," the young man replied in Cantonese. "You understand?"

Doug was acutely aware how vulnerable he was, standing naked on the steps of a pool of thigh-deep water. "Yes, I speak Cantonese."

"Listen closely, we have only a moment alone. Go to Fa Yuen Street south of Nelson Street in Kowloon; take the Mong Kok streetcar to Argyle Street, and go east. Near the Prince Edward Square there is a house with a yellow door, and wooden stairs up the outside wall to a balcony around the first floor. You will go to the second door from the rear, number 10. You will ask for Jin Shixin, and you will be told that she is not in, but the woman who answers will say she is her sister and can give her a message. You will give her this message:

"A shipment of samurai swords from Nagasaki is en route to Shanghai, and you would like to sell yours to Jin Shixin's patron. She will tell you that Jin Shixin would be most interested in purchasing one for her patron, and will name a price. You will tell her you will think about it and come back another time.

"Tonight, one of our people will come to your room, and you will tell them the price that the woman gave you."

"How long will it take to get to the house with the yellow door and back?"

"That is of no importance."

"I have to catch a boat at four o'clock. A harbor tour with my friends. It will look suspicious if I miss it."

A deep scowl crossed the young man's face, and his brow furrowed in irritation. He took a deep breath. "Did they reserve the boat through the hotel?"

"I don't know."

"We will take care of it. Leave now, do not wait any longer. The boat will wait for you. Go!"

Doug hurried out of the water, grabbed his towel, and dried as fast as he could. The young man had disappeared, and two middle-aged British men came through the door from the Hot Room, engaged in conversation about stock prices.

He hurried through the exit, which emerged into the massage rooms. Several Chinese masseurs were lined along the wood paneled wall, and one approached with a bow, and motioned toward an empty room.

Doug apologized in Cantonese, and explained that something had come up and he had to leave. He asked how to get back to the front.

The masseur directed him down a long hall, but tapped his arm as he hurried by. "It is not healthy to skip the massage."

Doug thanked him and rushed down the hall. He dressed quickly, hurried upstairs to the lobby, and exited the hotel. The doorman directed him to the streetcar stop a block away.

His heart pounded, but thankfully he had to wait only a few moments, and he hopped on and took the streetcar about a mile and a half. Along the way, they passed the open green space of King's Park, packed with revelers in red celebrating the Lunar New Year. It took nearly a half-hour to reach Argyle Street, and before the car even stopped Doug leapt onto the sidewalk and jogged a couple of blocks until he found Fa Yuen Street. He asked an old Chinese man in Cantonese where to find Nelson Street, and was pointed toward the south. He found the house with the yellow door after almost four blocks, and he bounded up the stairs to the balcony.

His heart fluttered as he approached the door to number ten. He told himself it was the rush to get here, but he knew his nerves were to blame. He steadied his shaking hand before knocking hard on the door.

An attractive Chinese woman about his age answered the door. "Yes, sir? May I help you?" she asked in heavily accented English.

Doug bowed and wished her good afternoon in Cantonese. "I am looking for Jin Shixin—is she at home?"

The woman shook her head. "No, Jin Shixin is not in, but I am her sister and I can give her a message for you."

"It is a business matter," Doug ad libbed, giving him a moment to take a breath before continuing with the script. "A shipment of samurai swords from Nagasaki is on its way to Shanghai, and I would like to sell one of mine to Jin Shixin's patron. I understand he might be interested."

"Yes, he is a collector. Jin Shixin would be most interested in purchasing one of your swords for her patron. She could pay ten thousand for it."

Doug nearly gasped at the large amount, far too much for a literal sword. He bowed to give himself a moment to recollect his composure. "Thank you. I will think about it and come back another time."

"Good day, sir," she said, and closed the door.

Doug's hands shook the entire time he walked back to the streetcar stop on Argyle Street. It was a bustling boulevard of hotels and stores, not unlike many in downtown Shanghai, but he was too distracted to pay much attention to the crowds out for their Saturday afternoon shopping.

He had just engaged in espionage.

For the communists.

He shuddered.

The streetcar deposited him near the quay at almost quarter past four. He spotted Kenny's tall frame near one of the docks, standing beside a two-level yacht, and he hurried toward them.

Julia saw him as he rushed down the dock.

"There you are, Douglas. We had given up on you."

"My apologies—I lay down for a nap, and I'm afraid I overslept."

"We called your room," Abbie said, standing up on her toes to kiss his cheek. "But you didn't answer."

"That must have been when I was in the bathroom, cleaning up."

Kenny shook his hand. "When you didn't answer your phone, I went up and knocked on your door at four o'clock."

"It's all worked out, in any case," Julia said, her imperious tone already grating on Doug's nerves.

"The boat pilot is having trouble getting clearance from the harbor master," Pete explained. "He has a permit to take us out at four, but for God only knows what reason, the blasted harbor master is being difficult. Something about his schedules. Damned if I know."

Doug kept his mouth shut. The others didn't need to hear about the long reach of the communists. "That's a real shame. Hopefully they get it cleared up soon." He suspected the situation would magically fix itself within moments.

He was right. Less than five minutes later, a thin middle-aged British man, tan with deeply-lined face, and dressed in the uniform of a ship's pilot, walked up to Pete and told him that the harbor master had just called, and they were cleared to depart.

"Let's get everyone on board before he changes his mind," Pete said to the group. "Come on, let's go, everybody. Chop chop!"

Doug had to chuckle at that little bit of Pidgin added at the end. He'd begun to notice that long-time foreign residents in China would slip Pidgin words or phrases into their everyday English. For some reason, that amused him.

They filed onto the yacht, and the pilot directed them to the main cabin. He pointed out the life vests and the liquor cabinet, wished them an enjoyable cruise, and disappeared up the stairs.

Pete was at the liquor cabinet pouring drinks before the pilot had even left.

"You first, Dougie," he said, handing Doug a gin and tonic. "I hope you got all rested up, we're planning to have some real fun tonight."

"Not as much as I would have liked," Doug said, and didn't elaborate.

"Then you can sleep in tomorrow and miss breakfast," Pete said as he mixed the next drink.

Doug took a seat next to Kenny and Abbie on a couch as the yacht backed away, and half-turned to look out the big picture window at the view of Victoria Harbor.

"Quite something, isn't it?" Kenny asked. "I wish we had this sort of view in Shanghai."

"It's beautiful!" Abbie gushed. "It almost makes me wish we lived here instead." Her tone sounded wistful.

Kenny scowled. "But my job is with the British Supreme Court for China—this isn't China, technically."

"I know that," she said, slapping at his arm. "It's a British colony. I was only saying."

The International Settlement and the French Concession in Shanghai might be self-governing entities, run primarily by their foreign residents with minimal input from the Chinese residents—but they were still part of China, sovereign Chinese territory. Hong Kong and the nearby Portuguese colony of Macau were not.

Boats of every style and size surrounded them as they moved toward the center of the harbor, one of the busiest in the world. Doug's ears were filled with the sound of boat motors and honking horns. Victoria Harbor was only a half-mile wide, but it stretched for two miles as it curved around the southern extreme of Kowloon Peninsula, in a perfectly-mirrored bend on the north shore of Hong Kong Island—it was as if a giant had run his finger in a swoop between the mountains and carved the harbor.

Their boat headed for the west, directly into the light of the setting sun, which glinted off the water in the few areas that weren't churned by boat wakes.

"A toast, everyone!" Pete shouted, raising his glass of bourbon on the rocks. "To Hong Kong, our fabulous host city for Chinese New Year. Cheers!"

The conversations and antics became increasingly raucous as they cruised the harbor and the drinks flowed. Doug made a conscious effort to sip his drink slowly, wanting to keep his head. A communist agent would come calling at his room later that night, and he didn't want to be slow-witted, or passed out asleep.

After forty minutes on the water, and a little more than a mile in distance, the harbor widened as it opened onto Wanshan Bay, the rocky coast of Kowloon Peninsula falling away to their right, and the mountainous coast of Hong Kong Island slipping away to their left. They had more room to maneuver, and the yacht's engines grew louder as the pilot accelerated. The sun was setting behind the crests of distant hills, bathing everything in a reddish glow.

Abbie sighed, and rested her head on Kenny's shoulder. "I love being out on the water," she said, that wistful tone returning. "I still miss that about Vancouver—sailing out into the bay on a summer evening, the sea breeze on our faces. It's so relaxing."

"I'll bet you went sailing a lot on San Francisco Bay when you were younger, eh, Doug?" Kenny asked, nudging Doug's arm with his elbow.

Doug pulled his eyes from the view and looked at his friends. "A few times," he said. "My parents didn't own a boat, but my friend Brent Aleshire's family had a yacht, almost as big as this one. I was their guest a few times. And you're right, Abbie—it is very relaxing. Peaceful, even."

"Yes, peaceful! That's exactly what I meant."

"You didn't seem so peaceful earlier, old chum," Kenny said, reaching out to put a hand on Doug's shoulder. "You seemed distracted. Everything alright?"

Doug faked a smile and nodded. He appreciated his friend's concern, but didn't want to get into any of it. *Couldn't* get into any of it, actually.

"Yes, I'm fine."

The yacht made a slow arc toward the south as dusk faded into twilight, and twinkling lights began to appear on shore.

The pilot's voice came onto the loudspeaker. "Back behind us are the lights of Victoria, which you'll see clearer after we come about. It's one of the loveliest sights you'll ever see."

Twilight slipped into total darkness as they came about in a wide arc—even this far south, dusk and twilight were still short in January—and as they turned back toward the mouth of the harbor, the curved shore of Hong Kong Island seemed to glow as if it were burning yellow embers, with little fingers of light running up canyons between the dark peaks.

"Oh! Isn't it gorgeous!" Betty said behind them, looking over their heads at the view across the water.

"Can you imagine how much electricity the British have to generate to power that?" George mused beside her.

Doug thought it interesting that George assumed that "the British" generated that kind of power, rather than the Chinese majority in the colony.

"Who needs another cocktail?" Pete asked, appearing beside George and putting his arm around his shoulders. "One, two, three, four—Doug? You still nursing that one?"

Doug shrugged in an embarrassed sort of way, and took a drink of his now watery gin and tonic. "I'll take another, after you've finished everyone else's."

"Douglas can't help it, really," Julia said to the group, as if she were explaining the mystery of life. "His mother's people were teetotalers, isn't that right, Douglas? Missionaries, weren't they?"

Doug nodded, suppressing his irritation. "That's right. My grandparents were missionaries in southern China, not terribly far from here, actually. They didn't approve of alcohol, and my mother still doesn't. But—" he stopped to down the last of his cocktail—"I am not my mother."

There was laughter all around, but Doug stared at Julia. There was a sort of triumphant gleam in her eye, he thought, and another enigmatic smile.

He had long gotten the feeling that she didn't like him much—or rather, that she didn't really *approve* of him for some reason. He couldn't put his finger on why, but it seemed more and more obvious all the time.

The yacht pulled into the docks at Victoria an hour later, and everyone poured off the boat and jaunted down the peer toward the quay.

A line of rickshaws stood waiting on the quay, and Pete grabbed the first rickshaw runner and asked him in Pidgin where to find the seafood restaurant they had chosen. Hearing it was only a couple of blocks away, he tipped the man and motioned for everyone to follow him.

"It's too bad Lucy couldn't be here to enjoy this," Abbie said as she fell into step beside Doug.

"She came here last summer with her mother," Doug said. "She spoke highly of Hong Kong, I'm sure she'd love to come back sometime. This is my first time here, though."

"Ours, too." Abbie slipped an arm through his, and then slipped her other arm through Kenny's. "Since she's not here, I'm the luckiest girl in Hong Kong, with *two* handsome escorts to dinner."

Twenty minutes later, the nine of them were seated at a long table next to a window, looking out over the busy harbor, the ships and boats now lights bobbing on the water in a sort of ballet. Pete ordered a round of drinks, everyone's usual.

Doug inwardly groaned, about to get his third gin and tonic of the evening. So far, he'd managed to keep from getting any sort of buzz from the alcohol, and he wondered how much longer he'd be able to pull that off.

Dinner was exquisite, with steamed fish in ginger and soy sauce. Doug ate with a fork instead of asking for chopsticks, in consideration of the company, self-conscious of being thought a show-off.

Pete ordered several bottles of white Bordeaux to go with dinner. Doug sipped his wine as slowly as he could without raising suspicion, but he still felt a touch of buzz coming on as dinner progressed. Of course, he was the least buzzed member of their party.

A pair of older, well-dressed British couples occupied the next table, and kept casting sideways glances at them. Toward the end of dinner one of the gentlemen, who wore a monocle over a thick white mustache, grumbled to his companions loudly enough to be overheard, "Hmmph! A typical bunch of loud, uncouth Americans, acting as if this were *Shanghai*." He said the name of the city as if it were distasteful.

"See here!" Kenny half-shouted across the table at him. "Some of us are Canadians, my good man."

The table laughed, and the maître'd had to come and ask them to please keep their voices lower.

Doug tried to laugh and joke along with the others, but his mind kept replaying the events of the afternoon, in spite of his best attempts to forget about it.

Abbie slipped her arm through his as they ate dessert, and leaned close. "Are you sure you're alright, Doug?"

"Never better." He was conscious he'd said that too fast, and the look on her face said she hadn't bought it, so he tried reassuring her with a big smile and patted her hand on his forearm.

"You just seem...distracted."

"I guess I'm just missing Lucy," he said. It wasn't untrue.

It was almost ten o'clock when they finally left the restaurant, and the air was chilly and breezy on the quay. Abbie, Julia and Betty wrapped shawls around their shoulders, while the men were forced to turn up the collars of their suit jackets, none of them having brought along an overcoat.

The Kowloon Ferry took them across the harbor a little while later, and Doug shivered in the nighttime chill.

Or perhaps it was more than the chill.

Once inside the lobby of the Peninsula Hotel, the group headed *en masse* toward the bar, but Doug waved goodbye and walked toward the elevator.

"Don't you want a night cap?" Pete asked him.

Doug shook his head. "Thanks, but I'm exhausted. I'm going to retire early."

"Alright, suit yourself," Pete said with a shrug and a bemused look. "Good night, Doug."

"Why did he even bother to come here?" Doug heard Julia say as he stepped onto the elevator, and he sighed.

"Maybe he's meeting a girl," Pete said, and Doug cringed at how loudly Pete's voice carried.

The elevator operator bowed his head and wished him good evening in accented English; Doug replied in Cantonese, and asked for the fourth floor.

As the elevator rose, Doug caught a glimpse of Kenny watching him through the gate with a concerned look. He felt guilty, but pushed it down.

He had a job to do, damn it.

Back in his room, he removed his jacket, but kept his tie on in anticipation of his unknown visitor. He paced the floor for ten minutes, and the sudden knock, when it came, made him jump. He grabbed his jacket from the back of the arm chair where he had tossed it, slipped it back on, and opened the door.

The diminutive young Chinese woman in the uniform of a Peninsula Hotel maid held out a stack of fresh towels. "Clean towel, sir?" she asked in English.

Doug took the towels with a bow of his head, and thanked her in Cantonese, then stood there awkwardly, waiting.

She stared at him. After several seconds, she asked in English, "You need bathroom cleaned? Okey-dokey sir. I clean for you." She gave him the sort of scowl that told him she thought he was a complete idiot, and he stood aside to let her in.

Once he'd closed the door, she spun around and stared at him with intense dark eyes, as if warning him that she was only here for one purpose.

He still felt uncomfortable just blurting out the information. He couldn't be too cautious about all of this, he told himself. "You came for something?" he asked in Cantonese, quietly, just in case curious ears were listening at the door.

She pursed her lips in apparent exasperation. "The price," she hissed back, also in Cantonese.

Doug nodded, trying to seem deliberative, that he was just making sure. "She said ten thousand."

The maid did not visibly react to the large sum. She only nodded her head at him, and strode to the door, letting herself out.

Doug stood in the middle of his hotel room and released a long exhale.

He jumped at another knock on his door, and his heart about leapt into his throat. He took a couple of deep breaths in an attempt to get his heart to stop racing, and composed himself before opening the door.

Kenny stood with his arms crossed, scowling.

"I was coming to check on you, since you were so subdued all evening," Kenny said with a frown, his irritation coming through in spite of the slurring of his words. "But I see that Pete was right. I didn't know the maids in this hotel offered that kind of 'service.' Or that you'd be the type to request it."

Doug had to laugh, as much from relief as from anxiety that Kenny had *almost* caught him doing something worse.

"No, nothing of that sort at all, I promise. She brought fresh towels and cleaned the bathroom."

Kenny looked suspicious. "Odd time of night to request a bathroom cleaning, Dougie."

"I was just about to take a hot bath, to relax before bed."

"Hmmm." Kenny pursed his lips.

Doug's pulse quickened again as the nerves returned. "Is that so strange?"

"I don't hear any water running."

"Oh!" Doug nearly laughed again as relief washed through him once more. "I hadn't started it yet. I was just about to."

Kenny stared at him for a moment with an unreadable expression, swaying a little. Then he grinned and tried to pat Doug's shoulder twice, missing each time. "Have a good night, old chum. See you in the morning."

Doug closed the door, and rested his forehead against the doorframe for a long moment. *How in the hell did I come to this*?

Sunday, January 26

Doug rose early, and he enjoyed breakfast while reading through the local English-language newspaper.

His friends trickled down one by one, each more bleary-eyed than the last, and ordered strong black coffee. Doug chuckled at each, and wished them a cheery "Good morning" in turn.

They replied with varying degrees of grumbling. Most of them stayed only long enough to eat a little something and head back upstairs to pack up and check out.

Doug found an open gift shop at the station, and purchased a post card showing traditional Chinese Junks sailing Victoria Harbor under the words "**HONG KONG**" in big bold letters. He turned the post card over and jotted a quick note.

> "L—
> Wishing you were here with me.
> I love and miss you,
> —Doug"

He bought one of the new airmail stamps, addressed it to Lucy at Vassar, and dropped it in the mail slot off the lobby. She'd get a kick out of the Hong Kong postage stamp and post mark.

The PanAm clipper had recently begun regular mail service between San Francisco and Manila, with stops in Honolulu, Midway, Wake, and Guam. There had already been regular mail service by amphibious plane between Manila and Hong Kong, and Doug found it amazing that his post card could get to Lucy half-way across the world in as little as a week.

The train ride home was quiet, which gave Doug too much time to stew over what he'd done the day before. His friends weren't very chatty, though things gradually returned to normal as the hours passed.

It was well past dark by the time they pulled into Shanghai station. Clearly all exhausted, they exchanged brief good-byes before climbing into cabs and going their separate ways.

And Doug was left with nothing to distract him from the knowledge that he'd done something he wished he hadn't.

Hutson

6

Thursday, February 20

Doug found Robert Hilliard near the gates of the race track, reading a newspaper. The morning's cold drizzle had gone, and the clouds were beginning to clear, allowing moments of bright afternoon sun to warm the city to nearly fifty degrees Fahrenheit.

"Good to see you, Bainbridge," Hilliard said, folding the newspaper and shaking Doug's hand.

"You as well, sir."

"I hope you don't mind the outdoor venue for our meeting," Hilliard said, motioning them toward the wide green space of the Recreation Grounds. They strolled across the still-damp grass of the bowling green. "Spring is starting to take hold here in the Yangtzee Valley, it seems a shame to miss the nice weather by meeting indoors."

"I agree, sir. Actually, the Recreation Grounds are convenient for me today. I'm meeting my friends for our twice-weekly basketball game in an hour."

"Ah, very good," Hilliard said, sounding pleased. "You play with Mr. Tolbert, Mr. Traywick, and Dr. Howerton, I presume?"

"Yes, and also Fred Perry and Stuart Vandermeer."

"That's six men."

Doug nodded. "Mr. Traywick is our reserve."

Even though six-foot-four Kenny was the perfect height for a basketball player, he wasn't very coordinated. Or really all that athletic. All gangly arms and legs. But he tried hard, and he filled in when one of the others needed a moment's rest. Pete and George were both six-two, plenty tall enough for basketball, and also more athletic than Kenny. They were good shooters. Fred and Stuart were each a touch shorter than Doug—five-ten or five-eleven—but they were young and quick, good at stealing the ball and passing it to Pete or George.

"We should have plenty of time before you have to meet them," Hilliard said. "Why don't we start with what you've learned from Miss Wong."

"Not much, sir," Doug said, feeling his cheeks flush. "She's very reticent. I've tried not to push hard, just being friendly, but there hasn't even been a crack in the wall she puts up."

Hilliard frowned. "That is disappointing." He hesitated, regarding Doug with an unsure expression for a moment. "The navy has a morality code, as you are aware...but I think sometimes the ends justify the means. I would not hesitate to do what you must, Bainbridge."

Doug felt his cheeks flush hot. "I don't think that will be necessary, Commander."

Hilliard nodded. "Probably not. This isn't a critical mission, as you know. Your purpose here remains immersion. Just remember what we discussed in November, about our shifting tactics in Asia. I don't know what role you'll be assigned by ONI after your immersion is finished, but keep in mind that a good intelligence officer may be expected to do things that most people—even most military men—might consider unsavory."

Doug felt his stomach tumble. "I've also spoken with Mr. Arthur Jones, the reporter," he said, changing the subject just enough. "He sometimes uses Miss Wong and the other members of her cell as sources, and has built some trust with them. I've kept my inquiries casual, as if I'm just curious. Mr. Jones has said that Miss Wong and her comrades have clammed up completely in the last few months."

He hoped that demonstrated that he could be flexible in his tactics. But he also worried that the lack of results might lead Hilliard back to what he'd implied before.

Hilliard nodded, and to Doug's relief didn't look displeased. "Our State Department liaisons at the embassy are coming up against the same dead-ends. Their contacts among the communists have stopped saying anything."

"That probably confirms they're involved in the Nakayama assassination."

"That is our assessment," Hilliard said. "But it doesn't give us any insights into what is coming."

"No, sir." Doug wondered how important that was to ONI. Their main mission was to gather intelligence about other nations' navies and their advancements. Political intelligence was the purview of the State Department's information officers at the embassies.

But because the U.S. Navy saw Japan as their most likely future adversary, the assassination of a Japanese sailor had piqued interest. Doug wasn't sure just how much, though.

"Is there anything else on that topic?" Hilliard asked.

Doug felt his stomach drop. For almost a month he had agonized over how much to say—if anything—about what happened in Hong Kong. Would Hilliard be upset at how far Doug had been drawn into the intrigue? Or would he see this as an opening to be explored?

It would be far worse if they found out some other way. Doug took a deep breath, and opted to gamble on the truth. "A few weeks ago— the night of the lunar New Year—Miss Wong's cell leader came to my apartment and asked me to do something for them."

He paused to await Hilliard's reaction. They were rounding the empty football/rugby field, walking toward the baseball diamond where two men threw a ball back and forth.

Hilliard stopped, but his expression gave nothing away. "Go on."

Doug glanced around, but there was no one closer than the two men on the baseball diamond, a good fifty yards away.

"He knew that my friends had gone to Hong Kong for the holiday, and he told me to join them; and then take a message to a certain house in Kowloon the next day, get an answer, and convey it to someone who would contact me at my hotel that night."

Hilliard's eyes narrowed, but not so much that he seemed angry. At least, that was Doug's hope.

"Did you agree?"

Doug couldn't discern anything from Hilliard's tone.

"He didn't give me a choice. He implied that if I didn't do as instructed, there would be painful consequences. I decided to go, and determine what to do once I knew what the message was."

Hilliard nodded, looking satisfied. "That was a wise course of action. What happened?"

Doug felt relief wash through him, and a weight seemed to lift from his shoulders. "I went to the place they instructed, the hotel spa, and a young man there gave me the message and directions to the house. He was in the uniform of an employee, but I can't say if he was a plant or a real worker."

Hilliard waved that off.

Doug continued. "He told me to ask for someone named Jin Shixin. The woman who answered would say that she was Miss Jin's sister, and I should tell her that a shipment of samurai swords from Nagasaki was coming to Shanghai, and I would like to sell one of mine to Miss Jin's patron. She would quote me a price, and I would give that price to someone who would contact me that night."

Hilliard looked away, frowning, deep in thought. "What did you make of that?"

"Nothing for certain," Doug said, hesitating. "It would seem to be a reference to Japanese maneuvers out of Nagasaki, coming to

84

Shanghai—but without specifics. The sale offer would be some sort of financial transaction pertaining to that. I couldn't help but wonder if the Reds were looking to hire a professional assassin, not one of their own."

Hilliard nodded again. "That's a reasonable hypothesis—but it raises more questions than it answers. Did you agree to take the message?"

Doug felt his heart skip a beat.

"Yes. The woman at the house said Miss Jin's patron would pay ten thousand for the sword."

Hilliard's eyes widened briefly. "That's quite a sum."

Doug was just glad Hilliard didn't explode with anger that he had agreed to do it. "What do you make of it, sir?"

Hilliard took a deep breath, and looked toward the baseball diamond, seeming to ponder it for a moment. "Ten thousand is way too much for a samurai sword—even an antique one. But, it is far less than an assassin-for-hire would charge for a job."

"I also wondered if the whole thing was a ruse," Doug confessed. "Perhaps they were just testing me."

Hilliard considered this for a few seconds, then shook his head. "I don't think so. Too involved. I'll see what I can learn about this Jin Shixin in Hong Kong. Good work, Bainbridge."

Doug allowed himself a relieved half-smile. "Thank you, sir."

"Have they contacted you since then?"

"No, sir."

"Typical," Hilliard muttered. They crossed the field, heading back toward the race track and administration building. "You may not hear from them again for months. But they will almost certainly be in contact again at some point. That's their *modus operandi*. When they do, I want you to contact me as soon as you're safe to do so. Understand?"

"Yes, sir."

Hutson

7

Wednesday, March 25

Longhua Park was packed with visitors from across Shanghai and the surrounding countryside for the annual Longhua Temple festival. Doug made his way through the crowd at the north end of the park with effort, trying to get a glimpse of the festivities. There were a few westerners on the fringes, observing, but the crowd was overwhelmingly Chinese.

At the far end of the park, where the crowd was densely packed, he could just see the curved tiled roof of the Buddhist temple, which from this distance almost looked like an ancient longboat. Beyond the temple, its famous seven-story pagoda towered over the festivities. Giant wooden dragons moved around the front of the temple, symbols of the invisible dragon spirits who were said to visit the temple on this holy day every year to grant the wishes of the worshippers.

Doug tried several vantage points to get a better view, to no avail. Disappointed, he turned away and strolled back to the northwest gate, breathing in the aroma of the blossoming peach trees.

As he was about to exit the park, he spotted a short, stocky bespectacled man in an expensive silk suit lounging against the trunk of a peach tree, staring at the crowd.

Doug's heart skipped a beat as he recognized the Japanese agent named Kawakami, who had threatened Doug at knife-point nine months before to demand Tim's files on the Korean Provisional Government in

Shanghai. The last time Doug had seen him, Kawakami killed two Chinese agents of the *Juntong*—the Chinese secret police. Then he disappeared from Shanghai.

As he walked by, Kawakami looked his way, and their eyes locked for a couple of seconds. A chill ran up Doug's spine; he had been recognized.

Doug nodded in acknowledgement, hiding his apprehension. He turned away from Kawakami and exited onto Tianyaoqiao Road. This was on the southern outskirts of the Chinese city, more than five miles from home in the International Settlement. As Doug moved north along the street, searching for an available motor cab, he glanced backward at Kawakami, now standing outside the park gate. Watching him.

His heart pounded, and he walked faster, but conscious not to speed up too much; he didn't want Kawakami to detect his apprehension. Where in the hell was a cab?

Finally he spotted one approaching from the direction of the park; Doug raised his arm to hail it, and hurried forward as it stopped. He gave the driver directions in Shanghainese, and as the car sped away, he looked through the rear windshield to see Kawakami still standing by the park gate, watching the cab.

Friday, April 10

Doug sat at the desk in the small office he rented on the third floor of a building downtown on West Peking Road, leaning back in his rolling chair, newspaper spread across his knees, his feet up on the desk next to the telephone that wasn't connected. It was a warm day, and he had the window open; the sounds of car horns, shouts of rickshaw runners, and conversations in Shanghainese and other Chinese languages drifted up from the busy street.

The frosted glass on the door behind him had the name of his father's company painted in gold lettering: **Bainbridge Imports and Fine Chinese Goods**. Officially, his story was that he was in Shanghai to operate an office for his family's business; he needed a fake office to make that believable, and last June Kenny had helpfully suggested a vacancy in the building where he had his office.

So when there was a knock on his door at four o'clock in the afternoon, Doug knew right away who it was—since he didn't actually conduct any business, Kenny was the only person who ever came by.

Not that Doug would tell him, that, of course.

He folded the newspaper and stashed it in a desk drawer.

"Ho there, old chum," Kenny said when Doug opened the door. "I need a drink in the worst way—care to close up shop early and join me?"

"You bet," Doug said. "Let me just put away what I was working on." He stepped back to the desk, picked up the manila folder that was full of pages of meaningless text, opened a drawer in the filing cabinet he kept for appearances, and stuffed the folder between several others that were also full of junk.

"Bad day?" He asked as he locked the door.

They walked toward the stairs, and Kenny groaned. "To put it mildly. I accidentally used the Canadian spelling for 'tire' in a brief to be filed today, and the barrister discovered it right before court and screamed at me for five minutes in the middle of the courthouse hall. Then we went into the courtroom, and the justices pointed out the 'misspelling' and reprimanded the barrister for it. So after court, the barrister had to scream at me again for another five minutes."

Kenny was a lawyer from Vancouver, British Columbia, and he'd come to Shanghai in 1934 to work as a solicitor representing Canadian citizens in criminal cases before the British Court of Shanghai. Canada didn't have its own diplomatic relations with the Republic of China, so Great Britain's extraterritorial rights were extended to Canadians, as part of the British Empire.

"I'm really sorry to hear that. That's terrible that he treated you that way. Your first drink is on me," Doug said as they headed down the stairs.

"You probably wouldn't understand this," Kenny said as they descended, "but we Canadians get tired of hearing the British tell us how 'American' we've become, and then hearing Americans complain about how 'British' we are. We're neither, of course. Can't we just be ourselves? Isn't that good enough?"

Doug hoped he'd never said anything to imply Kenny and Abbie seemed at all British.

A workman was painting Japanese *Hiragana* letters on the frosted glass of an office door on the ground floor as they passed—Doug couldn't read it, but he recognized Japanese *Hiragana* script when he saw it.

In typical fashion, the business name was written in *Kanji*, which was the Japanese script identical to Chinese script—so just as with different Chinese languages, Doug could read the meaning of the writing, but wasn't able to pronounce it—while the proprietor's name was written in the phonetic *Hiragana*, which Doug couldn't read.

"That's unusual for this part of town," he murmured as they passed.

"What's unusual?" Kenny asked, not paying attention to the work.

"That's Japanese he's painting on that door," Doug said, nodding backward as he held the front door open for his friend. "It's just unusual west of Honan."

Peking Road, like Nanking Road a couple of blocks to the south, had a much more Chinese feel west of Honan Road than east of it, where western-style businesses, boutiques, hotels, and restaurants predominated. Most of the Japanese businesses downtown were likewise in the eastern blocks, close to the river; and from Honan Road west to Thibet road, downtown was very Chinese. Doug liked that, and the fact that Kenny's office was located in this area had been one of the first things Doug had liked about him.

There was an American tavern on the corner of Peking Road and Honan that Doug and Kenny sometimes visited after working hours, and after leaving the building they turned east to walk the block to Honan Road.

Ahead of them, just rounding the corner from Honan, Doug spotted Kawakami walking toward them on the sidewalk, accompanied by a younger Japanese man, about thirty, taller and thinner than Kawakami.

Kawakami's eyes locked on Doug's for several seconds as they approached.

The younger Japanese man seemed to notice, and he looked from his older companion to Doug with a curious sort of expression. They both looked away just before passing the two young westerners.

Kenny had been talking more about the nasty British barrister, hands gesturing as he spoke, and hadn't seemed to notice the nonverbal exchange.

Doug wondered if the pair were headed for that office where the Japanese words were being painted. The thought of Kawakami in the same office building where he pretended to do business was not pleasant, to say the least.

They crossed Honan when the Sikh traffic officer in the intersection signaled, and entered the Liberty tavern, which was not yet full at this hour. Doug ordered their usuals—a gin and tonic for himself, and an Old Fashioned for Kenny.

Kenny took more than a sip of his drink before setting it down and sighing. "I'm sorry, Doug. I've been carrying on so about my day—how was yours?"

"Fairly uneventful, until the end," Doug said.

"Looking forward to this weekend?" Kenny asked, elbowing Doug playfully in the ribs. "Pete and I have it all planned out, and he's invited a whole lot of fun fellows to join us tomorrow night, all of our chums. If this isn't the best birthday you've ever had, I'll eat my hat on Monday."

Doug had to laugh at Kenny's earnest enthusiasm. It had been years since anyone had done anything special for his birthday—since his university days at Stanford, actually—and he was touched, even if he wouldn't have ever thought to plan a big celebration for turning twenty-six.

But this was Shanghai, after all, and big celebrations for any occasion were par for the course.

"I'm sure the only way it could possibly be better would be if you somehow brought Lucy across the Pacific to be here for it," he said.

"I would have if I could," Kenny said with a grin. "It won't be long now, though."

"No, it won't," Doug agreed, though it would seem like forever. "Less than two months to go."

"We should drink to that," Kenny said, raising his glass. "To Lucy, and her speedy arrival in Shanghai. Cheers!"

"Cheers!" Doug echoed, clinked his glass against Kenny's, and drank.

Saturday, April 11

The band in the third floor ballroom at the Paramount played swing while couples danced around the floor in the wild new style. Doug leaned against a corner of the bar, swaying not quite in time to the music, a half-empty tumbler of gin and tonic in his hand, not noticing the condensation dripping onto the knee of his pants.

His head buzzed with more than just the loud music, and a silly grin spread wide across his face. "Lucy loves to swing dance," he said to Kenny, his voice slurring.

Pete turned away from the bar with a fresh drink in his hand, and laughed. "You should go grab a pretty girl and dance, then."

Doug shook his head in exaggerated fashion. "I don't dance so well—not like that, I mean. I dance pretty good most of the time, but I don't do so good with those moves." He gestured toward the dance floor with his drink, spilling a little onto his shoe.

"How are you ever going to get better if you don't get out there and try?" Pete asked, taking Doug's glass from him and handing it to Kenny.

Peter Tolbert was perhaps the least shy or restrained person Doug had ever met, and he was always suggesting new and bold ways to have a good time. A few years older than them at twenty-nine, he had a 'work hard, play hard' attitude, and he had the uncanny knack of getting away with any crazy thing he suggested. At six-foot-two, he was almost as tall as Kenny, but probably had forty pounds more muscle, and roguish good looks, with thick dark brown hair, ruddy complexion, and hazel eyes.

"That one over there has been staring at you for a little while," Pete said with a wink and a crooked smile, and put his arm around Doug to turn him in the direction he was pointing with his glass.

An elegant Chinese woman in a silk ball gown was looking at him with an amused expression. It took Doug's addled mind a few seconds to realize who it was.

"I know her!" he said to Pete and Kenny. He motioned for them to lean close, and continued in an attempt at a whisper. "Her name's Lin-wen, and she's a bit of a tramp." Seeing their amused expressions, he added, "Trust me, I *know*."

Even as he said it, he was stunned at how easily something so indiscreet slipped out. That wasn't like him.

But why not? *Quit being such a goody-goody*, he told himself. "She gets *around*," he whispered, and then nodded with a knowing expression.

"Well! Then that settles it," Pete said, slapping Doug on the back. "You must go ask her for a dance."

Doug didn't particularly want to speak with Ming Lin-wen, but Pete's big hand on the middle of his back gave him a powerful shove forward, and he had to half-run toward her table in order to keep from stumbling and falling flat on his face.

"A pleasure to see you again, Bainbridge Douglas," she said in her crisp, bell-like Mandarin.

"Miss Ming," he slurred in Mandarin, and made a bow of his head. Then he looked at his empty hand. "I seem to have lost my drink."

She laughed. "I think perhaps you finished it, Bainbridge Douglas. I think you may have finished many drinks this evening. How long have you been here?"

"Not long," he said, holding onto the back of the empty chair next to hers. "We were at the American Club first." He looked up in thought, and counted on his fingers. "Then we went to the Cathay, then to the Park, and now here."

He left out the two hours spent at a burlesque hall between the Cathay Hotel bar and the Park Hotel.

Her eyes seemed to laugh, and he stared at her teeth as she smiled. "That is quite an evening. Must be a special occasion."

"It's my birthday," he said in a stage whisper.

"Oh? Well, allow me to wish you many happy returns of the day, Bainbridge Douglas."

"Thank you, very much," he said, pleased. Then he straightened, and pointed back toward the bar where his friends stood in a huddle, hands over their mouths, trying not to laugh out loud. "I have to return to my friends. Good evening, Miss Ming."

Her amused smile seemed dazzling as she gave him a genteel nod. "Good evening, Mr. Bainbridge."

He stumbled back to the bar, and tripped on his own shoelace. He fell forward, and Kenny caught him in both arms.

"Whoa, there! Careful, old chum, or you're liable to knock out a tooth."

Doug wrapped an arm around Kenny's shoulder and hoisted himself back up, leaning heavily on his friend. "Thank you for looking out for me," he said, patting Kenny's chest. "Now I think I need another drink."

"I think we need to get you some food," Pete said.

"Food and another drink," Doug replied as they turned him toward the door.

A large, wide-shouldered Chinese man was walking their direction as they started toward the elevator, and Doug recognized him immediately. Their eyes met, and the large Chinese man held his gaze as he passed.

"What was he staring at?" Kenny asked to no one in particular.

"I know him!" Doug said in a stage whisper. "He's the tramp's husband. And he's a real nasty character named Wu Shan. Stay away from him."

"The tramp's husband, huh?" Pete said, chuckling. "I can just imagine what a nasty character that would make him, Dougie."

Sunday, April 12

Doug's head pounded as he awoke to the sound of birds chirping, and his mind was fuzzy. His mouth felt as if it were full of cotton balls. He lifted his head to look around, and it took him a minute to realize he was outside, lying face down on the patio chaise on the rooftop courtyard of the Palace Hotel, between the two seventh-floor penthouses.

It took him a few more seconds to realize he was naked, and another couple of seconds before panic set in.

His clothes were nowhere near, though a lampshade lay on its side next to the chaise, disembodied from whatever lamp it belonged to.

He sat up too fast, and blood rushed painfully to his head. He squeezed his eyes shut and put his right hand on his forehead, while his left hand fished around for the lampshade. Finding it at last, he put it in front of his privates as he stood up—slowly—and walked to the glass door of the north penthouse.

He was relieved to find the door unlocked—*thank you, God*—and he let himself in. As he turned around, he spotted three Chinese people watching him with amused smiles from the window of the south penthouse—a man and two women, about his age, dressed in western attire. All he could do was give them a sheepish grin and a wave, then hurry behind the curtains.

Kenny sprawled across the nearest couch on his back, mouth open, one long arm dangling on the floor, the other stretched over his head. He was wearing boxer shorts, a necktie around his bare neck, black socks and garter; and Doug almost burst out laughing at the sight of him.

He might have, if his head hadn't felt like it would explode if he did.

Another figure in boxer shorts with his back to the room filled the other couch, and Doug recognized the six-foot-two frame and wavy black hair of their friend George.

He found his underwear and pants on the floor, on opposite sides of the large room from one another. As he tugged them on, he noticed a lamp without a shade, on the end table beside Kenny's head. He returned the lampshade to its rightful place, and resumed the search for the remainder of his clothes.

He counted six bottles of gin or whiskey scattered around the room, either empty or nearly so.

He found his shirt and shoes in the bedroom, and his necktie was tied to the doorknob of the open door. Fred and Stuart snored atop the bed in their underwear, an unknown naked Chinese girl curled in between them. Doug couldn't recall seeing her before. At twenty-three, Fred and Stuart were a few years younger than the others, and they wore the new-fangled briefs instead of boxer shorts.

Doug put his shirt on, draped his tie around his neck, and carried his shoes in his hand as he went back to the main room, searching for his missing socks.

When he went through the kitchen door, he found Pete sitting at the table with a steaming cup of coffee in a saucer. He wore a pair of plaid pajama pants and slippers, but his torso was bare.

"Good morning!" Pete said, far too loudly, and no doubt on purpose, judging by his ear-to-ear grin. "I'll bet you need some coffee after the night you had. And there's a bottle of aspirin on the counter." He took a cup and saucer from a silver tray, and poured coffee from a pot in the center. "I ordered room service a little while ago," he explained, handing the coffee to Doug. "Have a pineapple bun."

Doug looked around awkwardly for somewhere to put his shoes, and Pete laughed.

"Looking for these?" he asked, lifting up a pair of socks from the kitchen sink. "I'm afraid they're still damp."

Doug groaned. "Do I want to know?"

"Probably not."

There was one thing he did desperately want to know, though. "Did I do anything I really shouldn't have? I mean, there's a naked woman in the other room, and I woke up...well..."

Pete laughed again. "The other gal got up and slunk out about an hour ago. Don't worry, pal, you were a good boy. The most we could get you to do was play with their tits a little. You kept telling them about Lucy, and how beautiful she was, so after a while the other fellas, um, took over for you."

Doug felt a wave of relief wash through him.

"You were a hoot last night, Dougie," Pete went on. "You kept saying something about a Japanese spy following you, and the secret police trying to catch him, or something—but you didn't want the secret police getting *you* while they were at it. It was hilarious, we were all cracking up."

Doug felt his heart drop into the pit of his stomach. Something about Pete's words seemed awfully familiar—he could almost remember saying those things—and a deep sense of dread spread through him.

"God, I'm such an ass," he mumbled to himself.

Apparently his mumbling wasn't too quiet for Pete to overhear, for his friend chuckled and shook his head. "No, you're not. You *were* the most wasted I think I've ever seen you, though. The strait-laced Doug we all know and love would *never* strip naked and run laps around the courtyard, for instance. Kenny chased you for a minute, but gave up and sat down to wait for you to lose steam."

"Ugh!" Doug groaned, closing his eyes in shame and letting his forehead rest in his hand.

Pete chuckled again, and patted Doug's shoulder. "Good to see you loosen up—but maybe loosen up just a tad less next time, huh?"

"There were people in the next penthouse watching me when I woke up."

"Don't worry, I'm sure they were blinded by the sun reflecting off your pale ass," Pete deadpanned.

Kenny came stumbling into the kitchen a moment later. He'd put on his slacks, but not his shirt, and he was slipping his suspenders over his bare shoulders as he came in.

"Good morning!" Pete shouted, and both Doug and Kenny cringed.

"Sadist," Kenny muttered.

Doug pushed the aspirin bottle toward him while Pete laughed and poured another cup of coffee.

"How are you not hung over, Peter?" Kenny asked, blowing on the hot coffee.

Pete grinned and shrugged. "Guess I can just hold my liquor better."

"And he's been up longer," Doug said. "Who knows what he looked like earlier?"

"Nice try," Pete said.

"Not all of us are built like a linebacker, either, Peter," Kenny said.

Pete's expression took on an "aww shucks" look, and he shrugged again. Then he got up and patted them both on the shoulders as he walked past. "I guess I'd better go rouse the other fellas, and make sure that other dame hasn't rifled through everyone's wallets while they were knocked out."

After Pete left, Doug took a sip of coffee, and looked at Kenny, feeling a little sheepish. "I guess I acted like a total ass last night."

Kenny laughed. "I wouldn't say that. You were just having a good time."

Doug shook his head. "I'm not exactly proud of the things I said and did."

"You *did* decide to celebrate your birthday in your birthday suit— I'm just repeating your corny joke—but otherwise I don't think you have anything to be ashamed of."

"It sounds like I said some crazy things," Doug probed.

A strange look crossed Kenny's face. "About that, Doug—now that you mention it, I can't help but wonder—"

He was interrupted by Pete's return to the room, with Fred and Stuart in tow, both still in their jockey shorts, rubbing their eyes and scratching their crotches.

"Good morning, gents!" Kenny said with a broad smile.

Fred and Stuart both grunted as their only response.

"Aspirin?" Doug asked, sliding the bottle toward them.

Fred and Stuart each muttered "Thanks," and popped a couple of aspirin while Pete poured cups of coffee.

"I think we're going to need another pot," he said, and went out to the other room to order one.

George passed him at the kitchen door. He'd put on pants, but was still shirtless, and his suspenders dangled at the sides of his legs. "Good morning," he said in his deep, rich baritone voice, trying to sound cheerful and giving everyone a smile that wasn't quite convincing. "Hell of a party last night. How are you feeling this morning, Doug?"

He gave Doug a genuine grin, but then frowned at the coffee cup in his hand as barely any coffee dribbled out of the pot.

"Don't ask," Doug said.

"I can imagine," George replied. "Aspirin will help, but drink a lot of water this morning."

George was a physician, from Fort Wayne, Indiana. Twenty-eight years old, he'd come to Shanghai almost two years ago, not long after graduating from medical school. He worked a shift one night per week at St. Luke's Hospital in Hongkou, but otherwise had a private practice on Fouzhou Road downtown, just a few blocks from where they were.

Pete came back into the kitchen. "More coffee is on the way up, along with some more pineapple rolls for breakfast."

"Eggs and bacon would be healthier," George muttered.

"Then go order some, if you want," Pete said, letting some irritation show.

George stayed put.

"We've got an hour 'til we have to clear out," Pete said. "If anyone wants a bath before going home, better claim the tub now."

The sun was high above them when they exited the Palace Hotel onto The Bund an hour later, and Doug tugged his hat a little lower over his eyes, still a touch sensitive to the light. They crossed Nanking Road as a group, then Kenny and Doug said their goodbyes to the others, who all lived Uptown, and therefore waited in front of the Cathay Hotel for the westbound streetcar.

Doug and Kenny continued west along Nanking Road on foot. "Hey, Kenny—I'm sorry again about how I acted last night, making you chase me around when I was acting like an idiot."

Kenny waved a dismissive hand in the air. "Don't be sorry. I'm not."

"Thanks."

"I am curious, though," Kenny began, sounding hesitant.

Doug waited.

"You kept talking about '*Boring Doug*,' and not letting '*Boring Doug*' make an appearance—and I'm curious why you think you're so boring. I've never thought so."

Doug cringed, remembering now having said those words at the Paramount last night. "Let's just say I'm not usually the type of fellow to go to a burlesque show, let alone run around a courtyard in my birthday suit." He shrugged, trying to seem nonchalant. "Before I came to China, I used to have colleagues who said I was uptight."

Kenny laughed, though to Doug it sounded contrived. "Ha! You were hardly uptight last night." He patted Doug on the back.

"I think I need to settle somewhere in-between."

"I think you're just fine the way you are, old chum," Kenny said.

"Thanks."

"Though in-between is good."

They rounded the corner onto Honan Road and proceeded north toward Soochow Creek.

"The other thing I wanted to ask about," Kenny started, his voice quieter, and again hesitant.

"Yes?"

"Towards the end of the night, not long before you stripped off the last of your clothes and began running around, you started telling everyone that a Japanese spy was following you, and the Chinese secret police were trying to catch him, but you didn't trust them, either. It sounded like a tall tale for entertainment, and everyone was laughing—but I couldn't help remembering what you said Friday about the Japanese company moving into that office on the ground floor at work."

"I was just talking like a crazy person. A crazy *drunk* person, that's all." He glanced up at Kenny's face, but his friend didn't look convinced.

"I wouldn't have given it a second thought—the Japanese company, that is—but you pointed it out specially."

Doug shook his head and tried to look amused. "Don't worry about it, buddy, OK? I read that Graham Greene novel last week, and I guess it must have put things in my drunk head."

But Kenny still looked concerned. They'd reached the corner of Soochow Road South, just before the bridge, and stopped. Kenny and Abbie's apartment was a block back to the east, while Doug's neighborhood sat across the creek in Hongkou—officially the North District. Kenny stared at Doug for a moment, searching his face.

"What?" Doug asked.

"Doug—you'd tell me if you were in some sort of trouble, wouldn't you? I could help, you know."

Doug patted his friend's arm below the shoulder. "There's no trouble, honestly—but I appreciate your offer, I really do. Thanks, Kenny."

He touched the rim of his hat as he turned away and crossed the bridge toward home. He hoped everyone would just forget what he'd said.

Dear God, don't let this come back to bite me in the ass.

8

Friday, June 5

The First Class passengers were nearly finished coming down the gangway, without any sign of Lucy, when Doug finally spotted her, waiting behind the barricade on the Second Class deck.

He tried not to let his surprise show, and as she approached down the plainer Second Class gangway a few moments later, he waved and smiled. She beamed at him, then turned to the Customs Officer and handed over her declaration page and passport. Once he'd marked it off and returned her passport, she ran toward Doug and threw her arms around him.

"God, I've missed you!" she gushed in his ear, pressing her cheek against his and squeezing him tightly.

"I wrote you every other week, just like we said," he replied, stroking the back of her soft blonde hair. "I bet you thought I wouldn't."

"Ha! Maybe," she said, releasing the hug, but keeping her hands on his arms as she leaned back to look at him with a sardonic half-smile. "Ten months *is* a long time, and a fella can get forgetful."

"I could never forget you," he said, feeling giddy at having her here, seeing her and touching her for real instead of just in his dreams.

She gave him another quick hug, then took his hand and walked with him toward the collection of Second Class luggage waiting beside The Bund. "I did have faith in you, but a girl can't hang *all* her hopes on the fairy-tale ending."

She gave Doug the claim ticket for her luggage, and Doug handed it to the Chinese porter, who scurried off, returning first with a large steamer trunk, and then with two valises. Doug tipped him a quarter and thanked him in Shanghainese.

"You were able to reserve a room for me at the Astor House? Or am I staying at a different hotel until I find something permanent?"

"Actually, I found you an apartment a few blocks from mine," he said as the porter raised his arm to hail a rickshaw.

Her eyes clouded, and her lips tightened. "Doug, I can find my own apartment. I know what I like, and once I have a job I'll know if I can afford it."

Part of him had worried she'd react that way. "Just wait until you see it. If you don't like it, I'll cancel it. I really think you'll like it. Shall we go there first? Or would you rather stop for lunch?"

"Lunch would be marvelous," she said with a heavy sigh. "But maybe it would be best to go look first, and then go eat. I can always get settled in later."

Doug held her hand as she climbed into the back of the rickshaw, and hopped in beside her. He gave the runner an address on Soochow Road North, in Shanghainese.

Lucy looked around, face raised, her blue eyes glowing with excitement. "God, it's great to be back. You know, I really missed Shanghai while I was back in the States."

"I'm really glad you're back," he said, giving her hand a squeeze. "But tell me—why did you travel Second Class?"

She shook her head and rolled her eyes. "Long story—want the short version?"

"Sure."

"My father didn't really believe I was coming back, as it turned out. He thought it was a silly girl's fancy, and that I'd come to my senses and marry a good Chicago boy. When I came home for Christmas vacation, he made sure I was introduced to at least a dozen sons of business associates, all from 'very good families.' I had to keep reminding him that I was committed to you, and coming back to Shanghai. I don't think he really believed me until spring, when I wrote that I needed to arrange my passage from San Francisco. He wrote back that he wasn't going to pay one cent toward my 'folly,' and that if I were determined to go on with it I had to pay for it myself."

She released a long sigh. "I had a bit of money saved from little amounts my grandparents gave me over the years, and I used some of that to buy my ticket. I decided not to blow it all on a First Class fare, so I travelled Second Class on the train across country. It felt *very* bourgeois. Not as much privacy in the sleeping car, but it was tolerable. I hear in Third Class you don't even get a bed, so I wasn't so bad off."

Doug imagined she stood out like a sore thumb, with her elegant clothes and her Vassar-girl accent. "How was it on the ship? Was it very different?"

"The cabin was barely smaller than the ones Mother and I had last year in First Class, and maybe the furnishings weren't quite as nice, but really you could hardly tell the difference. It was the dining room that was really different—the tables, the place settings, even the food were not as nice. And there was no ballroom, either; so no dancing."

She looped her arm through his and leaned against him. "Not that *that* mattered. I would have only wanted to dance with you, anyway."

He felt his heart melt at that, and he kissed her forehead. "Welcome back," he whispered.

"I know there's so much I need to do—but for today, I plan to spend the rest of the day with you. Alone, if possible." She looked up at him, and gave him a smoldering gaze that made his heart flutter.

"No argument from me. Kenny and Abbie are eager to see you, and asked to have dinner with us as soon as possible—but I told them tomorrow night at the earliest." He put his arm around her and kissed her forehead again. "I want you all to myself for now."

"Good, we're of one accord, then," she said with a firm nod. Then her expression broke into a smile again. "I'm looking forward to seeing them again, too—Abbie was such a dear, she wrote me almost as much as you did—but tomorrow is plenty soon enough. I'm sure they understood."

"Of course they did."

They arrived at the building where Doug had found an apartment, and he tipped the rickshaw runner a quarter. Lucy stood on the sidewalk, looking out across the street and Soochow Creek beyond, toward downtown Shanghai. Houseboats bobbed in the water along both banks of the wide creek.

"Is this where I *live*, Doug? With this view?"

"You like it?"

"It's spectacular!" she gushed. Then she tried to look stern. "But the apartment had better be nice, too. I don't want to live in a hovel with a view."

He grinned. "Come on, let's get your key and take you upstairs." He picked up her trunk and hauled it through the front door while the rickshaw driver held it open. Lucy followed with a valise in each hand.

After introducing Lucy to the landlord and landlady and getting the key, he took her to her apartment—a third-floor walk-up in this four-story building, with windows facing the creek and downtown.

The windows were open, and a faint breeze shifted the white curtains, but the apartment was hot and stuffy. "The first thing you'll want to get is a bunch of fans," he told her.

While she stood in the middle of the living room, looking around and nodding, he dragged her trunk into the bedroom and plopped it on top of the creaky iron-framed bed. He went back to the living room, and found her looking out the window. He stood beside her and put an arm around her waist.

"This is wonderful, Doug, better than I could have hoped for, being a single girl in a new city. I can't believe you found this for me. But how do I know if it's within my budget?"

"Don't worry about that."

"Douglas Bainbridge, I *told* you I want to be independent. If I can't pay for it with my own income, I won't stay."

"Of course." In one of her letters that spring, she wrote about what kind of job she hoped to find. He had a few leads for her—but that could wait. He knew better than to suggest more than one challenge to her independence at a time. "You won't have trouble finding a job, and the rent in Shanghai is better than you'd think. Let's talk about it over lunch."

He felt her stir in the middle of the night, and he raised his head. "Are you awake?" he whispered.

She still lay curled against him, the way they had fallen asleep, and her white skin glowed in the moonlight that came through his bedroom window.

"I just need some water," she whispered back, getting up from the bed and stepping toward his dresser, where a pitcher of water sat next to a cup, a washing bowl, and a hand towel. There was enough light from the nearly-full moon that he could see a rivulet of sweat sliding down the crevice of her spine toward her backside.

After taking a long drink of water, she dabbed at her face with his towel, and then at the valley between her breasts. She looked over and saw him watching, and a hint of smile curled her lips. She sauntered back to the bed, and lay down facing him.

He reached out his hand, and ran his fingertips down her side toward her hip, and then back again. It made her shiver.

"Good lord, Doug—how do you sleep here without air conditioning?"

"You'll get used to it. It took me a while, too."

"I hope you're right." She shook her head. "I don't see how, though—this is miserable. I forgot how oppressive the heat is here, and the humidity. At least at the Astor House, we had air conditioning."

"You just have to sleep on top of the covers, not under them," Doug said, still stroking her side. "And always naked, with a fan blowing on you. You can get your pajamas out in October."

"You're the expert. Clearly."

He heard it in her voice, and his eyes moved back up to her face, saw the suggestive half-smile on her lips.

It might be too hot to sleep, but it wasn't too hot for other things.

Thursday, June 11

"I am so excited for you!" Abbie gushed when Lucy delivered the news about her new job. They were sitting side-by-side at the bar in the Cathay at five o'clock in the afternoon, with Doug and Kenny on either side of them.

"Thank you so much," Lucy said, accepting Abbie's hug. "I'm sure I wouldn't have gotten the position without your recommendation."

"Nonsense. You are supremely qualified, and the regents were impressed with you at your interview."

Lucy had been offered a position as a teacher of English and American literature at St. Anne's Academy, a co-educational Anglican high school down the street from St. John's University. Abbie taught Algebra and Geometry at St. Anne's, so when Doug mentioned the open position there, he posited it as Abbie's suggestion. He didn't mention that he'd asked if there were any openings.

"I can't see how, I was a nervous wreck the entire time," Lucy replied, blushing. "I've never taught before, and between us, I'm *terrified* that I'll be absolutely horrid at it."

"Don't worry," Abbie said with a dismissive wave. "You clearly know your subject, and you love it—so just tell the kids what's wonderful about the books you're teaching, and you'll do fine."

"I can't think of a better job for you than teaching kids to love books," Doug said, placing his hand on Lucy's. "You'll be wonderful at it, you'll see."

"Here, here!" Kenny said.

Lucy took a deep breath and shook her head. "I don't know how I'm going to teach Chaucer to Chinese boys and girls. It's hard enough for us. Or Shakespeare, for that matter."

"Relax," Abbie said. "Most of the Chinese students have studied English since they were six years old, and you'll be surprised how well they comprehend—every bit as well as the Canadian, American, and British students."

In addition to being co-ed—a significant plus to Lucy—St. Anne's Academy was also international and interracial, with more than half of the students being Chinese. It was also less than a mile from her new apartment, so she could walk there in good weather.

"You're all right, I'm sure," Lucy said, taking another deep breath. "I'm probably being silly about it."

"You should let us take you out to celebrate," Kenny said. "Tomorrow night, our treat—dinner at Velardi's, then a movie at the Majestic, and then maybe dancing at the Paramount. Sound good?"

"Sounds lovely—but you really don't have to, you know," Lucy said.

"Nonsense, we insist."

"Alright, if you insist. Thank you."

Doug gave her hand a squeeze. "And now you can write to your parents that you found a job already, and you're settling in just fine, thank you very much. That should be a load off your mind."

"You have no idea."

"Oh, I can imagine," Doug said.

"I'm afraid the curriculum is rather rigid and old-fashioned," Abbie said. "Nothing published this century, I'm sure. Nothing even the *tiniest* bit racy or controversial—so no 'Lost Generation' books. That's the downside of teaching at a religious school."

"I wonder if I could talk them into Pearl Buck's books," Lucy said. "She was the daughter of missionaries, after all, and there's nothing racy about her stories. But they're still modern. And being set in China, with Chinese characters—well, the students could relate to them, and come to really love reading because of that."

"It's worth a try," Abbie said. "Strike while the iron's hot, as they say."

"Speaking of racy," Lucy said, and then paused to look around. Everyone leaned close almost instinctively, and she lowered her voice. "I have a copy of *Tropic of Cancer*. My friend Eleanor bought several copies last summer when she was touring Europe. It's banned in the States—and in Canada, too, I think—but she said you can find it in France. She smuggled them back with her, brought them to Vassar and sold them to her friends. I bought one."

The look on Abbie's face was, Doug thought, 'deliciously scandalized.' Impressed, to say the least.

"Have you *read* it, then?"

Lucy almost giggled. "Yes! It's amazing! I'll loan it to you, you'll love it."

"Would you? Oh, how wonderfully *deviant* of you. And I love that about you, Lucy—you might be my best friend ever."

Lucy laughed. "My pleasure. I'll wrap it up and bring it with me to dinner tomorrow."

"Is it as racy as they say it is?" Doug asked.

She gave him a sly smirk. "It's rather candid," she murmured.

He felt himself blush, and wasn't sure why.

Friday, June 12

After dinner and wine at Velardi's, the four of them caught a motor cab to the Majestic, Shanghai's newest and sleekest movie theater. Kenny bought tickets to see *It Had to Happen*, staring George Raft and Rosalind Russell.

"I just adore Rosalind Russell," Abbie said as they took their seats. "She and Greta Garbo are my favorites."

"They're both wonderful," Lucy said, taking a seat between Abbie and Doug. "But I'm a bigger fan of Bette Davis. Have any of you seen *The Petrified Forest* yet? It was released a few months ago, about the same time as this picture."

"No, but I believe it's coming here next week," Kenny said, stepping around to take the seat on the other side of Doug. "We usually get pictures here about two or three months after their North American release."

"Then you must see it when it does," Lucy told them. "Bette Davis is spectacular in it, as this girl who dreams of going to France and being an artist. She's so relatable. And Humphrey Bogart—I have no words for how dramatic his performance was. Chilling—yes, that would describe it, absolutely chilling."

"Then I suppose we have no choice," Kenny said with a grin, leaning across Doug. "The four of us are seeing *Petrified Forest* next Friday night, right here."

Doug took Lucy's hand, smiled at her and winked.

The lights went down, the red curtain parted, and the familiar refrains introducing the Universal newsreel began. It was dated more than a week ago, having taken that long to cross the Pacific. There was nothing new for those who, like Doug, read the newspaper; but it was still interesting to actually see the news.

Images of strikes and street riots in Spain flashed across the screen, as the announcer proclaimed in dramatic voice how this demonstrated the collapse of law and order in the once-great country, with members of the outlawed Falange party attacking labor unionists and other supporters of the Popular Front government.

Doug couldn't help but see parallels to the fighting in China between the conservative Nationalist government, and the communists who controlled large parts of the interior. The Popular Front—a coalition that included socialists, communists, and center-left republicans—had won the February elections in Spain, and then outlawed the far-right Falange, who were now rioting.

A similar coalition in France—coincidentally also named the Popular Front—had more recently won the French general elections in May. Now there were communists in the ruling cabinets of both France and Spain; Doug wondered how much hand-wringing must be going on in the halls of Washington D.C. these days.

He had certainly heard nothing more from Commander Hilliard about getting close to Wong Mei-Ling and her comrades.

For some reason, he found that amusing, and began to chuckle. Lucy gave him a small jab to the ribcage with her elbow.

After the film, as they filed out of the theater into the brightly lit lobby, Kenny put an arm around Doug's shoulders. "We mentioned maybe going dancing at the Paramount—but what do you say to meeting Pete and Julia, and George and Betty at the bar at the Park? Lucy's not met them yet, has she?"

"No, I haven't," Lucy said, slipping her arm through Doug's.

"And we can always go on to the Paramount after a drink or two. Or the others may want to go there with us. We'll make a night of it."

"That's fine by me," Doug said, looking at Lucy. "Are you up for a big night on the town?"

"Yes, let's."

As they walked out the door, Lucy held back, tugging on Doug's arm. "Julia is the one you've written about in your letters, who acts like the Queen Bee, is that right?"

Doug laughed. "Yes, that's her."

"Oh, goodie," Lucy said, and they walked out the door to where Kenny and Abbie waited on the sidewalk.

"But her husband Pete is one of the friendliest fellows you'll ever meet. I guess it is true what they say, that opposites attract."

They caught a motor cab to the Park Hotel, the tallest building in China at twenty-two stories high, that towered over the race track and Recreation Grounds.

They found their friends in the bar, well into their cocktails.

Doug watched Lucy closely, worried she wouldn't like his friends. She seemed a little taken aback at first by Pete's gregarious reaction to being introduced to her. But she quickly adapted—or pretended to, Doug couldn't be sure—and put on a dazzling smile as she shook hands with all the new people.

Doug couldn't help but notice her reaction as she laid eyes on Dr. George Howerton, and a stab of jealousy sank into his gut as her eyes lingered a few seconds, sparkling.

"Something caught your eye?" he asked quietly a moment later when everyone else had returned their attention to their ongoing conversation.

"Pardon?"

"You sure stared at George for a while," Doug said, not bothering to hide his irritation.

She laughed out loud. The others looked at her, and she placed her hand flat on Doug's chest and continued laughing. They turned back to their conversation a few seconds later.

"What in God's name is so damned funny, if I may ask?"

"You!" she said, still laughing, and dabbed a silk handkerchief at the tears forming in her eyes. "Oh Douglas Bainbridge, I haven't laughed that hard in weeks. Now, why on Earth would you say that? You couldn't possibly be jealous."

"You stared at George," he repeated, scowling. "You were pretty google-eyed. It was obvious."

"Well, you never mentioned in your letters how handsome George is."

He didn't know whether to be irritated or relieved at the matter-of-fact tone she used. He looked over at George, who was no doubt the

113

handsomest man in their group, with his dimpled chin, clear white skin, wavy black hair, and strikingly blue eyes. Still, it made his blood pressure rise thinking of how Lucy had noticed it.

He looked back at her, and his cheeks flushed at her amused smile. He looked away, and raised his arm for the bartender.

"Don't worry, darling," she said, rubbing his arm. "You have absolutely nothing to worry about. For starters, you are the most interesting man I've ever met. And on top of that, you know as well as I do that George has nothing on your looks."

He looked back at her with an arched eyebrow. That was nice of her to say, but really?

"Oh, come on, Doug. You know you look like you just stepped out of the Sears Roebuck catalog. If you'd grown up in Los Angeles instead of San Francisco, they would have cast you in movies years ago."

"I can't act."

"As if *that* would matter, with your face."

He felt himself blushing, and looked away again, back toward the bartender. "Gin and tonic, please, and a champagne cocktail."

He kept his face forward while the bartender made their drinks, and when they were delivered a few minutes later he turned around to hand Lucy her champagne flute. He was startled at the searching look in her eyes.

"You really don't know that, do you?"

"Know what?" he pretended. Were they still talking about this?

"Surely you've been told before," she said, still staring at him with an intensity that made him uncomfortable.

"I don't know what you mean."

"Yes you do, don't play dumb. It's not becoming." The momentary cross look left her face, and the enigmatic expression returned. "Didn't your mother ever tell you how handsome you are? Or your sisters?"

"Good heavens, no!" Doug could never imagine his mother saying anything of the sort—she'd made moral pronouncements against vanity on many occasions, usually when her children insisted on buying the latest fashions.

"That really was a cold home you grew up in, wasn't it?"

He wasn't sure why that raised his hackles—it was the truth, after all—but it did. He frowned.

"But even so, Doug, surely you noticed how people are always drawn to you."

No, they were always drawn to Brent; I was always with him, along for the ride. "No, I never noticed."

His boarding school roommate and best friend, Brent Aleshire, had been without a doubt the handsomest boy at the country club dances, a tow-head blond with pale blue eyes, dimpled cheeks and chin, and an easy charm that came from an air of unquestionable confidence. Brent was always the center of attention, the proverbial Golden Boy, and Doug just enjoyed being part of the fun.

They'd had a bit of a falling out right before graduation, and in the fall of 1928 Brent went off to New York to attend Columbia, while Doug stayed in California and went to Stanford. David Yen had become Doug's best friend at Stanford.

Lucy gave up. "Well, you shouldn't worry." She took a sip of her champagne cocktail. "Besides, it should count for something that I came half-way across the world for you. That should earn me a little trust, at the very least."

He felt ashamed of his reaction. "Of course it does, I don't know what I was thinking. I apologize."

She smiled and took his hand. "Apology accepted," she said. "Now let's go mingle, or your friends will think I'm trying to keep you all to myself."

"We're out celebrating Lucy's new job," Kenny told the group a few minutes later.

"Congratulations!" Pete said, looking genuinely happy. "What sort of work will you be doing?"

"I'm going to teach, English and American literature."

"She's teaching at the same school I do," Abbie added, beaming.

"That's wonderful," Betty said, her smile warm and friendly.

"Yes, and best of luck," George said.

Julia's smile seemed almost cat-like. "Teaching is a wonderful profession," she said, sounding like she was making a speech. "I'm sure you'll find it very rewarding. It's a good job for educated women—if you *have* to work."

Doug felt his gut tighten. Julia had never worked, of course.

Lucy, though, seemed to take it in stride, and didn't miss a beat before replying, "Oh, I *want* to work. Independence is important, don't you think? No modern woman should be without a vocation in this day and age. So, Mrs. Tolbert—may I call you Julia? Thank you. So, Julia— what sort of work do you do?"

Julia's smile grew fixed, icy even. Doug suppressed a laugh, and the look on Kenny's face said that he was doing the same. Abbie looked at Lucy with wide, admiring eyes. Pete turned to the bartender to order a round of drinks, and George and Betty looked down.

"I volunteer with the American Red Cross, and I run our household." Julia paused and swirled the red wine in her glass. "We have a cook and a maid, you see, plus an active social calendar that must be maintained."

"That must keep you quite busy," Lucy murmured, and took a sip of her champagne cocktail. "Oh, thank you, Pete."

"More drinks for everybody," Pete said, a little too loudly, passing out cocktails left and right, and pretending there hadn't been an uncomfortable showing-up of his wife that just transpired.

"We're going up to the Paramount in a little while, to go dancing," Kenny said. "Anyone care to join us?"

"That sounds fun, count us in," George said.

116

"We'll all go," Pete said, back to his usual gregarious self. "We'll dance the night away, and not go home until the sun comes up."

"I suppose we could go to the Paramount," Julia said. "But no dancing for me, Peter." She looked at Lucy with a dazzling smile and patted her forearm. "They've started doing nothing but *swing* dance there the last several months. It's really quite something, if you're not easily scandalized. You should see it, the way everyone flies around, hips bumping, and with *no* regard for how high their skirts are twirling."

Lucy's face lit up with enthusiasm. "That sounds swell! I just love to swing dance—don't you Doug?"

Doug had to suppress a laugh for the second time that evening. "I do with you."

"I think that settles it," Kenny said. "After this round of drinks, let's head on to the Paramount."

Doug and Lucy caught their own cab outside of the Park Hotel and rode alone as the car took them west up Bubbling Well Road.

"Well, *that* was an interesting time," Lucy said as soon as the door closed and the cab pulled away from the curb. "I like your friends, Doug—I really do—but that Julia is a beast, isn't she?"

Doug chuckled. "She can be, sometimes. She was worse than usual tonight. She likes to maintain her social dominance, I think, and you were clearly a threat to her in that regard, darling."

"I can take care of myself, you know."

"Oh, I know, believe me—and after tonight, so do all of the rest of our friends."

She looked a little sheepish for a moment, and twisted a handkerchief between her fingers. "I hope I didn't embarrass you in front of all your friends."

"You didn't," Doug said, and took hold of her hand. "On the contrary, I was very proud to be with you tonight. My girl can stand up with the best of them."

She smiled, and a look of relief crossed her eyes. "That's the nicest thing you've ever said, Douglas Bainbridge."

He leaned in and kissed her.

"And besides, Julia is just jealous because you're so much prettier than she is."

Lucy laughed. "That's the second nicest thing you've said."

9

Friday, July 10

Doug came out of a grocery store a few blocks east of his apartment with a paper bag in the crook of one arm, and saw Wong Mei-Ling hurrying across the street, headed east toward Wusong Road.

That's odd. It wasn't her day off, and even if it were, why would she be heading toward Japantown? It made no sense.

He followed her.

She glanced around and ducked into a narrow alley half a block before Wusong.

Doug crept to the alley, staying by the entrance in case she turned around again, and he had nowhere to hide. She slipped along the back walls of the buildings that lined the west side of the avenue. She stopped at a door about halfway down, and knocked, paused, then knocked twice more. A moment later she disappeared inside.

Doug hesitated a second, then looked around to make sure no one else was watching that alley, and hurried down to the door where she had entered. It was nondescript, just a back door into a three-story brick building. There were dented trash cans beside the door that reeked of garbage and buzzed with flies, just like every other back door along both sides of the alley.

Doug counted the doors; this was the sixth building from the cross street. He went back down the alley, jogged over to Wusong, then up the west side of the avenue.

At the sixth door he slowed and took a look.

It was a hardware store named Chang's. Nothing about it seemed out of the ordinary—other than the fact that its name was Chinese, in a block that had turned increasingly Japanese in the last year. Looking down the street, Doug now saw more Japanese than Chinese names on this side of the Avenue, which marked the western boundary of Japantown.

Or used to, anyway.

Doug moved on after a couple of seconds, wary that Wong Mei-Ling would see him on the sidewalk, looking into the store. He could explain it away as window shopping on a Friday afternoon, but she'd remain suspicious.

He looped around the block and headed back toward home. This route took him past Mr. Chen Gwan's apartment building, where his friend Tim McIntyre had lived. Doug paused for a moment in front of the building, and looked up at the third floor window that had been Tim's.

He and Jonesy had sat there and gone through the files that ultimately led them to Tim's killer. Doug was about to turn away and continue home, when he saw movement in the first floor window.

Mr. Chen stuck his head out. "Hello, Mr. Bainbridge. How are you?" he said in Shanghainese.

Doug gave Mr. Chen a polite bow. "I am very well, thank you. It has been a while. I hope you and Mrs. Chen are well."

Mr. Chen smiled and nodded. "Long time, no see," he said in Pidgin.

"That's true," Doug said, feeling some guilt that he hadn't kept in better touch with the Chens after finding Tim's killer.

"Li Sung came by to see us yesterday," Mr. Chen said. "She is getting married next week. She's very happy. Mrs. Chen and I are happy for her. She has been through so much."

Doug nodded, feeling pangs of sadness along with happiness for Sung. It had been more than a year since Tim's death, and she deserved to move on with her life and find love with someone new.

"Is he Chinese?" Doug asked, and immediately wondered why that would matter. As if it would be less of an affront to Tim's memory if his replacement were different than he? That was silly.

Chen nodded. "Yes, he is Chinese. A young doctor she met at that church over on Tianjian Road, the one that helped her out last year."

"Yes, I know the place," Doug said. He occasionally visited the Presbyterian Church on Tianjian Road, and knew the pastor there. He didn't attend services regularly, but on the occasions that he did, he attended the English-language service rather than the Shanghainese one. He likely would have never seen Li Sung's fiancé.

He wished Mr. Chen a good day, bowed, and started back toward home. It was just a few blocks to his building, but he peeked into Mr. Hwang's store as he entered instead of immediately going upstairs.

Mr. Hwang himself worked the counter, and Doug wondered what excuse Wong Mei-Ling had given for why she needed to leave.

He paused mid-step. Perhaps he could get Mr. Hwang to say.

He went back to the store, and bowed at the landlord. "Good afternoon, Mr. Hwang. I came to speak with Miss Wong. Is she on a break?"

Mr. Hwang returned Doug's bow. "I'm afraid Miss Wong had to leave. I am covering the store this afternoon."

Doug feigned surprise. "Oh? I hope she isn't ill."

"No. A personal matter."

Did he know, and wasn't saying? Or was that all Wong Mei-ling had said, and he chose not to pry? Doug wasn't sure. Mr. Hwang's expression gave away nothing.

"Perhaps I can assist you, Mr. Bainbridge?"

"No, thank you. I'll speak with Miss Wong tomorrow. A personal matter."

Doug sat at his kitchen table at five o'clock with a pot of tea and the afternoon newspaper. He took both the English-language morning paper and the Chinese-language afternoon paper, and was often surprised at the different stories that ran in each.

The sounds from the street outside his open window grew louder as the work day ended and crowds made their way home.

Lucy would be home by now. She was going to cook dinner for them this evening, and he'd promised to arrive at six. He decided to leave a little early, and pick up some flowers for her from the florist around the corner from her building.

He washed up a bit, and walked out his door a little after five-thirty. The weather was stifling hot, the air heavy and so thick with humidity that it was hard to take a deep breath, and there was an almost total absence of breeze. The city's stench was particularly pungent this evening.

The Friday evening crowds were packed along Kiangse Road as he headed south toward Soochow Creek, and he stopped in the little flower shop just north of the bridge. A plump, middle-aged Chinese woman behind the counter bowed as he entered, and greeted him in Pidgin. He returned her greeting in Shanghainese.

He picked out a collection of white and pink lotus blossoms—which the lady behind the counter told him were grown in their own pond—and whistled to himself as he left the store and rounded the corner onto Soochow Road North.

He bounded up the stairs of her building in spite of the stuffy heat, and hid the flowers in his left hand behind his back as he knocked on her door.

Lucy answered wearing a white apron over a red house dress, smiled and kissed his cheek. She beamed when he brought the flowers from behind his back and held them out to her.

"Oh Doug, they're beautiful! Let me put them in some water."

Her apartment smelled of roasting poultry, and he took a deep breath to savor the smell.

"I stopped at the butcher down the street on my way home from the school, and bought a duck. I'm roasting it the same as I would a chicken," she said from the kitchen sink, filling a vase with water.

"It smells delicious."

"I hope it tastes delicious," she said, setting the vase in the middle of the table, and arranging the flowers in it. "I followed the same recipe I learned in home economics back in high school when they taught us how to roast a chicken. I can't tell you how many times I've made chicken this way. I just hope it works as well for duck."

"I'm sure it will," Doug said, putting his hands on her shoulders and smiling at her. "I've looked forward to this all day."

"Me too," she admitted with a sigh. "It will be nice to just stay in for a change on a Friday night."

"Just you and me," he said, and gave her a kiss.

"Music to my ears," she agreed. Then she winked at him and turned back toward the kitchenette. "Let me check the bird."

A sound like a distant gunshot echoed through the kitchen window, followed by another, and then two more in quick succession.

Lucy looked toward the window, then back at Doug as he hurried through the kitchen. "Firecrackers?"

"No," he said, and stuck his head out the kitchen window. The women in the courtyard had stood and were talking amongst themselves, ignoring their sizzling woks for a moment. Doug heard loud chatter from the street out front, and he ducked back inside and hurried across her apartment to look out the living room window.

"What's going on?" Lucy asked behind him, concerned.

"I'm not sure—but that was definitely gunfire."

"Where?" her voice sounded alarmed.

"Toward the east, I think. Hard to say with the way it echoed."

"Close by?"

She still sounded alarmed, and he pulled his head back inside and turned to face her, putting his hands on her shoulders. "Not too far, but several blocks, at least. I'll check it out."

"Why?"

"I'll see what I can learn."

"Doug, be careful," she pleaded, grabbing his forearm as he passed her.

He gave her what he hoped was a reassuring smile, and put his hand on top of hers. "I will." Then he gently removed her hand from his arm, grabbed his hat, and went out the door. He rushed down the stairs.

Crowds were milling along the sidewalk, and passersby shouted to rickshaws coming from the east, asking for information. "A shooting in Japantown," was all anyone said for a while.

Doug decided to get closer, and moved down the street a couple of blocks.

Just this side of the twenty-story Broadway Mansions Hotel, a Chinese businessman in a western-style suit stood surrounded by about a dozen people, all Chinese, and recounted in rapid Shanghainese what he had seen. He was about mid-thirties, and Doug noticed he had no hat. His expression seemed a little shaken.

"It was a deliberate attack," he said. "The killer wore an assassin's hood, a black one, and he shot a Japanese man at close range, right in front of him."

"Who was the man he shot?" someone asked. "Another sailor?"

The businessman in the middle of the circle shook his head. "It was a businessman, in a nice suit and hat."

"Who was it?"

"I don't know him, but the killer did—he called his name before he shot him." His expression was grave, but he also seemed to be enjoying the attention as those around him peppered him with questions. His tone became more grandiose, and his hands more expressive.

Doug turned back toward the west, and as he departed he heard the witness describing an axe on the assassin's belt. *That's a strange detail.*

"What's going on?" Lucy demanded as soon as he walked in.

"Someone shot a Japanese businessman over in Japantown," he said, setting his hat on the table. "There's a rumor it was a professional assassin."

"Is it true, do you think?"

Doug shrugged. "Possibly—one witness claims to have seen the attack, and he said the shooter wore a black assassin's hood, called the man's name, and shot the Japanese man from close range directly in front of him."

"Oh, my God!" Lucy's hand went to her mouth.

Just then, Doug remembered Wong Mei-Ling sneaking down the alley near the edge of Japantown. He hoped it was a coincidence.

"This happened once last fall. In November, a pair of Chinese men shot a Japanese sailor on Wusong Road. Two hundred Japanese marines patrolled Japantown for the next day, and the police launched a big investigation, but they never identified the killers."

"In November? Well that's been, what, eight months? Surely the two aren't connected."

Doug took a deep breath and looked up in thought a moment. "I suppose it's possible. Coincidences do happen. But my boss at the embassy in Nanjing thinks it was the communists who did the first killing, based upon a declaration they made last August at the Seventh World Congress in Moscow. I'd appreciate if you don't share that with anyone, though."

"I won't. You know you can trust me."

He smiled. "Yes, I do. So I'm going to tell you that my boss, Commander Hilliard, asked me to see if I could learn what the communists were planning by getting friendly with Wong Mei-Ling, who works in Mr. Hwang's shop below my apartment."

125

A strange look crept into Lucy's blue eyes. "That sounds an awful lot like spying, Doug. I thought you said you don't do that."

"I don't. Well, it's kind of a gray area, I suppose."

She wore a stern expression that took him by surprise. "I don't like it, Doug."

"Neither did I." He walked into the kitchenette and started removing dishes from her cabinet. "None of my attempts to get friendly with Miss Wong worked, and there hadn't been any other attacks since November, so it just kind of fell by the wayside, forgotten."

"But now?"

He looked over to see her standing beside him, and she placed a hand on top of his on the counter.

He shrugged. "I don't know."

"This Miss Wong, who works in the shop in your building—is that the round-faced girl I've seen sweeping the floor as I've gone by? About my age?"

Doug nodded. "I think she's a year younger than you, actually. But yes, that's her."

"How 'friendly' did they want you to get?"

He laughed a little. "Are you jealous?"

"Not at all," she said, sounding completely serious. "You know I don't get jealous. I'm not that insecure. And even if I were, I trust you. You know that, don't you?" Her expression didn't look angry or jealous, and her eyes looked at him with more of a questioning look.

He grinned and gave her hand a squeeze. "Yes, I know that."

"Good. Now go be a dear, and set the table."

It was late when Doug left Lucy's apartment, and made his way home up Kiangse Road. As he turned onto Huang Lei Road, a block from his apartment, he slowed down, as if on a leisurely stroll.

In truth, he was waiting for Constable Billy Dickinson to round the corner on his nightly patrol, but he didn't want to just stand and wait.

He pictured communist sentries at the corners, watching. It was irrational, but he couldn't push the image from his mind, and the nagging little fear wouldn't be pushed too far from his consciousness.

It was nearly ten minutes before Billy appeared around the corner, coming towards Doug's building, by which time Doug had been forced to hide in the shadow of his doorway.

"Good evening, constable," he said while Billy was still some distance away, to avoid startling him. He suspected the police on duty tonight were all on edge, given the day's activity.

"Oh, hallo there, Mr. Bainbridge, sir," Billy said, touching the rim of his police cap as he neared. "Hot night, isn't it? I suppose I wouldn't want to be inside a stuffy building, either, sir. Not much breeze to speak of out here, though."

"Seems we had some excitement over in Japantown this evening," Doug replied, cutting right to the chase.

"We did at that, sir," Billy said, nodding gravely. "Nasty business, actually. Were you there, sir?"

"No, I was at my girlfriend's apartment, down this side of Soochow Creek. I heard it, though, and went out to find out what happened."

"Now, that wasn't a very safe thing for you to do, Mr. Bainbridge, sir," Billy said, stern. "If anything like that happens again, I want you to stay safely indoors. I'm sorry to have to take that tone with you, Mr. Bainbridge, sir, but I'm afraid I must. Wouldn't be doing me job properly if I didn't. I hope you understand, sir."

Doug made himself appear chagrined. "Of course I do, Billy. And thank you for your concern. I'll think better next time, and not be so impulsive."

"Right-o," Billy said, touching the rim of his cap again and starting off. "Now if you'll excuse me, sir, best get back to me rounds. Got to stay on schedule, you see."

Doug fell into step beside Billy. "Just one more thing—I heard several witnesses say it was a professional assassin, and that he called the Japanese man's name before he shot him. Is that true?"

"I'm afraid I can't comment, sir," Billy said, his posture and tone growing stiff. "Ongoing investigation, you see."

"Yes, of course." Doug tried one more thing. "Did the Japanese community insist on Japanese detectives handling the case again, like the last time?"

"They did, sir."

"They never found the killer who got that sailor last fall, did they?"

"No sir, they did not." Billy's tone still sounded stilted; defensive, even. "Don't let that worry you, though, Mr. Bainbridge, sir."

"I'll try not to," Doug said and turned back toward the door. "Good night, Billy. Stay safe out here."

Monday, July 13

Doug went into his office late that Monday, and as he rounded the corner from Honan Road onto Peking Road, the stout figure of Kawakami came out of a shop door across the street. Doug ignored him, but as he walked the block toward his office building, he got the feeling that the Japanese man was following him.

Doug picked up his pace and reached the door before Kawakami. Once inside, he bolted up the stairs to the third floor. He hurried down the hallway, hearing heavy foot falls on the stairs below. He unlocked the door of his office, and slipped inside before Kawakami could reach his floor, locking the door securely behind him.

He sat at his desk, panting, turned around watching the frosted glass on his door while trying to calm his nerves.

Several minutes passed, and he breathed easier. Just when he thought he had worried for nothing, a shadowy figure appeared on the other side of the door, the unmistakable shape of the short, stout Japanese man with the silk hat.

He held his breath.

Kawakami stood there for a long moment, facing the door, not moving.

Doug sat perfectly still—but then became painfully aware that Kawakami could see the outline of his head silhouetted against the open window behind him.

Damn it!

Kawakami's right hand came up, and Doug gripped the arms of his chair. Kawakami's knock was heavy, echoing through the office.

"Who is it?" Doug called, trying to sound calm.

A second loud knocking on the door frame was the only answer.

"Would you come back later, please? I'm busy getting ready to meet with a client."

He heard some metallic scratching sound, followed by a click, and his breath caught in his throat as he saw the lock turn. The door knob turned, and his heart pounded in his ears.

Kawakami stepped inside the room, and used his cane to shut the door. He seemed to wear a permanent scowl, the only expression Doug had ever seen on the man's face.

"Greetings, Bainbridge Douglas," the Japanese man said in Shanghainese. "We have business to discuss."

Doug answered in English. "I'm sorry, I have a client coming by shortly, and I have to prepare for our meeting. If you write down your name and a phone number, I'll get back with you when I'm able."

"I know you speak Shanghainese, Bainbridge Douglas," Kawakami replied in that language. "Do not assume that we have not looked into your background. We know much about you."

"Who is 'we?'" Doug asked, in Shanghainese this time, apprehensive about the plural pronoun.

"That is not important. I am here to ask what you know about the death of Kayao *san* three days ago."

129

"Not much, I'm afraid," Doug said, which was mostly the truth. He had only learned the victim's name from the newspapers on Saturday— Kayao Kosaku, a Japanese salesman and long-time resident of Shanghai.

"Do not lie to me, Bainbridge Douglas."

Something clicked, and Doug glanced down to see a stiletto open in Kawakami's right hand, pointed toward him.

"It's the truth," he said, fighting to stay calm. "I know very little, and most of that I learned from reading the newspapers."

"Tell me what you know that was not in the newspapers."

Doug thought of Wong Mei-Ling, and her almost certainly secret trip into the Chinese hardware store on the edge of Japantown. He had to think of something else he could tell Kawakami that wouldn't incriminate her. Or her friends.

Then it came to him.

"One witness said the assassin wore an axe on his belt," Doug said, allowing a little bit of excitement into his tone. "That wasn't reported in the newspapers—the English or the Chinese ones."

Kawakami said nothing, just stared at Doug with unblinking eyes.

"It's a strange detail," Doug continued.

Kawakami grunted. "You went to Hong Kong in January. Why?"

The inquiry surprised Doug, and he wondered not only how Kawakami had learned that, but why he was curious about it. "It was just a short trip with some friends, for the Chinese New Year. We were only there a couple of days."

Kawakami grunted again. "Who did you meet while you were in Hong Kong?"

Doug gave him a confused look. "I don't know what you mean."

"Besides your friends, did you meet with anyone else in Hong Kong?"

Doug shrugged, keeping the confused look on his face. "I mean, the workers at the hotel, and the restaurants where we ate. I don't know what else you mean."

Kawakami's eyes narrowed, and he stared hard at Doug, unblinking.

"Did you stop in Wuzhou on your way to or from Hong Kong, Bainbridge Douglas?"

Doug was genuinely confused this time. "I don't remember—the train made several stops along the way, but I can't remember all of the cities."

Kawakami grunted again. "Tell me what you know about Wang Yaqiao."

"Who?"

"Don't lie."

"I'm not lying. I don't know who that is."

Kawakami's lips pursed. He took a step forward and held the stiletto out toward Doug. "Try to remember."

"I think you should leave," Doug said, trying to sound calm and confident. "I'll call the police."

"Your telephone is not connected, Bainbridge Douglas."

Kawakami took another step forward, and now the end of the stiletto was little more than a foot in front of Doug's nose. The sharp blade glinted in the light coming from the window.

"Wang Yaqiao visits Hong Kong often, Bainbridge Douglas. He has a residence there, in Kowloon. You stayed in Kowloon. His home is in Wuzhou, near Hong Kong, and his gang is based there. His gang has many members in Shanghai, and they wear axes on their belts at all times."

Doug stared at Kawakami with an open mouth. "I didn't know any of that. You must believe me—I have never heard of Wang Yaqiao, or his gang. Until Friday, I'd never heard of anyone wearing an axe on his belt. That's the truth, I swear."

Kawakami stared at him for a moment, then nodded and took a step back.

"Have you heard of Jin Shixin, Bainbridge Douglas?"

He remembered that name—the communist agent who approached him at the Peninsula Hotel, the spa attendant, had instructed him to ask for that person. The Chinese woman in Kowloon who had answered the door said she was Jin Shixin's sister.

He looked up in thought, hoping his eyes didn't betray him. "I don't think so."

Kawakami seemed to buy it; he grunted and nodded, then took a step back. The stiletto disappeared.

"Our office is downstairs, first floor. If you remember Miss Jin, come to us first. You may speak to me, or to my associate, Nakagawa *san*—no one else. You understand?"

Doug nodded. His throat had gone dry. "I understand," he croaked.

Kawakami turned toward the door, but stopped with his hand on the door knob. "If the *Juntong* come to you, asking anything, you will come to our office and tell us."

Then he walked out the door.

10

Doug went to the bar at the Cathay Hotel at noon, hoping to find Jonesy. He ate lunch and waited almost an hour, but Jonesy never arrived. Before he left, he asked the Chinese bartender in Shanghainese if he had seen Jonesy that day.

"Not today," the bartender replied. "Sometimes he doesn't come here for lunch. I can leave a message for him, if he comes later."

Doug declined, and left. It was a few blocks to the downtown building where the Associated Press had their Shanghai office, and he walked through the doors ten minutes later.

Gladys Sherman looked up from her typewriter with an automatic smile. "May I help you?" Then her smile grew more genuine as she recognized him. "Oh, Mr. Bainbridge, isn't it? What can I do for you?"

"I'm looking for Jonesy, have you heard from him today?"

Gladys nodded. "He was in for a bit this morning—filed a story, picked up his messages—but he left around eleven. He had some appointments with sources, but I don't know details. I can leave a message for him, he'll probably check in sometime this afternoon."

"Tell him I need to speak with him about something, today. Tell him to meet me at the Liberty Tavern, on the northeast corner of Honan and Peking Road, four o'clock."

"Will he know what this is in reference to?"

He'll probably guess. "I'm sure he will."

"If for some reason he doesn't check in before four o'clock, I'll send you a message at that location," Gladys said, tearing the sheet from her message pad and putting it into a slot marked "A. Jones."

"Thank you, Miss Sherman."

Doug found a message waiting for him when he arrived at the pub at four o'clock. It was on plain paper, in a woman's handwriting.

"Jonesy will meet you at 4:30."

Which probably means four forty-five. Doug settled in to wait.

It was about forty minutes past four when Jonesy came through the door. He raised his hand for the bartender as he took the stool next to Doug's.

"Martini, two olives, and another gin and tonic for my friend here."

"Thanks," Doug said.

"Thanks for contacting me," Jonesy replied. "I assume you want to talk about that Japanese salesman who was killed in Japantown on Friday night, Mr. Kayao."

"Yes. Hopefully we can help each other out."

Jonesy's green eyes narrowed. "You know something?"

"I heard the murderer wore an axe on his belt, which is the mark of a particular gang based in southern China."

"Yes, the Axe Gang, I know all about them," Jonesy said. "I also heard the assassin wore an axe on his belt. Doesn't necessarily mean he's part of the Axe Gang, though—someone could be trying to frame them for it."

"Who?"

"The Green Gang, for one," Jonesy said, and fell quiet as the bartender returned and set their drinks in front of them. When he'd gone, Jonesy continued. "The Axe Gang are their main rivals in the south."

Doug took a deep breath, and his brow furrowed as he processed that. "But why would the Green Gang want to kill a Japanese salesman?"

"Who knows?" Jonesy said with a shrug, and took a sip of his martini. Condensation already streamed down the sides of the glass. "Maybe he owed them money. Maybe he got in their way somehow. They kill lots of people, you know."

Doug didn't buy that, and shook his head. "No, this was a deliberate attack on a Japanese national, in the International Settlement, in the heart of the Japanese colony. It was meant to send a message. The Green Gang might have a motive to frame the Axe Gang for a murder, but they don't have a motive to kill Japanese nationals in such a public way—if anything, they have a disincentive to do that, given the reaction of the Japanese authorities here."

Jonesy appeared to consider that for a moment, and took another sip of his martini.

"Sure, the Jap big wigs are all up in arms over it—but they did the same back in November when that sailor Nakayama was killed, and diddly came of that."

"That's true—but it doesn't mean nothing will come out this time."

Jonesy shrugged, not looking convinced. "The fact that nothing came of the earlier investigation might itself be circumstantial evidence pointing toward the Green Gang," he said, quieter. "They're known to be slippery when it comes to arrest and prosecution. You and I know that as well as anyone, with everything we learned last year after Tim died."

Doug glanced around. The tavern was starting to fill up with the usual after-work crowd of mostly American businessmen. He leaned close to Jonesy and said just above a whisper, "There's more I have to tell you—but not here, not now that it's crowded."

Four o'clock would have been better.

Jonesy grunted understanding. "I'm covering a baseball game over at the Rec grounds in a little while; why don't you walk with me, and we can talk on the way. After we finish our drinks, of course."

Doug had no sooner agreed to the plan, than he heard his name shouted from the door. He turned and saw Kenny coming in, grinning and waving.

"I wondered if I'd see you in here," Kenny said as he reached them, shaking Doug's hand and patting him on the shoulder. "Mondays are rough sometimes, eh? I don't believe I know your friend—how do you do? I'm Kenneth Traywick."

"Art Jones," Jonesy said, shaking Kenny's offered hand. "I have a feeling we've met before, though I couldn't say where."

"I first met Kenny and his wife Abbie that night at Geoffries' suite," Doug interrupted.

Recognition dawned on Kenny's face. "I remember you—you're that fellow who shot Will Geoffries. Doug told me all about that business. What a nightmare, eh? I was terribly sorry to learn about it."

"Don't mention it," Jonesy said. "It was more than a year ago, and life goes on."

"It does indeed," Kenny agreed, head bobbing. He put his arm around Doug's shoulders. "In the last year, our boy Doug here has become one of my best friends. You'd never know we met on such a tragic evening, eh?"

Doug noticed a funny sort of twinkle had come to Jonesy's eyes, and a crooked smile upturned one side of his mouth. "How about that? Are you Canadian, Mr. Trawick?"

"I am. British Columbia."

"Recognized the accent. I'm from Detroit. Been over to Windsor, Ontario more than a few times in my day."

"Oh, very nice. I've never been there, myself. Once when I was about fourteen, my family took a train across the country to Ottawa one summer, but that was my only time in Ontario." He looked back at

Doug. "Before I forget—Abbie asked me to invite you and Lucy over to our place for dinner on Friday, if you're free."

Doug shrugged. "Sounds good to me, let me check with Lucy."

"Splendid," Kenny said, beaming. "Let me get a drink, and I'll be back with you in a moment." He walked toward the end of the crowded bar to get the bartender's attention.

Doug felt a little unnerved at the strange way Jonesy was looking at him. "What's the matter?"

Jonesy chuckled and shook his head. "Nothing, don't worry about it. We should leave soon, though, if we're going to have time to chat before I have to be in the bleachers."

"Sorry about the interruption," Doug said, nodding toward the end of the bar where Kenny leaned over talking to the bartender.

Jonesy waved that off and took a swig of his martini. "Don't be. Your friend seems like a real genuine fella, a good egg."

Doug nodded. "He is. I should say goodbye to him before we leave."

He got up before Jonesy could say anything, and met Kenny on the way back with his drink. "Sorry buddy, we have to leave. Mr. Jones and I have somewhere to be in a little bit."

"Aww, that's too bad. I was looking forward to chatting with you and your friend. Well, maybe another time, eh?"

By then they had returned to where Jonesy sat, draining the last of his martini and shoving the empty glass aside. He stood and put his bowler hat on his head, then turned to Kenny and shook his hand.

"It was a pleasure meeting you, Mr. Traywick. Listen, Doug and I are on our way over to the baseball game at the Rec grounds— American club versus the Canadians tonight. You should join us."

I thought you wanted to hear what I learned. Doug hid his bewilderment.

Kenny looked at Doug with an apologetic look. "I wish I could, but I have to get home to my wife soon. Thank you for the invitation, though. Rain check, eh?"

"Absolutely," Doug said, and patted Kenny's arm on the way out.

Out on the street, Doug put on his hat and fell into step beside Jonesy, walking south toward Nanking Road, and then west toward the Recreation Grounds. Doug let a little distance come between them and the non-Chinese crowds of eastern downtown before he spoke.

"I had a visitor this morning. You remember that Japanese agent who was looking for Tim's files on the Korean resistance last year?"

"Yeah, Kawa-something, wasn't it? He back in town?"

"Kawakami. Yes, he's been back since at least March. I've seen him a couple of times since then. This morning he picked the lock and let himself into my office to have a chat with me."

"Oh? About the attack on Kayao?"

"Uh huh. And this is where I need to ask you to make this strictly off the record, understand?"

"Sure, if that's the way you want it. We're off the record."

Doug took a deep breath and looked around at the crowd on the sidewalk. All Chinese, and no one who set off any alarm bells. Then he noticed they were walking past the Jade Dragon, the nightclub where Tim had last been seen alive. He looked away, lowered his head, and muttered out the side of his mouth.

"Kawakami asked me about my trip to Hong Kong in January. I told him it was a short trip with my friends, for Chinese New Year—which was all true. But he asked me if I met someone named Wang Yanqiao, who runs a gang out of Wuzhou."

Jonesy stopped, took Doug by the shoulder and pulled him up against the brick wall of a Chinese grocery. "Stop right there. We'll continue this conversation when we're off the street."

Doug nodded, and they resumed walking in silence. A couple of blocks later, they reached the wide boulevard of Thibet Road, which marked the western edge of downtown. On the other side of the street rose the twenty-two story Park Hotel, and opposite it were the horse track and the broad green expanse of the Recreation Grounds.

They crossed the street twice, until they were walking alone through an open grassy area just past the grandstands of the race track.

"Ok, let's talk. But keep your voice down, even here," Jonesy muttered, glancing around to be sure that no one was nearby. "That name you mentioned—Wang Yanqiao—he's the head of the Axe Gang. They're more than your usual criminal gang—not just drugs, gambling, and prostitution—they are professional assassins, and very deadly at it. They're the only ones brave enough to take on the Green Gang, if the price is right; and they've paid dearly for it, too. But they are not deterred. In addition to their feared axes, they're also well-trained in the martial arts."

He stopped and looked Doug in the eye. His expression was searching, perhaps even a touch worried.

Doug waited for him to speak again.

"This Kawakami fellow seems to believe the Axe gang is really behind the attack, if he asked about Wang Yanqiao. What I want to know is this—why in God's name did he ask if *you* had met with Wang?"

Doug took a deep breath, searching for the right words. "Because apparently I met with one of his associates." Now that he knew who Wang was, horror crept into his belly. "How Kawakami found out, I don't have any idea."

Jonesy looked down and shook his head, muttering something about "...just like Tim." When he looked back up, his expression was stony. "How did you come to meet with an associate of Wang Yanqiao? And tell me everything—leave nothing out, you understand? Nothing."

"Ok," Doug said, and took another deep breath before plunging into the story. "You figured out last fall that I was tasked with learning more about the Reds' plans in regards to killing Japanese."

"Right," Jonesy agreed, with one firm nod. "Go on."

"Well, I must not have been discreet enough, because their local leader called on me at home in January—the night of the Chinese New Year, January twenty-fourth. He knew my friends had gone to Hong Kong for the long weekend; knew where they were staying, even, and he told me to take the overnight train and join them."

Doug recounted the instructions he was given, and how events played out in Hong Kong. "That was it, and I never heard anything more about any of it—until this morning."

Jonesy's mouth had set in a tight line as he listened. "And this Kawakami fellow knew all about it?"

Doug shrugged. "He didn't seem to know all of it. He just asked if I had met with Wang Yanqiao. I said I hadn't—the truth, I'd never even heard of him before this morning—and he asked if I had ever heard of Jin Shixin. Of course I remembered that name, but I didn't admit it."

Jonesy shook his head, cursing under his breath. "You Intelligence boys need to learn to be more careful, if you're going to compete on the big stage. Yeah, yeah, I know—we're new at this. The British have been doing this cloak and dagger stuff for centuries, and they're old pros."

"I didn't ask for this, remember," Doug said, scowling and crossing his arms. "They came to me, and didn't give me much choice."

"Sure, I understand—but that won't stop the Japanese from torturing and killing you for what you did. Got that? Good—so be more careful from now on."

Doug swallowed hard, and his stomach fluttered. He licked his lips nervously. "I think he believed me, though. About not knowing Wang Yanqiao, that is. I think he could tell I was telling the truth."

"Let's hope so," Jonesy mumbled. "If he doesn't, you're going to have to deal with him."

"What do you mean by that?"

Jonesy stared at him for several seconds. "Have you thought about getting a gun?"

"Doug, I wasn't expecting you this evening," Lucy said when he showed up at her door.

"I wanted to talk with you about something. May I come in?"

She looked startled. "Yes—yes, of course. Come in. I was just doing some writing, that's all."

He noticed a notebook sitting open on her table, with a fountain pen next to it. He stood in the middle of her apartment while she closed the door, and she looked at him with worried eyes. "Is everything alright, Doug? You look awfully serious."

"I think you should sit down."

She held her breath, and sat on the edge of a chair. He took the seat opposite her. "I think I might be in some danger."

She exhaled hard. "I thought you were going to say you didn't want to see me anymore. Good Lord, Doug, don't do that again. Now what's this about being in danger? Are you serious?"

"It's a long story."

She scooted her seat closer to his. "I've got all evening."

"OK, here goes. You remember last summer, with everything that happened around the death of my friend Tim? You remember the Japanese man I told you about, Kawakami? He's back, and I may have done something that's gotten his attention."

He told her the whole story, starting with what Hilliard told him to do last November, going through the trip to Hong Kong, and finally to Kawakami's visit that morning. He ended with Jonesy's advice to get a gun.

She looked shell-shocked when he finished.

"What are you thinking?"

She took his hand. "I think you should get a gun, Doug. Don't take any chances. Get it tomorrow."

Tuesday, July 14

Doug went to the International Settlement's licensing and registration office downtown first thing the next morning. Even this early, the line at the reception desk held nearly a dozen people, most of them Chinese.

Two young Chinese women worked the reception desk, one in a short-sleeved blue dress, the other in a short-sleeved green dress. They greeted the Chinese customers in Shanghainese, the white ones in Pidgin.

"What paper wantchee?" the woman in the green dress asked Doug when he reached the front.

He answered in Shanghainese. "I'd like to apply for an application to carry a gun, please."

She grinned when she heard him speak her language. "Fill out this application. Do you have your passport?"

"Yes, I do."

"Then we can give you a license today. When you finish the application, take it to Mr. Kuykendall, second desk on the right. Next!"

Doug took a seat and filled out the application form, then signed at the bottom. He removed his passport from his jacket pocket, and took the completed application to the indicated desk.

A tall white man of about thirty-five sat at the desk in shirt and tie, but with his jacket hung on the back of his chair, perusing a folder with several pages of forms. Thin, light brown hair was parted on the left, and unoiled. He had pale blue eyes that held Doug's as he approached.

"May I help you, sir?" he asked in English.

"Mr. Kuykendall? I was told to bring this to you." Doug handed the bureaucrat his application and passport.

"You are in da right place. Please sit down." Kuykendall reviewed the application, reading aloud. He spoke English with a pronounced Dutch accent—faintly Germanic with a sing-song rhythm, and he pronounced his th's like d's, and his r's from the back of his throat.

"How long have you lived in the International Settlement, Mr. Bainbridge?"

"A year and two months," Doug answered.

"Have you lived anywhere else in China?"

"No."

"Then this should be fast for you. The fee is eight Shanghai dollars."

Doug handed him cash for the fee, and Kuykendall gave him back the change.

"Please have a seat in the front office, and I will call you in a little while."

'A little while' turned out to be almost forty-five minutes. For a while Doug listened to the customers requesting registrations for cars, boats, rickshaws, businesses—but after a bit he grew bored and tuned out. He wished he'd brought along a book.

From time to time an interesting accent in English caught his ear, and he amused himself by trying to guess what country the particular white person was from—Italy, Brazil, Sweden, etc. A few times, something was said to give confirmation of his guess, but most of the time he had to content himself with only the assumption.

Finally, Kuykendall called his name, and Doug went to his desk.

"Here is your license to carry a firearm, Mr. Bainbridge," Kuykendall said. "It is valid for three months, and must be renewed by fourteenth October, 1936. Please notice that it is only valid within the International Settlement. If you carry your firearm with you into the French Concession, or into Chinese territory, you will need a different license."

"Very clear," Doug said, taking the paper the bureaucrat handed him. "Do I come see you for the renewal, or is there a different process?"

"You must apply again in three months, the same as today, sir."

Typical. "Thank you, Mr. Kuykendall."

He located the gun store that Jonesy recommended, a few blocks away on Foochow Road.

"If you insist on buying one legally, that's the best place," Jonesy had said, after Doug declined his offer of 'unofficial' gun sellers. He wanted to keep this whole business strictly above board.

Baron Aleksandr Rustikov, the bearded fifty-ish Russian man who owned the gun shop, was knowledgeable about all manner of firearms, and after asking Doug a few questions about his intentions ("Protection," Doug replied), he showed him a few late-model pistols from the United States, Germany, and Italy.

Doug debated between a 1935 Browning Hi-power/FN GP35, and a 1934 Beretta; after test-firing a few rounds into a barrel of sand, he opted for the Browning.

The gun itself was expensive, and cost him twenty-five dollars, but a box of ammunition was only three cents. The incongruity both amused and bemused him.

He picked out a nice leather shoulder holster for another dollar.

Rustikov filled out the registration paperwork for the gun, and Doug signed it.

"I file paper tomorrow, you have registration by weekend," the Russian said in deeply-accented English.

Doug thought there might be a joke in there somewhere about using the gun tonight, and throwing it in the river before morning—but he kept it to himself.

He strapped on the holster over his shirt, placed the pistol in it, and slipped his linen jacket back on over it. The fit was imperfect—the linen suit having been tailored to him last summer, and therefore lacking extra room for the pistol—but it wasn't uncomfortable.

He tried stuffing the gun into the waist of his pants in back, as he'd seen done in countless movies, and found that quite uncomfortable, so in the end he put it back in the holster and decided to see if he could have his jacket let out a little.

He walked home, a trip of about a mile, and as he walked he imagined everyone he passed was looking at the not-entirely-subtle bulge at his side where the pistol was holstered. He tried to tell himself that people weren't paying that much attention, since they passed countless men with concealed weapons on a daily basis—but he still felt the eyes on him.

It made him self-conscious at first, but by the time he reached the Honan Road Bridge over Soochow Creek, something of a swagger had come to his stride, a feeling almost like a movie mobster. It was ridiculous, and he laughed at himself as he turned the corner onto Huang Lei Road and made for home.

Hutson

11

Monday, August 24

Doug was surprised by the knock on his office door in the middle of the afternoon, but was more surprised to see Jonesy standing in the hall when he answered.

"Jonesy, this is a surprise. How did you know where to find my office?"

"You know better than to ask me to reveal my sources," Jonesy said with a harrumph.

"What are you doing here?"

"Need to talk a few minutes, in private. Invite me in, maybe?"

Doug stepped aside, embarrassed at his momentary lack of manners. "My apologies. You caught me by surprise, that's all. I wasn't expecting any visitors—least of all, you."

As Doug closed the door, he watched Jonesy look around, peeking under lamp shades and behind the desk and the filing cabinet, and Doug arched an eyebrow in the unspoken question.

"When was the last time you checked this place for bugs?" Jonesy asked, without looking up from his search.

Doug was embarrassed to admit he never had—he'd never really needed to, honestly. Even with Kawakami and his associate periodically occupying an office downstairs, he'd never felt the need, given that he never discussed anything confidential with anyone here. At most, Kenny stopped by sometimes at the end of the work day, and they talked about evening or weekend plans.

He let his lack of answer be the answer.

After several seconds, Jonesy grunted as his only response, still looking in nooks and crannies around the small space.

Doug stood aside and let him finish.

"What about the phone?" Jonesy asked, picking up the receiver and unscrewing the caps on both ends.

"It's never been connected," Doug said. "It's just for show."

Jonesy checked them anyway, but found nothing there.

Satisfied, he turned around and sat on the end of the desk. "A couple of Japanese men were assassinated earlier today in Chengtu, out in Szechuan province. A pair of journalists this time, which is troubling— as you might imagine. Everyone at our office is calling up every source they know—out west, in Nanking, and here. It's exhilarating and depressing all at once."

"I can imagine," Doug said, picturing the Associated Press office as a hive of activity, phones ringing off the hook, reporters scurrying every which way.

"The *modus operandi* of the killer today was the same as the one that shot that salesman here about six weeks ago—the attacker wore a black assassin's hood, and an axe at his belt; an axe that he didn't use, I might add, since he shot the poor fellas."

Doug took a few seconds to ponder this. "The Axe Gang is active all through the Yangtze valley, isn't that right?"

"That's right."

"So it's plausible that they have a chapter in Chengdu, wouldn't you say? And Chongqing as well, which isn't far."

"I'm sure they do," Jonesy said. "What's less plausible is for one of their members to shoot a pair of victims instead of hacking them to death with his axe, which is their weapon of choice. Even less plausible is that *two* of their members—in two different cities on either end of the river valley—used a gun instead of an axe."

"I understand where you're going with that," Doug said. "We're back to the hypothesis that someone is framing the Axe Gang for the murders—either the Green Gang, or the Communist Party."

"That's one possibility," Jonesy said, sounding a bit cagey.

"What's the other possibility?"

Jonesy chuckled. "You should be able to guess, given your activity in Hong Kong."

Doug felt his stomach drop. His mouth went dry, but he managed to get out the words. "You think the communists have struck a deal with the Axe Gang, but using a hybrid style of attack? The Axe Gang's style of ambush, but with guns supplied by the Reds?"

"You said it, not me."

Doug's mind raced. "That would certainly confuse the authorities, and make it a lot harder to pin the crime on the true perpetrators."

"It would indeed—which seems to be the case, since they've never solved the previous two shootings."

Doug nodded, but his mind was occupied with unanswered questions. "Have you heard what type of gun was involved in today's shooting?"

"No," Jonesy said, sitting up a little straighter. "You think it's a Soviet-made weapon? Something the Reds would have provided to the assassin?"

Doug shrugged. "It's possible."

"But that would point the police straight to the Reds," Jonesy argued.

"Not necessarily," Doug countered. "There are lots of illegal guns floating around the black market, all over China. A professional assassin could have purchased a Soviet firearm just about anywhere—it wouldn't *have* to have been provided by the Communist Party."

"But *could* have been," Jonesy said, picking up on Doug's thread.

Doug nodded. "And any suspicion placed on the local communists wouldn't by itself put them in any greater danger, since they have to hide from the secret police as it is."

"But it would put them under greater scrutiny," Jonesy said. "They'd be in greater danger because of increased surveillance—or at least hindered in their activities because of it."

"True," Doug conceded. "But wouldn't that be a necessary risk, if this is part of a greater objective—to make war on the Japanese presence in China?"

Jonesy took a deep breath, looking up in thought, and slowly nodded. "You're probably right. The real question, then, is how to get them to reveal themselves. They're going to be extra cautious right now—and they're the most cautious sons-of-bitches as it is already."

That was a tricky problem, Doug agreed—but also not really his problem; it was Jonesy's.

On the other hand, the resumption of attacks on Japanese nationals—two in six weeks—might renew ONI's interest in the communists' plans, after eight months of quiet had dispelled their interest. Perhaps he was only being proactive by taking an active interest in Jonesy's inquiries. Commander Hilliard might even be impressed with his initiative.

"So we have to bring something to the table," he said.

Jonesy chuckled. "'We,' huh? Well, I'm glad to have you on board, sailor. We have to make them an offer—got anything particular in mind?"

Doug shrugged, thinking. "We could threaten to reveal what happened in January, and expose their agents."

Jonesy snorted and crossed his arms. "You should know better— they move around too much for that. They surely abandoned that house months ago, if not the day you were there. There won't be anything there for the cops to search, trust me."

Doug's face flushed, knowing Jonesy was right. "But we can identify several of their members locally. And once the secret police get ahold of a few of them, it's only a short time until one of them breaks and gives away the others."

Jonesy shook his head and rolled his eyes. "You really think they won't kill you before you even get close to someone to pass along your secrets? You'll be dead faster than you can say jiminy crickets, and they won't even blink."

Doug crossed his own arms, irritated. "Alright, smart aleck—what would you suggest?"

"It can't be a threat—they don't respond to those with anything but retaliation, and they don't mess around. No, it has to be something that gives them an advantage."

Doug tensed. "I'm not comfortable helping them with their conflict against the Nationalist government. Our government supports the Nationalists, and it would jeopardize my career to do anything contrary to that—not to mention putting *both* of us into hot water for espionage."

Jonesy scowled. "What do you think I am, stupid? *Of course* we can't get involved in that struggle, and not just for the reasons you mentioned. Think about how the secret police would react if we were found to have helped the Reds against them. They aren't any more forgiving than the commies, you can be sure."

"Then what?"

"I'm still working that out."

Doug released an exasperated sigh and started pacing the room. He thought of several possibilities, but selling out any of the communists' potential rivals—such as the Green Gang, for instance— involved the risk of putting themselves in the crosshairs, and making unnecessary dangerous enemies.

But one of those potential enemies was already a potential future enemy. ONI had been preparing for an eventual war against Japan for more than fifteen years. And Kawakami was already suspicious of Doug as it was.

It would be really easy to let the local reds know that Kawakami was onto them. He could even provide a few details about the Japanese agent, from what he had observed. Doug could then leave the rest to them, and let them use the information as they would—but in exchange for the tip, he could negotiate some information for himself and Jonesy.

The more he thought about it, the more he liked the possibility. *It just might work.*

He stopped pacing and turned to Jonesy with a smile spreading across his lips. "I've got an idea," he said.

Tuesday, August 25

Doug entered Mr. Hwang's store that afternoon, having waited almost a half-hour for the landlord to go back into his office and close the door, leaving Wong Mei-Ling alone in the front. Another customer was at the desk when Doug first walked in, a diminutive Chinese woman of about sixty, and Doug stood back while she finished picking up her clean laundry and paying the bill.

Fortunately, no one else entered while he was waiting, so when he approached the desk he only had to wait ten seconds for the old woman to exit and leave him alone in the store with Mei-Ling.

"Good afternoon, Miss Wong," he said in Shanghainese with a slight bow. He lowered his voice and continued more quietly. "I wonder if we might have a word in private?"

He saw the unspoken question in her mysterious dark eyes, and she glanced around. "We can talk now."

Doug stepped close to the counter, and leaned over it to whisper to her. "I'd like to meet with your boss."

"Mr. Hwang is busy in the office," she said. "He is recording the accounts for the week, and he does not like to be interrupted when he records the accounts."

"No, your other boss."

"I don't know what you mean, Mr. Bainbridge."

"Yes, you do."

She stared at him for a moment, and he couldn't read her expression.

The silence grew uncomfortable, but he willed himself to stay patient and wait. Finally, she spoke.

"He will find you."

"I could meet him somewhere tomorrow morning," Doug offered.

She shook her head, and her expression carried a note of disdain, as if she couldn't believe how stupid he could be. "He will find you when he is ready for you."

Doug nodded, stood back up straight, and gave her a polite bow. "Thank you for your assistance, Miss Wong. Good day."

Hutson

12

Saturday, August 29

Doug and Lucy sat across the table from Kenny and Abbie at Velardi's. They had a table by the large open windows that overlooked the sidewalk, and tonight there was a nice breeze coming off the water of Soochow Creek, giving the illusion of coolness in the otherwise hot and sultry evening.

It had been almost three weeks since Doug and Lucy had meet Kenny and Abbie for dinner, and Kenny was particularly giddy tonight as he greeted them, almost kissing Doug on the cheek after kissing Lucy's. His sudden embarrassment as he caught himself had brought laughter from all of them, and Kenny blushed several shades of scarlet.

After they sat, and their usual waiter Gino brought out four wine glasses and a carafe of chianti, Kenny immediately stood and poured them all, not giving anyone else a chance to grab the wine.

His behavior was odd, maybe a little jittery, but he seemed to be in a good mood—elated, even—so Doug doubted there was anything wrong.

He couldn't help but notice that Kenny barely poured Abbie's glass half-way full. He glanced sideways at Lucy, who was staring at Abbie's glass.

Abbie's gaze followed theirs, and her cheeks flushed. "I think the jig is up, Kenneth."

Kenny laughed, a nervous, overly loud laugh as he retook his seat. "I guess I'm not very subtle, am I?"

"I don't know what you're talking about," Lucy said, cool as a cucumber.

Doug reached for her hand under the table cloth, and she gave his a squeeze. *God, I love this woman*, he thought without hesitation.

Kenny looked at Abbie, and Doug noticed his hand trembling on the table. Kenny grabbed Abbie's hand and stared at her with a big goofy grin. "I suppose we should just up and say it, eh, dear?"

"You tell them," Abbie said, her smile and expression adoring.

Kenny exhaled sharply, almost as if he'd been hit in the gut, but he was still smiling.

Poor fellow. Poor scared, sweet fellow, Doug thought.

"We're having a baby," Kenny blurted, and his forehead beaded with sweat.

"Oh, that's wonderful!" Lucy gushed, as if she hadn't expected that in the slightest.

Doug couldn't help but chuckle at her reaction, but he covered it up by reaching across the table to shake Kenny's hand and pat his shoulder.

"Congratulations, old chum," he said. Then he stood and walked around the table to Abbie's seat, and leaned down to kiss her cheek. "What wonderful news. I'm thrilled for you both."

"Both of us are," Lucy added.

Abbie beamed across the table at Lucy. "I'm excited, too. When we were first married, I didn't want to have children right away, but now that it's happened I'm positively giddy about it. I'm just sorry that I'll have to stop teaching for the next several years."

"That is a shame," Lucy said, reaching across the table to squeeze Abbie's forearm. "I know how much you love it. But you'll love being a mother, too. It's just the beginning of another adventure."

"What a lovely way to put it," Abbie said, lighting up again. "Thank you so much for that."

"It's true," Lucy said, and raised her glass. "To the happy family."

"To the happy family," Doug echoed, and raised his glass as well.

"Cheers!" Kenny said, and they all tapped their glasses together and drank.

"We wanted to tell you two first, before the others," Kenny said, then caught himself and laughed. "Well, we cabled our folks a couple of weeks ago, so they were actually first. It cost me almost *fifty dollars* to send two trans-Pacific cablegrams, but we thought this news was worth that cost."

"It still amazes me that they got the messages within hours, halfway around the world," Abbie said, shaking her head in wonder.

"And with air mail now, you can get letters home in about a week. It is amazing," Lucy agreed.

"I had to send a cable to San Francisco last year, and even made a trans-Pacific phone call," Doug added. "It was very expensive."

"A *phone* call? Good grief!" Abbie looked truly amazed.

"Yes, well—the sound wasn't good, as you'd expect, and it cost Mr. McIntyre thirty-nine dollars for three minutes, so not something you would want to do on a lark."

Lucy knew this story, of course, and she knew it brought a note of sadness to his mood whenever he thought of Tim's murder, so she changed the subject. "When are you due?" she asked, reaching across the table to touch Abbie's hand.

"March the fourth," Abbie replied. "It should be about the start of springtime here."

Doug walked Lucy home from the restaurant a couple of hours later. It was a warm and humid evening, and they strolled leisurely, hand in hand. The low rumble of distant thunder promised rain later that night, but for now the air was still and heavy.

"That was exciting news, wasn't it?" Doug said as they crossed the bridge over Soochow Creek. "I wasn't expecting that. And how about them telling us before telling the others? They must like us the best, huh?"

Lucy laughed. "It's not hard to like us better than Julia."

Doug laughed too. "That's certainly true. Still, Kenny's been close with Pete since before I knew either of them. Perhaps we shouldn't let on that we knew first, once Kenny and Abbie tell everyone. Pete's not usually the type of fellow to get bothered by things like that—or by much of anything, really, he's so easy-going—but you never know. Julia, though..."

"I agree, our little secret," Lucy said. They walked in silence for a few seconds, and she leaned her head on his shoulder. "I'm so happy for Abbie, but sad for her at the same time," she said after a bit, as they neared the north end of the bridge.

"What do you mean?"

"After the first of the year, she's going to have to give up teaching for at least six years. Longer, if they have any more kids. I know she's going to miss it."

Doug made a grand shrug. "I don't know, I think you were right earlier when you said she's going to love being a mother. She'll be happy."

"Oh, I know. And I meant what I said—she *will* love being a mother. And you're right, she will be happy—but she'll also be a little bit sad, and that makes me sad for her."

Doug grinned. "She'll be too busy to be sad."

He felt her stiffen, and she stopped leaning on his shoulder as they strolled. She sighed in an exasperated sort of way.

"What is it?"

"Nothing," she said, in the sort of tone that told him it was anything but.

"No, really—what's the matter?"

She shook her head and looked away from him, toward the river as they rounded the corner onto Soochow Road North. He waited, and a moment later she looked back forward.

"Why are men so stupid sometimes?"

He felt his stomach clench, as if she'd poked her finger into his gut. "What on earth—" he began, but she cut him off.

"Why do men *never* understand what women want? Why do you have to make such boneheaded statements about motherhood, and its supposed joys? It's not as if *you'll* ever walk in those shoes."

His jaw clenched, and his shoulders squared. "Hey now, there's no call to get nasty with me, I didn't make the rules."

She stopped, and turned to stare at him, open-mouthed. Then her lips tightened into a straight line, and she put her hands on her hips.

"The rules? The *rules*, Doug? And just what *rules* are you talking about, pray tell?"

He swallowed involuntarily, a little taken aback by the severity of her reaction. "You know what rules—the ones that say she has to quit working before she has the baby, and that she can't go back to teaching until after all of her children are in school. I didn't make that up. It's not as if it's up to me."

"Oh, that's nice, Doug. Thank you for washing your hands of the situation. What's a little injustice if it doesn't apply to you, right?"

"Hey! Cut it out—you know perfectly well I care about justice, and equality between the races and the nations. I've spoken about it."

She turned away from him, shaking her head and balling both hands into fists, which she shook at her sides. A harsh growl came out of her mouth. "Arrrrrrr! You are the most exasperating man sometimes."

Then she stormed off, marching down the street toward her apartment.

Doug hurried after her, taking most of a block to catch up.

"Hey there, c'mon, let's calm down a little," he said, his voice as calm and soothing as he could make it. He reached for her arm, but she jerked it out of his fingers.

"Don't patronize me."

"I wasn't trying to patronize you. Please, would you just slow down a minute and let me talk to you?"

She stopped, spun on her heel and faced him, crossing her arms over her chest. Thunder rumbled closer. "Alright, we'll have it your way. Let's talk. Is that what you're going to expect from me someday? That I'll be happy stuck at home, in front of a stove, a baby on my hip stirring a pot?"

Doug's mouth hung open, and for a second he was speechless. Where on Earth had *that* come from? "I think we're jumping way ahead of ourselves here," he said, unable to come up with anything else.

Her lips pursed, and her brows knit together. He'd said the wrong thing.

"Haven't you thought about it, Doug? Our future? I know we haven't talked much about the future—marriage, children—but it has to have crossed your mind. Hasn't it? Otherwise, what are we doing? Just having some laughs?"

"No," he said, stung. "No, of course not. How can you say that?"

She shook her head, an angry laughing sound coming out her nose. "You wanted to talk."

"Yes, I did. I do. I'm just not sure where all of this is coming from, why you're blaming me for these things. I don't control what's going to happen to Abbie; and how can I say what's going to happen to you someday? Why are you pinning all of it on me?"

She exhaled hard, and appeared to deflate a little bit. Her arms uncrossed and fell to her sides, limp.

"I don't know. It's not you, Doug—well, not you personally. It's men in general, and you happen to be the closest representative of that suspicious group, so you get the brunt of it tonight. And you *did* bring it up."

He wasn't entirely certain how he'd brought it up, but he knew to keep his mouth shut.

They walked the rest of the way in tense silence. When they reached the door of her building, she stopped and turned to him. "Thank you for seeing me safely home," she said, her voice flat.

"I guess I'm not coming upstairs with you, then?" he asked, quietly, not hiding his disappointment.

He saw the hurt in her eyes, the hesitation. He imagined she suddenly felt bad about their fight.

But that was replaced by cool resolution. "Not tonight, Doug. I'll see you tomorrow, ok?" She hesitated a second, then stood on her toes and gave him a quick kiss on the cheek. "Good night."

He stood there for a minute, watching her run up the stairs before the door closed and obscured his view. He remained there for several seconds after, perhaps waiting to see if she turned around and came back down.

From the corner of his eye, he saw the light come on in her apartment. He turned heel and hurried off toward the corner before she could look out her window and see him still standing there, waiting.

Being pathetic.

His irritation rose as he rounded the corner onto Kiangse Road, and he stormed off toward home.

Hutson

13

Sunday, August 30

Commander Hilliard was already seated in the restaurant at the Cathay Hotel the next day when Doug arrived a few minutes early.

"Commander," Doug said as he sat, after shaking his superior's hand, civilian-style.

"Thank you for joining me," Hilliard said, as if Doug had a choice in the matter. "Tell me how things have been going for the last three months. What have you experienced?"

Doug filled him in on the highlights, since their previous meeting in late May—which had marked one year in Shanghai for Doug. He paused as they placed their lunch orders, and resumed when the waiter departed. He ended his report with what Jonesy had said about the Japanese journalists who had been murdered in Chengdu the previous week.

"Yes, that is troubling," Hilliard agreed, looking as if there were more he wanted to say.

"The attacks are clearly increasing," Doug said. "And spreading. What else do you know about them, sir?"

"Not much more than what you've said, to be honest," Hilliard said. "I'm more privy to the official Japanese reaction than you are—but suffice it to say the Japs have been leaning on the Nationalist government hard to apprehend and punish the culprits. There have been threats of military action. Of course the secret police are working on it. The fact that they haven't been able to make any arrests would seem to confirm a very organized network, as you've surmised."

"But whose network, sir?"

"That is the question, isn't it? As I said, we don't really know much more than you do, Lt. Commander."

"What more can I do, sir? How can I help?"

Hilliard put forward a fixed smile. "Just keep doing what you're doing. Your immersion is going well, so let's not spoil that. If you can manage to pick up some little tidbits of intelligence about the Japanese, or the communists, or that Axe Gang that might be involved—all well and good, pass that along to us as you can. But don't jeopardize your position, understood?"

Doug hid his disappointment. "Understood, sir."

"Good. Now, on to the rest of our agenda today," Hilliard said, straightening, looking very serious. "This is our last quarterly meeting, Bainbridge. My two-year stint in China has come to an end, and I have been reassigned to Manila, to work with the Asiatic Fleet. I'll depart on the first."

"The day after tomorrow."

"That's right. I'm not returning to Nanking. Later this afternoon at the consulate, I'll write up my report of our meeting, and send it to my superior in the diplomatic pouch."

"Who will manage my immersion for the next nine months?" Doug asked. "Will I meet with Commander Shock directly?"

Commander Thomas Shock was the American naval attaché at the embassy in Nanjing, Robert Hilliard's boss until now.

"They'll replace me soon enough," Hilliard said. "I'm not sure exactly when, and I have no idea who they'll tap for the position, but you'll be told in due time. Just worry about your own role, and leave the rest to the brass in Washington."

"Yes, sir."

One thing Doug hated about military life was the rigid roles, and the way responsibility and knowledge was filtered into specific silos.

Keep in your lane, sailor.

The navy had been good for him in many ways—not least that it had given him a job out of college in 1932, when he had no other prospects in the depth of the Depression. Plus, he had learned discipline of a useful and healthy variety—not the strict moral censure of his parents' discipline.

Still, it often seemed that someone who possessed intelligence, critical thinking, and creativity was as often as not stifled by military discipline, even in the officer corps.

Doug had felt stifled in his role in Washington. That was why he'd leapt at the opportunity to come to China and do one of the two-year immersions. It had definitely been the right choice.

And yet, still...

Doug glanced around to make sure that there were no waiters or water-fillers nearby, and he leaned across the table to ask quietly, "Do we still have someone in Shanghai, running agents in and out of Japan, sir?"

Hilliard leaned back, took a breath. "Yes," he said after several seconds, and didn't elaborate.

"Just one, sir?"

"For now."

Doug nodded, and leaned back from the table. "Is the civilian leadership still uncomfortable with that mission, sir?"

"That's my understanding."

Doug extrapolated. "But for now, they aren't interfering?"

Hilliard chuckled. "That's correct, Bainbridge. So as before, you may hear talk of Chinese agents being run to Nagasaki, Sasebo, or

Shimonoseki—just continue to act ignorant of it, and keep your own position first and foremost. Understood?"

"Yes, sir."

Their food arrived, and they spent the rest of the hour chatting about general news from the States, goings on in Washington, and general happenings of the Asiatic Fleet in and out of Shanghai. By the end, as they left the lobby of the Cathy Hotel and its air conditioning behind, and stood in the sweltering heat on the sidewalk beside Nanking Road, Hilliard extended his hand.

"It's been a pleasure working with you, Bainbridge," he said as Doug shook his hand one last time. "I expect we'll run into each other again in the future, after your time in Shanghai comes to a close. Best of luck to you, Lt. Commander."

"To you as well, sir," Doug said.

Doug walked back west along Nanking Road, hopping on the north-bound streetcar when he reached Honan Road.

Hilliard's reference to "after" his time in Shanghai came to a close had stuck with him. Perhaps it was because Hilliard himself was leaving China, but it really brought home to Doug—in a way he hadn't internalized before—that he would also have to leave Shanghai in nine months.

Perhaps he would stay in China, perhaps not, but it wouldn't be here.

Lucy's face flashed across his mind's eye, and a sense of melancholy settled over him.

When he first met her on the ship to China fifteen months before, he'd thought it was just a ship-board romance, a short-term lark. Then it became more, and by the end of two weeks in Shanghai he was willing to fight for her, for their future together. They made plans for her to come back to Shanghai in a year, and then made that happen.

And perhaps he had willfully ignored the inevitable end.

Perhaps that was why he hadn't allowed himself to think very far into the future—marriage, children. When she mentioned that last night, it seemed so out of the blue; but of course, it wasn't. Of course she had been thinking of those things. Of course he *should* have been thinking of those things.

But he had made a habit out of not thinking them. For years he avoided such thoughts, focusing on his own life, alone, a bachelor.

But that wasn't really *him* anymore.

He hopped off the streetcar by his neighborhood, and walked toward home, lost in his own mind.

What would Lucy say about the eventual end of his time in Shanghai? What would she want? His first thought was that she would come along where ever he was sent next, that she would want to be with him above all else—but was that fair?

She had made an excellent point last night, that men shouldn't make sweeping assumptions about what women want. She was building her own life in Shanghai. She had a job, a home. All on her own, she was becoming a regular customer at some of the shops and cafes in her neighborhood along the north bank of Soochow Creek.

Sure, they had their mutual favorites, places they liked to go together, places where they were both recognized. But just as he had his favorite places in his own neighborhood—such as the Cantonese teahouse—Lucy had hers in her neighborhood.

He found it difficult, though, to completely separate his own private life in his neighborhood from their growing life together with their friends. As he opened the door of his building and started up the stairs, he reminded himself that they had only really been "together" here for a little less than three months.

He couldn't just expect her to uproot her life for him and leave Shanghai at the end of the following May.

She's already done that once, though. That thought buoyed him. She had uprooted her life when she came to Shanghai. Would she be willing to do that again? The first time, her life was going to change anyway, with graduation from college. She just chose to make that change with him.

As he let himself into his apartment, melancholy settled over him and wouldn't shake off. He distracted himself by making a pot of tea, and then sitting down with a cup of tea and a book. It was an adventure romp, full of action and excitement—but his mood remained blue.

Deep down, he wasn't confident that she would follow him.

A lump came to his throat, and without warning his eyes blurred. Where in the hell had that come from?

He sniffed his nose, and angrily wiped away the tears that were starting to spill from the corners of his eyes. *Damn it man! Get ahold of yourself.*

A glimmer of hope appeared on the horizon of his mind—if ONI had someone in Shanghai running a network of Chinese agents into and out of Japanese ports, might they not have opportunities for him here when his immersion finished? Perhaps he wouldn't have to leave Shanghai at all.

It was a long shot, but for now he would cling to it, and cross the other bridges if and when he came to them.

14

Thursday, September 3

Doug sat in a chair reading a book beside a whirring fan later that week when a loud knock on his door interrupted him around nine o'clock. It was already dark out, and his first thought was that the leader of Wong Mei-Ling's cell was finally coming to see him, but then he changed his mind; the cell leader would be more cautious, and wouldn't knock so loudly.

He put his shirt back on, having draped it across the back of the chair when he assumed he was alone for the night, and he quickly buttoned it as he went to the door, pausing until all but the top button were fastened before he opened it.

Jonesy stood on the other side. "Sorry to disturb you, but this came over the wire this evening, and I knew you'd be interested."

He handed Doug a short piece of perforated paper with a few lines of type. Doug stood in the doorway and read it over once, then re-read it to make sure he hadn't missed anything.

It was brief, but he caught its significance immediately.

"*Japanese citizen Junzo Nakano killed 3 September by masked gunman in port of Pei-hai, southern China. No robbery, motive unknown.*"

"When did you get this?" Doug asked, incredulous.

"A little while ago," Jonesy answered, vague. "Seems to be another one of our deliberate assassinations, doesn't it? I'm on my way down there to see if I can interview some witnesses, and I thought you might be interested in tagging along."

Doug noticed a suit case sitting on the hall floor behind Jonesy. "Where is Pei-hai?"

"About three hundred miles west-southwest of Hong Kong, on the Gulf of Tonkin. About as far south as you can get and still be in China. In fact, it's closer to Hanoi than it is to Canton. Seeing as how you speak Cantonese and I don't, I thought you might be able to help me get some of the details that other reporters wouldn't be able to pull from witnesses in Pidgin. You act as my translator, and the AP will pay for your travel. What do you say?"

Doug hesitated. "When do you want to leave?"

"The last overnight train leaves in about an hour."

"That's not much notice," Doug said, scowling.

Jonesy just shrugged. "Sorry, couldn't do much better than that. Guess I'm just used to it. Well? Are you in?"

"How long would we be gone?"

"A couple of days, maybe three. Tick tock, buddy, I've got to know if you're coming or not."

Doug wanted to go, and knew he probably should, for the sake of his career—but he and Lucy had standing plans to spend the weekend together. And after their recent fight and make up, he was hesitant...

"Wait right here," he said, and hurried across the hall, knocking on Charlie and Bao's door.

Bao answered a moment later, shirtless and barefoot, wearing his tattered and faded blue trousers that were cut off at the knees. They were clearly in for the night as well.

"Oh, hello, Mr. Bainbridge."

"Hello, Bao. I wonder if you and Charlie would do a favor for me."

"Of course. Charlie finish up his bath, he be back in a few minutes. Come wait inside." He stepped aside and let Doug pass.

"I'm in a hurry," Doug said with an apologetic smile. "Could you please take a message to Miss Kinzler for me? I need her to know that I have to go somewhere unexpectedly, and won't be back until Sunday or Monday. Actually, could I write her a quick note?"

"Okey dokey, let me get paper." Bao went to a bureau on the far side of the room, and removed a pad of paper and a fountain pen from the drawer. As he returned, he looked surprised, then bowed his head and said, "Oh, hello."

Doug turned around to see Jonesy standing in the door. And he didn't like the look on Jonesy's face as his eyes fixed on Bao, looking him up and down.

"Hello there. I'm Art Jones, but you can call me Jonesy." His tone was altogether too smooth for Doug's taste.

"This is my neighbor, Li Baosheng," Doug said in introduction, a little too loud and too sharp, not bothering to hide his irritation.

Just then, Charlie emerged from the hall bathroom in his boxer shorts and sleeveless undershirt, a wet towel draped around his shoulders, and stood in the door behind Jonesy, who turned at the sound of footsteps behind him.

"Well hallo, Douglas," Charlie said with a smile. "This is an unexpected pleasure. And who is your friend?"

"Art Jones." Jonesy introduced himself with markedly less suaveness than he had a moment before, Doug noticed. But then he glanced over at Doug with a touch of amusement in his green eyes, before looking back at Charlie. "I've known Doug for more than a year. We had a mutual friend."

"You met my friend Tim McIntyre last year, not long after I moved in," Doug reminded Charlie. "He came by on my first Friday night here, the one who was killed. I met Mr. Jones at the funeral."

"Oh, yes, of course I remember. Mr. McIntyre seemed a very nice young man." Charlie looked back at Jonesy. "You and Mr. McIntyre were close, then, Mr. Jones?"

Doug was pretty sure he heard an unspoken question underneath the explicit one. But how in the hell would Charlie have surmised already that Jonesy was like them?

"Mr. McIntyre and I worked together," Jonesy replied, his tone carrying the practiced gravity that one learned to use when speaking of a close friend or relative long after he or she has passed away. "And he was a good friend."

"I'm so sorry," Charlie said, as always his sincerity shining through what would be a rote response from most people.

"Thank you, Mister...?"

Charlie flushed, and extended his hand. "Oh, apologies. Where are me manners? I'm Charlie Ford, and this is my companion, Li Baosheng."

Doug noticed immediately that Charlie showed no hesitation in using the word 'companion' to describe Bao in front of Jonesy, a perfect stranger. In the fifteen months he had known them, Doug had never witnessed such immediate openness from them.

"I need to send a note to Miss Kinzler, and I'm not able to deliver it myself," Doug said to Charlie, bringing the conversation back on topic. "I'm in a bit of a hurry, and I hope that you or Bao will be willing to run it over to her apartment for me."

"Oh, absolutely, Bao will take it for you," Charlie said.

"Here the paper, Mr. Bainbridge," Bao said, holding the pad and pen out to Doug.

Doug sat at the table, and wrote out a quick note.

> *"I have to take an unexpected trip south for two or three days. There has been another Japanese assassination, and I need to see what can be learned. I'll telegram when I get there. Love, Doug."*

He folded it and wrote her first name and address on the outside, then handed it to Bao, who had put on shoes and a dingy white shirt. "Make sure she gets this right away, and bring back any reply."

Bao grinned as he took the folded paper. "Can do, Mr. Bainbridge!" He turned and sprinted out the door, scampering down the stairs.

Doug turned to Charlie, who stood chatting with Jonesy. "Thank you, Charlie. I appreciate your help. I have to leave town on short notice, and unfortunately I have to cancel plans with Miss Kinzler."

"Glad to do it. I hope Miss Kinzler isn't too put out by it." Charlie turned to Jonesy. "She is a lovely person, our Miss Kinzler. Do you know her, Mr. Jones?"

"Only by reputation," Jonesy said. He pulled a cigar from inside his jacket. "Mind if I smoke this?"

"Not at all," Charlie said, pulling out a chair between the kitchen table and the open window to the fire escape.

Doug wasn't sure how to feel about the chumminess that his neighbor and Jonesy were showing. "I need to pack my things, so will you excuse me? Jonesy, should I come back here to find you before we leave?"

Jonesy looked at Charlie with raised eyebrows. "If you don't mind...?"

"Not at all! Please stay, and make yourself comfortable," Charlie said with a big, genuine smile.

As Doug walked out to the hall, he overheard Jonesy ask, "So, you and Bao are...?"

As he opened his own door, he heard Charlie's nonchalant reply: "Yes, been together more'n three years now."

How in the hell did they know? Was there some secret code he knew nothing about? He shook his head in mild irritation as he hurried to his bedroom to pack for the trip.

Twenty minutes later, Doug knocked on Charlie and Bao's door. Charlie answered, still with the damp towel draped around his shoulders and dressed exactly the same. Jonesy still sat at the kitchen table, legs crossed, spent cigar stubbed out in a bowl in front of him.

"Douglas! Welcome back. Do come in," Charlie said with a grin, and stepped aside to let Doug into the apartment.

"Ready to go?" Doug asked Jonesy.

"As ready as I'm going to get. But I thought you wanted to wait for a reply from your girlfriend."

Doug wasn't sure why that irritated him, but it did.

"I don't want to be late. I don't like having to rush through the train station." He remembered having to do just that in January, barely catching the train to Hong Kong.

"Alright then, let's go." Jonesy got up and turned to shake Charlie's hand. "Charlie, thank you for your hospitality. I hope to see you and Bao again soon."

"Call on us any time, Jonesy," Charlie replied.

Doug couldn't help but notice the familiar use of common names. *That was fast*, he thought, a touch cynically.

They reached the bottom of the stairs and stepped out onto the sidewalk, turning toward Honan Road to catch a streetcar or a cab, when Doug heard Bao calling. "Mr. Bainbridge! Wait one minute."

Doug turned, and Bao was running up Huang Wei Road, waving a piece of paper. He waited for Bao to reach them and breathlessly hand him the folded paper.

His name was scrawled on the outside, in Lucy's handwriting. He opened it and read:

"I'll come with you. I'll meet you in twenty minutes."

That was certainly not what he had expected. He looked at Bao. "What did Miss Kinzler tell you?"

Bao grinned, still breathing heavily. "She say she coming, too, as soon as she pack a bag. She say she take a cab, and be here not long after me."

Behind him, Doug heard Jonesy chuckling. "I guess we're waiting, then."

It was less than five minutes before a motor cab sped up the narrow street, and jolted to a stop in front of Doug's building, tires screeching on the damp stones. Lucy must have told the driver to step on it, he mused. The thought called to mind a *"Follow that cab!"* chase scene in a Hollywood caper, and he almost laughed before he stopped himself with just a smile.

"Wipe that goofy grin off your face, buddy," Jonesy said in *soto voce* behind him, close to Doug's ear.

The Chinese cab driver bolted from the driver's seat and rushed around to open the back door for them, then take their suit cases and put them in the trunk. Doug slid in beside Lucy, with Jonesy right after him.

"I didn't expect this," Doug said, smiling at Lucy and touching her hand. "Why did you decide to come along?"

"I recalled what happened to you the last time you looked into someone's murder," Lucy said with a sardonic look. "I didn't want that to happen again."

"There won't be any danger," Doug said, slightly defensive. "And if there were, I would hardly want you there. That would only put you in danger, too."

"Or save your neck," Lucy said with a wry half-smile.

"Are you going to introduce us, or do I have to introduce myself?" Jonesy's gruff voice asked beside him.

Doug stifled his irritation, and was momentarily distracted by the abrupt acceleration of the cab, tires squealing, throwing him back against the seat. "Lucy Kinzler, this is Arthur Jones, better known as Jonesy."

"Ah, Jonesy—I've heard all about you. How do you do? I'm Doug's girlfriend, Lucy."

"How do you do?" Jonesy replied, taking Lucy's proffered hand and shaking it.

They were nearly thrown against the left-hand door as the cab sped around the corner onto Honan Road, barely slowing to check oncoming traffic. A rickshaw operator shouted curses at them in Shanghainese for cutting him off, and Doug looked back to see the runner shaking his fist at them.

"We're not in *that* much of a hurry," Doug muttered to Lucy.

She looked nonplussed. "You don't want to risk missing the train, do you?"

"How do you know we're short on time?" Doug asked.

She gave him the sort of indulgent look that one would give to an inquisitive three year old who asks about everything. "It's almost nine-thirty, Doug—I know there aren't that many trains that leave later than ten."

"True." Doug shrugged and looked forward.

"So, while we have a few minutes, tell me about this assassination you're going south to investigate. Bring me up to speed, as they say."

From the corner of his eye, Doug could see an amused smile on Jonesy's face, and it irritated him. He could just imagine what Jonesy was thinking—that Doug was letting his girlfriend run roughshod over them, inserting herself without invitation. Imagining those thoughts in Jonesy's mind rankled all the more because it meant Doug was being emasculated by a 'sissy.'

Still, he was glad for Lucy's interest, and for her company. He chose to ignore Jonesy and focus on the bright and eager young woman sitting on his other side.

"We don't really know much about the victim, other than his name and that he's Japanese," Doug said. "And all we really know about the attacker is that it was a masked gunman. We're going down to see if we can interview some witnesses, and get more information."

"But on the surface, that sounds awfully similar to the others," Lucy pronounced.

"Yes, it does."

"And where exactly are we going?"

"To a town called Pei-hai, on the Gulf of Tonkin. I wasn't familiar with it until tonight."

Lucy looked a little confused. "The Gulf of Tonkin? Isn't that by French Indochina?"

"Partly," Jonesy said before Doug could answer. "But the north shore of the gulf is China's south coast."

"Ah, I see," Lucy answered, nodding to herself. "I remember we passed through it last summer on the coastal steamer that Mother and I took from Hong Kong to Saigon."

"From what I learned this evening, it's a small port, but it's become a bit of a resort the last several years," Jonesy said. "They say it's hardly known by westerners, and most of the tourists are Chinese, or other Asians. It's said to have one of the most beautiful beaches in China."

"So perhaps the Japanese man who was killed was an innocent tourist," Lucy said.

"Seems as good a guess as any," Jonesy agreed. "I say we start with the local police, and see if we can find out where the attack took place—if it was near the shore, we go there and canvass the hotels, see if Nakano was staying at any of them, and if anyone visited him or came looking for him."

They had just passed outside of the boundaries of the International Settlement, and were only a quarter mile from the train station, and Doug noticed that the taxi driver kept looking in his rearview mirror, more than was normal.

Doug asked him in Shanghainese if they were being followed.

The driver looked straight ahead and answered no.

Doug half-turned his head, facing toward Lucy, and looked from the corner of eye out the rear windshield. There were plenty of car headlights behind them, but it was a busy street, and there was no way for him to know if one was specifically following them, rather than driving to the train station.

"What is it?" Lucy asked.

"Probably nothing," Doug said.

He wondered if the driver understood what they had been saying to one another; most locals spoke Pidgin, but did not understand English. It wasn't unusual to find educated Chinese who spoke fluent English, however; and while this taxi driver probably wasn't highly educated, Doug decided to test him.

"How did you communicate with the driver when he first picked you up?" he muttered to Lucy out of the side of his mouth.

"In Pidgin," she murmured, and seemed to search his face for clues to what he was getting at.

As the train station came into view a block in front of them, Doug leaned forward and spoke to the driver in Shanghainese. "I hear the weather in Qingdao is lovely this time of year. Do you know that city?"

"I have never been," the driver replied in Shanghainese, and then honked at another cab that cut him off just before the entrance to the drive in front of the train station.

"My friends and I have heard that the Tsingtao Brewery gives tours. Perhaps we will go there one day instead of to the beach."

The driver just grunted, checked his blind spot, and gunned the engine to pull into the circular drive, then slammed on the brakes near the door. He gave Doug no reaction to his statement about the brewery in the former German colony some three hundred miles to the north.

"Station here," he said in Pidgin, hurrying out of the car to open Lucy's door. Then he popped open the trunk and removed their suit cases, setting them on the sidewalk beside the cab.

"I already paid him the fare," Lucy told Doug when they were outside.

Jonesy thanked him in Pidgin, handing him a dime. Doug thanked him in Shanghainese, and handed him a quarter.

"Show off," Jonesy muttered as he picked up his suit case and marched through the front doors of the train station.

Inside the station, Doug read the boards in Chinese script over the ticket windows, and found the destination city of Beihai in Guangdong province—which had obviously been Romanized as Pei-Hei, a typical mispronunciation.

"I found the city we're looking for—it's pronounced 'Beihai,' not 'Pei-Hai.'" He gave Jonesy a reproachful stare.

Jonesy just shrugged, unfazed.

"It's a twenty-five hour trip," Doug continued. "We won't be there until late tomorrow night."

"Then I guess we'd better get going," Jonesy replied.

At the ticket counter, Lucy got in front of Doug and requested one First Class ticket with sleeping berth.

"Make that two, please," Doug said, stepping up beside her and getting out his wallet.

"Douglas Bainbridge, I can get my own ticket," Lucy said, slapping his hand away. "You didn't ask me to come, I invited myself, so I'll pay my own way, thank you very much." She looked at the confused Chinese woman behind the counter, and smiled. "Just one, please. How much?"

Lucy took her ticket and stepped aside, putting her change into her purse while Doug got his ticket. As he stepped away a moment later, and Jonesy stepped forward, the stocky reporter smirked at him.

Doug couldn't resist glaring at him.

They boarded the train with ten minutes to spare, and put their luggage into the sleeping berths. Lucy's berth was directly across from

Doug's on the bottom, while Jonesy had a top berth farther down the aisle.

"We could share one, you know," Doug murmured to Lucy while Jonesy was out of earshot.

She shook her head with a rueful smile. "You are incorrigible, you know that?" Then she put her arms around his waist and kissed him. "It's one thing for you to spend the night at my place, or for me to spend the night at your place—but in public, on a train, you just keep to your side of the aisle, Mr. Bainbridge."

"Killjoy," Doug said, faking a pout.

Jonesy came up to them just then. "Anyone care for a nightcap? I'm heading to the club car for a drink, if anyone wants to join me."

"I'm game," Lucy said.

"Sure, why not?" Doug said, and offered Lucy his arm.

The train had begun moving by the time they got settled, and the lights of Shanghai flew by. It was late, and the club car was fairly empty, with only a few other people—mostly westerners—conversing in the booths.

A Chinese waiter brought their drinks—a martini for Jonesy, a gin and tonic for Doug, and a champagne cocktail for Lucy.

"Here's to finding out what the hell's going on," Jonesy said, raising his martini glass in a toast and taking a drink.

Doug scowled at Jonesy's language. *He* knew that Lucy couldn't care less about a man swearing, of course; but Jonesy didn't know that about her. It was bad form to swear in front of a lady, especially a lady one had only just met.

"Language—we're in mixed company, Jonesy," he muttered.

Jonesy looked at Lucy. "Did you mind what I said?"

"Not at all," Lucy replied, nonchalant. She lit a cigarette and took a long pull, releasing the smoke above them. "That sort of thing doesn't bother me in the least. You can relax."

"I appreciate that," Jonesy said, giving Doug an 'I told you so' look.

Doug and Lucy left Jonesy in the club car after one drink, and walked back toward their sleeping car. It was after eleven o'clock, and the interior of the train was mostly silent, with only the rhythmic clackity-clack of the wheels along the track, punctuated by the occasional whistle from the steam engine far ahead of them.

The aisle through the sleeping cars wasn't wide enough for them to walk side by side, so they held hands while Doug took the lead and Lucy followed. As they passed a dozy Chinese porter sitting on a stool by the end of their car, Doug touched his hat rim and wished him good night in Mandarin.

Doug stopped just inside their car.

Kawakami, dressed in a dark silk suit and top hat, with a red carnation in the lapel, had just entered the car at the other end, and came strolling down the aisle toward them, tapping his cane against the floor as he went.

"What is it?" Lucy asked.

"I'll tell you in a moment," Doug whispered, keeping his eyes locked on the stout middle-aged Japanese man approaching them.

Kawakami stared back, unblinking.

As he passed them, Kawakami nodded to Doug, and touched the rim of his top hat at Lucy. Then he opened the connecting door and stepped into the next car, headed in the direction of the club car.

Doug watched him go, and Lucy followed his eyes.

"That man," Doug started, still whispering.

"Yes?"

"That's the Japanese agent I've told you about—Kawakami *san*."

"Oh!" Lucy sounded startled. She looked at Doug with wide eyes. "What do you suppose he's doing on this train?"

Doug shook his head, taking a deep breath. "It's possible he's just doing what we're doing—going down to Beihai to see what he can learn. That would be reasonable, since it was another one of his countrymen who was killed."

"That's true," Lucy said, unsure. "Do you think so, Doug?"

Doug shook his head again. "I honestly don't know." He hesitated, unsure if he wanted to tell her about his premonition in the cab.

"What is it?" she asked, slightly above a whisper this time.

He motioned with his hand for her to keep her voice down.

She nodded, and continued in a whisper. "There's something more you're not saying. Tell me."

He shrugged. "It's silly, really. Just a feeling I had while we were in the cab earlier, that we were being followed. It seemed that our driver kept looking back more often than normal, and for longer. I tried to find out if he was listening to us, but could never determine if he understood English or not."

"You don't really think our taxi driver was working for this Kawakami, Doug," Lucy whispered, sounding reproachful.

"Not likely," Doug agreed.

"Not likely at all," Lucy insisted.

Doug nodded. She was right, of course. He was more concerned that someone watched them get in the cab, and then tailed them to the station.

The communists were the most likely to do that. They seemed to always have someone watching; or at least, often enough. Kawakami or one of his agents was another possibility, though.

But why? What was the motive to follow them?

It could always be someone following Jonesy, and that could be wholly unconnected to what they were doing now. Some other story Jonesy was working on, or had recently written.

Even as he thought it, it rang false. No, if they'd been followed, it was because of where they were going.

"I'll sleep lightly tonight," he muttered to Lucy as they made their way to their berths in the middle of the car. He kissed her, and they wished each other goodnight.

As Doug sat on his bed with the curtain drawn, slipping into his pajamas, it occurred to him that Kawakami was likely going to the club car—where Jonesy was still relaxing with a second martini.

He had a moment of panic. Even if he were still dressed, he wouldn't be able to get there before Kawakami to warn Jonesy. But he told himself to relax—for one thing, he had no evidence that Kawakami knew who Jonesy was. And Doug wasn't in Jonesy's company often enough to worry that Kawakami or one of his spies had seen them together.

He lay down, closed his eyes, and took several slow, deep breaths, trying to relax enough to get sleepy.

It didn't work. He was still awake some time later when he heard the unmistakable heavy stride of Jonesy returning from the club car. He listened to the steps, which went farther down the car before stopping about where Jonesy's berth was. Doug nodded in satisfaction that he'd identified correctly. He listened as Jonesy clambered into his upper berth—an amusingly awkward image coming to mind—and then the faint rustle of curtain and bed sheets.

He felt himself relaxing toward a light doze, when he was jolted awake by other heavy footsteps coming through the car, these with a much more purposeful stride. It was only a few minutes since Jonesy returned, he was certain, which meant Kawakami had to have been following Jonesy from the club car.

Coincidentally? Or on purpose? It could easily be either. His mind tumbled with images of Kawakami watching Jonesy in the club car with that relentless stare of his, and then following him through the train with a menacing glare, his hand grasping the stiletto in his jacket pocket.

The stiletto! The thought sent a shiver up Doug's spine, and sent his pulse through the roof. Kawakami might slip into their car in the middle of the night and silence them forever with a few practiced jabs of the deadly weapon. It would be all too easy. He might also have to kill an observant porter in the process, but since the porters were all Chinese, Doug doubted Kawakami would have any scruples about that.

He lay awake for hours, staring at the dark ceiling of his berth.

When he finally did drift into sleep, it was fitful, and interrupted by disturbing dream images of Kawakami creeping through the darkened sleeping car, his face cartoonishly long and garish, the extended stiletto in his hand. He made an evil laugh as he slowly tugged back the curtain of Doug's berth, then threw his hand over Doug's mouth and jabbed the stiletto toward his throat...

Doug bolted upright the second Kawakami's dream knife touched his throat. He was covered in sweat, soaking through his pajamas, and he breathed hard, his chest heaving.

He heard a faint knocking near his pillow. He pulled back his curtain a few inches and saw Lucy crouched in front of his berth, a concerned look on her face.

"Doug? Are you alright, dear?" she asked, her voice dripping with worry.

He glanced behind her, where a few Chinese faces peeked out from behind curtains, looking at them.

"You yelled, and it woke me up. I came right over to see what was wrong."

Doug swallowed hard, tried to calm his trembling hands. "I'm fine. Just a bad dream. What did I yell?"

She stared at him for a second before answering, her blue eyes looking unconvinced. "Nothing particular—it was just a sound you made, really loud. It sounded like something was happening, so I had to check on you."

Doug glanced behind her and noticed that all of the curtains but hers had fallen back into place, the occupants no longer interested.

"I just—it was just a bad dream, don't worry. I'll be fine, once I calm down."

"Are you sure?"

He attempted a smile. "I'm sure."

"Do you need anything?"

He wasn't really sure why—perhaps it was the adrenaline from his vivid scare, now that he knew it wasn't real—but his dick was hard as a rock. *Really, now?*

"You could sneak in here and cuddle with me until I fall back to sleep," he said, trying to sound shaken rather than lustful.

She looked up and down the aisle before whispering for him to scoot over. She climbed in beside him, curled up against his side, and put her arm across his chest. "Is that better?" she whispered into the skin of his neck below his ear.

It sent a tingle down his spine, and gave him goosebumps.

"Much better," he whispered. He took her hand and slid it down toward his crotch.

She startled. "Douglas!" she hissed. "Shame on you! Here I thought you were scared and needed comfort."

"I was. I do. It's just, you know, now that it's over and it wasn't real, well..." He left the rest to her imagination.

"There are people just feet from us, who woke up when you shouted," she whispered. "They'll hear us."

"No they won't. We'll be real quiet, I promise. I'll be quiet if you will."

"We both know that's not possible." But he noticed that she hadn't moved her hand.

"Yes it is. You'll see. Haven't you ever wanted to do it on a moving train?"

He heard her soft laugh. "I take it you've given this fantasy some thought."

"Haven't you?"

"I'll plead the fifth on that."

It was his turn to laugh. "I thought so." He moved his hand to the waist band of her pajamas. "I'll stop any time you tell me to."

She didn't tell him to.

Friday, September 4

The train cut across green fields of rice and soy all of the next morning. Verdant mountains to the west provided a gorgeous backdrop as Lucy and Doug had a leisurely breakfast in the dining car, and they lingered over coffee long after they finished eating.

They'd been there for an hour and a half by the time Jonesy came down for breakfast. They were sitting at a table for two, so he nodded to them as he passed, and took the open table right behind them.

"You two look chipper this morning," he said, and shook his head. "Morning people, eh?"

Doug shrugged. "I suppose I've learned to be. I take it by your late arrival that you aren't."

"Not in the slightest," Jonesy said, then turned around as the Chinese waiter came to take his order. "Black coffee, orange juice, two eggs over easy, buttered toast, and two strips of bacon, please."

"It's good to see you have an appetite," Lucy said. "Doug didn't order much this morning."

"How long did you stay in the club car last night?" Doug asked, lowering his voice and hoping Jonesy got the hint and did likewise.

"Not long, just long enough for one more drink. Why do you ask?"

"Did a portly Japanese man in a silk suit come in not long after we left? About fifty, probably, top hat, red carnation, silver-tipped walking cane?"

Jonesy gave him an appraising look. "Yes, I remember that fella. Came in and sat on the other side of the car. Ordered some sake, I think. It had Japanese writing on the bottle. Why?"

Doug glanced at Lucy, then looked back at Jonesy. "That was our old friend Kawakami. He passed us on our way back to our berths."

"You don't say?" Jonesy looked up in thought for a moment. "What do you suppose he's doing here, on this train?"

"That's exactly what I was wondering."

"Could be a coincidence," Jonesy said. "That he's on this specific train, I mean. Not that he's headed down to Beihai, with what happened down there. We all know that's why he's going. The question is, did he pick this train because of us, because we were on it? I don't know—it's possible. I sure as hell wouldn't rule it out."

Doug cringed and looked at Lucy—old habit, he supposed—but she didn't react to the swear word. That was one of the many things he loved about her.

"We've got all day on this train," he said, not relishing a long trip with a potential hostile party on board with them. "So I guess that gives us plenty of time to figure it out."

"Is that a silver lining?" Lucy asked.

Jonesy lit a cigar as the waiter brought him a steaming cup of black coffee. He puffed on it a few times, and set it on the edge of the silver ashtray. He looked at his wrist watch. "We've got about thirteen hours to go. What do you have in mind?" He picked up the coffee cup and blew across the surface before taking a small sip.

Doug had no idea. He hadn't really thought it through. Nothing came immediately to mind, so he had to shake his head and shrug, saying nothing.

Jonesy chuckled and took another sip of his coffee. "You're still no Sam Spade," he said with a rueful half smile. "But at least you've got some gumption. That's why I asked you to come along with me."

As usual, Doug found Jonesy's manner irritating. "Do you have any bright ideas?"

Before Jonesy could answer, Lucy interrupted. "Why do we have to do anything at all?"

Both men stared at her.

"What I mean is, why not let him come to us? Why go looking for trouble, when there's no escape if you find it? It's not as if there are that many places on this train for him to go—if we stay right here, or go to the club car, either way we're bound to run into him sometime over the course of the day. Wouldn't you agree?"

Jonesy nodded. "Sounds good to me. I'm in no hurry."

Doug thought about it for a moment. It made sense. And if Kawakami never interacted with them at all, then maybe he just happened to have picked the same train to Beihai, and there was nothing more to it.

Perhaps Kawakami was wondering the same things about them, if they were following him to see what he was up to. That might work to their advantage.

"I say let's do exactly that," he said, reaching out to take Lucy's hand on the table. "Then, when we get to Beihai tonight, if he's avoided us, or just failed to engage, then maybe we consider tailing him to see what he's up to."

Jonesy looked at Doug with newfound appreciation. "I told you I brought you along for a reason." He took a long draw on his cigar, blowing the smoke toward the ceiling. "No reason we can't split up once we get there—I'll go find witnesses to talk to, and you can track Kawakami."

Doug wasn't comfortable with Lucy coming with him while he tailed a Japanese secret agent—but he couldn't suggest that he and Jonesy trade tasks. Interviewing witnesses was Jonesy's actual job; he was going to Beihai for a story, and that was all.

"You take Miss Kinzler with you," he said, reluctantly.

From the corner of his eye, he saw Lucy stiffen. "No, I'm coming with you, Doug."

He squeezed her hand. "It's not safe for you to tag along with me," he said, gently. "It's likelier to get dangerous, should he discover me following him, and I can't subject you to that."

"I'm sorry—did you say '*tag along*' with you?" She let go of his hand, and stared at him with an expression somewhere between annoyance and incredulity.

He struggled to find the right words. "Lucy, you know what I mean—"

"I'm not some starry-eyed little girl, tagging along on a school-girl adventure, Doug."

"I know that, I just meant—"

"I know what you meant, Douglas." She crossed her arms and gave him a look of defiance. "I'm coming with you."

Doug knew better than to argue with her. He'd try to change her mind later.

With thirteen hours until they arrived in Beihai, there was plenty of time for that.

Hutson

15

They didn't see Kawakami that morning. They left the dining car after a while, and met up in the club car later. Jonesy had a deck of cards, and the three of them played Eights for a while, until Doug got tired of playing and went back to his berth for a book. When he got back to the club car, Jonesy and Lucy were playing Gin Rummy.

Long train rides always bored Doug. It was one of the reasons he had so rarely returned to San Francisco for a visit after he moved to Washington in 1932.

One of many reasons.

When they hadn't seen Kawakami by the time they finished lunch, Doug began to wonder what was going on. He said something to Jonesy about it after the waiter cleared their table.

"Maybe somebody knocked him off," Jonesy joked.

"Don't even joke about that." *Because maybe someone did.* Doug couldn't help that thought.

"We would have heard if someone had found a body," Lucy pointed out. "That gossip would have flown through this train like a carrier pigeon."

Jonesy chuckled. "Like *'Murder on the Orient Express,'* huh?"

Lucy blushed. "Yes, I suppose so. I read that one a couple of years ago. Maybe I had its plot on my mind, since we're on a train and going to investigate a murder."

"I read that one, too," Doug said. "I didn't like the ending."

Lucy looked surprised. "Oh? Really? I thought it was brilliant."

Doug shrugged. "I can't decide what I think of Agatha Christie's mysteries. They're very clever, but sometimes I think just a little too clever."

"Don't listen to him," Lucy said to Jonesy, waving a hand in Doug's direction. "He likes Hemingway, for heaven's sake."

"Really?" Jonesy said, giving Doug a funny look. "Well, I suppose that shouldn't surprise me."

Doug frowned. "What do you mean by that?"

Before Jonesy answered, something caught his attention, and he stared behind Doug. "Don't look now," he mumbled under his breath.

Doug had to stop himself from turning around. "Kawakami?" he whispered out of the side of his mouth, looking toward the side, across the opposite table as if he were looking at the scenery on the other side of the train.

"Uh huh," Jonesy said, casually, and lit a cigar.

"Well then, I suppose we won't need a Hercule Poirot, will we?" Lucy said with a bright smile.

Jonesy chuckled and took a drag on his cigar.

Kawakami's wide form passed them, and he took a seat at a small booth at the far end of the dining car, opposite side of the aisle, and sat facing them.

Doug supposed it was part of Kawakami's regular practice to sit facing the entire room, and probably had nothing to do with facing them in particular.

Perhaps he should start making a habit of that himself.

"Let's go," he said, nodding toward the exit, and they got up and left the dining car.

"I think I'm going to take a nap," Lucy said as they made their way through the train. "I feel like a little girl saying that, but I'm tired."

"A nap sounds good to me, too," Doug said.

Lucy gave him a stern look, and he could imagine her thinking that he'd better not have any ideas.

"I'm going to sit in the club car and read for a while," Jonesy said. "If anything interesting happens, I'll let you know after your naps." The sardonic look on his face told Doug that he didn't believe their excuse.

He ignored it. "It's a deal. See you in a bit." He took Lucy's hand and they went back to their sleeping car.

Once in his berth, he checked his suitcase to be sure no one had riffled through it, but found no evidence that anything had been disturbed, beyond the porter making the bed. He relaxed, loosened his neck tie and unbuttoned the top button of his shirt, and lay down with his hat over his eyes.

He slept hard, and when he awoke and checked his wrist watch, he was stunned to see he'd slept almost two hours. Irritated with himself, he sat up, buttoned his collar and tightened his neck tie before pulling back the curtain.

Lucy's berth was empty. He was briefly irritated that she didn't wake him when she awoke, but he told himself that was silly; it was thoughtful of her to let him sleep.

When he walked into the club car, he spotted her sitting with Jonesy at a table near the bar. They were laughing and chatting like old friends, and for some reason this really annoyed Doug. He took a deep breath before he reached their table, and put on a friendly smile.

"Well hello there," he said, trying to sound cheerful. "I thought I might find you two here. What's so funny?"

Lucy waved her hand. "Oh, nothing really. Jonesy was just telling me some amusing anecdotes from his years covering the news in Shanghai."

"There are some interesting characters in our fair city," Jonesy said with an amused grin, and took a long pull on his cigar.

"I wish I'd gotten here sooner," Doug said, sliding into the booth beside Lucy. He put his hand on her knee. "I hope you had a good nap."

"I did, thank you," she said, cheerful. "When I got up, you were out like a light, so I just let you sleep. I know you didn't sleep well last night."

"And just how do you know that, pray tell?" Jonesy asked, which elicited startled laughter from Lucy, and open-mouthed shock from Doug.

"What a scandalous thing to say, Jonesy!" Lucy said, hand on her chest, but she kept laughing.

"Are you offended?" Jonesy inquired, one eyebrow cocked in exaggerated mock curiosity.

Lucy shook her head, still laughing. "Not in the least. And I suppose it serves me right, setting you up like that, after the topics we've discussed this afternoon. Shame on me."

Jonesy chuckled.

"I might have been a little offended," Doug said, a little huffy.

Jonesy chuckled again and looked at Lucy, pointing at Doug with his smoldering cigar. "See? What did I tell you? Uptight, isn't he?"

Lucy laughed, and looked at Doug with an affectionate expression, shaking her head. "Oh, he has his moments, believe me."

Doug scowled hard. "I don't like the tone of this conversation."

Lucy gave his hand a squeeze. Jonesy shook his head and said, "Thanks. Keep proving my point, Doug."

Doug decided not to dig himself any deeper into the hole, and changed the subject. "Have you seen our old friend Kawakami?"

"Not since the dining car," Jonesy said. "I expected he'd show up here this afternoon, if he was really following us."

"Unless he's trying to throw us off," Doug suggested. "He probably guessed we're onto him, so he's giving us some space while we travel, letting us relax and look the other way. When we get to Beihai, I think we'll see him show interest again."

"Unless he really isn't interested in us at all," Jonesy said.

"If you want *my* opinion, I think Jonesy's right," Lucy said. "His presence on the same train as us is a coincidence."

This irritated Doug more than he expected—not that her opinion disagreed with his, but rather that it agreed with Jonesy's.

"Well, we've got seven hours to find out," he said. "We'll act like he's not here, and see what happens after we get to Beihai."

The train pulled into the Beihai station shortly after ten-thirty.

They had seen little of Kawakami, just a glimpse of him arriving in the dining car for a late dinner, around the time that they finished eating and were preparing to leave. He didn't seem to pay much attention to them, so they ignored him and went about their business.

Doug had thought the heat and humidity of Shanghai was oppressive, but when he stepped off of the air conditioned first class train cars and into the tropical air outside, he felt as if he were standing under a wet blanket. A very hot, wet blanket. He fanned himself with his passport, but got no relief that way.

He and Lucy stood together on the platform, and waited a couple of minutes for Jonesy. The stocky reporter wiped his brow with his handkerchief as he joined them.

"Keep your eyes out for you know who," Doug muttered.

"I need to exchange some currency, and I'm sure you two do as well, since we didn't have time back in Shanghai," Jonesy said. "Then we need to find a suitable hotel. Probably near the beaches, in the tourist areas, since our victim was in all likelihood a tourist."

They found the currency exchange window in the lobby of the station, thankfully still open. Lucy stepped up, and in expert Pidgin she exchanged some Shanghai dollars for Chinese currency. Doug was impressed at how quickly she had mastered Pidgin, and only wished she'd learned Shanghainese as well. But Shanghainese would be of no use here.

He stepped up to the window when she was finished, and greeted the young woman behind the window in Cantonese. She smiled at the unexpected use of her language, and he slid across one hundred Shanghai dollars.

As he waited for her to count out the appropriate amount of Chinese currency, he leaned against the counter and looked over the small station lobby.

Kawakami marched through just then, carrying a small valise, looking straight ahead—or so it seemed—and marched through the exit doors.

"Give my money to this young lady," Doug instructed the exchange clerk in Cantonese. Then to Lucy in English, "Hold my money for me, and take my luggage. I'll find you two as soon as I see where he's going."

He hurried after Kawakami.

"But Doug, I was going to come with you," Lucy protested behind him, but he was already at the door, and ignored her as he hurried through.

He stood on a short stretch of sidewalk in front of the station, along a narrow street. He looked both ways, and saw Kawakami in a rickshaw that had just pulled away.

He hurried after them, watching the street for another rickshaw. An empty one passed, going the other direction, toward the train station, and he shouted at the runner in Cantonese, waving his hand.

The rickshaw operator did an immediate one hundred and eighty degree turn, and Doug hopped in the back before he'd come to a stop.

"Follow that rickshaw right there, the one with the passenger wearing a top hat," he said in Cantonese, pointing ahead at Kawakami's rickshaw. "But don't let them see you following—stay back a ways. Just don't lose them, and I will pay you double."

"Whatever you want, sir," the runner said in a dialect that sounded a bit like Cantonese, but not quite. He was shirtless and dripping with sweat, the waist of his pants soaked several inches.

They had already gone a couple of blocks when Doug realized he had no Chinese currency to pay the rickshaw operator. Hopefully the runner wouldn't be too livid if he paid in Shanghai coins. But he would worry about that later.

The streets were dark, the only illumination coming from the edges of shuttered windows. There was heavy cloud cover, so no moonlight or starlight, and that served to hold in the oppressively hot, wet air. While the darkness made it difficult to see Kawakami's rickshaw ahead of them, it also made it nearly impossible for Kawakami to see them following.

They rounded a corner onto another nearly deserted street when it began to rain—big, heavy drops, a few at a time at first, but within minutes it turned into a torrential downpour.

Monsoon season, Doug thought with a groan. He should have known better, he reminded himself. He'd been in China long enough to know that the south coast was heavily affected by the summer monsoons from June through September.

Ahead of him, Kawakami put up a black umbrella, and Doug sighed in frustration.

He turned up the collar of his linen suit jacket and tugged his hat lower over his face in a vain attempt to ward off the wetness that took only seconds to penetrate to his skin. At least it wasn't windy, he thought with grim satisfaction.

Kawakami's rickshaw took a couple of additional turns onto streets that were now deserted. Doug's rickshaw operator kept right with them, never complaining about the weather. If anything, Doug thought, the runner might welcome the rain to wash away the sweat.

Doug got the impression from what he'd seen before the rain that Beihai wasn't exactly the hopping scene after dark that Shanghai was.

Not many places were, of course, but Beihai was a small city, with nearly one hundred thousand people; whereas Shanghai had more than three million residents from all over the globe.

Kawakami's rickshaw stopped at a dark store front not far from the harbor, and the portly Japanese agent got out, carrying his valise and open umbrella, and disappeared around the back of the two-story brick building.

His rickshaw did not pull away.

Doug told his runner to wait at the corner, and he jumped out and stood in the limited cover of some thick hedges. He crouched behind the big waxy green leaves and watched.

He no longer envied Kawakami his umbrella, being soaked sufficiently that he couldn't get any wetter as he stood in the pouring rain. At least, he thought so; rivulets of rain water ran from the rim of his hat, and from time to time he had to wipe a drop from his eyes as it soaked through onto his forehead.

Now he couldn't get any wetter than he already was.

When nothing happened for several minutes, he crept forward slowly, keeping to the relative cover of the hedge, until he reached the pathway that Kawakami had used. It led along the side of the building, beside a small garden enclosed on three sides by the hedge. A marble fountain stood in the center of the little garden, and flowers of every color imaginable surrounded it.

Doug crept along the wall, keeping out of sight of anyone who might happen to look out the second story windows. When he reached the back corner of the building, he peaked around. His head moved at glacially slow speed, as he imagined some big goon standing just around the corner, watching, waiting for an opportunity to punch anyone spying on them.

Or worse.

He found no one standing there. *Of course not*, he thought, glancing up at the rain falling in torrents from the dark sky. There was a narrow alley behind the building, but it was deserted. Doug hurried toward a door in the center of the back wall, but it was solid with no windows. He briefly considered trying the handle to see if it were locked, but ruled that out immediately.

Don't be an idiot, he told himself. What could be gained that would outweigh the risk involved in trespassing?

Instead he went around the other side of the building, half-expecting to find Kawakami standing there talking with one of his minions. Instead it was just a narrow passage between buildings, barely three feet across, and it was empty save for the metal trash cans standing guard at the rear entrance.

He slipped past the trash cans and dashed up the narrow passage toward the street.

Kawakami's rickshaw was gone.

Doug looked up and down the street, but only his own rickshaw stood at the corner, its operator stoic in the heavy rain.

"Damn it!" he muttered, his right fist hitting his left palm in frustration.

He ran down the street toward his rickshaw, oblivious to the darkened storefront that he ran past.

"Did that man come back out after I went around the building?" he asked the rickshaw runner in Cantonese.

The man nodded.

"What did he do?"

"He got back in the rickshaw, and they went away."

Doug huffed in exasperation. "Where did they go?"

The runner nodded down the street. "They went left at the next street, toward the harbor."

"Let's go," Doug said, scrambling into the seat. "Go where they did, as fast as you can."

The operator picked up the handles and ran. His short break had given him a bit of additional speed, and they reached the next street in little more than a minute.

It was two blocks from there to the harbor, and the street was deserted. When they reached the harbor, the runner stopped, waiting for direction. Doug looked up and down the harbor front, but there was no sign of Kawakami or the rickshaw.

"Damn it!" he muttered again. He'd been had.

"Take me to the hotels near the beach," he told the runner.

The third hotel he tried confirmed that Miss Kinzler and Mr. Jones had checked in about thirty minutes before. "They said you would be here soon, Mr. Bainbridge," the middle-aged desk clerk said in standard Cantonese, and handed him a brass key. "You are in room seventeen."

"Thank you," he said, with a bow. "Did Miss Kinzler happen to leave anything for me?" He hoped she had put his Chinese currency in an envelope and left it at the desk for him.

"No sir, she did not."

"Would you by any chance be able to exchange some coins from Shanghai currency to Chinese currency?"

The clerk hesitated. "I'm afraid I do not know the exchange rate, sir."

"I understand," Doug replied with a bow of his head. "Would it be possible to advance me some currency, charged to my room, so that I can pay my rickshaw?"

"Yes, sir. The fare from the train station?"

"No, more than that. We made two stops." Doug decided not to estimate. "Wait just a moment, let me ask him."

He ran out to where the rickshaw runner stood under the awning in front of the hotel lobby. He asked him how much the regular fare would be for their trip.

When the runner quoted him a fee, Doug deducted twenty percent for the obvious mark-up quoted to an 'ignorant tourist,' and then doubled that lower figure, since he'd promised double. He offered the runner that amount, and they haggled for the next thirty seconds before settling on a price.

Doug went back inside and asked the desk clerk for that amount. The clerk gave him a look bordering somewhere between sympathy and pity. "You are being overcharged," he said as he handed over the coins.

Doug hurried out to pay the runner, and went upstairs.

The hallway was clean, but plain, and very stuffy. Unlike the fancier hotels of Shanghai, there was no air conditioning here, and a single open window at the top of the stairs was the sole ventilation.

He found room number seventeen almost at the end. He unlocked the door, but stopped in his tracks when he saw Jonesy lounging with a book on one of the twin beds, in a bathrobe, wet hair plastered to his forehead.

Jonesy's wet clothes hung from the back of a chair, while his suit jacket and hat hung from nearby pegs, with a fan blowing directly on them. All of them were dripping, with puddles forming on the floor.

"There you are," Jonesy said, sitting up and closing the book.

"I'm sorry," Doug said, cheeks flushing. "I must have the wrong room." He looked at the number seventeen on the outside of the door, in both Arabic numerals and Chinese script.

"No, you're in the right place," Jonesy said. "We're roomies tonight. Lucy's in the room next door, number sixteen. I called for the maid a little bit ago, and she's bringing more towels. You'll want to get out of those wet clothes."

"No thanks," Doug said, terse.

Jonesy gave him a dubious look, arching an eyebrow. "Suit yourself. Did you find out what Kawakami is up to?"

"No, he ditched me." It irritated Doug to have to admit that.

Jonesy thought about that a moment, and nodded. "He's too smart to let himself be followed, not once he'd seen you on the train."

He leaned back against the propped up pillows and opened his book.

"I'm going to check on Lucy," Doug said, stepping out the door.

"She might not be back in her room yet," Jonesy said, not looking up from his book. "She said she was going to take a bath, and I haven't heard her return."

Doug hesitated in the doorway. "Where is the bathroom?"

"Down the hall to the right—but I've got dibs on it after she's finished." Jonesy glanced over Doug's way. "You can go third."

Doug closed the door, and found number sixteen next door. He knocked twice, but heard no sound within, so he turned back, and found the bathroom door at the end of the hall.

He knocked quietly.

"Occupied!" Lucy's voice called from inside.

"Luce, it's me," he said in a stage whisper through the key hole.

She was silent for a few seconds. "I'm in the bath," she said, sounding a bit awkward for some reason.

"Can I come in?" he whispered through the key hole.

"Doug!"

He wasn't really sure why that would shock her. "Why not?"

"You can't be serious. Doug—we'll talk about it later. Now let me finish my bath."

Irritated, he turned away and started to go back to his room—but an awkward silence with Jonesy hardly sounded appealing, so he went down to the lobby.

"Good evening," he said to the clerk in Cantonese, with a polite head bow. "Would it be possible for me to rent my own room, separate from Mr. Jones?"

"I'm sorry, Mr. Bainbridge," the clerk said, returning the head bow. "We have no vacancy. You and your companions took our last two available rooms. I hope it is satisfactory."

"Yes, it is satisfactory, thank you," Doug said, resigned to sharing the room with Jonesy—unless he could talk Lucy into letting him share her bed. He bowed, and turned back toward the stairs.

He passed the maid at the top of the stairs, a diminutive Chinese woman of about fifty, removing a stack of white towels from a linen closet beside the open window. She nodded, and offered him a towel in Pidgin. He thanked her in Cantonese, and took a towel.

As he walked back to number seventeen, she followed him with a stack of towels in her arms, almost covering her eyes. As he unlocked the door, she waited behind him. When he walked in the room, she followed him.

"Lots towel, Mista Jones," she said, and set the stack onto the little writing desk that sat opposite the two twin beds.

Lucy passed their open door as the maid was leaving, her pink bathrobe tucked tightly around her throat. "The bathroom's available," she said.

"Thanks," Jonesy said, jumping up. He laid a towel on the puddles that had formed under his still drippy clothing, and draped another towel around his neck as he walked out.

Doug went to Lucy's door, which she was about to shut before she saw him.

"I don't suppose I could come in while you get dressed?" he asked with a wry smile.

The funny look on her face confused him.

"Really, Doug—do you want to get us kicked out of this hotel?"

"They won't kick us out of the hotel."

"I wouldn't count on it," she replied, crossing her arms. "I'm registered under my own name, and you're registered under yours. We're clearly not married—different last names—and this isn't

203

Shanghai. They might take offense and throw us out in the middle of the night. It would only take one other guest to report us, and we'd be done for."

He hated that she was right about that.

"What if I snuck in here in the middle of the night?" he asked. "Leave the door unlocked, I would tip toe, no one would hear me."

She shook her head. "And what if someone happened to open their door at that moment, needing to go to the bathroom? We can't take that chance. On the train was one thing—it can't happen again while we're here."

Doug felt his gut clenching, in both disappointment and discomfort.

"Are you listening to me, Doug?"

"Yes, I hear you," he said, short. He instantly regretted his tone, and softened it. "Sorry. I know you're right, I just hate the thought of sharing a room with Jonesy."

She laughed, and shook her head. "Don't be such a fuddy duddy," she said, and closed her door.

Doug went back to the room he was going to have to share with Jonesy, and while he had it to himself he stripped off his sopping wet jacket and tie, and loosened his collar. He found an empty peg to hang them, along with his hat, and spread a towel under them to catch the drips.

He was relieved to take off his soaked shoes and socks, and then wiped his feet on the towel he'd spread on the floor.

He stared at Jonesy's wet clothes, blowing in the breeze created by the fan a few feet in front of them. His own jacket and tie a few feet farther away also fluttered. Still, the air was heavy with humidity. *They'll never dry by morning.*

He had a spare shirt in his suit case, along with clean underwear and socks—but the thought of putting on a damp suit in the morning made him shiver, in spite of the stuffy heat in the room.

Jonesy returned a little while later, wet hair now combed, and the damp towel draped around his neck.

"All yours," he said, and opened his suit case to remove a fresh pair of boxer shorts.

Doug turned away. "Thanks," he muttered as he grabbed a towel and removed his pajamas from his valise, carrying them both to the empty bathroom.

Doug didn't normally bathe in the evenings—but at home he only shared a bathroom with his neighbors Charlie and Bao, so he didn't have to fight for bathroom time in the morning. Here, he shared the bathroom with the occupants of eighteen rooms, and the line in the morning would be horrendous.

Besides, he hadn't had a full bath this morning, since the train only had a water closet, what Americans would call a "half-bath."

He ran the faucet, and was actually a little relieved that only tepid water came from the spout. He slipped into the cool water after it filled the tub, and enjoyed the relief from the hot and muggy air.

He dressed in his pajamas after the bath, and thought to himself that they had been far more comfortable for sleeping on the air conditioned train.

For whatever reason, he'd expected that he and Lucy would share a room, and so he wouldn't have to sweat through his pajamas.

He let himself back into room number seventeen, and scowled when he saw Jonesy lounging on top of his bed in nothing but a pair of boxer shorts, his book propped open on his bare torso.

"Aren't you going to get dressed for bed?" he asked, irritated.

Jonesy looked at him like he was from Mars. "In this heat? Are you kidding?"

"It's unseemly," Doug snapped. "You're practically naked."

Jonesy laughed. "'*Practically* naked?' Are you serious?"

"Cover yourself."

Jonesy's face set in a determined scowl. "I'm as covered as I'm going to get tonight, thank you. I'll get dressed in the morning. Until then, this is how I'm going to sleep. If you've got a problem with that, it's your problem, not mine."

"It's not polite."

"What's not polite?"

"The way you flaunt it."

Jonesy laughed again. "Flaunt it? You are a piece of work. Don't pretend you've never seen a man in underwear before. Hell, we both know you showered with the fellas at that fancy boarding school of yours, so you've seen 'em in nothing at all. Don't get all prudish with me."

"That's different."

"How?"

"They weren't..." Doug didn't finish.

An uncomfortable silence fell between them. For a second, Jonesy's green eyes looked stung, but then went cold.

"You really are up-tight," Jonesy muttered. He pointed his finger toward Doug. "Do you have any idea how many times a day you interact with men like me, and don't even know it?"

Doug scoffed. "I think I would know."

"Maybe sometimes you know it, but most of the time you don't. It happens every day, and you have no idea. And you don't feel threatened, so stop being threatened by me."

"I'm not threatened."

"Uh huh." Jonesy's condescending tone rankled Doug. "You at least know your neighbors are 'fans of the YMCA,' don't you?"

"I beg your pardon?" Doug had no idea what Jonesy was talking about.

"They're gay, you slow poke," Jonesy said with a sardonic half-smile and head shake. "You *do* know your neighbors, Charlie and Bao, are a couple, right? And I don't mean a couple of pals."

Doug scowled, uncomfortable. "Of course I know that. Do you think I'm stupid?"

Jonesy chuckled, and Doug's irritation grew.

"No, I don't think you're stupid. I figured you probably knew—but also thought you just might be obtuse enough to not put it together. People miss it all the time, you know."

"I don't know what you mean. I figured it out the first time I met them."

"Good for you. But since they live together, the clues were a little less hidden," Jonesy said. "You miss it most of the time, just like everyone else."

"Don't exaggerate."

"I'm not," Jonesy said, pointing a finger again. "You *are* just that obtuse, even when it's right under your God damned nose."

Doug felt his annoyance rising as his cheeks flushed. "What are you getting at, Jonesy?"

"Well, take your tall friend, for instance—Kenneth, right? He's so hopelessly in love with you he can barely see straight. Acts like an adoring puppy every time he's with you. And you should see his eyes whenever he sees you."

Doug's temper flashed. He felt affronted on behalf of his friend, and had to resist the urge to punch Jonesy right in that smug mouth of his.

"Don't be ridiculous! Kenny is completely in love with his wife. They're expecting a baby, by the way. How would that be possible if what you said were true?"

Jonesy laughed out loud. "You're as naïve as everyone else," he said through his laughter.

Doug crossed his arms and glared.

Jonesy stopped laughing, and his expression grew serious. "You have no idea how many men with wives and children take any opportunity that comes their way to have an encounter with a man.

Happens all the time. And that don't necessarily mean they're gay—there are lots of people who like both men and women. I've known plenty of fellas that adore their wives, love them for real, but they're also desperately in love with their best friends, and never tell them. That's your friend Kenneth for you."

"I don't have to listen to this," Doug said. He pulled the lamp cord, and the room fell dark, except for a sliver of moonlight coming through the window and reflecting on the end of Jonesy's bed. He didn't care that Jonesy had been reading. *He and his damn book can go to hell*.

Doug flopped onto the bed, and turned his back to Jonesy.

16

Saturday, September 5

Doug rose early the next morning, having barely slept most of the night. He blamed it on the stuffy heat, but part of him suspected his anger at Jonesy had fueled his restless dozing.

He made sure Jonesy's eyes were closed and his breathing even before he went into the farthest corner to change out of his pajamas and into his clothes. As he'd feared, his jacket was still damp when he slid it on over his fresh shirt, and the feeling made his skin crawl.

He heard Jonesy stirring as he fastened his necktie, so he grabbed his hat and hurried out the door before the stocky reporter could get up from bed.

As he'd suspected, there was a line for the bathroom stretching halfway down the hall. He slipped over to Lucy's door and knocked.

"Just a minute," she called from inside.

"It's me," he said.

A moment later, she unlocked the door, dressed in a navy blue dress with white polka dots and collar. She grabbed her purse from the bedside table, and locked the door behind her.

"Is Jonesy joining us for breakfast?" she asked as she took his arm and they walked down the hall.

"No, he's still asleep. I didn't want to wake him. He said he's not a morning person."

"That's true," Lucy said as they went down the stairs. "Still, it would be a shame if he had to miss breakfast."

"He'll be fine," Doug said. "He's a reporter, he's resourceful."

An older man stood behind the front desk this morning, and he nodded at them as they walked through the lobby. Large front windows sat open, allowing in the breeze off the beach, and for the first time since getting off the train ten hours before, Doug felt a touch of coolness as the air moved over his sweaty forehead.

Doug approached the desk, bowed, and asked in Cantonese where they could find a good place for breakfast.

The man smiled at the sound of his language from Doug's mouth, and gave directions to a tea house a couple of blocks away.

They strolled down the shorefront road, taking their time and enjoying the cool-ish breeze off the Gulf of Tonkin.

"I was surprised last night that the desk clerk spoke good English," Lucy said. "I was prepared to use Pidgin with everyone, but it was nice to not have to for a change. Still..." she let her voice trail off.

"What?" Doug asked.

Lucy gave him a sheepish grin. "It's probably silly, but if there are people around who speak English, we won't be able to discuss things amongst ourselves without worry of being overheard."

Doug patted her hand on his arm. "Don't worry about that. If we need to, we'll just talk quietly and make sure no one is within close proximity."

"So you *have* done this before," she said with an almost triumphant tone.

He shook his head. "Not really. Not nearly as much as you probably think, anyway."

"But you clearly know what you're doing, better than I do."

There was a distance in her voice that bothered him.

"Only a little bit. You could really exaggerate how much we do this kind of thing. Most of my experience, actually, was from discussing Tim's death with Jonesy last year."

This seemed to satisfy her, as she nodded and didn't respond. She did hug his arm a little tighter, and looked out toward the beach, which was nearly deserted this time of morning. An elderly couple threw pieces of something to the sea gulls near the surf, and a trio of fishermen repaired a torn net near the spit of sand that extended out into the water as the shore rounded into the harbor.

"I hope we have some time to enjoy ourselves while we're here," she said. "I know you and Jonesy have your work to do, and I'm here to help in any way I can; but I do hope we can have a few moments of vacation before we have to go back."

He hoped that, too.

They took their time at breakfast, enjoying each other's company, and holding hands while they drank tea and ate pineapple buns with red bean paste.

He yawned a few times, and she asked him why he was so sleepy.

"I didn't sleep well last night."

"I'm sorry to hear that. Why not? Surely you were exhausted from traveling."

Doug shrugged, not wanting to get into it. "It was too hot, and I couldn't get comfortable."

She gave him a knowing look, and he had to look away.

"Couldn't get comfortable, huh? Because Jonesy was in the room?"

He hated that she figured it out. And he loved her for being able to figure him out.

He didn't answer directly. "He lay around in his boxer shorts, for heaven's sake."

He thought that explained everything perfectly well, but her amused half smile and the gleam in her eyes told him otherwise.

"What?" he asked, a little irritated.

"That hardly seems strange to me, with how hot it was last night. At home, you would sleep naked. I think that was perfectly respectful of him, under the circumstances."

Doug scowled and looked away. "You wouldn't understand."

"Why wouldn't I?"

"Because you're not a man, that's why." His tone was a little sharper than he'd intended, and he instantly regretted that. It wasn't her fault she couldn't understand it from a man's perspective.

"Oh, I see," she said, her voice flat.

"Don't be that way." He reached out to take her hand in both of his. "I only meant that it's different for men. Women don't have to worry about that sort of thing, not in the same way."

"I'm not really sure what you're inferring, Doug," Lucy said, her brows knitting above her nose in consternation. "You surely can't think that Jonesy would try to take advantage of you. That's the silliest thing I've heard in ages."

"Men aren't like women," he said, which only caused her scowl to deepen.

"And what is *that* supposed to mean, Doug? Are you implying that men can't be trusted to keep their hands to themselves if someone attractive is nearby? Are you saying I shouldn't trust you when I'm not around, and other beautiful women are?"

"Of course not! Don't be ridiculous. I didn't mean anything of the kind. Stop putting words in my mouth."

"OK, then what exactly *did* you mean?" She crossed her arms and stared at him.

"Only that men are more aggressive about going after what they want, that's all. I didn't mean that all men can't be trusted. I only meant—"

"But apparently you think Jonesy can't," she interrupted. "Even though he's given you *no* reason to not trust him. If anything, he's given you every reason to put your trust in him, after everything he's done for you—with Tim's death, and since."

He couldn't argue with that, and she wasn't seeing his point anyway, so he looked away and drank his tea in silence.

She didn't let it go. "And I'll have you know that women are every bit as capable of going after what they want as men are. I got you, didn't I?"

"That wasn't one-sided—I got you, too. As I recall, I went after you in Chongqing."

The amused twinkle came back to her eyes. She lit a cigarette and took a long pull on it.

"Oh, yes, you did—and I suppose I had *nothing* at all to do with that."

Doug's mouth hung open for a second, stunned. "Are you trying to imply that you manipulated me into going after you?"

"Don't be such an ass," she said, waving a dismissive hand in the air. "There was no manipulation. You came for me because you wanted to. But you can't say I had nothing to do with it. I'd at least planted the seeds, which grew into you wanting to."

That felt better; and it also rang true, if he were being honest.

"Do you suppose we should get back and see if Jonesy's ready to find witnesses to interview?" she asked, and took another pull on her cigarette.

He nodded. "He might be awake by now."

"Then let's go," she said, and stubbed out her half-smoked cigarette in the ash tray. "Now don't be an ass to Jonesy today, you hear? He's a nice man, and it was kind of him to ask you to come along. Don't forget that. The rest is just silliness."

"Yes, ma'am."

They found Jonesy sitting in an arm chair in the hotel lobby five minutes later, arms crossed, watching the door.

"About time you two got back," he said, rising from the chair.

"You're not used to having to wait for us, are you, Jonesy?" Doug said with a friendly jab. "It's always the other way around."

"We had breakfast. Are you hungry?" Lucy flashed Doug a warning look.

"Yes, thanks. I'll grab something fast from a street vendor, though. Let's get going."

Jonesy led them out to the street. "After Lucy and I checked in, but while we were still waiting for you last night, I asked if Nakano had stayed at our hotel, and was told they haven't had a Japanese guest in a while," Jonesy said. "Seems most of the guests are Chinese— except for a French couple, we're the only foreigners staying there right now."

Doug nodded. "We need to know first where the shooting occurred. That's where we'll find the best witnesses. Later, we can find out where he was staying, and see what we can learn about him there."

"Good thinking," Jonesy said with a firm nod. "You might just make a good investigator yet." He raised his arm to hail an empty rickshaw.

"Where to?" Lucy asked as she climbed in and sat on Doug's lap. It was tight quarters.

"The police station," Jonesy said.

The rickshaw brought them to the Beihai Police Station fifteen minutes later, and Doug told Lucy to wait while he and Jonesy went inside.

"Why can't I come with you?" she asked, folding her arms and glaring at him.

"Because I need someone to hold the rickshaw while we're inside, and I need to go with Jonesy so I can be his translator."

Lucy's glare melted, and a sheepish half smile replaced it. "Oh, of course. Sorry."

"We'll be back as soon as we can."

Truthfully, Jonesy could have made due in Pidgin, if there weren't anyone at the police station who spoke English. But Doug might still be able to help out; and even if not, he wasn't about to settle for Jonesy's second-hand account.

The police weren't forthcoming at first, but Jonesy slipped the sergeant a few coins, and information began flowing.

Nakano had indeed been shot less than two blocks from the beach, as they had suspected. The police knew the hotel he was staying at, and searched his belongings after the attack, but found nothing to provide a clue as to why he had been targeted. He was, to all appearances, a tourist on vacation.

"But he was staying alone at the hotel?" Doug asked the sergeant in Cantonese.

"Yes, he was staying alone."

"Were there other Japanese staying in that hotel at the time?"

"No, he was the only Japanese at that hotel."

No friends, family, or significant other on vacation with him. Doug found this fishy. He translated the interaction for Jonesy.

"What do you think of that?" Jonesy asked, dubious.

"It seems improbable to me," Doug muttered.

"I agree. Ask him if they've notified Nakano's family, and where they are."

Doug translated.

"Yes, we located his family in Japan, and his wife in Shanghai, and they have been notified," the sergeant said, expressionless.

Doug felt a thrill rush through him. "It seems he might have lived in Shanghai," he muttered to Jonesy, and translated the sergeant's words.

Jonesy didn't react much, only nodded and jotted something in his notebook. But a slight flush of his cheeks, betrayed his excitement at the news.

"Get the names of the witnesses the cops interviewed," Jonesy said.

After Doug translated, the sergeant hemmed and hawed a little, until Jonesy slipped him another coin. Then he bowed and went through a door, returning a few minutes later with a list of names and addresses.

Doug thanked him in Cantonese, took the list, and bowed. He and Jonesy hurried out to the waiting rickshaw, and Doug gave the runner the first address on their list.

"Well?" Lucy asked as Doug got in beside her.

"We might have hit pay dirt," Jonesy told Lucy as he climbed in after Doug. "Seems Nakano was a resident of Shanghai."

"Or at least, he has a wife in Shanghai," Doug said. "And she was not here with him. Neither was anyone else, apparently."

"And you're not buying it," Lucy said.

"Not in the least," Doug replied.

"Me neither," Jonesy echoed.

"Good, me neither."

"Do we need to keep going?" Lucy asked as they left the home of the fourth witness two hours later. "It seems we have a pretty clear picture."

"*I'm* not finished," Jonesy said, gruff. "You never know what one little detail you might get from the last person on the list."

"If you want to go back to the hotel while we finish up, that would be fine," Doug offered. "We'll come back and pick you up before dinner."

"No, I'll stay," Lucy said, her voice flat.

They took a rickshaw to the next address.

After glancing at the runner pulling the rickshaw, Lucy leaned close to Doug and spoke quietly. "Everything we've been told by the witnesses matches the other murders—there was an ambush, and Nakano was shot by someone wearing an axe on his belt, and a hood hiding his face. Doesn't that confirm our suspicion that these are connected? What more detail are we looking for?"

Doug was about to agree with her, but Jonesy interrupted him as he opened his mouth.

"Additional details could make the connection stronger," Jonesy said in a gruff whisper. "So far, we don't have a solid account of any martial arts moves, which could cement this as an Axe Gang job. We also don't know if anyone spied any accomplices lurking nearby. And there's no explanation of how the attacker got away."

When they rounded the corner onto their destination street, a Black Ford idled in front of a house. A man in the uniform of a Chinese Army captain stood near the passenger side, smoking a cigarette.

"Let's wait a moment," Doug whispered to his companions, and then told the rickshaw operator in Cantonese to stop where they were.

"What do you make of that?" Jonesy asked Doug.

Military intelligence, Doug thought, but instead whispered, "Let's wait and see who comes out of the house."

There was a good possibility the captain standing by the car had already spotted them, but he didn't seem to be paying them much mind. Nonetheless, Doug told Jonesy to go up to the house where they were parked, and pretend to be asking directions.

Jonesy gave him a dubious look, but climbed out without a word and walked to the house.

Lucy leaned against Doug, kissing his cheek. "You don't think that's the secret police, do you?" she whispered in his ear.

She was good. Cool as a cucumber.

He stroked the back of her hair and looked at her long enough to kiss her forehead and whisper before looking back, "No, not in uniform."

From the corner of his eye, he saw a satisfied half-smile spread across Lucy's lips. "I thought the same thing," she murmured.

To their right, Jonesy was talking to a middle-aged Chinese man in Pidgin, and he pretended to look that way while keeping his eyes on the house with the military car in front. The address on that door was the one they were looking for.

Jonesy drug out his conversation as long as he could—far longer than Doug could have—and he shuffled back to the rickshaw, clearly taking his time.

Their patience was rewarded then, as two military men emerged from the house and put their hats on. One was a colonel, the other a major who followed a step behind.

Doug recognized the face of the colonel immediately.

The only time he had seen him, he was wearing civilian clothes, and was dressed up for the lunar New Year, but it was unmistakable.

"That's colonel Ming Zhonghu," he muttered as Jonesy climbed back into the rickshaw.

"I remember that name," Jonesy said, pausing for several seconds. "He's with the Blue Shirts Society. He's the brother of—"

"Yes," Doug interrupted him. He wasn't comfortable bringing up Ming Lin-wen in front of Lucy.

"Jackpot," Jonesy muttered.

The elderly Chinese man slammed the door in their faces when Doug asked him about the shooting.

"Friendly fellow," Jonesy muttered. "I think we can thank Colonel Ming for that reception."

Doug nodded agreement. "He certainly looked terrified."

Jonesy made a frustrated grumbling sound as they walked back to the rickshaw. "No use asking around anymore. We won't get another peep out of anyone down here, mark my words."

17

Wednesday, September 9
Shanghai

Doug was undressing for bed when a noise in the kitchen disturbed him. He still had his boxer shorts on, so he hurried out to the main room and turned on a lamp, then stopped cold.

The communist cell leader stood in the center of his kitchenette, while a young man climbed through the kitchen window from the fire escape, knife in hand.

"Keep silent, Bainbridge Douglas. We mean you no harm, as long as you cooperate with us," the leader said in Shanghainese, staring at Doug with unblinking eyes.

"What do you want?" Doug asked, keeping his voce as steady as he could. It was two weeks since he'd asked for a meeting, and much had happened since. He wished he'd grabbed his gun before running out of the bedroom.

"You were in Beihai a few days ago, with Mr. Jones and Miss Kinzler," the leader said.

Not for the first time, Doug was disturbed by just how much these communists knew about his comings and goings. He nodded, but stayed silent.

"While you were there, one of my counterparts in that city was murdered by a Japanese agent, who disappeared after committing the crime." The leader's voice was as cold and level as his stare. "The police are useless, but we already know who did it. It is someone you are acquainted with—Kawakami Takahiro."

Doug took a second to absorb this information. Then he nodded slowly. "I am acquainted with Kawakami *san*, but I am not familiar with him."

"He is an operative of the Japanese Secret Service," the leader said, his gaze level and unwavering.

Doug nodded again. "I suspected that. Last year, he had an interest in a murdered reporter friend of mine who had written about the Korean Provisional Government." *And he also killed two Juntong agents.* But he left that unsaid.

The comrade seemed to appraise him for a moment before speaking again. "When was the last time you saw Kawakami *san*, Bainbridge Douglas?"

Doug decided it would be imprudent to say nothing. Or to lie.

"I saw him on the overnight train to Beihai, five days ago."

The comrade's eyes narrowed. "What was he doing?"

Doug glanced at the young man standing behind the leader, playing with the blade of a nasty-looking knife. He swallowed hard and shrugged.

"Nothing out of the ordinary. He seemed to be traveling by himself, and he kept to himself, as far as I know."

The leader seemed to ponder this for a moment. "You are aware that the Japanese Secret Service has rented an office in the same building as your office, Bainbridge Douglas?"

"Yes, I am aware of that. They are not often there, though."

"You are acquainted with Kawakami *san*'s underling, Nakagawa Haruto?"

Doug shook his head. "No. I have seen him, but have never met him." He paused a second before adding, "I've only once before heard his name."

The leader's eyebrow moved an almost imperceptible amount up, before his expression returned to placid. "Who told you Nakagawa *san*'s name?"

Doug swallowed hard, regretting that he'd mentioned that. "It was Kawakami *san* who told me Nakagawa *san*'s name."

The comrade took a step forward. The young man behind him also took a step forward, staying just behind the leader's shoulder, and his eyes gleamed.

"When did you speak with Kawakami *san*?"

Doug swallowed again, and felt his upper lip start to sweat; he hoped it wasn't obvious in the dim light of a single lamp.

"It was in July."

"What were the circumstances of your conversation, Bainbridge Douglas?"

Doug's heart pounded. "He came to see me. He broke into my office while I was there, and he asked me questions about my trip to Hong Kong in January, why I had gone and whom I had met. He asked about someone named Wang Yaqiao, and about Jin Shixin."

An angry scowl fell across the leader's face, and he got up in Doug's face, his breath sour with stale garlic and soy. "What did you tell him?" His voice carried venom.

"Nothing," Doug said, trying to sound calm. "I mean, I told him that I'd never heard of Wang Yaqiao, which was true at the time. And I said that I didn't know Jin Shixin."

The leader stared at him without a word.

Doug grew increasingly uncomfortable under his unwavering gaze. He found himself saying more without really meaning to. "He seemed to know that I had met with someone in Kowloon, and he was trying to make a connection with Jin Shixin and Wang Yaqiao. I admitted to nothing."

Please God, let him believe me. He didn't pray often, but he found himself praying hard now.

The leader took a step back, and seemed to be appraising Doug again.

He was silent for almost a full minute before an almost imperceptible move of his head caused his young comrade to come forward, grab Doug by the nape of the neck, and position the blunt surface of his knife directly under the outline of Doug's penis through his boxer shorts. He lifted the knife, just enough that Doug could feel the coldness of the metal through the thin fabric, and a shiver ran through his genitals and up his spine.

The leader's eyes were cold and hard. "Why were you on a train to Beihai on Friday, Bainbridge Douglas? Do not lie."

Doug swallowed hard, twice, and finally found his voice. "An acquaintance of mine is a reporter for the Associated Press—Arthur Jones—and he had learned of the killing of Nakano earlier that day. He was on his way down to interview witnesses for the story, and he asked me to come with him, since I speak Cantonese."

The leader stepped forward again, inches from Doug's face. "Tell me why you agreed to go with Mr. Jones."

Doug wasn't one hundred percent sure. It had seemed a good opportunity. But how much could he say about that?

"I don't know," he said after hesitating a second. "It seemed like a chance for a free trip, without having to do anything difficult. He said he'd pay for everything." That was partly true, anyway.

"Why did Miss Kinzler join you?"

This was easier. "For a vacation together." That was a partial truth, anyway; the fact that it was a good cover was a bonus.

"Did you know that Kawakami *san* would be on that train?"

"No, not until I saw him on board, after we'd departed."

"Did you know that Kawakami *san* was going to Beihai?"

"No. It was a surprise to see him."

The leader took a step back again and stared at Doug. After a moment, he nodded, and the young man released Doug's neck, removed his knife from the front of Doug's boxer shorts, and stepped back.

The leader crossed his arms. "I believe what you have said to me, Bainbridge Douglas. And I trust that you know the penalty for betrayal. I have one more question—what did Kawakami *san* say to you about Wang Yaqiao when he broke into your office in July?"

Doug thought for a moment. "He said Wang Yaqiao lives in Wuzhou, but has a house in Kowloon, Hong Kong. He said his gang is based in Wuzhou, but it has many members in Shanghai; and that they wear axes on their belts, just like the man who had killed Kayao *san* a few days before then."

"That is all?" the leader asked.

Doug nodded. "Yes, that is all he said. I didn't know any of it before then."

The leader motioned to his young comrade, and he exited the kitchen window onto the fire escape. The leader followed, but paused at the window to look back.

"Kawakami *san* has disappeared. If you see him, you will inform Wong Mei-Ling immediately. Good night, Bainbridge Douglas."

He slipped out the window and disappeared into the night.

Doug released a long breath, and collapsed into an arm chair.

Thursday, September 10

Doug left a message for Jonesy with Gladys at the Associated Press office the next morning, asking to meet at Doug's office before lunch if possible; or if not, then at the Cathay for lunch. He asked Gladys to mark it "urgent," and she said that she'd give it to him as soon as he checked in.

Jonesy knocked on Doug's office door shortly before eleven.

"What's so urgent?" he asked, cigar clenched in his teeth, a stream of smoke circling behind him.

"Close the door and have a seat," Doug said.

223

"Sounds serious," Jonesy said, and searched in vain for an ash tray, holding his hand under the long ash at the end of his cigar.

"I got a visit last night, from our local communist commander," Doug said, and held out an empty trash can.

Jonesy took the trash can, flicked his ashes into it, and set it on the ground next to the legs of his chair.

"Interesting. What did he want this time?"

"He asked a lot of questions about Beihai, and about Kawakami. They believe Kawakami killed one of their leaders down there."

Jonesy seemed surprised, but barely. "Interesting," was all he said. Doug wondered if he was ever truly surprised by anything.

"He was suspicious of our motives, why we were on the same train as Kawakami, what he was doing, did we speak with him, etc. I was as truthful as I could be without telling him all of our business. It took some convincing, but he believed me when I told him we had no idea Kawakami was going down there."

Jonesy nodded, looking up in thought. "That doesn't sound too bad. What's so urgent?"

"There's more," Doug said, annoyed. "He wanted to know about my earlier interaction with Kawakami, and so I told them about how he seemed to know what I was up to in Hong Kong in January, and how he told me about Wang Yaqiao. At the end, they instructed me to inform them right away, through Wong Mei-ling, if I see Kawakami anywhere."

Jonesy nodded again. "Seems simple enough. Do it. What do you need to run that by me for?"

This irritated Doug all the more. "I'm not running it by you—I asked you here so I could ask you to also let me know right away if you see Kawakami anywhere. He's gone underground for now, which makes sense if he killed that communist cell leader down in Beihai. But he's bound to turn up in Shanghai again sooner or later."

Jonesy chuckled. "You want me to come to you with that information? Wouldn't it be more efficient if I went to Wong Mei-Ling herself?"

Doug kept forgetting that Jonesy had a working relationship with her. "Do what you think is best," he said, terse. "Either way, I'd like to know myself if he's back in town, so I can be prepared for any potential run-in with him."

"Fair enough," Jonesy said, flicking more ash into the trash can. He pushed his chair back as he stood. "Was there anything else?"

Doug stared at the middle-aged reporter, and the enigmatic look on his face. Something about the gleam in his green eyes disturbed Doug; it was as if Jonesy wanted to get into the conversation that Doug was avoiding.

"No, nothing else," Doug said, looking away.

Jonesy chuckled, that annoying knowing chuckle that said he knew exactly what was going on in Doug's head. He stuck his cigar back in his mouth, put his pen and notepad back in his jacket, and grabbed the doorknob.

"A pleasure as always, Douglas." He put his hat on as he exited.

Doug sat on his desk, pondering the unspoken conversation that part of him wanted to have, and the other part desperately avoided. His face flushed with anger, and he banged his fist against the side of the desk.

Friday, September 11

Doug tried to slip out of the building unnoticed that afternoon. It wasn't yet four o'clock, and he'd thought he would get through undetected, but Kenny's office door was open. It was only about ten feet from the stairs on the second floor, and his chair faced the door; as he sat with his feet propped up on his desk between stacks of paperwork, reading over another stack of papers in h s hand, he glanced up and spied Doug going down the stairs.

225

He waved enthusiastically, and the characteristic big grin suddenly didn't seem just warm and friendly, like it used to.

Damn you, Jonesy! If he'd never said anything, Doug wouldn't have become uncomfortable with his best friend's affection. Things could have stayed normal, and they could have gone on about their lives.

"Hey there, old chum! I haven't seen you all week. Come in, have a seat and let's chat a bit, eh?"

Doug had made it a few steps below the second floor, but he dutifully went back up and down the hall to Kenny's door.

Kenny stood, and clapped Doug on the back as he entered the cluttered attorney's office. "That chair there is clear, have a seat; take a load off, as they say."

Doug took the indicated chair. "I've been really busy this week with work, sorry I haven't been able to stop by."

"And you were gone all weekend," Kenny said. "Abby and I wanted to ask you and Lucy to dinner on Saturday, but Lucy's landlady said she hadn't seen her since Thursday night. We went to your building to look for you two, and your neighbor Mr. Ford said that you and Lucy had gone south for a long weekend. You hadn't mentioned it, so we were a bit taken aback. Everything alright?"

"Yes, fine," Doug said. "We just needed a little time away, and it was a last-minute decision."

"That sounds like fun. Where did you go?"

"A little place called Beihai, down on the south coast," Doug said, uncomfortable. He found it hard to meet Kenny's eyes. "We didn't even know where we were going until the night we left. It was really last minute."

"Abbie and I used to go on little adventures together like that, back when we were at university. Some of the happiest moments of my life, actually." Kenny looked wistful, reveling in the remembered joy. "Wish we could still do that. Real life calls, though, eh? It's nice that you have the freedom to decide to do it. I envy you two."

226

Doug shrugged, still not meeting Kenny's eyes for more than a second or two. "Well, it was probably our last opportunity for a while, since school will be resuming soon, and Lucy will be back to work."

"Yes, Abbie is looking forward to the new semester. It will be her last for a long time, so I think she's going to savor the experiences this time."

Doug thought about what Lucy had said, the night they fought about women having to leave work when they had babies, and the mixed emotions that caused.

"Is Abbie sad about leaving teaching?"

Kenny shrugged. "A little, I think—but she's happy about the baby. We both are, but I think it's different for women. The maternal instincts kick in, and everything else is subsumed by them. It's ingrained in them, you know, by nature. She's thrilled, already planning the nursery, window shopping baby clothes and baby bumpers—and there's still five-and-a-half months to go."

"Congratulations again," Doug said, trying to muster enthusiasm and falling short.

Kenny gave him a concerned look. "Doug, what's wrong?"

"Nothing," he said, too quickly. A doubtful look crossed Kenny's eyes, and Doug looked away in a hurry.

"Something's bothering you, old chum," Kenny said, sounding worried. "Is there something I can help with?"

"No, honestly." Doug looked down at his hands. He wanted nothing more than to get out of this room as soon as he could. His stomach seemed to be tying itself in knots from anxiety.

"Well, even if I can't help, I can listen." Kenny pulled his chair forward. "Tell me what's bothering you."

He reached out and touched Doug's knee, and Doug flinched at the intimate contact.

Kenny noticed. His eyes grew guarded, and his cheeks flushed bright red in embarrassment. He sat back, posture stiff.

"I don't mean to pry," he said, in a tone that was both distant and slightly sad. "I just thought it might help to talk it out with a sympathetic ear, that's all. It's something friends do."

Doug nodded, feeling bad for his reaction. He hadn't been able to help it, though; it had been automatic, a reflex, not intentional or thought out. He glanced at Kenny's face, saw the hint of heart-break in his eyes, and looked away in a hurry.

"I'm sorry, I'm not trying to be evasive," he mumbled. "I'm just not big about talking things through."

"I understand," Kenny said, but his tone indicated that he didn't. Doug didn't know how he could explain it in a way that wouldn't offend his friend.

His friend. Kenny *was* his friend. His best friend. Kenny had been there for more than a year, always available, always ready to offer a hand or a sympathetic ear, as he said. And it had been a long time since Doug had had a good friend.

Too long. He latched onto Kenny's friendship last summer out of a deep and gnawing need for it, and this realization made him fidget in his seat. He'd been lonely in Washington, lonelier than he would care to admit, and so when Kenny showered his admiration and affection his way, he'd relished it more than he would have expected.

Had he known all along? Had he willfully ignored it, suppressed all thought of it, in order to preserve a friendship that he so badly needed?

So then, what did that mean now? He didn't know the answer to that, and wondering made his head hurt.

"I was on my way out," he said, motioning toward the door. "I have somewhere to be soon."

"Right, I won't keep you," Kenny said, standing up and letting Doug pass.

He extended his hand, and Doug looked up at his eyes for the first time in a while. There was sadness in them, for certain, but there was also a resolute hopefulness that made Doug's heart break even more. His hand stayed out, steady, waiting.

Doug took it and gave him a handshake.

Kenny nodded and looked away, but not before Doug saw a hint of tears forming at the corners of his friend's eyes. Kenny cleared his throat.

"If you're around in about an hour, maybe meet me for a drink at the pub?" Kenny asked.

Doug considered it for a second. "If I can get back this direction in time, I will. I can't guarantee it, though." He glanced sideways at Kenny, who nodded, resigned.

"See you soon, then, Dougie."

The familiarity struck him like a stack of books. Kenny had called him that countless times, and until now it had seemed natural, and Doug hadn't given it a second thought.

Doug walked down the stairs with a giant lump descending into his stomach. He cursed himself.

What the hell was wrong with him?

Hutson

18

He stopped by Lucy's apartment on his way home. Her door stood open, probably for air flow as she worked around the apartment. She had an album spinning on her new record player, and she was dancing around as she cleaned.

One of the new swing albums. He looked at the cover sitting on her kitchen table. The Benny Goodman Orchestra. He'd heard of them. One of the hot new hit acts in the States.

The tune coming through the speaker sounded familiar, and he wondered if they'd heard it at the Paramount one night when they went dancing. He was usually concentrating too hard on his feet, trying not to miss a step, to pay much attention to the music itself beyond the general feel of the beat. As he stood in her doorway listening, though, he realized he really liked the sound, beyond the easy-to-dance-to beat.

A moment later she noticed him leaning against the door frame, and a startled "Oh!" escaped her, and she touched her chest and laughed. "Good grief, Doug! You startled me. Don't sneak up on a woman like that, you about gave me a heart attack."

He laughed, too, and stepped forward to give her a kiss on the mouth. "Looks like fun." He took her hands and danced with her. She grinned as he tried a few of the moves, but kept kicking the living room chairs in the small space. He finally gave up, and they both laughed at their awkwardness.

"What brings you by so early?" she asked, turning the music off and walking into the kitchenette. "Want some tea? I can make some."

"That would be swell, thanks." He took a seat in the arm chair as she filled the tea pot with water and plugged it in.

She sauntered over and took a seat beside him on the arm of the chair, leaning her side against his shoulder and putting an arm around him.

"I'm glad to see you. I assumed you'd meet Kenny for drinks after work, and didn't expect to see you until later. Is he busy tonight? Other plans?"

Doug shrugged. "I don't think so. I just wanted to leave early, and come see you, spend a little extra time with you."

He slid his arm around her waist, and pulled her tighter against him. He tilted his head up and reached for her lips with his mouth. She obligingly came down to meet him, and they kissed for several minutes. When she pulled away after a long time, her face was flushed, and she fanned herself with her hand and laughed.

"Whew! You got me a little worked up, Douglas Bainbridge!" she said. "What brought that on?"

He shrugged again. "I don't know, I just missed you, I guess."

"You just saw me a couple of days ago," she said, standing as the tea pot began to whistle. He watched her backside sway as she walked into the kitchenette. She unplugged the tea pot, and took a pair of cups and saucers from the cabinet. She poured them each a cup, brought them back, and his eyes roamed up her entire form as she approached.

"My face is up here," she said with a rueful half-smile as she handed him a cup and saucer. "I know what you have on your mind."

He patted the arm of the chair, and she sat back down, but didn't lean against him this time, instead sitting up as she sipped her steaming tea. He put his hand on the small of her back and gently rubbed it.

"Is that so wrong?" he asked.

"Depends on whom you ask."

"Ha! That's true," he said, laughing. "But what do you think?"

She batted her eyelashes over the top of her tea cup, and looked down coquettishly. "Why Mr. Bainbridge, I never!" she said in a vamped southern belle drawl.

He laughed out loud, and leaned his head against her side. "I just adore you," he said through his laughter.

"And I you," she said, setting her cup and saucer on the nearby stand. Then she folded her hands in her lap and looked at him seriously. "Now tell me what's going on with you and Kenny."

He felt himself stiffen, and tried to force himself to relax his shoulders. She could always read him like a book, and he hated that he gave her such easy clues.

"Nothing's wrong," he said, but when he glanced up at her eyes, she was looking back at him like a stern teacher staring down a lying pupil. "I mean it."

"Hmmm," she said, and crossed her arms. "Do you really think I don't know you, Doug? I've lived here for three months, and I know you and Kenny get together for drinks after work every Friday night, without fail. You get together for drinks at least two or three times a week—but this week, you haven't even mentioned his name. If that doesn't mean something's wrong, then I've stepped into the looking glass."

He looked away, aware that his mere avoidance was confirming what she'd said. *Damn it!* "It's just something Jonesy said in Beihai," he muttered.

"Speak up," Lucy commanded, every bit the stern teacher at that moment.

"It's something Jonesy said to me when we were in Beihai last weekend," Doug repeated, at full volume.

She arched an eyebrow. "Tell me what it was. I want everything, don't leave anything out just because you think it's embarrassing."

How in the hell did she guess that? He wondered sometimes if she could read his mind instead of just his face.

"Jonesy claimed that Kenny is 'in love' with me," Doug said, cross. "I don't know where he got that idea. He gets all of these strange notions about men sometimes. It's annoying. I think he does it on purpose to aggravate people."

Lucy's expression was strange, enigmatic, and Doug wondered what was going on behind her bright blue eyes.

"What?" he asked.

"Jonesy shouldn't have said that," she said, quietly. Perhaps even a little sadly. "He should have known better."

"Exactly! I tried not to think too much about it, but I couldn't get it out of my head. And it's just made things awkward with Kenny. Every time he touched me—" he stopped, having not intended to say that.

She shook her head. "I knew it would ruin everything if you ever found out," she said, still quiet.

He sat bolt straight and glared at her. "You knew?"

She waved a hand in the air. "Of course I knew. I may not be the jealous type, but any woman can tell when someone is in love with her man. It's almost a sixth sense." She hesitated before adding, "And besides, Abbie told me there was interest last summer, before I returned to Vassar."

Doug's mouth hung open, incredulous. It took him several seconds before he could summon words. "You knew for more than a year? And you never told me?"

She crossed her arms, stern. "I knew you'd react just like this. I told Abbie you wouldn't be understanding, let alone open."

That confused him. "What do you mean?"

She shook her head and stood up. "You really can be obtuse sometimes, Doug."

He felt the irritation rise through him, and his ears burned hot. He was getting tired of hearing people call him that word.

"I am *not* obtuse, and I really wish people would stop saying that to me."

"It's an appropriate word for someone who misses what's right in front of him, because he doesn't want to see it."

He snapped. "What exactly am I missing? What's so damned obvious that I don't want to see?"

"Apparently, Jonesy already told you," Lucy said, glaring at him. "And he shouldn't have. I'll have to give him a piece of my mind, the next time I see Mr. Arthur Jones."

She crossed the room, her back to him, and stood by the window for a moment, looking out.

"So that's it? *That's* what I'm so obtuse about?"

She turned around, shaking her head. "You want the whole story, Doug?"

He scowled. "Of course."

"Are you sure?"

He felt his irritation rising again, and had to force himself not to snap at her. "Tell me what you've got to say."

"Alright, fine. What I meant before was this: Abbie told me last summer that she and Kenny are both bisexuals, and they admitted it to each other years ago, back in college when they were dating. It only made their relationship stronger, she said."

Doug felt his stomach turning sour, and he looked away from her and stared at the living room floor.

Lucy continued, in spite of his avoidance. "She told me they never stray, but that from time to time they...shall we say, 'enjoy the company' of other couples—Kenny pairs off with the husband or boyfriend, and Abbie pairs off with the wife or girlfriend. She confided that they discussed propositioning us, but Kenny was hesitant about it— even more than usual."

Doug felt cold inside. He didn't know how to feel, so he felt nothing.

"What did you tell her?" he asked, his voice flat, without emotion.

"I told her I was flattered," Lucy said. After a few seconds, she added in firm tone, "And I told her that I wouldn't categorically say no to such an idea, but that you would never be open to it. And I told her that you'd react pretty much as you are right now. We agreed to keep the conversation strictly between ourselves—which I have now for more than a year."

He sat still, staring at the floor, his eyes not wavering from a particular knot in one of the wood boards.

She sat on the arm of the chair beside him, and he felt her hand on his back. She rubbed in a circular pattern, slowly, soothing. "It doesn't take a genius to figure out that the reason Kenny was more hesitant than usual is because he really cares about you, Doug, and didn't want to ruin your friendship."

He didn't move. He didn't even look at her.

"I'm sorry, Doug. I hated keeping a secret from you, and there were times that it ate me up inside that I was hiding something from you. But I knew it was for the best, and I would have carried this to the grave if it meant you would keep your best friend. I couldn't take that away from you, and one secret between us was a price worth paying for that."

He felt numb, and he sat in silence, staring at the knot in the floor board. But after a minute, in a tiny place deep in his gut, the numbness began a slow but steady retreat, and an aching pain radiated from that microscopic spot.

He stood, and turned to face the door, glancing at her from the side of his eyes. "I've got to go. I need some air. I've just—I've got to go."

"Alright," she said, quiet. "I'll be here if you need me."

He stormed out the door and down the stairs, thrusting his hat on his head as he shoved the building door open and slammed it shut behind him.

19

Saturday, September 12

Doug lay in bed long after waking up the next morning, staring at the ceiling. Stewing.

He felt as if his world had been turned upside down. Kenny and Abbie were not what they seemed. Were others? Pete and Julia, George and Betty—he felt his chest constrict.

Don't be ridiculous. Guilt by association would implicate him as well, and that was all this was; so he dismissed those thoughts.

Jonesy said he interacted with men like that every day. He couldn't stop thinking that. He couldn't help but think about Fred and Stuart, and how they picked up Chinese girls together. And took them back to their one-bedroom apartment.

He bolted from bed, shaking his head hard in a vain attempt to banish the unwanted images.

Damn you, Jonesy!

He threw on some boxer shorts, grabbed a towel, and stormed off to the bathroom to shave and clean up.

He unlocked his office an hour later. The building was empty, thankfully, but he locked the door behind him nonetheless.

The office equipment might be a ruse, but the typewriter was functional. He fed a piece of paper into the machine and began pecking at the keys.

CONFIDENTIAL

Commander Shock,

As you are no doubt aware, I was tasked by Commander Hilliard to learn what I could about the involvement of the Chinese Communist Party in the assassination of Japanese nationals in China. To that end, I recently journeyed to Beihai (a.k.a. "Pei-hai") on the 4th of this month, to see what could be learned about the fatal attack on Junzo Nakano the previous day.

Mr. Nakano was a Japanese resident of Shanghai. While in Beihai he appeared to be a tourist on vacation, but he came alone and left his wife behind in Shanghai.

While on the journey to Beihai, I encountered Takahiro Kawakami on the train. As I am sure Commander Hilliard briefed you, we believe Mr. Kawakami to be an agent of one of the Japanese secret services. After arrival in Beihai, I attempted to follow Mr. Kawakami at an appropriate distance to determine his intentions, but he performed an evasive maneuver, and I lost the trail.

My conclusion is that Mr. Nakano was a Japanese agent, dispatched to Beihai on a clandestine mission of unknown purpose. It is unclear if his attacker was a communist agent, or a member of a criminal element in southern China known as the "Axe Gang." Motive is unknown.

Respectfully submitted,

Lt. Commander Douglas P. Bainbridge.

He folded the report and slipped it inside a blank envelope. He hid the envelope in his jacket pocket. Even though it was Saturday and the building was dark, he took care to make sure no one was around when he exited his office and went down the stairs.

After what he wrote about Kawakami, the last thing he wanted was to encounter the man in a dark hall or stairway.

It was barely half a mile to the U.S. Consulate, but he glanced around constantly to make sure no one was watching or following. Perhaps it was all of the recent talk about spies and spying, but he felt a touch cloak-and-dagger as he walked through downtown Shanghai carrying a confidential missive in his pocket.

The reality was far less clandestine, of course, and he walked openly through the front door of the consulate ten minutes later.

He presented his passport to the middle-aged black man who sat guard inside the door.

"I'm Lt. Commander Bainbridge, United States Navy," he said. "I need to have a confidential message sent to the embassy in Nanking. Can you direct me to the consular official who sends the diplomatic pouch?"

"That would be Mr. Callaghan, but he ain't here today. He'll be in on Monday."

"Would it be possible for me to leave the message in a secure place? Maybe inside his office?"

The guard looked at him suspiciously. "You got your military ID card on ya?"

Doug shook his head. "No, and the reason I don't is classified. I'm sure you understand."

The guard's suspicious look deepened. "Ya got somebody can vouch for ya, sir?"

Doug nodded, and reluctantly gave the name. "Commander Shock at the embassy can vouch for me, if Mr. Callaghan requires that. The message is for him, and it is important that it reach him."

"You'll hafta speak with Mr. Harris about that," the guard said, and pointed down a corridor. "Second door on your left."

Doug found Robert Harris, the consular officer in charge, to be eager to help, once Doug explained the situation was classified. He took Doug's sealed envelope and promised to have Mr. Callaghan include it in the week's diplomatic pouch to the embassy. He stamped it "CONFIDENTIAL" in Doug's presence and set it in his out-box.

Doug left the consulate a few minutes later, tipping his hat to the guard as he walked out the door. He was in a good mood as he walked toward the streetcar stop, but as he waited for the streetcar to come he noticed a man standing in a nearby doorway reading a newspaper, who kept glancing over the paper at him.

Doug watched out of the side of his eye for several minutes, and he was rewarded when his observer was forced to move by a well-dressed Chinese couple emerging from the door he was standing in front of.

The newspaper came down to reveal the face of Kawakami's assistant, Nakagawa.

Doug had a moment of panic, wondering if the Japanese agent had been following him from the consulate, or if he'd followed him there earlier.

He took a breath. There was nothing inherently suspicious about an American visiting his country's consulate. He had done nothing to suggest otherwise, so Nakagawa had nothing to report on him.

But this was confirmation that they were watching him.

Thursday, September 17

"Telegram for Douglas Bainbridge."

"I'm Mr. Bainbridge." Doug signed the American Express delivery, and gave the Chinese delivery boy a dime.

The message was from Nanjing. He opened the envelope after closing his door.

WISH TO CANCEL ORDER OF RED SILK STOP

WILL DISCUSS FUTURE ORDERS FROM YOUR FIRM
NOVEMBER STOP
    SINCERELY,

    T.S.

Doug knew exactly what the message meant. No more investigation of communist involvement.

Along with an overwhelming sense of relief, he was surprised to also feel a touch of disappointment. It had felt useful. He couldn't deny a slight sting that the higher-ups didn't value the intelligence he'd gathered, enough to want more.

But this would make his life simpler.

Saturday, September 19

Doug stepped out of a Chinese grocery on West Nanking Road late in the afternoon, carrying a paper sack full of Chinese vegetables. He and Lucy were going to try a traditional Shanghai shrimp and vegetable stir-fry this evening instead of going out.

He'd suggested they eat in for the last two weeks, primarily to avoid accidentally running into their friends somewhere and having to explain why he had been a hermit recently. It was a conversation he didn't want to have, and besides, he appreciated the extra one-on-one time with Lucy.

As he waited for the Honan Road street car, he saw Jonesy approaching.

"That's a stroke of luck, running into you here," Jonesy said, removing his hat long enough to wipe his brow with his handkerchief. "I was just on my way to see you."

Doug arched an eyebrow. "To see me? Or Wong Mei-ling."

"You—although I wouldn't argue with a chance to ask Miss Wong a question or two right now."

"I have plans this evening, so I'm not really free to be one of your sources."

Jonesy grunted and shook his head. "There was an assassination in Hankou today, about mid-way up the Yantgze valley. A Japanese cop. They have a Japanese concession in Hankou, and the reports are a Chinese gunman or gunmen shot the cop at point-blank range while he was patrolling the concession."

He paused to let the news sink in.

Doug's nerves tingled, intrigued. It was barely two weeks since the attack on Nakano in Beihai. Things were escalating.

"Was the gunman wearing an axe?"

"Don't know. I'm heading out there to see what I can learn. The train leaves in an hour, and gets there before midnight. I was coming to see you so I could ask if you wanted to come along. We made a pretty good team in Pei-hai, and I thought we might repeat that in Hankou."

Doug shook his head. "Can't, sorry. I have plans this weekend." He was loath to admit that part of him wished he could go. But orders were orders.

"Break 'em. We've got a golden opportunity here. For both of us."

Doug shook his head harder. "I can't. I'm sorry."

Jonesy's eyes narrowed, and he stared at Doug for several seconds.

"Aren't you even a little curious what's happening? Or have you got inside information that I don't?" He added that last in a lower voice, gravely and grumbling.

"No, nothing like that, I assure you," Doug said.

Jonesy's expression turned bitter. He eyed the paper bag in Doug's arm. "Making dinner with your girlfriend? Or your boyfriend?"

"Shut up, Jonesy." Doug had to stop himself from dropping the groceries on the ground and slugging the smug reporter.

"Have it your way," Jonesy huffed, removing his hat to wipe his brow again. Then he shoved it back on his head and stormed off.

20

Wednesday, September 23, 1936

The calendar might say it was fall now, but it still felt like summer. The temperature that day had risen above eighty degrees Fahrenheit, and so Doug spent the early evening reclined on his bed in his underwear, fans blowing on him.

Fortunately, sunset came earlier now, so as dusk settled and the temperature cooled, he got dressed and ventured out for dinner.

There was a traditional Shanghainese restaurant he liked a couple of blocks away on Kiangse Road, about midway between his place and Lucy's, and she had said that she'd meet him there tonight at seven-thirty.

He arrived a little early, not surprised to see the place packed; it was *dang hun* tonight, one of four nights each month when locals of modest means ate meat or fish with dinner. On the second, eighth, sixteenth, and twenty-third of each month, the markets of Shanghai all sold out of meat and fish early in the day, so families of less modest means went out to eat.

A deep blue twilight had settled over the city when Lucy arrived promptly at seven-thirty, looking gorgeous in a light blue dress, her blonde hair pulled back in a bun, revealing pearl earrings that matched the string of pearls around her neck.

He kissed her cheek, and held her seat as she sat.

After they'd exchanged pleasantries about their respective days, Lucy asked if he'd heard anything from Jonesy.

Doug shook his head. "Not a word. I left a message for him at the AP office yesterday, so either he hasn't checked in with them, or he's still mad at me for not going."

"Which do you think it is?"

He made a face. "Given that Hankou is not much more than three hundred miles from here, I'm sure he's come back already. It's less than a day by train, for heaven's sake."

"You don't suppose he got into any trouble there?" Lucy asked, looking a little concerned.

Doug had considered that. Given Jonesy's penchant for probing deep for a story, he might have angered the wrong people, asking questions about an assassination. *Another* assassination. Still, Doug had dismissed the thought, falling back on the likelihood that Jonesy was still angry at his refusal to join him.

"I don't think so," he told Lucy, putting his hand on top of hers on the table. "He's a pretty resourceful fellow, you know."

"Even resourceful people get themselves into trouble sometimes. Maybe we should check on him?"

"It's only been a few days," Doug said, but even as he said it he knew that wouldn't placate her.

"Long enough for a 'nosy reporter' to get himself in trouble."

He nodded, resigned. "Alright, after dinner we can call his apartment, and see if he's in."

They finished eating dinner and were discussing the possibility of ordering dessert, when a series of gunshots echoed through the restaurant's open windows. There were five shots fired, and Doug determined from the sound that they were a few blocks away.

Japantown, he thought, and glanced at his wrist watch. Eight-twenty.

Murmurs of concern rippled through the restaurant, and waiters stood frozen in place for a few seconds. Outside on the street, shouts rose all around.

"Better skip dessert tonight," Doug said to Lucy, who looked startled. "Let me get you home." He raised his hand to call for the waiter.

"Can you understand what they're saying out there?" she asked, nodding toward the front windows, and the street beyond where crowds had gathered.

He shook his head. "Too many people talking all at once. I can't pick out much—but it sounds like a lot of speculation." He requested the check from the waiter in Shanghainese.

They walked out the door ten minutes later, and Doug took Lucy's elbow and steered her south, toward Soochow Creek and her apartment building.

Then a squad of Japanese marines ran up the street, bayonets fixed to the front of their rifles.

"What's going on?" Lucy asked, looking at Doug with wide eyes.

"Japanese marines," he muttered out of the side of his mouth, and steered them to the wall to give the squad ample room to pass.

"But this isn't Japantown," she protested.

"They're clearing the street," he said as the squad approached, the sergeant shouting to the crowds while the marines under his command fanned out, using the threat of their bayonet points to move people along.

Doug extended his arm in front of Lucy's chest, stood close to her and pressed both of their backs against the wall. They stayed there for several minutes, watching the Japanese marines file past, until one pointed his bayonet-tipped rifle at them and motioned with it for them to move along.

"C'mon, let's move." He clasped her hand as they rushed down the sidewalk toward the creek.

A larger squad of Japanese marines was moving west down Soochow Road North as they reached the corner; rushing toward Honan Road. Doug and Lucy waited at the corner for the last of them to pass, before turning right and hurrying the last several yards to her building's front door.

Lucy exhaled hard as she closed the apartment door behind them, and slumped back against the frame. "I haven't been this glad to be home in ages," she said, breathless.

Doug went to the window, and parted the curtains to look out. A pair of police constables on the corner engaged in an animated conversation with four Japanese marines, voices raised, and Doug wondered if they even understood each other.

"I'm sorry about all this," he said as he turned around.

"What?"

"I'm sorry to have gotten you into all of this. By moving here, I mean. The crime since you came, I didn't anticipate that."

She laughed. "Oh Doug, I grew up in Chicago, for goodness sake. There were mafia gang shootings more often than this when I was growing up. You go about your life, and you get through it."

That eased his mind more than he anticipated. He hadn't realized how much that thought had been weighing on him.

"Of course, we never had to worry about foreign marines occupying our neighborhood," Lucy added.

He laughed in spite of himself, and shook his head. "No, I'd bet not."

"I think you'd better stay here for a while," she said, and moved toward the kitchenette. "I'll put on some tea."

"Good idea," he agreed.

In truth, though, he was conflicted—he wanted to stay and make sure Lucy was protected, but on the other hand this was a perfect opportunity for him to go out and observe Japanese maneuvers, and report them to the Naval Attaché.

Perhaps he could do both, he reasoned. He could stay with Lucy until the confusion and panic subsided, and then he could leave on the pretext of going home for bed; if he "happened" to take the long way home and watch the Japanese marines along the way, then so be it.

Lucy came back with two steaming cups of tea, and handed one to him by the saucer. He blew on it and took a sniff; it was the jasmine tea that she favored.

"This is when I wish I had a radio," she said, taking a seat and blowing across the top of her tea cup.

Doug nodded. "I'd like to know what's going on."

"Once I've saved enough, I'll buy one," she said, taking a sip of her tea. "I'm surprised you don't have a radio, actually. Why is that?"

He shrugged. "Just haven't gotten around to getting one, I suppose." He didn't want to tell her that it had seemed a waste to spend that much money on something he could only keep for two years.

"I know there's an English language radio station here," she said.

He nodded. "There is. Most of our friends listen in after dinner. I'm sure they've already broken into their regular program to report the news."

"So our friends know we're stuck at home, then," she mused, and took a sip of her tea. "I have to say, it feels a little like being under siege."

"Oh? You've been under siege?" Doug teased, putting his arms around her waist. "Some rival dormitory surround yours at Vassar?"

She swatted at his hand, but smiled. "Stop being an ass. I've read in books about castles under siege. I image this is what it feels like."

"I suppose it might."

Her expression grew serious. "Do you think the Japanese are trying to provoke a war?"

"I don't know. But our navy has believed for years that our next war would take place in this part of the world, to counter Japanese expansionism. This could be how it starts."

"What would that mean for you?" she asked, her big blue eyes steady, but betraying more than a little worry. He imagined them staying strong with effort.

"I don't know," he admitted. "I don't see the United States going to war just to defend China from Japanese aggression, unless American interests here were threatened. I guess it depends on how far the Japanese are willing to push things. If worse came to worst, I might be summoned to the Asiatic Fleet in Manila, or I might have to go back to Washington. Hard to say."

She slid down into his lap and lay her head against his shoulder. "Just when the future looked so promising for us."

He kissed her forehead and put his arm around her shoulders, squeezing her to him. "I'm sure there's nothing to worry about," he whispered, and wished he believed that himself.

**

A little while later, the sounds of men's shouts in Japanese came from the street, and Doug crept toward the window and peeked out.

"What is it?" she asked from the kitchenette, where she was washing their tea cups.

"A handful of Japanese marines," he said. He watched them moving up the street in pairs and trios, slowly and deliberately, looking around. "They seem to be on patrol. Or else they're searching for someone."

A few minutes later, they heard the sound of a fist banging on a door downstairs, followed by muffled shouting coming up through the floors. This was followed in another few minutes by more banging on another door, and more muffled shouting.

Lucy's eyes widened. "What on Earth? They're not going to search apartment by apartment, are they?" She sounded both incredulous and indignant.

"I don't know. Possibly," Doug said, lips tight. In addition to being a violation of due process, it was hardly the most effective method for tracking down an assassin.

Several minutes later, heavy footsteps marched up the stairs, and then loud bangs on the door echoed through Lucy's living room. A man shouted something in Japanese.

Doug held up his hand toward Lucy, telling her to remain where she stood. He strode to the door and threw it open, standing in the opening with straight back and squared shoulders. "Can I help you?"

A Japanese marine shoved him out of the way and marched past, followed by a companion. Without so much as a second glance at either of them, they looked over the room, then one of them stomped to the kitchen window and looked out onto the fire escape.

Then they marched down the short hall to her bedroom.

Doug crept over to Lucy's side, and took her hand. He felt helpless, and the imposed impotence in front of his girlfriend infuriated him.

They heard her closet door thrown open, and then the sounds of furniture scraping across the floor as it was moved.

"Just let them do it," he muttered to Lucy. "Don't do anything to provoke them, and they'll leave soon." He hated saying the words, somehow making the whole experience seem more real.

The two marines came back to the living room a few minutes later, and moved the couch from its place along the wall to look behind it. Satisfied, they returned to the door.

The first one who had entered, whom Doug now noticed was a corporal, stood in front of Doug and stared at him. "You Engrish?"

"Americans," Doug said.

"Speak Japanese?"

"No." Doug hesitated, then asked the corporal in Mandarin if he spoke any Chinese.

The marine's dark eyes narrowed. Then he brushed past them, deliberately knocking Doug's shoulder on the way out, and went down the hall to the stairs and went up to the fourth floor.

"Charming fellows," Lucy muttered, stepping over to close the door. Then she sighed as she looked at Doug. "That wasn't too horrible, I suppose."

"Let's see how much damage they did in your bedroom closet," Doug advised, and followed her down the short hall.

"Could've been worse," she said as they stood in the doorway, surveying the hanging clothes strewn all over her bedroom. Her dresser and nightstand had been moved from the wall, but otherwise were undisturbed.

Her closet was a shambles.

Every hanger had been pulled out and thrown haphazardly, along with hat boxes and shoes. Doug wondered if the marines thought a midget were hiding there, the way they had emptied it.

"I'll help you put it all back," he said, putting a hand on the middle of her back and rubbing slow circles between her shoulder blades.

"How far away from Japantown do you think they're searching?" she asked, taking an armful of dresses from the floor and spreading them out on top of the bed. She checked the hangers, and put them back inside the shoulders when she found one askew.

Doug thought of the squad of Japanese marines he'd seen earlier, rushing west toward Honan Road. That was more than a half-mile from Wusong Road and the edge of Japantown; how much farther would they go in search of an assassin?

He didn't voice his thoughts aloud, and only shrugged as he restacked her hat boxes on her closet shelf.

"I mean, really—we're several blocks from there, and this isn't a bad neighborhood. How could they possibly think they'd find their suspect here?"

"I don't think they're concerned about the quality of the neighborhood," Doug said. *Only how far the killer could run.* These marines were moving fast, and fanning out from the scene of the crime.

He thought of Wong Mei-ling and her comrades, and wondered if she knew who the killer was. Would she perhaps even hide him?

He pictured Japanese marines finding a young Chinese man in drab gray hiding behind a shabby couch while Wong Mei-ling screamed at them. In his imagination, a Japanese sergeant back-handed her across the face, and drug her by the hair to the hall, while she kicked and screamed.

He could check on her, if he knew where she lived. He only knew that she walked to work from somewhere nearby.

"Penny for your thoughts," Lucy said, looking at him with an amused half-smile.

"Sorry," he muttered, cheeks flushing, and put the last hat box back on a shelf.

"You had an awfully grim look on your face. And a very far-away look in your eyes."

It embarrassed him that his girlfriend had caught him thinking about another woman, specifically one in whom he might have once been interested. *As if that has anything to do with your current concern about her*, he reminded himself. It wasn't as if he had any feelings for Wong Mei-ling beyond friendly concern.

Still, his mind endeavored to separate her from Lucy.

"I should probably get back home soon," he said as they finished working. "For all I know, they've come searching my building, too."

"It wouldn't surprise me. Go, I'll be fine. Thank you for staying with me." She kissed him on the cheek. "I hope your apartment is fine. Come see me tomorrow, OK?"

"I will," he said, putting his hat on his head, then giving her a quick kiss on the lips at the door.

**

251

Instead of taking Kiangse Road back to his neighborhood—the most direct route—he detoured west, past the Shanghai Post Office, before turning north a block shy of Honan Road.

Ahead, Japanese marines were entering buildings. He moved slowly, and kept to the shadows along the front of the buildings, avoiding passing under the periodic street lamps.

The less they observed him observing them, the better.

Not until he got close to where a lone Japanese marine stood guard in front of a building that was being searched, across the street from a compatriot guarding another building being searched, did Doug normalize his gait and walk directly down the center of the sidewalk.

The guard closest to him lowered his rifle and shouted something in Japanese.

Doug stopped and faced him.

"I'm on my way home," he said in English, pointing up the street toward his neighborhood. "I live up that way a few blocks."

The guard shouted something over his shoulder, through the open door of the building. A moment later, a corporal stepped out. "Engrish?" he asked.

Doug assumed he was asking more about language than nationality, so he just said, "Yes."

"Cur-few," the corporal said, slowly and deliberately, as if he had practiced saying the word several times.

Doug pointed again. "I'm going home now. I live just up there. Three blocks."

The corporal didn't seem to understand, so Doug repeated it in Shanghainese, then again in Mandarin.

That time, he saw a spark of recognition. "Go!" the corporal ordered, pointing up the street. "Go now. Curfew."

Doug touched the rim of his hat and nodded, hurrying up the street. He went straight home, knowing better than to get caught on the street a second time. His luck might not hold out.

He rounded the corner onto his street. Japanese marines stood guard in front of his building and the one across from it. *Here we go again*, he thought with a groan.

The marine across the street saw him first, when he was still twenty yards from his building's door, and shouted at the marine on Doug's side of the street. The latter turned and aimed his rifle at Doug, shouting a blistering stream of Japanese commands.

Doug stopped and raised his hands in the air. "Do you speak English?" he asked.

"I speak English," another voice said behind him, in good pronunciation, but with a Japanese accent.

A figure in the blue uniform of the Shanghai Municipal Police came around his side and stood in front of him. He said something in Japanese to the marines, who both lowered their guns and returned to sentry duty.

"A curfew has been imposed in the Hongkou district, sir," the Japanese police officer said.

"I know, a couple of marines informed me a few minutes ago, as I was on my way home. I live in that building right there," Doug said, pointing at the door.

"Then you should get inside immediately," the police officer said, and turned aside and held his arm out toward the nearby door.

"Thank you," Doug said, touching the rim on his hat and nodding deeply. "Where are Constable Dickinson and Constable Patel this evening? They usually patrol this neighborhood."

"They are not on duty tonight," the Japanese officer said. "I will patrol this neighborhood."

"And you are?"

The constable stiffened briefly, but bowed his head in deference. "I am Constable Yamashita, East District Precinct. Good night, sir."

It was a dismissal, and Doug took it with a graceful bow of his head, and hurried inside his building, barely glancing at the marine sentry by the door.

East District—they brought in Japanese police constables from Yangtzepoo. And the normal police patrols had clearly been suspended. He surmised that only Japanese constables were allowed to patrol in Hongkou tonight.

After bounding up the first half-flight of stairs, he thought better and slowed down, listening for sounds of confrontation between Japanese troops and the building's residents. Angry voices came from upstairs, and as he passed the second floor he heard Charlie's voice protesting.

Doug reached the top of the stairs and looked through his neighbors' open door to see two Japanese marines standing between Charlie and Bao. One held Bao by the arm, while the other held Charlie back with a palm on his chest and his gun lowered.

Charlie's face was strained and bright red, his eyes brimming with tears of frustration. Doug saw bruises around Bao's eyes, and blood coming from one of his ears.

"What's the meaning of this?"

Charlie looked startled, then momentarily relieved as he looked at Doug. "Oh! Douglas, thank goodness you're here." Then his expression turned to anger. "These *gentlemen* are searching for someone, and they've been altogether too rough with Bao. I keep telling 'em he hasn't done anything, and they don't bloody listen!"

His working class English accent seemed to have exaggerated into almost a caricature.

Doug fixed the two marines with his most intimidating glare, stretching his torso as tall and imposing as he could and puffing out his chest. "Who is in charge here?"

"Sergeant not here," said the Japanese corporal who had been holding Charlie back.

"Then *where* is he?" Doug demanded, crossing his arms and glaring at the corporal.

The corporal fixed him with a scowl, and glanced at Charlie, then Bao. "You home here?"

He's figured out about Charlie and Bao. And Doug's gut tightened at the implication of the corporal's question.

"I'm their neighbor," he said, and nodded his head toward his apartment. "I live across the hall."

"Go home," the corporal said, and then rattled off something in Japanese to the private who held Li Baosheng's arm.

"For what reason are you mistreating that man?" Doug demanded, ignoring the order to return home. He didn't exactly want a confrontation with armed Japanese marines, but neither did he want to take orders from them.

The marines stared back at him without comprehension.

He repeated the question in Mandarin.

Their eyes showed comprehension. The corporal replied in halting Mandarin, "We search for young Chinese men who attack Japanese tonight. This man no..." his voice trailed off as he searched for the word.

"Alibi?" Doug offered in Mandarin.

The corporal showed no sign of comprehension.

His Mandarin Chinese is barely better than his English, Doug mused. "Excuse?" he tried.

That worked. The corporal nodded, one firm motion. "Yes, this man no excuse tonight."

"I was home all evening, with Charlie," Bao said to Doug in Shanghainese, his voice and his eyes pleading. "I cooked dinner. We had Geng. We were still cleaning the dishes when they came to the door."

Doug looked at Charlie. "They say Bao doesn't have an alibi for this evening," he said in English. "Bao said he was home with you, having dinner."

"Yes, that's right," Charlie said, sounding breathless. "We *told* them that already."

"They probably didn't understand what you were saying," Doug said. *Or didn't want to.* "There seems to be a bit of a language barrier."

He turned back to the marines and addressed them in Mandarin, scowling and crossing his arms for emphasis. "I know these men, and I attest that they are honest and law-abiding citizens. The young Chinese man cooked dinner tonight, as he does every night, and they had just finished dinner before you came. He is not one of the men you are searching for."

A tense, silent moment followed. Everyone stared at the Japanese corporal.

Then he grunted, dropped his hand from Charlie's chest, and nodded toward Doug. "We search your home next," he said in Mandarin.

The other marine let go of Bao's arm and followed after his corporal, but at the last moment turned back and gave Bao a hard shove into the wall.

Bao hit the wall hard, and the air came forcefully out of his lungs as he slid down onto the floor in a seated position. The marine spat out angry, most likely insulting, words in Japanese, and marched out.

Doug had to stop himself from raising his arm to strike the man. Charlie rushed to Bao's side, and Doug gave them a sympathetic look before he turned back to the two Japanese marines who waited at his door, rifles pointed in his general direction.

"Just a moment," he said in Mandarin, fishing his key from his pocket. He wondered what they would have done if he hadn't come home. *Busted down the door, probably.* His timing couldn't have been much better.

Unless he'd come home in time to intervene when they roughed up Bao.

He dismissed the thought and unlocked the door. There was no way he could have known, and little reason to suspect.

As the marines shoved past him and began searching his apartment, using almost identical tactics as the other marines had at Lucy's apartment, he supposed he could have wondered what would happen if those that searched his building figured out Charlie and Bao's relationship. The thought never crossed his mind.

It had never had to.

Charlie and Bao didn't have that privilege. He was sure they thought of such things often.

He wondered about Charlie's gun. The Japanese were searching for a person—or persons—so they weren't opening drawers or kitchen cabinets, and likely didn't find the gun, or its permit. *Thank God for small miracles*. He hated to think what might have happened.

When these two finished looking behind furniture and emptying his closets, they left without a word, only cursory nods. Under normal circumstances, Doug supposed he might feel slighted by their lack of politesse—but given the situation, he counted himself lucky for their mere indifference.

He took a few minutes to put his apartment back together—far easier than when he'd found it ransacked his second week in Shanghai, more than a year ago. Then he went back across the hall and knocked on Charlie and Bao's door.

"It's Doug," he said before they had a chance to answer, to set their minds at ease that it wasn't another hostile invasion.

Charlie opened the door, and gave Doug a weak smile. Then his eyes darted past Doug, checking the hallway before motioning him inside.

"Douglas, thank you so much for your help earlier," he said as he closed the door behind them. "I don't know what more might've happened had you not been here. They might've drug poor Bao out into the street, hauled him away to God only knows where."

Doug blushed and shrugged. "I didn't do all that," he said.

"Oh! But you did. We owe you so much. You are a wonderful neighbor. And a good friend."

A wave of guilt swept through Doug's belly. A really good friend would have anticipated the situation and come sooner, he thought. But he banished that thought almost as soon as he had it. How could he have known, really? He'd never experienced anything like this before, so he couldn't have known. This was a whole new experience.

"How is Bao?" he asked, as much to change the subject as to find out how the young man was recovering.

"Oh, he'll be fine. A bit rattled, as you might expect. But he's resilient, he is. In the bath right now, gettin' himself cleaned up. He should be back shortly." Charlie's cheerful smile seemed forced, and Doug felt a wave of sympathy wash over him. "Can I fix you a drink? Gin and tonic?"

"Yes, thank you," Doug said. He watched Charlie hurry over to the liquor cabinet in the corner, then rush over to the ice box to chip off a couple of pieces into a tumbler. Doug supposed the activity kept Charlie's mind off what had happened.

And off what more might have happened.

Charlie finished mixing the drink, and turned with a smile and handed it to his guest. "There you are, Douglas. I'm afraid we're fresh out of limes, mate."

"That's quite alright," Doug assured him. He raised the glass in his host's direction. "Cheers."

Bao came through the door as Doug took a drink, and his eyes lit up. "Oh, hello, Mr. Bainbridge. The Japanese didn't hurt you?"

"No, they didn't hurt me. They're gone now, we can relax."

Bao nodded, a sad sort of smile on his lips. He shuffled past Doug and went down the hall toward the bedroom. He returned a moment later wearing fresh clothes.

A soft knock at the door caught their attention, and they all looked at each other for one tense second before they realized that if the Japanese had returned, they would bang on the door with fists or rifle butts, not knock politely.

A sheepish smile crossed Charlie's mouth as he hurried to open the door. "Oh, good evening, Mr. Hwang."

Their landlord gave them a polite bow from the doorway, but did not enter the apartment. "The Japanese have left the building," he said in careful English. "Did they do any damage while they searched?"

"Nothing that won't heal in short order," Charlie said with false cheerfulness.

Mr. Hwang seemed not to catch the implication. "The Japanese have declared martial law in all of Hongkou district," he said, voice matter-of-fact but expression grim.

This surprised Doug—though later it would seem obvious in hindsight. He'd known that the Japanese had occupied Hongkou, clearly. But a declaration of martial law was a serious step.

"For how long?" he asked, unable to keep the incredulity entirely from his tone.

Mr. Hwang shook his head. "Until they find the men they are looking for."

"What does it mean for us?" Charlie asked, staying close to Bao.

Close, but not touching him, Doug noticed. *Not in front of Mr. Hwang.*

"There is a curfew, and no one is to go outside until morning," Mr. Hwang said in his slow, careful English diction. "Then tomorrow we go about business as usual, except there will be Japanese troops everywhere. They can stop and search anyone, and they can arrest anyone for anything. We must be extra cautious in everything we do."

"And if they kill someone, the Japanese court will never punish them," Doug said to the room at large.

Charlie looked aghast. Bao didn't react.

"That is true," Mr. Hwang said, very grave. "I pray that your ancestors will watch over you extra closely until the Japanese withdraw." He bowed to them. "Good night."

"Good night, Mr. Hwang," Charlie and Doug said, in unison.

Once the landlord had departed, Charlie turned away. "I think I need a drink meself." He poured himself a gin over ice, took a long pull on the tumbler, and then topped it off again and took another sip.

Doug had seen him drink gin before, but this might have been the first time he saw him do so in distress.

"It should be over soon," he told Charlie and Bao, trying to sound reassuring.

Charlie looked skeptical. Bao's expression was unreadable, as usual.

"Mr. Hwang was vague, of course," Charlie said, waving his glass toward the still-open door. "He probably thinks the Japs'll be here a while—but he won't commit to that out-loud."

Doug shook his head. "It's a demonstration, that's all. They want to show the Chinese that they'll take matters into their own hands if the local authorities don't apprehend the culprits who have been preying on their citizens. A day—two days at most—is all they'll need to make their point."

"I hope you're right," Charlie said, quiet. He took another long drink of his gin.

Doug was about to say that they had less to fear than the Chinese, since the Japanese wouldn't want to provoke a crisis with the United States or Great Britain—but he remembered Bao wasn't so privileged, and he shut his mouth. The Japanese looked down on the Chinese as inferior.

Bao might well be trapped in this apartment for the next few days, not safe to walk abroad.

"Well, I'd best get back home," he said, setting his half-empty tumbler on the table and taking a tentative step toward the still-open door. "It's been a long day, for all of us. If either of you need anything, anything at all, just knock."

"Thank you," Charlie mumbled, seeming distracted.

"Thank you, Mr. Bainbridge!" Bao called as Doug walked out.

Doug thought it best to retire immediately, turning off all the lights and undressing in the near-dark. He feared the Japanese might investigate any well-lit abodes, and it was best not to tempt the hand of fate when it held a rifle and bayonet.

He was tired, and plopped onto the top of his bed as soon as he'd stripped out of his sweaty clothes. But sleep would not come, even after he closed his eyes and counted sheep.

His mind kept reliving the events of the evening, from the sound of the shots fired while they were at the restaurant, to the Japanese marines roughing up Charlie and Bao in their own apartment.

After a while he got up and walked naked to the window, pulling the curtain back just enough to look out onto the street.

A Japanese marine stood at each end of his quiet block, marching back and forth from sidewalk to sidewalk, rifles at their shoulders. After a while, a police constable strolled past, saluting the marines as he passed and greeting them in Japanese.

Doug stepped away from the window as the constable passed, letting the curtain fall back into place.

He wondered if Lucy was sleeping, or if she were as restless as he. In times like these, he wished he had a telephone. *Not much good that would do*, he thought, *unless she had one too.*

Tomorrow was Thursday, a school day, so she'd walk to work early in the morning, to get there before the students. Surely the Japanese wouldn't bother an American woman on her way to work, he assured himself. The most they would do would be to search her handbag.

Lucy can take care of herself. It was true, of course. But he still couldn't banish the little inkling of worry at the back of his mind.

And it wouldn't let him sleep.

He lay awake listening to the eerie silence from the city. Even late on a weeknight, there were usually sounds from Honan Road, revelers coming home late from a night on the town. But tonight all was still; silent save for the occasional sound of shoes on pavement as the Japanese police constables patrolled.

A sort of delirium settled upon him. He had been awake, restless, frustrated at the lack of sleep. Then, somehow, he was out on the street in front of his building, and it was hot as midday, but dense fog blanketed everything, making him feel closed it, almost suffocating.

Bao said hello to him, smiled and waved, and he waved back. Mr. Hwang came out of his shop door, and yelled at them to get inside, motioning with his arm in an exaggerated way.

A shape moved in the fog. Doug could see the shifting of the mist in a weird, sweeping motion that disappeared on itself, only to reappear a short distance away, curving around and disappearing again.

Bao was facing Doug, and suddenly his eyes grew wide and his mouth dropped open. He pointed behind Doug. "Mr. Bainbridge! Look out!" he yelled, and then turned tail and sprinted for Mr. Hwang's door. Mr. Hwang himself had disappeared.

Doug wanted to turn around, but he couldn't make himself do it. Fear gnawed at his belly, and he wanted to run for the door, but his feet seemed glued to the cobbled stones on the street.

A dark form slid past him on the left, and he looked over to see a long, slithering, red-scaled body. He faced forward again, and curving around to look at him was the giant head of a great red dragon.

He felt his heart pounding against his chest, and his breath came short and fast.

The dragon opened its jaws and revealed shining, dagger-like teeth.

He tried to scream, but no sound came from his open mouth.

Suddenly the dragon flew towards him, mouth gaping, a giant hole of blackness. A low growl emanated from deep inside its snake-like body, and grew steadily louder as it filled the space between them. Doug could feel its hot breath on his face, and then the darkness of its mouth consumed everything as the growl became a roar rushing through his ears—

He bolted upright in his bed, sweat dripping from his face onto his bare legs. It took a moment for him to realize it was just a dream.

Not the dragons again. He moaned and wiped his face with his hands. *Please God, don't let me start dreaming of dragons again.*

In the days following his friend Tim's murder in June of last year, he had dreamed several times of a great shimmering green dragon. The one tonight looked the same, only red and less shimmery.

The feeling was the same.

God, he remembered that feeling. He hated that he remembered that feeling.

He got up and walked to the pitcher on his dresser, and splashed some water on his face, then on his chest. *Get a grip on yourself, Doug.*

He went back to bed, and lay awake until dawn.

Hutson

21

Thursday, September 24

Doug dozed for a few hours after the break of dawn, and finally got out of bed around ten o'clock. He washed and got dressed, and knocked on his neighbors' door.

Bao answered, and his black eye looked worse than last night.

"Hello, Mr. Bainbridge."

"Hello Bao. I'm checking to make sure you and Charlie are alright."

"We alright," Bao said. "Charlie went to work, left twenty minutes ago."

Doug nodded. That was good. "I'm going to my office downtown—do you need me to bring you anything?"

"No, thank you Mr. Bainbridge. Have a good day, and stay safe from the Japanese." Bao smiled faintly as he closed the door.

Doug went down the stairs, and poked his head inside the shop on the ground floor. Wong Mei-Ling stood behind the counter, as she did almost every day, but her face looked more guarded than usual.

"Good morning, Miss Wong," he said, trying to sound cheerful and failing miserably.

She looked at him with a vacant expression. "Good morning."

"Did you have any trouble getting to work this morning? Because of the Japanese, I mean."

"No trouble," she said without elaboration, and looked away.

He nodded and turned back toward the door.

The street seemed strangely empty, and he turned right toward Honan Road, where he could catch the street car.

A Japanese marine stopped him shortly before he reached Honan Road, and demanded to see his identification papers. Doug showed his passport, and his Shanghai resident identification paper. The marine scrutinized them longer than was necessary, and finally thrust them back at Doug and motioned him through.

No one stood at the street car stop, and a quick inquiry of the old Chinese men sitting on the stoop of a building revealed that the street car was not running. Doug thanked them and walked toward the bridge. It was only a mile to his office, and the stroll would be fine, even in the oppressive heat.

Several Japanese marines stood sentry at the Honan Road bridge over Soochow Creek, and pedestrians on both sides lined up to be inspected. Doug stood in line for a few minutes, and when it was his turn the marine demanded his identification papers, and this time also demanded that he turn out his pockets and show the inside of his suit jacket. Doug complied without protest, suffering the indignity in silence, and after a moment he was on his way, crossing the creek into downtown.

He stopped to buy a newspaper on the south side of the bridge. Newspaper boys had been conspicuously absent north of the bridge, in Hongkou. The front page headline shouted in bold, capital letters:

JAPANESE SAILOR TOMOMITSU TAMINATO ASSASINATED!
YOSHITANE YAWATA AND YOSHIMI IDERIHA SERIOUSLY INJURED

Doug entered the office building on Peking Road ten minutes later, and noticed that the Japanese export office on the ground floor—the one Kawakami had opened last spring—was not open. He imagined Kawakami and his protégé lurking around the alleys of Hongkou, hunting communist assassins.

As he passed the landing on the next floor, he considered walking down to Kenny's office to check in, but he continued on to his floor. He wasn't quite ready to pretend.

He let himself into his office, sat in the chair and put his feet up on the desk, and opened the newspaper across his knees.

The front page of the English-language Shanghai Times was nothing but the assassination.

The dead sailor was First Class Seaman Taminato from the cruiser *Izumo*, in port. He had come ashore with three companions, and they were believed to have dined in Japantown. They were walking along Haining Road, and at eight-twenty PM they approached the intersection with Wusong Road, when they were fired upon from behind. Witnesses variously saw four or five shooters, but all agreed them to be Chinese men, firing pistols from the shelter of a stationary bus.

Three of the four Japanese sailors—Taminato, plus First Class Seaman Yawata, and Second Class Seaman Ideriha—were hit by bullets and seriously injured. Their unnamed companion, plus several Japanese civilians who witnessed the attack, brought them inside the Shiseido Bookstore, where Taminato collapsed and died.

Yawata and Ideriha were in serious condition, and were returned to their ship for medical attention. No further information was available at time of print.

In response, the Vice Admiral commanding the Japanese naval ships in the port of Shanghai had ordered more than 2,000 marines to land at eight-thirty PM, to occupy the whole of the Hongkou district and apprehend the assassins.

At eleven PM another 100 Japanese troops landed, along with armored vehicles and tanks.

This last caused Doug to raise his eyebrows in surprise. He hadn't seen any armored vehicles or tanks. He wondered if they were guarding the boundaries of Japantown.

He resolved to get as close as possible to Japantown that afternoon.

The paper noted that this was the largest Japanese troop presence in Shanghai since the 1932 Sino-Japanese War, which had caused much damage to the Chapei District in the Chinese municipality, north of the International Settlement.

It also reported that President Chiang Kai-shek asked War Minister He Yingqin by telegram to be in a state of readiness for war.

A small thrill ran up Doug's spine at the prospect. He had trained to observe war maneuvers, and this might be his first real chance. But within a second he reconsidered his initial excitement, as he thought of the danger to his friends and to Lucy of a battle in the streets.

The newspaper concluded the story with a mention that hundreds, perhaps thousands, of Chinese civilians had fled the Hongkou District overnight.

A bit of an afterthought, he noted. The English-language newspaper in the International Settlement bore the prejudices of most of the Anglo and American residents, unfortunately.

There was a knock on his door a while later, while he read the rest of the newspaper. When he answered the door, he wasn't surprised to see Kenny standing in the hall.

"Oh, thank God you're alright!" Kenny stepped in the office uninvited and touched Doug on the arm as he walked past. "Abbie and I have been worried sick about both of you since we heard the commotion from across the creek last night, and saw the Japanese troops from our window. How is Lucy?"

"She's fine," Doug said. "We're both fine. You don't need to worry about us."

"I'm so glad. I'll call Abbie and let her know, she'll be relieved." Kenny looked relieved himself. "She called the school this morning, and they told her not to come in. They advised all students and teachers from other parts of the city not to try to enter Hongkou today."

Doug had to admit that was wise advice. "Lucy went into work this morning."

"I suppose she would, wouldn't she? She already lives in Hongkou."

In spite of the matter-of-fact tone, Doug thought he detected a hint of worry in Kenny's eyes.

"We're carrying on with our lives," Doug said. "This will all be over soon."

"I hope you're right about that." Kenny's eyes lit up with excitement. "Did you see it? The shooting, I mean."

Doug shook his head. "No, we were dining at a restaurant at the time. We heard it, though."

"We didn't hear it." Kenny sounded a tad disappointed. "Or, we didn't know it if we did. It wouldn't have been as loud at our place, so we might have mistaken it for something else. Or maybe the tea kettle was whistling at the time, and we missed it altogether."

Kenny's excitement irritated Doug. He didn't know why, but it did. He turned away and walked to his desk.

"This was the biggest one yet," he said as he took his seat.

"And well-planned," Kenny added, taking a seat on the corner of Doug's desk. "They hid in an empty bus and waited until the sailors passed by."

Doug stared at Kenny's knees, dangerously close to his own, and scowled.

"It was pistols, no axes."

"Wasn't that first one shot?" Kenny said. "The one last November, you remember. Hideo something."

"Nakayama," Doug answered.

"That's right—Hideo Nakayama. He was also a sailor in their navy. And he was also shot, I'm fairly certain. Almost the same location, too, I believe—Wusong and Haining."

It irritated Doug further that Kenny was right about all of those details.

"You think it was the Reds?" Kenny asked.

Doug nodded. "Yes, seems most likely."

"What do you make of the different methods?" Kenny asked, leaning forward and looking earnest. "The ones here in Shanghai have been shot, the locations almost the same—but the others in Chengdu, Hankou and Pei-Hei were killed with an axe, weren't they?"

Doug shook his head. "The assassins *carried* axes, but the victims were shot." *Which muddies the waters a bit.*

"No axes spotted on the killers last night," Kenny said. "Or, at least, the paper didn't report that. So what do you make of that? Not connected? Two separate crime sprees?"

Doug's mind jumped back to his assignment in Hong Kong last January. He couldn't share that.

Or its implications.

"You look like you swallowed something distasteful," Kenny said, eyeing him curiously.

Doug shrugged, looked away. "The whole matter is distasteful," he muttered.

"No argument from me," Kenny said, cheerful again. "Say, why don't we go get some lunch? It's been a while since we lunched together. I've missed our conversations."

Doug tried to think of an excuse. "I've got a lot of work to do. The Japanese action has caused some difficulties for a few of our suppliers, so I'm scrambling to find alternate routes." That sounded plausible enough.

Kenny looked disappointed. "Maybe tomorrow, then?"

"Yes, maybe. We'll see how it goes," Doug said. Kenny's eyes darted to the folded newspaper on his otherwise-empty desk, and a veil seemed to fall over them.

"Right. I'll check in on you later. Have a good afternoon, Doug," he said, and let himself out.

"Damn!" Doug cursed under his breath. He should have had some of his fake files spread out on the desk. He should have anticipated that Kenny would come by to check on him, under the circumstances.

He hadn't planned that very well, and he castigated himself for it.

After waiting a while, to be sure that Kenny had gone to lunch, Doug locked up his office and left. He stopped at Kenny's closed office door on his way downstairs, and taped a note to the door saying:

"Kenny, I have to meet suppliers, will be gone the rest of the afternoon. – Doug."

He felt a momentary pang of guilt at the lie, but it was necessary.

He walked along Soochow Road South, heading toward the river. He tugged his hat lower and hurried past Kenny and Abbie's apartment building, hoping he wasn't spotted, and dreading the sound of Abbie's voice calling his name. He didn't relax until he was more than a block past their building.

The street lining the south shore of Soochow Creek was more full than usual, with plenty of multinational gawkers standing on the bank staring across the wide creek—small river, really—toward the Hongkou district and the Japanese troops stationed at regular intervals along Soochow Road North.

Doug cast plenty of glances across the creek wherever the crowds were thin enough to allow him a good view; but he never paused, not wanting to appear to be observing.

271

He made it all the way to the Garden Bridge, just short of the Huang Po River—a walk of almost a mile—without ever seeing armored vehicles or tanks on the other side of the creek. Only troops, individually or in small groups.

He noticed a conspicuous absence of Japanese guards on the other side of the Garden Bridge—the location of the swanky high-rise Broadway Mansions Hotel and the prestigious Astor House Hotel, not to mention the Soviet consulate—so he turned left and crossed over here.

Japantown lay a couple of blocks to the north, so in one way it was surprising that Broadway was not under occupation like the rest of Hongkou, given the proximity to the Japanese colony—but given the wealth and influence of the residents of these blocks, it was hardly shocking on second thought.

When he got to the north side of the bridge, in the shadow of the towering Broadway Mansions, he glanced left. Japanese marines were posted a half-block to the west.

He paused, considering whether to just go through the check-point to his left, and try to loop around toward Japantown, or continue up Broadway, past the actual mansions secure behind their walled compounds. Where Ming Lin-wen likely sat entertaining the ladies at afternoon tea.

He continued up Broadway.

For the second time that day, he tugged his hat lower as he hurried past the home of someone whom he'd rather not see him.

When he reached the end of Broadway and cut over toward the entrance to Wusong, he encountered a Japanese check-point, manned by an entire squadron of marines.

Behind them, some fifty yards distant, was the first of the armored vehicles he had read about.

These marines were more suspicious than the previous ones he encountered—if that were possible, he mused. They stared hard at him, and peppered him with questions about where he was going, where he was coming from, and why.

"I'm coming from downtown," he said in English, having already attempted to explain himself in Shanghainese, without success. At least two of the marines in this squad seemed to speak English with relative fluency.

He pointed to the address on his Shanghai identification paper. "I'm on my way home, on Huang Lei Road in Hongkou, not far from here."

The sergeant leading his interrogation narrowed his eyes, and glared at Doug. "Why you enter Hongkou here? Why you come through Japantown? Kiangse Road Bridge closer to your home."

Ordinarily he might say he wanted to have lunch at one of the Japanese restaurants along Wusong Road—but under the circumstances, he thought better of that. "I had lunch at the Cathay Hotel, so this bridge was closer."

He prayed that his stomach wouldn't growl and give away that he hadn't eaten yet.

The sergeant continued to stare a hole through him. "Why you not walk Soochow Road to Kiangse Road?" he demanded. "Why you come to Japantown?"

Doug could only think of one plausible explanation for that. "I stopped by the home of a friend who lives on Broadway."

The sergeant's lips tightened into a short, thin line, and his brow came together almost imperceptibly more.

He's not buying it, Doug thought. "My friend—her name is Ming Lin-wen—she lives at number 18 Broadway. You can check with their butler, I stopped by ten minutes ago, but she was not home."

He was almost certain they wouldn't take the time to check with a Chinese butler at the mansion of a Chinese aristocrat, just to verify the excuse of a random American passing through their check-point.

Almost certain.

Several seconds of uncomfortable silence elapsed, Doug's heart seeming to flutter as he waited. Finally, the sergeant turned away and barked something at his squad in Japanese. When he turned back to Doug, his expression was plain military stoic, no more glare.

"You take that street there, go back Soochow Road, take to Kiangse Road. You not go near Japantown, understand?" He pointed toward the narrow side street that ran behind the walled compounds of Broadway, two blocks toward Soochow Road North.

Doug nodded and touched the rim of his hat. "Thank you." He hurried on his way.

The prescribed route took him less than half a block from Lucy's apartment, but it would be at least an hour until she got home from the school, and probably longer. Besides, his stomach felt as if it would gnaw on his insides if he didn't get something to eat soon, so he took Kiangse Road north toward his neighborhood.

He was stopped one more time by a Japanese patrol about a block from home, but a quick check of his passport and identification paper was all the two marines did, and they waved him on.

He filed away in his memory the patterns of patrols he had seen around Hongkou, from this morning, and from now. When he had a chance—after the occupation ended—he would file a report with Commander Shock.

He knew better than to write anything down right now.

He wished he kept more food in his icebox, but he managed to put together enough bits of leftover dinners to have a passable lunch, and washed it down with a pot of Oolong tea. After lunch, he went downstairs to Mr. Hwang's store, hoping to find Wong Mei-Ling alone.

"Good afternoon, Miss Wong," he said in Shanghainese, bowing his head. "Is Mr. Hwang in the office?"

"He has gone home for lunch," she replied. "He will be back soon, probably fifteen minutes."

Good. Doug nodded, and leaned against the counter, affecting a friendly, casual posture. "You live near here, don't you? Did the Japanese search your apartment, too?"

She didn't immediately respond, but after severa' seconds she nodded. "The Japanese searched everyone's apartments. No one was spared."

"I suppose not. It was a disagreeable experience. Did they do any damage to your belongings?"

"No."

"Did they get rough with you?"

She fixed him with a hard stare for several seconds, and he wondered what she was thinking behind her dark, almost black eyes.

"They did not hurt me, or my flat-mates," she said, matter-of-fact. "They were insulting, that is all. And very thorough."

Doug nodded. "I'm sorry to hear that they insulted you."

"It is the Japanese way," she said, a note of bitterness in her voice.

"Yes, that is what I hear. I suppose, at least, since you had nothing to hide, you had nothing to fear from them."

She cocked her head slightly as she stared back at him, an enigmatic look on her face.

"You had nothing to hide, of course," he pressec, carefully.

She stiffened, took a step back, and glared at him.

He hadn't really expected anything more from her. Her reticence was a constant in their many interactions. Still, he had to try.

He glanced around to be certain they were still alone, and leaned across the counter. "If you know something, perhaps I can help."

"I do not know anything," she said, crossing her arms.

He didn't believe her. He saw the shifting of her eyes—barely perceptible—and the way she pressed her crossed arms against her torso a bit more tightly than seemed normal.

She was lying.

She knows who the killers are, but she won't say. His real concern was whether or not the Japanese would discern her connection, and arrest her. Maybe even torture her until she gave up the names of her comrades.

He glanced around again, and leaned farther over the counter, so that the corner of it dug uncomfortably into his abdomen. "If you need help, please come to me."

Her expression went blank, her arms fell to her sides, and she bowed her head. "You are most kind, Mr. Bainbridge. Good day."

He reached the top of the stairs a moment later and was startled to see Jonesy standing outside his door, waiting.

A wry sort of half-smile crossed Jonesy's mouth. "Get what you wanted out of Miss Wong?" He chuckled at Doug's reaction. "Didn't think so."

"Where have you been?" Doug asked, unlocking his door.

"Why? Did you miss me?" Jonesy asked in amusement.

Doug scowled, and motioned the reporter inside with an impatient wave of his arm. "No, but Lucy was worried. I told her you were fine, but you know how women are."

"If you say so," Jonesy said with a shrug.

Doug could have smacked his own forehead. He'd walked right into that one.

"Well, we hadn't heard from you, and of course it could be dangerous asking around after a political assassination. So, you see, Lucy was worried about you."

"I'm used to it."

"I told her you were," Doug said, closing the door. "I said you did this a lot, and that you know what you're doing."

"Thanks for the vote of confidence," Jonesy said. "And tell your girl I appreciate her concern. Got anything to drink?"

"I can make a pot of tea."

"Got anything stronger?"

Doug should have known. "I think I've got some gin left, and some tonic. I don't keep vermouth, so I can't make you a martini."

"Gin and tonic is fine," Jonesy said, and he took a seat while Doug went into the kitchenette to mix the drink.

"What brings you by?" Doug asked as he handed over the beverage.

"I'm interested in what you've seen and heard since last night," Jonesy said, and took a long pull on the cocktail.

"Were you around last night?"

"Define 'around.'"

Doug sighed, suppressing his exasperation. "Were you back in town?"

"Yes, I got back to Shanghai night before last."

"Hmm." Doug wasn't too surprised. He'd assumed Jonesy was mad at him for not going to Hankou. He didn't look mad now, though.

"Why don't you tell me what you learned in Hankou first. Then we can get into last night. Let's stick to chronological order."

Jonesy shrugged. "If you insist." He took a long drink, leaned back and looked up at the ceiling, as if composing his thoughts.

"For starters, they haven't arrested anyone there. The Japanese Concession was locked down pretty tight for a few days, but nothing remotely on the scale of what they've done here." Jonesy looked Doug in the eye. "*That's* the real story."

"I'm sure you've talked to lots of sources about what's happened here," Doug said. "Why do you need my version?"

Jonesy threw back the last of the gin and tonic. "Because you'd notice things a civilian wouldn't."

Doug couldn't argue with that, but he stayed silent.

"Well?" Jonesy stared at Doug with one eyebrow arched.

"You haven't told me much about Hankou yet," Doug replied, holding Jonsey's gaze.

Jonesy grunted. "Fine, you win. The victim was a Japanese policeman—"

"We already knew that much," Doug said, letting his impatience show.

"I was getting to the rest, don't interrupt me," Jonesy replied, testy. "There was either one or two shooters, the witnesses I talked to varied. Also, the witnesses I interviewed didn't agree on whether or not there was an axe on his belt—some said yes, and others said no."

Doug scratched his chin and looked up in thought. "Perhaps, if there were two, one of them had an axe, and the other didn't."

"Yeah, I thought of that," Jonesy said. "The trouble is, when I map out the purported locations of the witnesses I talked to, it seems incongruous that there could have been two assassins, and yet some of the witnesses in a clear line of sight only saw one."

"What do you make of that?" Doug asked.

"That memory is as faulty as ever," Jonesy said, and held up his empty glass. "Make me another?"

Doug scowled. "You're going to finish my gin," he snapped. He instantly regretted saying that. His mother would scold him for inhospitality if she'd heard.

"Fine, I'll take some tea, then," Jonesy said, crossing his arms and making a show of being put out.

Doug made a pot of tea, and while he waited for the water to boil, he peppered Jonesy with questions.

"Where have you been in Shanghai since you got back?"

"Around," Jonesy said.

"Have you been in Hongkou ever since last night's shooting?"

Jonesy shrugged. "I've been in and out."

Doug wondered how he could have slipped in and out of Hongkou, with the Japanese troops occupying the entire district. He let that go for now. "The people you've interviewed here—have you talked with any of the local communists about last night's attack?"

Jonesy crossed his arms and leaned back. "You know I don't reveal my sources. I'm not going to start now."

The teapot began to whistle, so Doug didn't have to think of an argument. He concentrated on pouring two cups, and carried one to Jonesy.

"Let's get back to what you've seen and heard since the shooting," Jonesy said, and blew across the top of his steaming cup. "I know you're interested in the Japanese troop maneuvers—not to mention the tanks and armored vehicles. You're probably in heaven right about now." He ventured a careful sip.

Doug took a deep breath, gathering his thoughts and contemplating what to reveal.

"Lucy and I first encountered the Japanese marines after leaving a restaurant last night, which is where we were when we heard the shots. They were clearing the streets at that time, which was maybe ten minutes after the shooting.

"Shortly after we got back to Lucy's apartment, they began going door to door and searching everyone's apartments. They never said what they were looking for. They weren't rude or destructive, at least not to us. They were pretty rough with my neighbor Bao."

Jonesy's eyebrows rose. "How rough?"

"They hit him," Doug said, anger rising at the memory. "They bruised his cheekbone, right here, just below his eye."

"Jap bastards," Jonesy muttered, and his face flushed dark red.

"Wong Mei-Ling said they were insulting to her and her roommate when their apartment was searched, but no one was hurt," Doug added.

"That means they don't know she's a red," Jonesy said, seeming a little distracted. "But why would they? She's safe enough." He stared past Doug, out the kitchen window. After several seconds, he added, "But Bao and Charlie aren't safe. They know about them."

A sense of dread settled into Doug's belly. He didn't want to know what Jonesy was imagining. "What can we do?"

279

Jonesy stared out the window in silence for a long moment. Then his eyes lit up, he snapped his finger, and looked back at Doug.

"I'll switch apartments with them, just for a few days. They can stay at my place uptown, and I'll stay here in Hongkou."

22

"My mother would have a fit if she knew a Chinese man was staying in my apartment," Lucy said under her breath to Doug, after showing Bao around.

"I might pay to see the look on her face," Doug replied with a grin.

Lucy slapped at his arm, but laughed. "Truthfully? So would I."

"Thanks for taking him in. I would have taken him to join Charlie at Jonesy's place, if I could have gotten him across the creek."

When Doug and Bao had approached the Kiangse Road bridge to downtown, Doug noticed the Japanese weren't letting any Chinese nationals cross Soochow Creek, so they detoured at the last moment and walked half a block to Lucy's building.

He just needed to get Bao away from his own apartment, where he and Charlie were known. He'd be safer here.

"I'm happy to help." Lucy collapsed into her couch with a heavy sigh. "My God, Doug, you wouldn't believe the day I've had."

Doug took a seat next to her. "I can imagine." He put his arm around her shoulder and pulled her toward him. She laid her head on his chest and sighed again.

"My poor students," she said. "They're old enough to understand what's going on, at least on a base level, and you can tell they're all frightened. The boys try not to show it, of course, which only makes it more obvious they're scared to death."

"How many students did you have?"

"Maybe five or six in each class. Only about a quarter of our students came to school, the rest stayed home. Mr. Higgins sent several of the male teachers out to escort the students inside. I watched from the windows. The Chinese students in particular took a lot of harassment from the Japanese troops stationed down the block, searching their book bags and dumping them out on the street. Papers scattered, and some of the girls were in tears."

She sat up and looked him in the eye. "I couldn't help noticing the white students didn't get treated the same way. Their bags were searched, but much faster, and without dumping them out."

Doug squeezed her shoulder. "I know, it's unfair. The Japanese don't want to antagonize any of the other countries on the Municipal Council, so they take a lighter hand with our nationals. With the Chinese, the opposite is true—they *want* to antagonize China right now. They're making a point."

"With *children*? That's inhumane."

"With everybody," Doug said. "They hate the Chinese. They always have. They like to feel superior for some reason. Miss Wong, who works in Mr. Hwang's shop, she told me the Japanese were very insulting to her, and to her roommate, when they searched their apartment last night. And I've told you how they treated Bao."

Lucy glanced around. She whispered, "I just assumed that was because of him and Charlie."

Doug shrugged. "It was. I mean, I'm sure that's most of it—but you notice they didn't hit Charlie."

Lucy frowned. "I hadn't put that together, honestly. I'm a bit angry at myself for not noticing that until you said so." She shook her head. "It's strange, isn't it? To think about Asians being prejudiced against other Asians. In America, they're all lumped together."

Doug nodded and kissed her forehead. "It's not so different, really. Think about how many white people are prejudiced against Jews, who are fellow white people."

"I suppose you're right." She laid her head back on his chest. "It's all so depressing. Just hold me and tell me it's going to be alright."

He wrapped his arms around her and held her tight to him. "It's going to be alright."

Now if only he could get himself to believe it.

Bao returned from taking a bath a few minutes later, his hair damp.

Doug stood to meet him. "I'm sorry I couldn't get you to Charlie," he said. "When I get back, I'll call them from Mr. Hwang's phone, and tell them what happened. I'll make sure Charlie knows you're safe here."

Jonesy had gone to the theater downtown where Charlie worked, and convinced him to go back to Jonesy's apartment for the night. The two of them would be waiting there for Doug to bring Bao.

"Thank you, Mr. Bainbridge," Bao said.

His gratitude sounded genuine, but Doug also heard sadness in his voice. "This will all be over soon," he said, trying to sound reassuring.

"I hear you like to cook," Lucy said. "We can make dinner together. Won't that be fun?"

Bao nodded. "Yes, thank you."

"I'd best be on my way," Doug said, and leaned in to give Lucy a kiss. "Curfew starts before dark. I'll come by and check on you both first thing in the morning."

"We'll be fine," Lucy said. "Don't worry about us."

Doug made his way home in the sultry evening heat, and was stopped once by a Japanese sentry asking to see his identification.

As he rounded the corner onto his street, he saw Kawakami standing in the shade of an awning, pretending to window shop.

Doug stopped, hid behind the corner, and watched. The awning under which Kawakami stood was half a block from his building, and on the opposite side of the street. After a while of staring into the same window, Kawakami moved down to the next shop, and stared into its window.

He's waiting for me. Doug looked around for any Japanese patrol. It would only be a matter of time before one came by—either marines, or SMP constables—and he would have to explain why he was standing against a building, peering around the corner.

He checked his watch. Curfew was less than fifteen minutes from now. Before long, he would have to break cover and go home, even if no patrol approached. And then Kawakami would see him.

The door to Mr. Hwang's shop opened, and Wong Mei-Ling exited. She turned west—away from Doug's position—but after half a block she turned left and disappeared down the side street.

A figure stepped out of the shadows a little farther down Huang Lei Road, folding a newspaper under his arm, and followed her.

Doug recognized Kawakami's assistant, Nakagawa. He nodded at Kawakami as he passed, but the older man didn't look his direction.

Doug kept his eyes on Kawakami, who pretended to stroll idly toward the corner around which Wong Mei-Ling and Nakagawa had gone. Then he stood there, waiting.

Time was ticking by, and curfew approached. Boots clapped on the bricks up the road, and he stepped out of his hiding place and walked as casually as he could toward his building.

His movement caught Kawakami's attention, and the Japanese agent turned his head to watch Doug move up the block and open the door to his building. Doug acted as if he didn't notice, but kept a careful watch out of the corner of his eye, until the door closed behind him.

He knocked on Mr. Hwang's office door, and the proprietor answered a moment later.

He gave his landlord a polite bow. "Good evening, Mr. Hwang. I wonder if I might make a local phone call on your telephone?"

The landlord agreed, accepted the nickel Doug gave him, and stepped out to give Doug a moment of privacy.

"Hello?" Jonesy's gruff voice answered after the operator put Doug's call through.

"Jonesy, it's Doug."

"Where the hell are you?"

"I'm calling from my landlord's office."

"What the hell's keeping you?" Jonesy demanded, irritated. "Mr. Ford and I have been stuck here waiting. Christ, look at the time—you won't be able to make it before curfew now. And I won't be able to get into Hongkou now, either. You've waited too long. What was the hold-up?"

Doug let Jonesy blow off steam before he answered his string of questions.

"I wasn't able to get Bao out of the district. The Japanese weren't letting any Chinese nationals cross the bridge. But he's safe. Tell Charlie that Bao is staying at Lucy's apartment tonight, and she's looking out for him."

He heard the scrape of Jonesy's hand covering the mouthpiece, followed by muffled conversation. Then the hand moved and Jonesy said, "Mr. Ford said to thank you both for your help. He and I are going out to dinner. I'll check in with you tomorrow, when I can get over there."

He hung up the line without saying good-bye.

Doug shook his head and went upstairs to his apartment. He couldn't blame Jonesy for being irritated. For a moment he wondered if he hadn't hidden behind that corner for ten minutes watching Kawakami, would Jonesy have had enough time to catch two street cars and get to their building before curfew?

Not at all likely. He couldn't blame himself for that.

So he turned his thoughts to Kawakami and Nakagawa as he reached his floor and entered his apartment.

They're spying on Wong Mei-Ling.

Which meant she was in danger. Either they thought she was involved in the attack, or they believed she knew the attackers, and following her would lead them to the culprits.

But Kawakami hadn't followed Mei-Ling. Only Nakagawa had. Kawakami had moved from his earlier position—but only to the corner.

Doug peeked out his front window. Kawakami still stood on the corner, motionless.

The real question was, were they also watching him?

23

Friday, September 25

Doug rose before dawn, and hurried to Lucy's apartment as soon as curfew was lifted.

She stepped out of her building as he rushed around the corner from Kiangse Road, pulling on her white gloves. He called her name, and she turned and waited.

"Bao's fine," she said as he kissed her cheek, the rim of her hat knocking his own hat off his head. He stooped to retrieve it from the sidewalk. "I wish I could stay and chat, but I really must hurry. I need to get to the school before the students start to arrive, however many there are today."

"I understand. Mind if I go up and check on Bao?"

"Be my guest," she said, turning to walk away. She called back over her shoulder, "The door's locked, but I'm sure he'll let you in."

There was no response when Doug first knocked on Lucy's door, so he knocked again and spoke through the key hole.

"Bao? Open up, it's Doug Bainbridge."

The lock clicked a moment later, and Bao opened the door. "Hello, Mr. Bainbridge. How are you?"

"I'm well enough, Bao," Doug said, stepping inside and closing the door behind him. "The question is, how are you holding up?"

Bao shrugged, a sad sort of look in his eyes. "I am fine. I wish Charlie is here."

Doug felt bad for the young man. "I understand, but the important thing is that you're both safe. The Japanese will leave any time now, and you can go home and get back to your normal lives. You'll see."

Bao nodded, but Doug wasn't sure he looked convinced. "You want some tea, Mr. Bainbridge? I make tea for us."

"No, thank you, Bao. I'd best be off. Mr. Jones will probably go to our building this morning, and I'd like to be there to meet him. I just wanted to check in first and make sure you were well."

He started to let himself out, but paused in the doorway and turned back toward Bao. "I wouldn't be surprised if Mr. Jones has a message for you from Charlie, so he might come by here later to deliver it. Don't let anyone else in, other than me and him, understand?"

"I understand, Mr. Bainbridge." Bao closed the door, and the lock clicked into place.

There was a commotion near the end of his street when Doug rounded the corner from Kiangse Road, and he walked past his building to see what was going on.

A small crowd gathered near the corner of the side street where Wong Mei-ling had gone last night, half a block from his building.

The same corner where Kawakami had stood, long after Doug went to bed.

A trio of Japanese police constables kept the crowd back, batons in their hands and cold stares on their faces.

Doug asked one of the women in Shanghainese what was going on.

She answered in a voice quiet enough that he had to lean down to hear what she said. "There is a dead man behind the trash cans, down that way. People are saying he's Japanese, but the police say nothing. They made us leave, and won't let us back in."

Doug immediately thought of Kawakami and Nakagawa.

He stood on his toes and craned his neck to look over the crowd, but all he saw were police constables down the alley. If he could only get close enough to see the body...

A squad of Japanese marines came around the corner from Kiangse Road, marching a quick step, rifles with bayonets aimed at an angle in front of them.

The crowd of Chinese scattered.

Doug rushed across the street to stand under Mr. Hwang's awning. Within half a minute, the street was empty.

The squad rounded the corner and fanned out along the length of the alley.

Doug was about to go inside, when he spotted Jonesy walking up the street toward him, staying close to the wall.

A constable shouted at Jonesy in Pidgin, asking where he was going. Jonesy answered back in Pidgin, pointing at Mr. Hwang's storefront.

The Japanese constable turned away with a scowl, and said nothing more.

"Touchy bastards," Jonesy muttered when he reached the doorway.

"There was a body found down that alley," Doug said, nodding rather than pointing. "The rumor is it was a Japanese man."

"You don't say? Did you hear shots fired?"

"No."

"Hmmm," Jonesy said, looking up in thought.

"What?"

Jonesy shrugged. "Makes me wonder if it was an axe murder, that's all." He looked toward the corner. "The Jap marines seem to have taken over the scene. That's interesting."

The district's under martial law, Jonesy. "How so?"

"The other times, they let the police do their work, and only cleared the street around the scene. They didn't take over. This is different somehow."

Doug suspected that Kawakami was part of the Japanese secret services. He presumed Nakagawa was, as well. If one of them were killed in a Shanghai alley, high ranking officials might well send in military forces to "clean up."

He saw Jonesy staring at him, and he looked away. "I've got Bao's key, I can let you into their apartment." He walked through the door and started up the stairs.

"Thanks," Jonesy muttered as he followed.

Doug unlocked Charlie and Bao's door and opened it, but stayed out in the hall, handing the key to Jonesy.

Jonesy took the key slowly, staring at Doug for a minute. "You know something."

Doug looked away. "Is there any message from Charlie to Bao that I can pass along to him when I see him later?"

Jonesy nodded, but continued to stare at Doug.

"Are you going to tell me what it is?" Doug asked, irritated. "I can't read your mind, Jonesy."

Jonesy crossed his arms. "Sure, I'll tell you—as soon as you tell me what you know about that Jap corpse down that alley."

Doug glanced around to make sure no one was in the stairwell, then nodded for Jonesy to go into Charlie and Bao's apartment. He followed, and closed the door. "I don't *know* anything, exactly."

"But you think you might."

Doug nodded. "You remember that Japanese agent from the train?"

"Yes. Kawakami."

"I recall we discussed that he's probably in the Japanese secret services in some capacity."

"That's right." Jonesy's eyes narrowed. "Go on."

"I've often wondered if the proximity of their office to mine was no accident, that they were keeping tabs on me." Doug paused, hesitant to reveal too much.

"They were here last night?" Jonesy asked.

"Not *here*—not in the building. I saw Kawakami loitering near the corner where those police constables were standing guard just now. His associate Nakagawa was hidden at first, but I saw him follow Wong Mei-ling down that alley when she left work. That was the last I saw him, but I looked out my window a few times, and Kawakami stayed on that corner. At least until after I went to bed."

"What time was that?"

"About eleven-thirty."

"How recently had you looked for him before that?"

"Right before," Doug said. "I turned my light off, looked out, saw him still there, and lay down to go to sleep."

"Hmmm..." Jonesy frowned and looked off in thought. "Have a seat, let's talk this out."

Doug sat on the couch, and Jonesy sat in a chair facing him.

"So the Jap spy services have figured out Wong Mei-Ling's connected to the Reds—or, at least they suspect as much."

"That was my assumption as well," Doug agreed.

"They must have reason to believe she's connected somehow to the Taminato affair, or knows who is."

"I agree."

"So we have to find out if they interrogated her, or if they're just watching her to see who she meets with." Jonesy paused and looked Doug in the eye. "Is she working today?"

"She should be," Doug said. He should have dropped into Mr. Hwang's shop to check on her. But Jonesy's arrival had interrupted him.

Jonesy looked at his watch. "If she's busy working, it won't be the best time to talk—but we need to know if she's there, or if she's gone missing. Let's go."

He leapt from the chair. Doug followed him downstairs, having to keep up.

They found her talking to a middle-aged Chinese couple whom Doug recognized as residents of the second floor. Their conversation in Shanghainese stopped when the two white men entered, but after giving them a cursory glance, the older couple turned back to Mei-Ling and resumed talking.

She interrupted them, nodding toward Doug and mumbling that he understood Shanghainese. They immediately clammed up.

"Apologies," Jonesy said, bowing his head at the three Chinese.

"It OK," Mei-Ling said. "We talkee long, 'bout Japanese."

"My savvy it bad pidgin talkee 'bout Japanese now," Jonesy said in Pidgin. "My catchee another time."

"My breakee pidgin two clock," she said, to Jonesy, but glancing at Doug.

Jonesy bowed to her. "My catchee then."

As they left the shop, Jonesy nodded in satisfaction. "That answers the most important question. She's not in Japanese custody. Or dead."

Doug frowned. "The Japanese wouldn't kill her if they thought she knew something. They're too efficient to make that mistake."

Jonesy snorted. "They'd kill her if she attacked them with a weapon, trying to escape."

Doug scolded himself for not thinking of that possibility. He always thought of Wong Mei-Ling as a quiet and mild-mannered young woman, if sometimes a little sullen. But she was also a member of a communist cell, so it made sense she could wield a weapon to protect herself if needed.

"You think she's armed?"

"No doubt in my mind," Jonesy said. "She's probably got a knife concealed somewhere in her trousers, if I had my guess." He glanced at his wrist watch. "It's almost five hours until her break. We could get some breakfast, and then go see Bao."

Doug agreed, and they went out to the street. A group of five Japanese police constables marching toward the front of the building gave them pause, however, and they stood at the corner of the building and watched.

When the constables entered Mr. Hwang's shop, Jonesy motioned for Doug to follow him back inside.

As they opened the door, Doug looked back. Kawakami stood on the corner of the alley, exactly where he had been last night.

But this time he was staring at the storefront. His eyes met Doug's and held them, his expression inscrutable.

Doug broke contact first, and followed after Jonesy, who had gone through the interior door to the shop. The middle-aged Chinese couple were in the process of scurrying out, and they rushed past Doug and hurried up the stairs, silent.

Doug stood in the doorway. The five policemen surrounded Wong Mei-Ling, in front of the counter. Two of the constables man-handled her arms into handcuffs while she struggled, cursing them in Shanghainese and telling them she had done nothing wrong.

"What are you arresting her for?" Jonesy demanded in English, but the constables ignored him.

Jonesy stepped right up to the police, towering over all of them, and Doug noticed he'd puffed out his chest, taking full advantage of both his height and his stocky build.

"Tell me why you're arresting her, or I'll report in tomorrow's newspaper that you're harassing random Chinese girls. I know the commissioner—it would be a shame if I had to tell him you fellas were uncooperative."

At least one of the Japanese policemen understood English, for he held up his hand to his compatriots, who had begun to drag Wong Mei-Ling toward the door.

"She is arrested for murder of Japanese businessman."

Jonesy opened his notepad and began scribbling. "What was the victim's name? When did this murder allegedly happen?"

The constable stared hard at Jonesy for a moment before deciding to answer. "She kill Nakagawa Haruto last night, at the door to the building where she live. She is under arrest for murder."

"No!" Wong Mei-Ling shouted in English. Or Pidgin, more likely, Doug reasoned. "Mista Jonesy, my no kill nobody. My go myside from pidgin, my no leave until come pidgin morningside."

The police dragged her to the door, and out into the street. She screamed at them in Shanghainese the whole time, protesting her innocence.

Doug believed her.

Jonesy marched behind the counter, and disappeared into the back of the shop. Doug hurried after him.

He found Jonesy pounding on the door of the office. "I know you're in there, Mr. Hwang. Open up. Get your cowardly butt out here and answer some questions, damn it!"

Jonesy's face was red with rage, and he kept pounding on the door, harder each time.

The door finally opened, and the diminutive proprietor stood straight-backed, his face pale, and stared up at the furious reporter blocking his path.

"The japs are gone, you're safe now, you big coward," Jonesy practically spat out.

"I must mind my shop," Mr. Hwang said in his slow, deliberate English. He tried to slip past Jonesy, but the big reporter extended his arm, and didn't move.

"She's worked for you for nine years, and you let her hang. Tell me why."

"I don't want trouble with the Japanese," Mr. Hwang said. "I could do nothing to help her. If I tried to stop them, they would arrest me, too."

"She says she didn't do anything," Jonesy said, through gritted teeth. "Do you believe she killed that Japanese man?"

Mr. Hwang's expression stayed passive, stoic even, in the face of Jonesy's hostility. "I do not know."

"How can you say that? You've known her since she was a girl."

Mr. Hwang straightened, but his expression didn't change. "We are known by the company we keep, Mr. Jones. Miss Wong probably did not kill that man herself, but she keeps company with dangerous radicals. I have spoken to her about it many times."

"Then why not fire her?" Jonesy demanded, even angrier than before.

Mr. Hwang stayed silent, and his face was unreadable.

Doug stepped in to defuse the tension. "Your loyalty to her is admirable, Mr. Hwang. You have always been good to her. She knows that she owes much to you."

There was a flash behind Mr. Hwang's dark eyes, quick and sudden like a bolt of lightning on a moonless night, and was just as suddenly gone. He nodded his head in polite acknowledgment.

"Thank you, Mr. Bainbridge. But with Miss Wong's arrest, at least there will be no further visits from the secret police."

Doug was taken aback. "The *Juntong* have visited recently?"

"Not recently," Mr. Hwang clarified. "They have come here a few times, infrequently. I think that Miss Wong was a person of only minor interest to them."

Jonesy's green eyes had narrowed as he looked back and forth between Doug and Mr. Hwang during the exchange. Now he fixed his stare on the Chinese proprietor.

"We know the *Juntong* came to you asking about Mr. Bainbridge last June, and you let them search his apartment" he said, lips tight. "We didn't know they were also asking about Miss Wong."

Mr. Hwang shook his head. "Not then. They asked about Miss Wong on their next visit. I don't want trouble with the *Juntong*, or with the communists, so I only told them what they could find out elsewhere."

"They should hire you onto the diplomatic corps in Nanking," Jonesy muttered. Mr. Hwang ignored him.

"What have they asked you about Miss Wong?" Doug asked, giving Jonesy a side-eyed glare.

"It would not be prudent for me to say," Mr. Hwang said with a bow of his head. "Please excuse me, gentlemen. I must attend to my shop in Miss Wong's absence."

Jonesy stepped aside with a slight huff, and Mr. Hwang hurried to the counter.

"Let's go," Doug said, and nodded toward the front door.

As he stepped outside, Doug noticed Kawakami had disappeared. *He called in the police.* But who was Kawakami's informant?

They walked in silence for a moment before Jonesy spoke. "I believe her when she says she didn't kill that Nakagawa fellow."

Doug nodded, looking down at the street. "I believe her, too."

"Good," Jonesy declared. "Because I'll need your help to prove her innocence. I can't do it by myself, not in time to save her, anyway."

As much as he didn't relish the prospect of working closely with Jonesy on another project, Doug had to admit it was the only way they could clear Wong Mei-Ling of the murder.

"We'll need to come up with a plan," he said.

"Yeah, I'm working that out in my head," Jonesy said, sounding distracted. After a few seconds, he snapped his finger. "Follow me."

He picked up his pace, and Doug hurried to keep up with him. "Where are we going?"

"We're going to get breakfast," Jonesy said with a sly grin. "I hope you're hungry."

Jonesy led him on a circuitous route mostly northward, and eventually Doug realized they were circling around the North District

Police station on Kashing Road. *Avoiding Japanese patrols*, he thought with a touch of admiration.

They came to a restaurant named The Dutch Village Inn, and Jonesy held the door open. When Doug entered, he found the restaurant full of Shanghai Municipal Police constables and sergeants in uniform. In fact, they seemed to be most of the customers.

"This place is always popular with the cops," Jonesy said near Doug's ear. "But since they've been pushed aside by the Japs the last couple of days, they're probably bored."

"Mr. Bainbridge, sir!" a familiar young British voice called from across the room, and Doug looked over to see Constable Billy Dickinson waving from a table in the far corner. He recognized Constable Patel sitting across from him.

Doug held up a finger to Jonesy, and walked over to their table. "Hello Billy, Constable Patel."

"Haven't seen you in here before, Mr. Bainbridge," Billy said with a grin.

"This is my first time here."

"Good place for breakfast, sir. No one makes pancakes better than a Dutchman, ain't that so?"

Doug nodded and agreed, though he had no opinion on the matter.

"Are you here with Mr. Jones, sir?"

"Yes." Doug hesitated, and then said, "We've just come from my building, where Miss Wong who works in the ground floor shop was arrested."

"That's a real shame, sir," Patel said in his lilting Punjabi accent. "I know the young woman you're referring to."

"What was she arrested for?" Billy asked.

"She's accused of killing a Japanese man, but she insists she's innocent."

Billy and Patel exchanged a glance.

"Begging your pardon, Mr. Bainbridge, sir—but the perpetrators always say they're innocent," Billy said. "Especially the Chinese ones, they never admit it."

Doug ignored the subtle racism in the statement. "I know Miss Wong well, and I believe she *is* innocent."

"She is a quiet one," Patel said, and Doug wondered what he meant to imply. "Do you know which police officers arrested her?"

Doug shook his head. "No, we didn't ask their names. I believe they were all Japanese, though."

Billy smirked. "'Course they were. That's all what's workin' in Hongkou right now, sir."

"I noticed," Doug muttered. "Mr. Jones is waiting for me, I'd best get back to him. It was nice seeing you both. I hope you're back on patrol in the neighborhood soon."

"We do, too, sir," Billy said. "Have a nice breakfast."

"Did you find out anything?" Jonesy asked when Doug got back to the front.

Doug cringed. *Of course* Jonesy came here to talk to cops, so he expected Doug had been pumping Billy and Patel for information.

"They assume she's guilty," he said. "They asked the names of the officers who arrested her, and I told them we didn't ask."

Jonesy gave him a strange look. "No—but I got their badge numbers."

Doug cringed again. "I wish I'd thought of that."

Jonesy just chuckled. "Let's get a table." He raised his hand, and a middle-aged man approached, probably forty-five to fifty, with light brown hair specked with gray on the sides. He was several inches shorter than Doug, and thin, though with a pronounced gut that was visible from the side.

"Good morning, Mr. Jonesy."

"Morning, Mr. Van. My companion and I would like a table for two, near Sergeant Masterson."

298

Doug pretended not to notice the flash of silver as Jonesy shook the proprietor's hand.

They were halfway through their stacks of pancakes when a police sergeant rose from a nearby table and sauntered over.

"Mr. Van said you might want to see me, Jonesy?" the man said in a working-class English accent. He had thick brown hair and blue eyes, a narrow chin, and a face that might have been handsome were it not for the crooked nose that had clearly never been set after a break.

"Yeah, a couple of Jap constables arrested a Chinese woman this morning, Wong Mei-ling, for the murder of Nakagawa Haruto. I got their badge numbers."

Jonesy slipped Masterson a folded piece of paper. The sergeant half-opened it, glanced inside, then refolded and pocketed it. He nodded toward Doug. "Who's this? He a, uh, 'friend' of yours?"

Doug felt his gut tighten, and he glared at the sergeant without thinking.

Jonesy gave Doug a warning glance before turning back toward the sergeant. "He's an interested party."

"What do you want me to find out?"

"I need details about the murder, for starters," Jonesy said. "Weapon, wounds, method of attack, the works. And anything you can find out about the victim."

Masterson's lips pursed as he considered Jonesy's request. "The Japs are extra sensitive right now, might take a little longer than usual."

"How much longer?"

Masterson shrugged. "Six o'clock. You know where to find me."

Hutson

24

Doug let himself into his apartment, a little sleepy from the pancakes that sat heavy in his stomach. A nap sounded like a great idea. He loosened his tie as he closed the door behind him, and had unbuttoned his collar when he turned around and came face-to-face with Kawakami.

The stout Japanese man still wore his hat, in spite of the stuffy heat indoors, and in his right hand he held a stiletto toward Doug's midsection. He stared at Doug with intense, dark eyes, but said nothing.

"What do you want?" Doug managed to croak after a few seconds.

"Sit," Kawakami ordered, and motioned with the knife toward the kitchen table.

Doug obeyed, glancing toward the kitchen window, open to the fire escape. Would he be fast enough to escape that way before Kawakami could act, or would he take a knife to the backside as he scrambled over the windowsill?

"What do you want?" he repeated as he sat, his voice steadier this time.

"We talk about Wang Yaqiao."

"Who?" Doug asked.

"How you know Jin Shixin?"

"I've never met her," Doug answered.

Kawakami grunted, and his eyes narrowed further. "Why you tell her we come Shanghai from Nagasaki?"

Now Doug was really confused. "Who?"

"You tell Jin Shixin, I and Nakagawa come Shanghai. She tell Wang Yaqiao."

The price of the samurai swords from Nagasaki, Doug thought, remembering the message he'd passed eight months ago.

"I don't know what you mean. I never met Jin Shixin."

A quick slash of Kawakami's hand. A flash of crimson in the corner of Doug's eye, making him look down. A shallow cut across his forearm, blood oozing.

It began to hurt when he saw it. He got up to grab a towel, but Kawakami thrust the stiletto toward his face.

"You talk first."

Doug swallowed hard, his forearm beginning to throb, but sat back down. Obviously Kawakami knew about his delivery, so there was no sense continuing to deny it.

"I didn't tell her that. I didn't know you were back in Shanghai until I saw you at the festival in the spring." Even so, he hardly knew Kawakami's comings and goings in any case, but thought better of saying so. "And it's the truth that I never met Jin Shixin. I was told to deliver a message to a house, and say it was for her. They didn't explain what it meant."

"Who told you take message?"

"I don't know his name."

Kawakami eased the knife forward, grunting.

"He runs a communist cell in Shanghai," Doug said, voice trembling in spite of his best efforts to keep it steady. He was treading into dangerous territory just revealing that much. "But I've never heard his name. I don't know anything about him."

"Describe."

Doug took a deep breath, trying to decide how detailed to be. "He has a little mustache, and short hair—very short, like this." He held his fingers a half-inch apart to demonstrate. "He's very thin, and tall for a Chinese—about my height. Probably thirty or thirty-five years old."

Kawakami grunted. "Zhu Xian."

Doug shrugged. "I don't know his name."

"He order for kill Nakagawa *san*."

That didn't surprise Doug in the least. He just hoped the next hit wasn't ordered on him for spilling the beans.

He was a little surprised that Kawakami knew that, though. Who were his informants?

"I don't know anything about him," Doug said, clasping his right hand over the cut on his left forearm before the blood ran onto the table. He nodded his head back toward the sink behind him. "May I get up to clean my cut?"

Kawakami stared him hard in the eye for a second, then jerked his head once toward the sink.

Doug jumped up from his seat, ran a ragged dishtowel under cold water, and pressed it down on his wound.

The latch of his front door clicked, and he turned his head. Kawakami had slipped out. Doug crept to the front window and peered out from behind his curtains.

Kawakami emerged from the front of the building a moment later.

Almost immediately, the communist cell leader—Zhu Xian, Kawakami had called him—materialized from the shadow at the entrance to the alley across the street where they had found Nakagawa's body.

"Kawakami *san*!" he shouted. "That is your real name, isn't it? A word, please."

Kawakami turned to bolt away, but he was surrounded by four Chinese men in black pants, all shirtless, their upper bodies ripped with sinewy muscles.

Doug spied axes hanging at their hips.

For one tense moment, the scene seemed to hang in suspended animation as Doug watched.

Then Kawakami sprang into action, surprisingly agile for a man of his girth, and kicked at the side of the man who blocked his most direct path to Japantown. The man blocked his kick with a rotation of his own leg, and he brought his arm up to chop at Kawakami's right hand, which held the stiletto.

It skittered across the pavement. Kawakami's forearm hung at an unnatural angle.

Doug watched as if in slow motion as the other three men converged on Kawakami; one swept the Japanese agent's legs out from under him, while another swung his ax.

It made a sickening thud and squish as it buried in Kawakami's midsection. Blood gushed.

The four men in black pants flipped backward like circus performers. They sprinted down the alley where Zhu Xian had stood, and disappeared.

Doug was startled and amazed to see that not one had left a bloody footprint.

Kawakami's head moved from side to side, and his good arm clutched at his bleeding middle. His right arm twitched at his side.

Doug sprinted out of his apartment and down the stairs. As he passed Mr. Hwang's door, he shouted into the store, "Call an ambulance! That man's hurt."

Kawakami's breathing was shallow and ragged when Doug reached him, and crouched over him. His eyes focused on Doug with effort.

"Help is coming," Doug said, careful not to touch him.

He heard police whistles from the direction of Honan Road, coming closer, accompanied by angry shouts in Japanese.

Doug stood and took a step back as a trio of Japanese police constables ran toward them, followed closely by a squad of Japanese marines.

"I saw it happen. I can identify one of the—"

One of the constables shoved him against the wa l. He shouted something furious in Japanese.

Doug felt his stomach drop.

Kawakami's eyes had closed, but his chest moved with short, shallow breaths. The pool of blood around him spread rapidly across the cobblestones.

Shouts in Japanese rose all around, accompanied by more whistles, and then the wail of an ambulance siren.

Two police constables took Doug by the shoulders and hauled him down the block. As they neared Honan Road, Doug recognized the police sergeant from earlier.

"You were found crouching over the body," the sergeant said, in English with a Japanese accent.

"I saw who attacked him," Doug said, but the sergeant cut him off.

"Silence! I am told there was no one else except you. You are under arrest."

He gave an order in Japanese, and one of the constables put handcuffs around Doug's wrists. They grabbed him by the arms and hauled him to a waiting police wagon.

Hutson

25

They took him first to the North District Police station, where a Japanese corporal sat at the front desk. Doug couldn't understand what any of them were saying, since every police officer in attendance spoke Japanese. Then they took him to another room, where a detective came in and told him in English that he was being charged with the attempted murder of Kawakami Takahiro.

Attempted murder. So Kawakami was alive. Doug wanted to ask how he was doing, but thought better of it.

His name was entered into a large book, along with the charge. Doug noticed that the detective made entries in both Japanese and English. *For the American Court.* The Japanese might have imposed martial law on the Hongkou district, but extraterritorial rights were still in force for privileged foreigners such as himself.

They took him back to the wagon and closed him in. Through the barred window in the back, he watched as they drove him downtown. They didn't even pause at the military checkpoint on the bridge.

The wagon pulled into the dock of a large brick building. After it stopped, two constables—one Chinese, the other British—opened the back, and the British constable directed Doug toward a large wooden door, that opened when he approached.

Here, an Indian constable in a red turban took his arm and led him to a cold, windowless room of concrete blocks painted white. A tall middle-aged man in the white uniform of a medical orderly, with a thick curly brown beard and piercing blue eyes took a sheet of paper from the Sikh constable.

"Douglas Bainbridge, American?" the orderly said in a Russian accent.

"Yes."

"Undress, please."

The Sikh constable unlocked the handcuffs, and stood a few feet from Doug, hand on the baton at his hip, watching as Doug removed his clothes.

Once his clothes sat in a pile on the floor, Doug faced the orderly with his hands clasped in front of his privates. He wasn't sure which gave him more unease—his nudity, or the obvious cut on his forearm that had scabbed.

"Step on scale, please."

Doug complied. Cold metal touched his scalp and shoulder blades, and he watched as the orderly shifted weights until the scale balanced.

"One hundred eighty centimeters, seventy-five kilograms," the Russian orderly recited, recording the figures on a form. "Go through here, please."

He motioned toward a door that the Sikh constable opened, leading into another white-walled windowless room. Doug glanced back longingly at his clothes still piled on the floor of the first room, and then the door slammed behind him.

"Mr. Douglas Bainbridge?" a Chinese man read from the form the Sikh officer handed him. He was dressed in brown slacks and blue dress-shirt, with a navy blue necktie; he wore a white coat, and a stethoscope hung around his neck.

"I am Dr. Tang. Stand here. Open mouth. Ahhhh."

Doug did as ordered, and the doctor probed the back of his mouth with a tongue depressor. He looked in Doug's ears, then tilted his head downward and combed through his hair, roughly.

The scalp and hair exam lasted about a minute, but the humiliation seemed to make it last far longer than that.

The doctor's stethoscope on his chest and back was so cold it brought goosebumps.

"Arms up, legs spread."

Doug again did as ordered, casting a side glance at the Sikh constable who stood nearby, keeping close watch. The doctor's hands slid over his body, and Doug felt his cheeks flush hot at the invasiveness of the inspection.

As if it couldn't get worse, the doctor then ordered him to grab the sides of the exam table and bend over. He couldn't help the undignified cry that escaped his lips at the shock and discomfort of the doctor's finger probing inside his anus.

The doctor was more than thorough.

"You are fit and clean," the doctor declared, scribbling notes onto the form in his clipboard.

The Sikh constable opened yet another door, and took Doug by the arm into the next room.

"Mr. Bainbridge, is it?" the thin, mustachioed officer in the next room said in a working-class English accent, reviewing the forms the constable handed him. "A yank, eh? I'm Sergeant Bickford, and I'll be your gaoler for the next few weeks, 'til they get you to trial. You'll be in the Foreign Section. Let's get you into a uniform." He turned to the red-faced man behind him and read off Doug's height and weight.

Doug continued to stand in humiliating nakedness while Bickford read him the jail's regulations. When his assistant finally brought forward a jail uniform, Doug slipped it on gratefully. It was coarse wool, gray, not very comfortable against his skin, but he didn't utter a complaint.

"Just remember where you are, an' we won't have no trouble, understand?" Bickford concluded.

Doug nodded, eyes downcast, but said nothing. He concentrated on sliding his feet into the black slippers.

The Sikh constable handcuffed him again, and took him by the arm. A double set of heavy wooden doors unlocked in turn, momentarily closing them into a tiny atrium in-between, and then opening to a long corridor lined with barred cells.

The cold air conditioning was replaced by stifling heat, accompanied by the stench of body odor, urine and feces. Doug thought he would gag for a moment, but he focused instead on the beads of sweat trickling down the side of his face, and down the center of his back, and the feeling passed.

Inmates shouted in numerous languages, and from time to time Doug's Sikh guard would swing his baton against cell bars, silencing those inside with a loud metallic ring. Once it elicited a sharp cry from an inmate who didn't move his fingers fast enough, followed by a string of curses in what sounded like Italian.

About three quarters of the way down the corridor, they stopped. The guard removed a large key-ring from behind his sash, and unlocked a cell.

It was tiny, about ten feet deep and six feet wide; the metal frame of two bunk beds occupied half of the width. A wooden bench, bolted to the floor, sat opposite, leaving a narrow passage down the center of the cell. A big-built tan-skinned man with curly black hair lounged against the gray plaster wall in back, next to a mildewed toilet, picking at his fingernails. He was shirtless, glistened with sweat, and his black chest hair clung to his skin, soaked.

He straightened and looked at Doug with a careless expression.

"Carvalho, this man is Bainbridge," the Sikh guard said in a lilting Punjabi accent. "New cell mate."

With that, he removed Doug's handcuffs, relocked the cell door with a big brass key, and returned the key-ring to its hiding place behind his heavy embroidered sash.

"Does he speak English?" Doug asked before the guard could move away, just louder than a whisper.

The guard shrugged. "Perhaps. Perhaps not."

Doug felt his stomach drop. "What is he charged with?"

The guard regarded him with an enigmatic look for a moment, then said without inflection, "Raping and beating two Chinese prostitutes last month." With that, he turned and strode back the way they had come.

Doug turned away from the bars, and his new cell mate—Carvalho, the guard had called him—again leaned against the back wall, his massive arms folded over his even more massive chest. He stared at Doug with an expression somewhere between curiosity and faint hostility.

"I'm Doug Bainbridge." He stopped, feeling awkward.

"Joaquim Carvalho."

Doug wasn't sure if his cell mate's tone was indifference, or annoyance. "I'm an American," he tried.

Carvalho gave him one curt nod of understanding. *"Do Brasil."*

Not sure what to do next, Doug pointed at the two bunks, and gave Carvalho a questioning expression.

Carvalho muttered something in Portuguese, now definitely sounding irritated, and pointed from Doug to the lower bunk.

Doug lowered his eyes and nodded, shuffling to the side of the lower bunk and sitting, elbows on his knees, chin in his hands. He stared at the far wall, unblinking.

What a nightmare.

Doug stayed like that for a long time, silent with his thoughts, and Carvalho went back to picking his fingernails. After a while, he moved from the wall, dropped his pants to his ankles, and pissed into the open toilet; shameless.

Doug looked away, and counted the number of cells across the corridor that had a clear view into their own cell. Three, at least.

There was no way he was going to be able to go to the bathroom. He mused without humor that he might die of an exploded bladder first.

Without clocks or windows, the passage of time became a maddening guessing game. After a long time, Doug gave up. His stomach told him he was hungry, but he didn't know if it was evening yet.

Eventually a Russian guard came by with a cart. They could hear its squeaky wheels stopping and starting at each cell for a long time before it showed up in front of them. Carvalho perked up as it drew near, and went to the bars, hanging his arms out in a careless sort of eagerness.

The Russian guard slid two small bundles wrapped in brown paper into their cell, along with two tin cups. Carvalho crouched immediately to retrieve one of each, then sat on the bench to unwrap and eat the sandwich.

Doug got up to fetch the other one, and returned to his bunk. His stomach growled as he unwrapped the paper—but then it turned sour when he looked at the sandwich inside.

One corner of the coarse brown bread had a bluish-green mold; when he turned it over the opposite piece of bread was moldy along one edge. He opened the sandwich to see what was inside, and the sight of wilted brownish lettuce and some mysterious thin slice of grayish meat made him gag.

He tossed it onto his bunk and looked away.

"*Você não quer*?" Carvalho asked in Portuguese, pointing at Doug's discarded food, eyebrows raised in anticipation.

Doug shook his head. "You can have it."

Carvalho leapt from the bench and snatched Doug's sandwich off the bunk before he could change his mind. With his thumb and forefinger, he pinched off the moldy parts of the bread and threw them on the floor, then took a huge bite of the remainder.

Doug looked away, suppressing a gag.

How long would he have to be stuck in here before hunger drove him to similar desperation?

After another long but indeterminate amount of time, a buzzer sounded, and a moment later the lights went out in all of the cells. The corridor lights remained lit, casting eerie shadows from the bars into the semi-darkened cells.

Doug slipped his shirt over his head, balled it up to supplement the thin pillow, and stretched out on top of the covers. He didn't trust the cleanliness of the sheets. He doubted he could sleep anyway, given the way the day kept replaying in his mind.

And there was no fan to alleviate the effects of the hot air that hung heavy and still.

Plus the corridor light cast its beam not far from where his eyes rested, barely within the wall's shadow.

In the semi-darkness, he saw Carvalho step over beside the bunks. Standing barely a foot from where Doug lay, he dropped his pants and kicked them off his feet. He stayed there for a moment, buck naked, while his raised arms tugged at the covers on the upper bunk.

Doug froze, and his heart pounded. His mind raced. The guard had said Carvalho was locked up for rape. And that he'd been here a month. A month with no women. And he was standing right next to Doug, naked, his penis swinging back and forth with every movement he made.

Doug's mouth went dry. He scooted as close to the wall as he could, gaining a couple of extra inches of distance. His racing mind came up with no good options should Carvalho decide to press his physical superiority.

His pulse pounded in his ears.

The big Brazilian stepped onto Doug's mattress, his toes digging into Doug's side. Doug held his breath. Then Carvalho hoisted himself onto the top bunk, and settled onto the mattress.

The rusty metal springs screeched their protest at his weight, and Doug's eyes grew wide at how far they sagged in the middle.

Those springs and a two-inch mattress were all that kept him from being crushed by a Brazilian who might as well have been carved from stone.

He wouldn't get a wink of sleep.

26

Saturday, September 26

Doug was awakened by a loud buzzer. A few seconds later, the lights clicked on in the cells, and he squinted against the sudden brightness.

He was shocked he'd slept at all.

Carvalho's thick legs swung over the side of the bunk, and his naked frame jumped down into the narrow space between Doug's bunk and the wooden bench. He stood there and stretched for several agonizingly long seconds. Then he turned, scratching his balls, and walked the few steps to the toilet and began to piss.

The sound made Doug's own bladder ache, though he'd barely touched the cup of bitter tea served with dinner the night before.

Carvalho returned to the side of the bed a moment later, still nude, and tugged at the sheets of the upper bunk. It was a repeat of the previous night's performance, though making the bed this time.

A few moments later, guards came down both sides of the corridor, batons banging across the cell bars as they went.

"Wash time!" British and Indian voices shouted at regular intervals as they went.

Doug got up, conscious that his cellmate stood in the center of the little cell. He averted his eyes while he smoothed the covers of his bunk—beds were to be neatly made every morning, Sergeant Bickford had instructed yesterday.

A cart came by, and a bearded Russian guard passed out ragged towels. The British guard who accompanied him scowled at Doug.

"Drop your trousers, inmate."

Doug had to stop himself from asking why, and did as ordered. He clasped his hands in front of his privates and stared at the floor.

The British guard made an exasperated noise. "You daft? Don't leave the bloody things around your ankles, inmate! You'll look like a baffoon tryin' to walk to the washroom that way, wontcha?"

Doug's face flushed as he crouched down to slip his pants off his feet. He kept his eyes on the ground when he tossed them onto his bunk. He took the towel offered by the Russian guard without looking up.

He supposed these guards had a thousand ways to humiliate new inmates. Petty despots ruling over an incarcerated kingdom.

They were ordered out of the cell, and joined a double line of two dozen inmates in the corridor, all in the same state of undress. Doug held his towel in front of himself in a meagre attempt at modesty.

The wash room sat around two corners from their cell block. Its concrete floor was damp, but felt cool against the soles of Doug's feet. Six wash basins lined the far wall, and they sorted into six lines of four each. A long plank of bare wood formed a sort of shelf over the sinks where they could lay their towels. They were allowed just two minutes apiece to splash themselves with water from the faucets, and hand-scrub arm pits, chests, crotches, butts.

Doug got sorted at the end of a line, behind Carvalho. When finished, those in front circled out to the corridor where the guards waited, and those behind them stepped forward.

Doug was second in line when he noticed the diminutive man directly beside him in the line to the right was looking at him. His eyes seemed focused on Doug's chest. He was short and slender, and his complexion was a shade darker than Doug's, but a shade lighter than Carvalho's. He looked away when he saw Doug watching him.

Doug's throat tightened, and he scowled.

Less than a minute later, he caught the young man staring at him again, and this time his dark eyes wandered slowly downward. When he caught Doug watching him this time, he didn't look away, but held Doug's gaze for a second, a hint of smile on the corners of his lips.

Doug scowled again and looked forward.

Their turn came, and he stepped up to the sink. He felt awkward setting his towel on the shelf, leaving himself fully exposed to his neighbor's unwanted inspection.

Which he noticed that he received.

The young man looked furtively back at the doorway, where a Sikh guard stood facing more outward than in.

He splashed water under his arms and took the opportunity to glance over at Doug. "*Bonjour*," he said, quiet. Then he added, still quiet but less tentative, "Hello."

"Hello," Doug muttered, facing forward.

"I am Laurent," the young man whispered.

Doug considered ignoring him, but after a few seconds he replied with just first name. "Doug." He kept his eyes on the sink and the running water.

The guard announced time was up, and Doug shut off the tap and quickly dried, then hurried to take his place in the corridor.

He could barely believe it, but he felt relieved to get back to his cell a moment later. He doubted he'd ever dressed so fast in his life.

About an hour after breakfast—which consisted of a small bowl of thin gruel and a tin cup of bitter tea—the guards came down the corridor unlocking cells. "Exercise time!" they shouted at each cell.

They lined up in the corridor again, clothed this time, but the same two dozen inmates in the same two lines. They were led out, past the washroom and through a double set of heavy wooden doors to an enclosed yard—surprisingly large and open, Doug thought.

"No talking, you nits!" an English guard shouted at them as they emerged into the sunlight.

Doug raised his face toward the sun and savored it for one precious moment, and then walked around to work the stiffness out of his legs. He looked up at the brick walls around the yard, and wondered behind which one Wong Mei-ling was kept.

He spotted the young Frenchman glancing at him from the corner of the yard, and studiously ignored him. Doug walked in random concentric circles, minding his own business.

The Frenchman—Laurent—started walking in seemingly random patterns as well, though Doug noticed that they passed frequently. Each time, Laurent tried to catch his eye, but Doug always looked elsewhere.

After a while, on one of their close passes, Laurent whispered "You are very pretty." His French accent made the stage whisper sound comical, but Doug wasn't amused. He walked toward the edge of the yard and leaned against a wall.

From here he could observe the other inmates. They were a mixed bunch, though all but one were white. Most were English or American, judging by the surnames the guards called them by. A few wore thick, long beards; clearly Russians. One was Japanese. A few others had surnames that sounded vaguely Italian or Spanish.

He noticed little clusters that gradually coalesced, never too close, never obvious, but clear enough if you paid attention. Whenever the guards were looking elsewhere, they would whisper for a moment, and then look down and kick the dirt when the guards' gaze returned their way.

Doug hoped he wouldn't be here long enough to crave that tiny bit of human contact. *Please God, get me out of here soon.*

The lone Frenchman—Manigault, the guards called him—stood beside the groundskeeper's shed, almost opposite from Doug; and from here he kept an obvious eye on Doug. Doug tried to avoid eye contact, but once he caught Laurent's eye as he looked around. The young man nodded, in the direction of a narrow gap between the shed and the wall. As Doug watched, he looked around quickly, then disappeared into the darkness of the gap.

Doug could surmise the young man's intentions. He would *definitely* never be *that* desperate, he told himself.

Not long after they had been locked in their cells after an hour of exercise, a sandy-haired guard came by and unlocked their door.

"Bainbridge, your lawyer's here to see you," he said in a harsh working-class English accent.

After a second's surprise, Doug got up from the cot and stepped into the corridor. He could guess who the attorney was. The guard relocked the cell, and led Doug through the double wooden doors at the entrance to the cell block. From there, he led him to a room with a big window.

Kenny sat at the metal table, wearing his best black suit and matching necktie.

The gaoler Bickford stood next to the table, chatting in a manner that would appear amiable to someone who didn't know better.

"Ah, Mr. Bainbridge, do come in," he said, overly solicitous. "Mr. Traywick here has presented himself as your attorney. I'll leave you to it. Take as much time as you need, and knock when you're finished."

"May I assume that window is sound-proofed?" Kenny asked Bickford, his tone short, suspicious.

"Of course, sir."

Kenny looked at Doug. "Mr. Bainbridge, would you please return to the corridor for a moment? Sergeant Bickford, remain here please, and close the door."

Doug waited outside with the guard, and watched through the window as Kenny and Bickford talked for a moment. Then Kenny looked at the mirror and waved them in. Bickford opened the door.

"Mr. Bainbridge, did you hear anything Sergeant Bickford and I said just now?"

"No, not a word," Doug said, shaking his head.

Kenny nodded at Bickford, firm, dismissive. "Thank you, sergeant."

Bickford's nod was curt, and he closed the door.

"I can't begin to say how glad I am to see you," Doug said with a big grin, taking the seat across the table from Kenny. "How did you find out I was here?"

"Your landlord saw your arrest through the front windows," Kenny said, sounding short, professional. Hardly friendly. "The Japanese lifted the curfew last night and withdrew to their ships, in case you hadn't heard."

Doug shook his head. How would he have heard that, when he'd been in jail the whole time?

"Arrests have been made for each Japanese assassinated this year, so they announced that their martial intervention had been successful, and they pulled back. With the restrictions on movement lifted, Lucy went to your place and Hwang told her what he saw. She called me straight away."

"How is she doing?"

"She's worried, as you might imagine."

"Of course," Doug said, quiet. He hated worrying her. "What did you tell her?"

"I told her I would take on your case, at least long enough to get you out of jail." He opened his briefcase, pulled out a manila folder and opened it. "It took some doing, but I managed to get the police records about the crime, and your supposed involvement in it. It was a little difficult—there was a lot of confusion at the North District Precinct, with the shift from a temporarily all-Japanese constabulary to the regular staffing."

Doug managed a half-smile. "I can imagine."

Kenny looked down, and concentrated on the papers in the folder. "The good news is, the evidence against you is thin, and all circumstantial. You were seen with the victim, and within a few moments of his attack, given the state of blood loss. No one else was in the street at the time. However, there wasn't even a trace of blood on your clothes, aside from a tear on your sleeve that corresponds to a cut on your own arm—which makes it unrealistic to suppose you were the attacker. And only a small amount at the tips of your shoes, which would be consistent with where you were standing."

He closed the file, folded his hands on top of it, and looked at Doug with a gaze that was cool, professional.

"The Japanese are being cagey about supposed motive—but we shouldn't have any trouble getting the American Court to dismiss the charges. We've got a hearing set for this afternoon at three o'clock. The American judge has already signed the Writ of Habeas Corpus, so I should have you released very soon now."

The wave of relief that washed over Doug was almost overwhelming. He felt his eyes start to well up, and a lump form at the back of his throat. He managed to croak "Thank you, Kenny."

"Happy to oblige." Kenny sat stiff in his chair, his hands still folded on top of the manila file, and his face was stony.

An awkward silence fell over them for a moment.

"You're a little sun burnt," Kenny said at last. He moved one finger to point up at Doug's face, without unfolding his hands.

Doug hadn't realized, but supposed he shouldn't be surprised. "We were allowed an hour of exercise outside. I wasn't given a hat."

Kenny nodded, and fell silent for a few more seconds. "Have they treated you well, otherwise?"

No, they humiliated the hell out of me, wouldn't let me talk with anyone outside of my cell, and fed me slop suitable for swine. Doug managed a weak smile instead and said, "Well enough, but I won't be sorry to leave."

Kenny nodded, but his expression remained fixed, his lips a tight line. "That's understandable."

Something was wrong. Doug couldn't imagine Kenny was this stiff and formal with every client, least of all a friend. It was beyond mere professionalism.

"Is everything alright?" he asked, raising one eye brow and scrutinizing Kenny's face.

"I'm sure it will be, once we have that hearing this afternoon. There's nothing to worry about. I think it's a pretty open and shut case."

Doug's heart sank a little. He nodded, looking down at the table as a faint sense of sadness dampened the joy he had felt a few moments ago. "That's good."

"Do you have any other questions for me? About your case, or the hearing?"

That last was tacked on deliberately. "No, I don't think so."

"Good. Let's get you released, then. The gaoler should have processed the Habeas Corpus by now." Kenny stood and motioned toward the door. He knocked, and a guard opened it.

Doug walked out the front door of the jail next to Kenny a half-hour later. It felt good to be back in his own clothes. It felt even better to know that he was free again.

"I can't thank you enough, really," Doug said, taking his friend's hand and shaking it with enthusiasm. "I know American law isn't your forte, but I appreciate your help more than you can know. Really I do."

He clasped his other hand on top of Kenny's for a moment, and briefly shook it with both hands.

Kenny pulled his hand away. He gave Doug a formal nod of acknowledgment. "Anything for a friend," he said, though his tone was far from friendly.

Kenny's manner still nagged at Doug. He'd been stiff and formal during the entire process of signing Doug out, bordering on coldness.

This was more than would be warranted solely by Kenny's role as his attorney.

Obviously Lucy spoke to Kenny last night, to ask his help after learning of Doug's arrest—but he was sure she wouldn't have told Kenny that Doug knew about his feelings.

No, Lucy wouldn't betray his confidence.

"Come back to my office," Kenny said. "We need to go over the details of your case, to prepare for your hearing at three o'clock. We shouldn't have any trouble, but it can be difficult to predict what the judge might ask."

"I'd like to go see Lucy, if there's time," Doug said as they started walking.

"She'll be at your hearing this afternoon."

They walked in silence for several blocks. It was awkward, and Doug couldn't shake the uneasy feeling that Kenny knew that he knew. But how? He was *certain* Lucy wouldn't have betrayed his confidence. He trusted her.

When they got to their office building, Kenny opened the door, and for an awkward second hesitated in place before taking a step back to motion Doug in first. When they got to his office one floor up, he was stiff when he opened the door and held it for Doug.

Inside he got right to business, almost brusque.

"First things first—I don't believe you attacked that man, this Takahiro Kawakami. But I do believe that you know him, and the judge is certain to ask that. I can't advise you to lie."

"I understand," Doug said, not elaborating.

Kenny waited a few seconds, and when Doug didn't add anything he continued. "I assume he's some sort of spy, given the few things you've said in the past. The next logical conclusion is that you must be some sort of spy yourself, Douglas. Is that an unreasonable conclusion?"

Doug sat perfectly still. "I'm not a spy."

Kenny's eyes narrowed, and he regarded Doug with some suspicion for several seconds. Then he sat forward and folded his hands on the desk, again stiff and formal.

"Remember that this conversation is privileged, and cannot be repeated to anyone without your consent. I need for you to be completely truthful and forthcoming with me, so we can avoid any surprises in court."

Doug stared back at Kenny, holding his gaze until his tall friend looked away. "If Kawakami were a spy, the Japanese would hardly admit that, would they? It's about as likely to come up at my hearing as my relationship to you."

A pained look flitted across Kenny's face for half a second, and was gone almost as soon as it appeared.

But to Doug it spoke volumes.

Kenny took a deep breath. "The victim—Mr. Kawakami—is alive, but unconscious at St. Luke's Hospital. He lost a great deal of blood, but according to George there was minimal internal damage. He should live." Doug's surprise must have registered in his eyes, because Kenny explained. "I called George last night and asked him to check in at the hospital. He said that the axe missed any vital organs, thanks to Mr. Kawakami's extensive girth."

Doug nodded, but said nothing.

"Since he's in a coma and can't identify his attacker, there is no solid evidence linking you to the attack. Is it safe to presume he won't name you as his attacker if and when he awakens?"

Doug nodded again. "He won't name me, I assure you."

Kenny attempted a smile that didn't reach his pale green eyes. "Then this should be a piece of cake. You needn't worry about re-arrest, or going back to that jail cell."

"I'm glad of *that*!" Doug said with a grin, attempting levity. But Kenny's smile remained fixed, cool.

Doug had grown increasingly uncomfortable with Kenny's manner since the jail. He couldn't take it any longer. "Kenny, why are you acting so distant? Something's wrong that you're not telling me."

Kenny attempted a laugh and looked away, but Doug stared at his face until he looked back.

Kenny's mouth was set tight, his eyes flashing. "Alright, for starters, you've been blowing me off for two weeks now, with no explanation. No communication, even. You're supposed to be my best friend, Douglas—I can't remember any time in the last year when we've gone more than a couple of days without speaking, let alone two whole weeks. So it seems you should be telling *me* why, not the other way around."

Doug deflated. He couldn't argue. "I don't know what I can say."

Kenny was fired up now, his voice raised. "*You're* the one who's been distant lately, not me! And with *no explanation!* Why are you so surprised that I would react in kind?"

Doug shrank back in his seat. The virulence of the verbal assault took all of the wind out of him.

And so did the truth of it.

"Kenny," he began, but then stopped, unsure how to proceed.

"Do go on," Kenny said, his eyes cold and hard.

Doug hesitated, at a loss for words. He looked down at the table. What could he say? Definitely not the truth. Kenny would be mortified, and Doug wasn't sure he could get the words out of his mouth in any case.

He squirmed in the silence.

"I mean...there's not really a good reason. I just...I don't know how to describe it...it's just..." He let his voice trail off, and shrugged, not sure what else to do.

When he glanced up, he saw fear in Kenny's eyes, despite the stony set of his lips and jaw.

He knew.

Doug's heart broke for his friend, and for a moment he forgot to be offended. His voice was quiet as he said, "I don't know what to say, Kenny."

The terror spread from Kenny's eyes to the rest of his face. "Doug—" he began, voice cracking. He looked away, then leapt from his seat and faced out the window.

He stood there for a long moment, perfectly still.

When he turned slowly toward Doug, he seemed to be holding himself together with great difficulty. His hands trembled. "How did you find out?" he asked, barely above a whisper.

Doug stayed silent, not wanting to confirm.

"Pretending you don't know what I'm talking about only prolongs my torture, you know." Kenny began pacing, hands fidgeting.

Part of Doug wanted to tell his friend that Jonesy had figured it out and blabbed, to end the torture of uncertainty; another part of him hadn't the foggiest idea how to begin to say those words. While the conflict raged on the inside, he sat still, silent.

Almost paralyzed.

"I know this makes you uncomfortable, and I'm sorry," Kenny said, finally looking at Doug. His eyes were pleading, and there was a faint tremble in his voice. "The last thing I would ever want to do is make you uncomfortable. That's why I never—" his voice trailed off.

All Doug could manage was a weak half-smile.

"Well...you know what I mean. I know you do, so don't even deny it. I wish things were different, you know. I wish I didn't feel—" Kenny's voice caught, and a startled sort of look came to his face. He took a deep breath, and continued slowly and deliberately—"the way that I feel. I'd change it if I could, you know."

"I know," Doug said, barely above a whisper.

"You believe me, don't you, Dougie?"

He managed another half-smile. "I believe you."

Kenny started pacing again, though not as agitated this time. Words tumbled out of his mouth like water over the cobblestones during a thunderstorm.

"When we first met at that party at the Sassoon House last summer, and you spent a while talking with me and Abbie—you were so nice, and I was drawn to you. You have to know how magnetic you are. You were interesting, and handsome, and you were interested in talking to *me*. And since you came with that reporter friend of yours, Mr. Jones—I mean, I could tell right away what sort he was, and so I thought maybe there was a chance, you know? I mean, just in the back of my mind, that's all. You know what I mean, don't you? Oh God, I'm putting this badly. It's just, I wanted to get to know you after that—*we* wanted to get to know you. Abbie and I. Both of us. And of course I figured out right away that I'd been...overzealous in my assumptions about your association with Mr. Jones. And we really did come to care for you as a dear, dear friend.

"And then we met Lucy, and she was wonderful, and everyone could see how meant for each other the two of you are, and so—well, I just buried it, you see. It didn't have to mean anything. It doesn't have to mean anything now, does it?"

He stopped suddenly, and stared at Doug, his eyes pleading.

Doug shrugged, no idea what to say. He felt overwhelmed.

Kenny started pacing again. "Abbie knew, of course. She knows everything. She figured it out in no time, and I don't hide things from her. I told her not to say anything to Lucy, that it would surely ruin our friendship—and you *have* to know that I value that above almost anything—but Abbie isn't easily deterred when she gets a notion to do something. You know how she is, you've seen it."

Doug had to chuckle. "I've seen it."

The look of relief that washed over Kenny's face, and the way his shoulders sort of sagged from the release of tension, made Doug's heart break.

"I can't help it, you know. It's always been this way. *I've* always been this way. Since adolescence. I never could decide who I wanted more, the girls or the boys."

Doug felt himself tense, but willed himself to relax. This couldn't be easy for Kenny to admit out loud. He wouldn't make it worse by appearing uncomfortable.

"Of course I always knew only one was realistic. Well—*usually* only one was realistic. There were some, I mean...oh, never mind. But Abbie was the first person who made me feel like I wasn't a freak for it. I didn't tell her, you know—she guessed. She always figures everything out. One of the smartest people I've ever known, and she never misses *a thing*. Well, you know her."

Doug nodded. "That's true."

"And she helped me know I wasn't alone." He stopped, stood very straight and tall as he faced Doug, shoulders squared. "It doesn't have to be a dichotomy. It's a lot more common than you think, Dougie. That's all I'll say."

Doug found that doubtful. But then he thought about everyone he'd known over the years, from Brent Aleshire at boarding school, to Washington D.C. and the young men he had interrupted in a public men's room on the National Mall; and now in Shanghai with Jonesy, Charlie Ford and Bao, Kenny and Abbie—hell, Lucy had admitted she'd experimented, and wasn't averse to further exploration.

It all seemed too much. He went numb.

"Thank you for your honesty, Kenny," he said, quiet. He didn't know what else to say.

Kenny looked sad, but just nodded and quietly said, "You're welcome."

After a second of awkward silence, Doug stood and extended his hand toward Kenny, but wouldn't look him directly in the eye. "Thank you again for getting me released. I really appreciate all the work you've done for me today. I won't forget it, I promise. I owe you one, Kenny."

Kenny nodded, a sort of resignation coming to his face. "You're welcome, Doug. Still friends?"

Doug faked a smile and nodded more vigorously than was needed. "Of course we are."

Doug spotted Lucy as he and Kenny walked into the downtown building used by the American Court for China. She had her hands clasped on a little purse in front of her, knuckles white, and her eyes looked worried.

When she spied him approaching, her expression melted, and she rushed to meet him. She threw her arms around him and squeezed so tight he couldn't take a deep breath.

"Oh my God, Doug, I was so worried!" she whispered, breathless. Then she pulled back far enough to look in his face, and the concern returned to her eyes. "Are you alright? Did they mistreat you?"

"I'm fine," he said, giving her a reassuring smile. "No mistreatment, I promise. Kenny here wouldn't have allowed it."

She let go of Doug long enough to give Kenny a kiss on the cheek and thank him again, and then slid her arm through Doug's and held it tightly.

Inside the courtroom, Doug and Kenny checked in with the bailiff, a stocky mustachioed fellow probably in his mid-thirties. The bailiff marked Doug off on the list, and directed him to sit in the front row. Kenny was told to take a seat in the gallery, and he sat next to Lucy.

A handful of other defendants waited in the front row. All but one of them was white, while the other was a young black man. Doug had only seen a few black men in Shanghai since he'd arrived more than a year ago, and he supposed that made this young defendant conspicuous; he wondered how difficult it would be for him to get an acquittal.

He didn't recognize any of these men from jail, and assumed they must have been kept in a different cell block.

The judge arrived—a dour-looking man in black robes, about fifty years old—and he read a general statement about the presumption of innocence and the burden of proof.

Two cases were called before Doug's—both burglary, and neither represented by a lawyer. Both were granted bail in the amount of two hundred dollars. The amount seemed high to Doug, and given the way both men were dressed, probably prohibitively so to them.

The judge must be in a bad mood, he surmised. Perhaps because he was forced to work on a Saturday.

Butterflies appeared in his stomach as if from nowhere when his name and case number were called.

They settled down a bit when Kenny stood at his side.

"Kenneth Traywick, counsel for the defense," Kenny said, and Doug noticed an absence of his usual Canadian accent.

"How does your client plea?" the judge asked, not sounding particularly interested.

"We are moving for immediate dismissal," Kenny said, and Doug wasn't sure he'd ever heard his friend sound more forceful. "Mr. Bainbridge had no weapon, and none was found at the scene. There was no blood on Mr. Bainbridge's person or his clothing, making his personal involvement in the attack impossible."

"There was blood found on his shoes," the prosecutor replied.

"Which is consistent with kneeling beside an injured man to determine life or death, as Mr. Bainbridge did."

The judge asked a few more questions, and then dismissed the charges with a bang of the gavel.

Lucy looked overjoyed when Doug turned around. She rose to meet him, and took his arm. Then Doug saw Jonesy sitting in the back row by the door. The reporter rose as they passed him.

"I've got to file for a copy of the dismissal," Kenny said as they walked through the doors. "I'll meet you back here in ten minutes."

Jonesy followed them out, and Kenny walked down the hall.

"I'm glad you've been cleared." He sounded a bit perfunctory. "I'm not surprised, but these things are never a guarantee."

"I'm surprised to see you here, Jonesy," Doug said. "I didn't think bail hearings were your beat. I can't imagine papers in the States being interested in that kind of story from the wire service."

"I'm writing a feature about all the arrests for Japanese assassinations, smart ass," Jonesy said, gruff. "Yours is part of that. Readers in the States will be *very* interested in an American being swept up in this business."

Momentary panic swept through Doug's midsection. He could just imagine Commander Shock's reaction to Doug's name being in the papers.

Especially being associated with a Japanese secret agent. Even if that part wasn't publicized.

He stopped and grabbed Jonesy's arm. "You have to leave my name out of it."

Jonesy scowled at Doug's hand on his forearm. "I can't. It's news."

Thinking again of Shock's reaction, Doug tried a bit of a bluff—one that was actually realistic. "If you try it, they'll make your service pull the story before it ever gets sent. *And* they'll have you on the next ship to the States. So long, Shanghai. You want that?"

Jonesy's eyes narrowed. "That would violate the First Amendment, and you know it."

"You think they'll care?" Doug held Jonesy's stare, and refused to blink.

After a long moment, Jonesy broke the stare, and swore under his breath. "Can I give you an alias, at least?"

"No," Doug said, keeping his voice firm, commanding even. "And no mention of Kawakami, either. Nothing about him at all, understand?"

"Can't you talk to those sons-of-bitches you report to? Let me at least print a little something?"

Doug shook his head. "Not a chance."

Jonesy swore under his breath again. Then he looked at Lucy and apologized.

Lucy waved it off. "It would take stronger language than that to shock me, Jonesy." Her tone was matter-of-fact, even brusque. Doug wondered if her attitude toward Jonesy was lingering anger about what he'd said.

Jonesy gave her a curious stare for a few seconds, then turned back to Doug.

"Maybe I have something to bargain with."

Doug arched an eyebrow. "Oh?"

Jonesy smirked. "Yeah. I've learned a thing or two about Wong Mei-Ling and that Japanese agent she's accused of killing. Wanna hear it? Then you've got to give me something in return."

27

It ate Doug up inside that Jonesy knew something about Wong Mei-Ling's innocence—or guilt—that he didn't, but he couldn't do anything about it.

"I can't make any guarantees, you know that."

Jonesy chuckled, and faked an innocent look. "Then I guess I'll have to keep it to myself." He turned to walk away, but lingered nonetheless.

Doug held out as long as he dared, and noticed that Jonesy was barely shuffling away.

"Alright," he called, and waited for Jonesy to come back. Ignoring the smirk on Jonesy's face, he continued quietly, "If you tell me what you know about Mei-Ling, I'll tell you what I saw when Kawakami was attacked."

He ignored the scowl on Lucy's face.

Jonesy seemed to weigh this. "Maybe what you saw isn't news to me," he said, eyeing Doug with an enigmatic expression. "*Maybe* what you have to tell me is worth something, and maybe it's not—so you go first, and we'll see if it's worth telling you what I know."

Damn it, Jonesy! "I reckon I don't have much choice, do I?"

Jonesy crossed his arms. "Nope."

"Alright then, here's what I saw from my apartment window. Four men surrounded Kawakami when he left my building. They wore black pants, axes strapped to their belts, and they were bare-chested. The only man I recognized was Zhu Xian, the Communist cell leader. He was dressed in gray, as usual. He called to Kawakami by name, and said something about that being his real name. When Kawakami tried to fight his way out of the circle, they ganged up on him and took him down with an axe to the gut."

Jonesy stroked his chin, looking up in thought. "Interesting. Axe Gang, then? Or meant to look like Axe Gang?"

"I wish I knew," Doug said.

"Either the Reds are working with the Axe Gang, coordinating efforts—or they're framing a criminal element to diffuse attention from themselves. Either could fit."

"Wouldn't it make more sense that they're cooperating?" Lucy asked. "Maybe they weren't at first, but once they realized they both want the Japanese out of China, they started working together. Isn't that the most logical?"

Jonesy's eyes narrowed. "It's one logical option. But not the only one."

"But isn't it more likely?" Lucy insisted. "Why assume the communists would frame a criminal gang?"

"Because the Reds are good at that," Jonesy said.

Lucy looked unconvinced. "Do their interests align?"

"We don't know for certain," Doug said.

"Oh, come on, Doug! You think they don't both want the Japanese gone from China?" Lucy crossed her arms. "That seems to be pretty universal. Communists, Nationalists, criminals, and every other Chinese down to the peasant rice farmers in little villages across the country—the one thing they all have in common is a hatred of the Japanese. Isn't that right?"

She turned her ire to Jonesy. "And if the communists wanted to frame a criminal gang for the assassinations, wouldn't it make more sense for them to frame the Green Gang, who has ties to corrupt government officials? That would kill two birds with one stone, don't you think? Why frame a different criminal gang—an enemy of the one allied with their Nationalist enemies? How would that advance their cause? Who was it who said *'The enemy of my enemy is my friend?'"*

Doug and Jonesy both stared at her, momentarily speechless.

Lucy gave Doug a wry half-smile. "Close your mouth, darling."

"That's an ancient proverb," Jonesy grumbled.

"And as true today as ever, I should think," Lucy retorted.

Doug recovered from the momentary shock of Lucy's demonstration. "OK, let's say we assume that the communists are in fact working with the Axe Gang, coordinating attacks on Japanese citizens in China—now what?"

Jonesy pointed his cigar at Doug. "What if I told you the murder of Nakagawa didn't fit with that pattern?"

That piqued Doug's interest. "Go on."

"Sergeant Masterson did some digging—don't know his sources, don't care. What he found is pretty interesting. First, there were no witnesses, so no way to know if the killer had an axe with him or not. Nakagawa was shot twice at close range. The ballistics suggest a very small pistol, easily concealed. No one in the building heard the shots, so the gun probably had a suppressor. That ain't cheap. As far as I know, the local reds don't have any."

"Then that should clear Miss Wong," Lucy said.

"The *Juntong*?" Doug ventured.

"Seems plausible to me," Jonesy said, and put his cigar back in his mouth with a satisfied nod.

"Then Mei-ling's the scapegoat." Doug's stomach sank.

"Mind if I stay with you tonight?" Doug asked Lucy as they reached her building.

Partly he just wanted to spend the night with her, since they hadn't had the opportunity during the Japanese occupation of the district. But also, he wasn't sure he wanted to go back to his apartment yet.

"Not at all," she said, a gleam in her eye as she smiled at him. "I figured you'd want to."

He fell asleep curled up behind Lucy, his body wrapped around hers like a perfect puzzle piece. A feeling of contentment washed over him as he drifted off, and he slept soundly, even in the warm and muggy night.

Sometime in the middle of the night he dreamed that he was back in the jail cell. Guards were shouting orders at him, and he couldn't seem to obey fast enough. His heart pounded, and he felt his hands tremble. Their orders grew ever more preposterous, and flew at him like darts in an English pub.

At some point, he looked down at the floor and realized with alarm that he was naked. He turned around, and Joaquim Carvalho leaned against the wall in the corner, picking his fingernails; but he looked up at Doug and leered at him. Then he dropped his trousers, kicked them off, and sauntered toward him.

Doug fled as far as the bars on the cell door. He could feel the cold metal against his skin. He called to the guards for help, but they seemed to have disappeared.

"Don't worry Dougie, I'm here," Kenny's voice said. Doug turned around and saw his friend standing there in his best suit. They were in a white room now, and Kenny smiled and patted his bare shoulder. "I'll get you home, buddy."

Then they were in Doug's apartment, in his bedroom. Doug was in bed, facing the window, just as he had fallen asleep at Lucy's apartment. Only Lucy wasn't wrapped up in his arms. He wondered where she'd gone, and turned his head and saw Kenny crawl into bed behind him.

"Don't worry, Dougie, I'm here for you."

Kenny was naked, too. But Doug didn't look away, and he didn't feel afraid, either. He felt calm, peaceful, safe even. Kenny wrapped his arms around Doug and pressed up against him. Doug could feel Kenny's skin on his. He could feel the texture of it, soft and warm, but different from Lucy's with little hairs.

Kenny's hands rubbed his chest, sending tingles down his spine. His hands moved down Doug's abdomen, and Doug felt his stomach flutter. Then Kenny kissed his neck, and his lips were soft.

"I knew you loved me, Dougie," he whispered. Then his hand slid down to Doug's groin...

Doug bolted upright in Lucy's bed, body drenched with sweat, gasping for breath. It took a second to remember where he was. He noticed with irritation that he was aroused, and not just a little.

He took a deep breath, closed his eyes, and tried to relax. Try as he might, he couldn't avoid the memory of how Kenny's skin had felt next to his, how his hands had felt on his body.

Son of a bitch!

"Doug? Are you alright?" Lucy's sleepy voice asked in the darkness.

A wave of panic swept through him, and it took a second for him to reassure himself that she had no idea what he had just dreamed.

"I'm fine," he said, too harsh.

She sat up, and in the dimness he could see the outline of her head, looking at him. "Are you sure?"

He had to smile at her concern, and he stroked her arm. "I'm sure." His penis was still rigid, so after a second's hesitation he rolled on top of her.

"Oh!" she said, almost a small squeal. "Again?"

"Why not?" he whispered, and nibbled her ear.

She relaxed under him, and her legs moved to wrap around his. "Why not, indeed."

He knew how to get that dream out of his mind.

Hutson

28

Sunday, September 27

Doug awoke earlier than he would have liked. His sleep had been fitful, and once the daylight streamed around the edges of the curtains he wasn't able to stay asleep.

Lucy stirred while he was getting dressed. She looked at the clock on the bedside table.

"It's only eight o'clock," she murmured, sleepy. "Come back to bed."

"I can't," he said, leaning down to stroke her hair. "I have things I need to do today."

"On a Sunday?" She sat up and gave him a curious look.

The sight of her bare breasts made him reconsider for a moment.

"My eyes are up here." She crossed her arms and arched an eyebrow.

Chagrined, he had to smile. He met her gaze. "I need to find out who tried to kill Kawakami, or I won't be entirely off the hook. And perhaps at the same time, I can prove that Wong Mei-ling didn't kill Nakagawa."

"I'm coming with you." She threw the sheet back and bolted from bed.

"You don't have to," Doug said as she slipped into her bathrobe. "You can stay in bed, and I'll come see you this afternoon."

"Don't be silly," she said, and kissed him on the cheek. She grabbed her bath kit and walked out.

"Where to?" she asked as they left a short while later.

"The alley where Nakagawa was killed."

"What are we looking for?"

"I'm not sure," Doug admitted. "I hope something stands out when we get there."

"And if not?"

He shrugged. "Maybe we can talk to Wong Mei-ling's roommates, or bribe her landlord to let us into her apartment."

When they reached the spot in front of the building, they spent a few minutes looking closely at the ground, but nothing stood out. A middle-aged Chinese woman came out with a wooden spoon in one hand. She crossed her arms and looked at them with suspicion.

"What wantchee?" she asked in Pidgin.

Doug bowed and answered in Shanghainese. "I am a friend of Wong Mei-ling, who lives in this building."

A look of surprise crossed the woman's eyes, followed by a veil of wariness. "She is not home."

"I know. She's in trouble, and I'm trying to help her." Doug wasn't sure how much the woman knew.

She uncrossed her arms and wagged the wooden spoon at him. "I don't want more trouble with the police."

"I'm not with the police. I just want to help my friend."

The woman's eyes looked over his shoulder, and he turned around to see Jonesy standing a few feet away.

"Doug, Lucy—what are you two doing here?"

"Probably the same thing you are," Lucy said, demure.

Jonesy chuckled. "How's that going?"

Lucy made a face. "Don't ask me—Doug's speaking Chinese again."

Jonesy looked at Doug and shook his head, a 'Tsk, Tsk' sort of look on his face. "Why not just use Pidgin like everyone else? Then we could all understand what's going on. You big show-off."

Jonesy addressed himself to the Chinese woman beyond Doug. "Hiya, Missy Deng."

"Hiya, Mista Jonesy."

Doug supposed he shouldn't be surprised that Jonesy and the woman knew each other.

"Wong Mei-ling catchee bad pidgin, savvy?" Jonesy asked.

The woman nodded. "Savvy."

"My wantchee talkee Missy Fu and Missy Yang. Them have got?"

The woman shook her head. "No, them no have got. Two piece."

"Two piece? What fashion?"

She shrugged. "No savvy."

Doug never used Pidgin, so he had to work hard to keep up with the conversation. He turned to Jonesy. "She says they haven't been here for two days?"

Jonesy smirked. "That's right. Miss Fu and Miss Yang are Miss Wong's roommates, in case you weren't aware. Seems they disappeared about the time Miss Wong was arrested. Mrs. Deng here is the landlady, and she doesn't know where they went."

"They probably felt they were in danger," Lucy said. "Not that I can blame them."

Doug wasn't feeling as charitable. "They left Mei-ling to take the fall," he muttered.

Jonesy gave him a strange look. "We don't know that for certain."

Doug felt his irritation rising—as it usually did when Jonesy was around for any length of time. "Then what do you suggest?"

Jonesy ignored him and looked back to Mrs. Deng. "My wantchee go topside, my three piece." He indicated himself, Doug and Lucy with a circular motion of his finger.

The woman stood passive and silent, until Doug saw a coin slide between Jonesy's fingers. The woman took the coin in a smooth motion and put it in the pocket of her apron, then motioned them to follow her into the building.

It never ceased to amaze Doug how easily things came for Jonesy.

The girls had clearly not expected to abandon the apartment. There were dirty dishes in the sink, and all of the cabinets and dresser drawers were full. A bookshelf in the living room was packed with academic books—but when Doug removed one, it was actually a wooden box, filled with pamphlets in Chinese espousing communist ideology.

Lucy came up beside him. "That's interesting. What were they hiding?"

"Communist literature."

"Good hiding place."

She was right, of course. Doug starting pulling books off the shelves, most of which were actual books. But a few others were wooden boxes like the first one, and inside he found different communist pamphlets.

He flipped through the pages of the real books, and in a few he found folded papers stashed, with handwritten Chinese script. None of them made any sense. *Must be in code.*

"What do they say?" Lucy asked over his shoulder.

"I'm not sure. They seem like random words, but there has to be some sort of pattern to them."

Doug had some training in code-cracking, but it would take a considerable amount of time to do it. He collected the folded messages, and stashed them inside his jacket pocket.

"Those might give us clues about some of the recent assassinated Japs," Jonesy said from the far side of the room, where he was looking through kitchen drawers. "Do you think you can figure them out?"

"Maybe," Doug said. "If it's true that she wasn't involved in Nakagawa's murder, then there's not likely to be anything about it."

"Unless one of her roommates killed him," Jonesy said.

Doug considered that a moment, but dismissed it. "She'd have known. I believe she was telling the truth about not knowing anything."

After a few seconds, Jonesy nodded. "Yeah, I believe her, too." He shut the drawer and stood in the middle of the room, hand on his hips, looking around with a dissatisfied expression. "Not much, I'm afraid. Not that I was expecting much—the Reds are a pretty discreet bunch. Those messages are about our only lead, assuming you can decipher them."

"Where to next?" Lucy asked.

Doug was proud of how committed to this she was, and he couldn't help the smile he gave her.

"I'm gonna talk to the neighbors," Jonesy said. He eyed them warily. "I work better alone."

Doug looked at Lucy. "Let's go talk to the police."

Corporal Dunegan became a whole lot more cooperative after Doug slipped him a silver dollar. He flipped open the arrest log and ran his finger down the list.

Then he frowned. "You said the twenty-fifth?"

"That's right. It was this last Friday."

"And you said the name was Wong Mei-ling, female, about twenty-one."

"Yes. She was arrested for murder." Doug watched Dunegan's finger run down the log again, more slowly this time.

"I'm sorry, sir. There's a couple of Wongs here, but they're both blokes, and neither arrested for murder."

Doug felt his heart sink.

"Is there any chance there's an entry under the victim's name?" Lucy asked, hopeful.

"Surname's Nakagawa," Doug said. "Haruto Nakagawa—or perhaps Nakagawa Haruto, the way the Japanese would have written it."

"No, sir. I'm afraid there's nothing." Dunegan looked at him for a second, and Doug wondered what he was thinking. "You sure it was this precinct?"

"Positive," Doug said with a firm nod. "The arrest was in my building, right in the heart of Hongkou."

Dunegan made a face. He glanced around, and motioned for Doug and Lucy to lean close.

"You know they brought in Jap constables and detectives from other precincts during the lockdown, right? Wouldn't let the rest of us out on patrol. I s'pose it's possible they processed her at their own precincts."

Doug gave the corporal a dubious look. "Did they do much of that?"

Dunegan shrugged. "Not that I could tell, sir. Worth a try, though, ain't it?"

By the time they'd trekked out to the East District precinct in Yangtzepoo, and then back-tracked to the Central District precinct downtown, Doug and Lucy were exhausted. After striking out both places, he had no appetite for going uptown to the West District precinct.

"It's clear the Japanese have hushed this up," he muttered to Lucy as they exited the Central precinct. "We're not going to find any records anywhere." *Because Nakagawa was a Japanese spy.*

"Isn't the jail nearby?" Lucy asked. "We could at least try to visit her. Even if she won't tell us anything we don't already know, it would be good to encourage her, don't you think?"

Doug agreed, and they walked to the jail.

"We've got no prisoner by that name," the young British woman wearing a gaoler uniform and a stern expression told them. She had black hair pulled back from her face and tucked under her hat, giving her a severe look.

"Was she released?" Doug asked, incredulous. Surely the Japanese wouldn't have allowed that.

"That information would be in the Records Department." The woman folded her arms across her chest in a way that said she would accept no further inquiries.

Lucy gave her a frosty look. "Thank you. Have a *lovely* day."

Doug grew concerned when the Belgian officer at the Records Department found no release or transfer documents of anyone named Wong Mei-ling. Not surprised any longer, but increasingly concerned.

How could the Japanese make a prisoner disappear? The Shanghai Municipal jail was downtown, well outside of their military occupation of the Hongkou district.

"Is there any other place that a prisoner would be held?" Doug asked.

"No, sir," the officer said in an accent that sounded vaguely French. "If the suspect was arrested in the International Settlement, she would be brought here."

A thought occurred to Doug. "Would a Chinese national be transported to the jail in the Chinese municipality?"

"No, sir. Prisoners who are arrested in the Chinese municipality are taken to their jail, but we do not transport across our boundary."

Doug thanked him, and took Lucy's arm.

"What are you thinking?" Lucy whispered from the side of her mouth as they walked out the door.

Doug waited until they were alone in the corridor. "If the Japanese police handed her over to the *Juntong*, they would have taken her into Chinese territory."

"Because she's a communist."

Doug nodded in silence.

Lucy squeezed his arm tighter, and leaned against him. "If the secret police have her, there's not much hope, is there?"

"No." His voice sounded as grim as he felt.

"We should get some lunch," Lucy said as they stepped out of the jail into the muggy heat of the early afternoon. "Let's find a tavern, and get a sandwich or something."

They walked in silence. Doug's thoughts tumbled around his head, and he struggled to make sense of them. *Something* didn't add up, though.

And then it hit him. He stopped dead in his tracks.

"What is it?" Lucy asked, looking and sounding concerned.

"No one had been in Mei-ling's apartment before us," he said. "It looked like it was just as she and her roommates would have left it."

"That seems right," Lucy said, not seeming to get his meaning.

He pulled her close. "The police hadn't searched it," he whispered. "They should have ransacked it, looking for evidence to convict her of murder. But they didn't."

Lucy looked confused. "I don't understand. I mean, it *is* odd, but I don't know where you're going with that."

"They don't need to get evidence to convict her if they don't take her to trial," Doug said. His brain was racing, formulating the hypothesis. "If the *Juntong* took her, their real aim is to bust the communists in this district. They could kill two birds with one stone if they tell the Japanese they've punished Nakagawa's murderer."

Lucy looked doubtful. "Won't the Japanese demand a public trial? That would mean evidence."

"No," Doug said slowly, still thinking it through. "The *Juntong* will torture her until she reveals the names of her comrades. Once they have no more use for her, they'll kill her. Then they show the body to the Japanese consul, say 'This is Nakagawa's killer,' and everyone's happy."

"Everyone except Wong Mei-ling," Lucy said, crossing her arms and scowling. "I have to say, Douglas Bainbridge, you're being very cavalier about this."

Doug barely heard her, his mind racing ahead, formulating a plan. "Sorry," he said, absently.

She watched him for a moment before asking, "What are you thinking?"

He took her by the shoulders and looked into her eyes. "I think I know how to find out if the *Juntong* have her—but you have to trust me. Will you?"

Hutson

29

"I am glad to hear from you, Bainbridge Douglas."

"It's been a long time, and I've thought about you a lot recently," Doug replied in Mandarin.

"That is kind of you. I have often thought of you, as well." Doug thought he heard a smile in Ming Lin-wen's voice.

He took a breath to steady his nerves. "Months ago, you invited me to tea...and I never accepted."

"That is true."

Doug could imagine the sly smile on her lips. "I'd like to accept your kind offer."

"I'm happy to hear that, Bainbridge Douglas." Now Doug could definitely hear the smile in her voice. "Perhaps Tuesday at three o'clock?"

Doug cringed. That was two days away. Wong Mei-ling had already been missing for two days, and time was not on their side. He closed his eyes and took another breath to steel himself.

"I'd like to see you sooner."

The seconds of silence that followed tied his stomach in knots.

"You are as eager as I am!" She sounded surprised and pleased. "Then, shall we say tomorrow at eleven o'clock? You remember the address."

"Yes, I do. I will be there at eleven tomorrow."

"I look forward to it," she said, and the line clicked off.

Doug returned the receiver to its cradle on Mr. Hwang's desk, and turned around to face Lucy, who stood in front of the closed door. He couldn't read her expression. "It's done."

"I'll have to take the day off work," she said, short.

He arched an eyebrow. "Will that be ok?"

She nodded, her lips set in a thin line. "Now we have to see if Jonesy is on board."

"Oh, you bet I'm in," Jonesy said after Doug explained the plan. "I've got some thoughts on the execution of this whole thing, too."

"Go ahead."

Jonesy explained what he had in mind. "I just wish we had more than twenty-two hours to prepare, but it'll have to do."

Doug had to agree, but it had a good chance of working. "Let's do it."

30

Monday, September 28

Doug could feel his heart in his throat as he raised his hand to knock on Ming Lin-wen's front door.

He leaned his ear to the door after knocking, and listened to the muted footfalls on the polished marble floor of her grand foyer. It wasn't the crisp step of a leather-soled butler—with any luck, Ming Lin-wen had sent away most of the servants, any she couldn't trust to be in the house when she was alone with a male visitor.

He was stunned when the lady of the house herself answered the door. She wore a form-fitting cream and gold *qípáo* that showed every curve to its best appeal, with short sleeves and a hemline at the knees. Her hair was pulled back from her face, and lotus blossoms adorned the clasp behind her head.

"Mr. Bainbridge, welcome," she said in careful English. "I am glad to see you."

"Thank you," he replied, sticking to English for the moment. He glanced around the open central hall, and the balcony of the upstairs hall visible at the top of the double stairs, but saw no one. He looked at her with affected surprise. "Do we have the house all to ourselves?"

She switched to Mandarin, but Doug noticed she lowered her voice. "I sent everyone away—all of the household servants and the gardeners. Only the guards remain, because they do not work for me, and I cannot direct them."

Doug wasn't concerned about the guards; he and Jonesy had taken turns observing the mansion's security detail from a room on the 11th floor of the Broadway Mansions Hotel a half-block to the south. At her own suggestion, Lucy rented a room on the fifth floor of the Astor House Hotel that faced onto Broadway and observed from a different angle.

Doug was confident in the guards' positions and movements around the compound.

"May I mix you a drink?" Ming Lin-wen asked, motioning toward the drawing room where he had taken tea with her and several other people on his last visit, more than a year ago.

"Yes, thank you," he said, keeping the timeline in mind.

"As I recall, you prefer gin with tonic."

Her memory impressed him. "Yes, thank you."

He stood near the window of the drawing room, pretending to admire the grand piano while she mixed his cocktail. If he'd noted their patterns correctly, one of the guards would pass by within the next few minutes; he just needed to keep Lin-wen in here until then so he could confirm.

She sauntered over with his drink a moment later, a cat-like smile curving up the corners of her mouth. But instead of handing it to him, she set it on an end table.

"You should take off your jacket, Douglas," she purred, and slipped her hands under his lapels and up to his shoulders, then took hold of his linen jacket and slid it down his arms. Her smoldering gaze held his while she draped it across the back of a nearby couch, and then handed him his cocktail. "Loosen your tie, make yourself comfortable."

He was conscious not to look nervous as he loosened his necktie and unbuttoned the collar of his shirt. Still, he couldn't help thinking of Lucy.

Lin-wen sat on the couch, still holding his gaze, and crossed her legs in such a way that the hem of her dress slid halfway up her thigh. She took a sip from a glass of wine, and patted the seat next to her.

He sat where indicated, but kept watch on the window from the corner of his eye. From a seated position, he hoped he would still see the top of the guard's head as it passed. He glanced at his wrist watch.

"I hope you are not in a hurry, Douglas," Lin-wen said with a playful swat at his arm.

"Not at all. I need to be back at my office at one o'clock, I'm expecting a shipping manifest."

Just then, the top of the guard's head moved slowly across the bottom of the window, heading toward the front of the compound. He'd round the front of the mansion in a moment, and then they would have twenty minutes.

But Lin-wen had slid toward him. Her knee pressed against his, and her fingers found his shirt buttons and opened the front halfway. Her hands slid over his bare chest, her thumbs rubbing slowly against his nipples, and back again.

His stomach fluttered, and for a second he lost himself in the sensation, as electricity shot through him. Then he forced himself to focus.

"I am glad you called yesterday," she cooed, eyes running down his half-exposed torso.

"I hoped you'd want to see me," he forced himself to say, while he counted seconds in his head until he could politely make his excuse. "May I use your restroom? Before we get too involved, and it becomes, well, difficult."

She gave him a knowing look and nodded. Her hands withdrew, and she pointed toward the door. "Go right from here, to the back of the house, and turn right. You'll find a water closet down the kitchen hall."

He remembered where it was, but thanked her with a bow of his head before hurrying out the door to the hall, re-buttoning his shirt as he walked.

He locked himself inside the WC a moment later, and hurried to the window, which was higher and smaller than the other windows on the ground floor. The window was cranked open, and he stepped onto the commode to look outside.

His timing was perfect. Jonesy was just arriving below the window, with Lucy right behind him.

She wore black slacks and a loose tan blouse, and Jonesy knelt down and locked his hands together to boost her up to the open window. Doug took her hands as she came toward him, and helped her through the narrow opening. He stepped down from the commode as she shimmied through into his arms, and landed lightly on the tile floor.

"Jonesy's right—he'd have a hard time coming in that way," she murmured.

"We haven't got much time," Doug whispered, and gave her a quick peck on the cheek. "Come on."

He opened the door slowly, and glanced around the hall to make sure his hostess hadn't followed him. Assured they were alone, he motioned for Lucy to follow him. They stopped at the corner of the central hall.

"The kitchen must be back that way, and I assume that's where you'll find the back door. The drawing room is that door just there, on the left; that's where I'll be with Miss Ming. The big room opposite it is the dining room. I don't know what's down that corridor over there, so start there once you get Jonesy inside."

"You're sure you'll be alright?" Her eyes looked worried, and she glanced at his loosened necktie.

"I'll be fine. You take care of Jonesy. I've got to get back before she wonders where I've gone."

"Good luck," she said, and gave his hand a quick squeeze as he pulled away.

He unbuttoned his shirt halfway, just as it was when he left a few moments before, and he smiled at Ming Lin-wen as he walked back into the drawing room. "My apologies for the interruption," he said in Mandarin, and retook his seat next to her on the couch.

"No apology needed." She gave him a sly look, and her hand slid up his thigh toward the fly of his pants. "I thought you might return without re-buttoning your trousers." Her fingers worked the buttons through their holes.

Doug's heart pounded. He had to slow her down without seeming to put on the brakes. "Has it been a long time since you were with a man?" Part of him hated himself for asking such a rude question, but he had to slow things down somehow.

Predictably, she withdrew her hand from his fly and slapped him across the face, hard. He'd been expecting it, but it still stung.

"What in impertinent thing to ask!" she hissed, and slid away from him. "It is said that Americans have no tact, but I never believed it."

"Forgive me," he said, making himself look and sound suitably contrite. "I just...well..." He thought fast. "I thought it might be exciting if you described him, and what he did, and then I could picture him here with us." He wanted to cringe.

Her eyes widened in surprise, but then her mouth curved into a pleased smile. "*Together*, Douglas? I am surprised that would interest you."

He made himself look down as if bashful. "Have you...have you ever done that?"

"Oh!" she exclaimed, but sounded more amused than shocked. "You *are* a naughty one!"

Doug felt his confidence return, and he slid his hand across the couch to touch her knee with his fingertips. "What was he like, the last one? Was he blond like me? Or was he dark and handsome, like a Frenchman or an Italian?" *Keep her talking, as long as possible.*

"No, he was not like you. You want me to tell you?"

"Yes, very much."

The look on her face said she had a new appreciation for him. "You must be discreet, of course…"

"Of course." He took her hand in both of his and stared into her dark eyes.

A sly look came to her face. "Would it shock you if I said he was Japanese?"

31

Doug didn't have to fake surprise. "I thought all Chinese hated the Japanese."

She laughed. "That is just politics, Douglas." She slid close to him again, her thigh pressed against his, and undid the rest of his shirt buttons. She slid her hands up his abdomen and circled his pectoral muscles. "He was very handsome—and built much like you. The same muscles. But his skin was darker than yours." She gave him an appraising look as she slid his shirt over his shoulders and down. "You would look striking side-by-side, the two of you."

Doug swallowed the distaste that welled up at the image. "Perhaps sometime soon."

A flash of ice crossed her eyes for a second. "No, that would not be possible."

Doug wondered at the coldness in her voice. "Did your husband find out about him?"

Her cheeks flushed with anger, and her posture stiffened. "We should not discuss my husband."

Idiot! He scolded himself. Of course she wouldn't want to talk about her husband, not under these circumstances. He needed to get it back to that topic, no matter how uncomfortable it made him.

"Let's pretend your Japanese friend were here with us, on this couch. What would I call him?"

The sly smile came back to the corners of her lips, but her eyes remained guarded. "You like this fantasy, I see. I did not give you enough credit, Douglas. I thought you were conventional, but you are like me—you are naughty underneath the proper exterior."

She looked pleased, and he wasn't about to contradict her. Then she waved a dismissive hand. "But Haruto was not good. He tried to boss me, and I am always my own boss." She took Doug's hand, and slid it up her thigh and under her skirt.

His breath came short and fast. He was running out of ways to slow this down.

"I have to tell you something," he blurted.

Her hand stopped pushing his, and she sat very still. "What is it?"

He paused a few seconds, trying to look unsure, but buying himself a little time. "I have a girlfriend," he confessed.

She gave him an amused half-smile. "I know all about her. But I am much prettier than she is. And I am not a filthy communist."

He stared at her for a moment, stunned. She still thought Wong Mei-ling was his girlfriend.

And she knew Mei-ling was a communist.

Lin-wen slid forward, and unfastened his belt. "I am no longer concerned about her," she whispered in Doug's ear, and began to nibble on his ear lobe.

He pulled back before thinking. "I don't like you talking about her that way."

She regarded him with a suspicious frown. "You Americans are far too idealistic, I think. It makes you naïve about certain things."

Doug scowled. "I'm not naïve. I'm here, aren't I? I just don't like you calling my girlfriend a 'filthy communist.'"

"I'm sure she didn't tell you she was a communist," Lin-wen placated, patting his knee. "But she definitely was. Now, let's forget about these unpleasant things, and go back to pleasurable things." Her hand rubbed the length of his penis through his pants.

"I think I need more to drink," Doug said, scooting forward and reaching for his cocktail. He was banking on her sense of hospitality to not get thrown out.

She grabbed his shoulder and pulled him around to face her, spilling his gin and tonic on the rug. Then she grabbed his crotch and squeezed, hard.

"I do not like to be told no, Douglas. I would have thought you'd remember that from last time."

"He said no, so get your hand off of him," Lucy's voice said. He looked over to see her standing in the door, an enormous hardback book in her hand. She was at the couch in two steps, and wacked Ming Lin-wen on the side of the head with the book, hard enough to knock her onto the floor.

Doug jumped up in surprise. Tongue-tied, he couldn't make himself say anything.

Lin-wen's arms moved, and she began to slowly push herself up from the floor, obviously disoriented.

Lucy stepped around the couch and thunked her on the back of the head with the book.

Lin-wen collapsed onto the floor and didn't move.

"Bitch," Lucy muttered, staring down at the sprawled figure. She looked up at Doug, and the corner of her mouth twitched. "Pardon my language."

Hutson

32

"Of course," Doug managed to get out, though his mouth was dry. "I didn't expect you."

"I thought you might be having some trouble," Lucy said, her lips stretching into a half-smile. "Jonesy said he didn't need help, and he agreed with me that you might."

Doug chose to ignore that. "Did you two find anything?"

"We found Wu Shan's office. The door was locked, but I used one of my hairpins to pick it." She wore a satisfied smile. "Jonesy was impressed. Maybe I should be the spy, instead of you," she teased.

"Ha, ha," he replied. "Then what?"

"We found several filing cabinets—all locked, of course. The hairpin came in quite handy. Once we had them all open, Jonesy sent me to check on you while he stayed."

"And you were careful not to leave any fingerprints?"

She gave him a look. "Of course."

"Let's go see what Jonesy found."

Lucy nodded toward Ming Lin-wen's figure on the floor. "What about her? Shouldn't we tie her up or something?"

Doug shook his head. "I don't want her found that way, if we have to leave in a hurry and can't untie her."

"You're the expert," she said with a tiny shrug, and turned toward the door.

Hardly, Doug thought as he followed her out, re-buttoning his shirt.

"You brought him back with you, huh?" Jonesy said, barely glancing up from the pages he'd spread out on a desk. "Must've been in trouble."

"You were right," Lucy said.

"Where's Ming Lin-wen?" Jonesy asked, looking up to fix Doug with a narrow-eyed stare.

"She's knocked out. Miss Kinzler's handiwork."

"Damn," Jonesy muttered, giving Lucy an appreciative look. "Unfortunately, that's going to be a problem for us once she comes to, and tells her husband's security detail."

"We'll have to worry about that later," Doug said, grim. He nodded toward the pages on the desk. "Found anything useful?"

"Lots of photographs of prisoners. Of course, I can't read a damn thing about them, since it's all in Chinese. No photos of Wong Mei-ling, though...yet."

"You can't read any Chinese at all? How many years have you been in China?"

"Four—and don't be a snob."

Doug nodded at the group of documents. "Let me see those." He perused the prisoner descriptions, including the distasteful descriptions of the tortures they were put through, and the information they coughed up. "These are all recent—all in the last three days. And I recognize this one...this one, too. They were comrades of Mei-ling's. I've seen them with her."

"They're sweeping up the cell," Jonesy said, grim.

"Does it say if the *Juntong* got their names from Miss Wong?" Lucy asked.

"No, it doesn't say who betrayed them."

Jonesy frowned. "And Wong Mei-ling wouldn't have betrayed them. She wouldn't crack that fast, she's too strong for that."

Then something caught Doug's eye, and he pulled a folder from a stack on the end of the desk.

"Hey!" Jonesy snapped. "I kept those in order so maybe Wu Shan wouldn't know anyone had looked at them."

"This file is labeled 'Nakagawa Haruto,'" Doug said. His heart pounded as he opened it and read through the pages.

He couldn't believe what he was reading.

"What is it?" Lucy asked, and he realized his mouth was open.

"Ming Lin-wen was spying on Nakagawa."

Hutson

33

"*What?*" Jonesy asked, clearly stunned.

Lucy's mouth hung open, speechless.

"She pretended to be his lover, and copied documents from his office for five months," Doug said. "She stole Japanese military secrets, and intel Nakagawa and Kawakami had on the Chinese government and the communists. You name it. Seems she was her husband's best spy."

"Anything on you?" Jonesy asked.

Doug flipped through the remaining pages, skimming. "No. If Kawakami and Nakagawa had anything on me, she kept it to herself."

"What about Miss Wong?" Lucy asked. "Is there anything about her in there?"

Doug held up a finger while he finished reading.

Then his heart sank.

"You found something," Jonesy prodded.

"Doug, you're white as a sheet," Lucy said, and touched his arm.

Doug felt his throat constrict, but he managed to get the words out. "Wu Shan's report says that after the Taminato assassination on the twenty-third, 'Agent Ming' supplied Nakagawa with the name of a communist agitator in Hongkou..." His throat constricted more, and he swallowed hard. "...whom she identified through observation of an American resident of the area. Agent Ming informed Nakagawa that Wong Mei-ling was the mastermind who planned the attack and hired Axe Gang assassins for the job."

That explained why he'd seen Nakagawa and Kawakami on the street corner that night.

"Oh my God! Doug," Lucy put her hand on his arm and squeezed.

"Damn it!" Jonesy swore. Then he shook his head in resignation. "Well, that's that."

"There's more," Doug croaked. He swallowed again. "Wu Shan wrote that 'Agent Ming eliminated Nakagawa Haruto while he pursued the communist target.' She left evidence by Nakagawa's body to frame Wong Mei-ling."

"Good lord!" Lucy exclaimed, touching her hand to her throat.

"What's it say about her arrest?" Jonesy asked.

Doug read the remainder of the report, then shook his head. "It only says she was arrested, not what happened to her, or where she went."

"She will not come back to Shanghai."

They all spun toward the door at the sound of Ming Lin-wen's voice in English. In her hand she held a 25-caliber ACP Baby Browning.

Just the type of pocket pistol that had killed Nakagawa.

"The Shanghai Municipal Police gave her to the *Juntong*," Lin-wen added, still in English. "They do not let communist agitators return to Shanghai."

"She's innocent," Doug said. "And you framed her for killing Nakagawa."

Ming Lin-wen shot him a condescending scowl. "She is not innocent—she is a communist. They have killed a great many people, Douglas."

"But you killed Nakagawa, she didn't."

"Nakagawa Haruto was a bad man. He deserved what he received."

"But Wong Mei-ling didn't deserve what she got."

"We disagree." Ming Lin-wen's eyes were cold.

"What do you want from us?" Lucy asked, stepping closer to Doug.

"Are you going to turn us over to your husband?" Jonesy asked, and Doug noticed he had begun inching toward Ming Lin-wen.

Lin-wen was looking at Doug, and didn't notice. A strange sort of smile came to her lips. "There is a story in Shanghai that an American spy has Chinese agents go to Japan to watch Japanese navy moves." She looked at Doug. "No one knows who the American is, but they say he speaks excellent Mandarin."

Jonesy glanced at Doug before looking back at Lin-wen. "I've heard that rumor, too."

Lin-wen barely glanced at Jonesy before looking back at Doug. "I am sure there is much information in these pages that this American spy would want. I could look the other way, for a price."

She thinks I'm the spook. Doug decided not to correct her. This could work to their advantage. "What price?"

A salacious gleam came to her eyes, which gave him a quick up-and-down. Then she addressed him in Mandarin. "Your lover is not coming back, Douglas. You will come see me every week, bring me gifts, and do what I ask. Then when I am satisfied with you, you may come here and photograph a file."

"Wong Mei-ling was not my lover." Doug almost said that Lucy was, but stopped at the last moment; that would only put her in unnecessary danger.

"Drop your gun!" Jonesy said, and they all looked over to see him standing a few feet from Lin-wen, his own gun pointed at her head.

It only took her a second to train her pistol on his chest. "If you shoot, we shoot each other, Mr. Jones."

While Lin-wen's concentration was locked on Jonesy, Doug took Lucy's hand and pulled her behind him. Then they slipped around behind Lin-wen's back.

She heard their shuffling feet, and spun around to face them, the pistol momentarily un-aimed.

Jonesy brought his hand up, and dropped it hard, slamming the butt of his gun on Lin-wen's hand.

She cried out in pain. Her pistol dropped to the floor, and fired a shot into the door, sending splinters flying.

Doug kicked the gun away, and it skittered into a corner. He grabbed Lin-wen's arms and held them behind her back.

While Lin-wen struggled against Doug's grip, and cursed them in Mandarin, Lucy hurried to the corner. She took her handkerchief and picked up the Baby Browning.

"I say we turn her over to the Shanghai police as Nakagawa's murderer. With the evidence we found, she'll hang for it."

A derisive laugh escaped Lin-wen's mouth, and she stopped struggling against Doug. "You think I will stay in jail? The 'evidence' you give to the police will be confiscated by the *Juntong* before morning, and I will be free. Then the *Juntong* will come for you. You will not be able to hide from them."

"Then we kill you, dump your body in the river, and get on the next boat to Manila," Jonesy said, cold as January, and Doug wondered if he were serious instead of bluffing.

"Perhaps we can come to a better arrangement," Doug offered. He switched to Mandarin to mutter in her ear, "I will not do what you asked earlier, under any circumstances." Then back to English, "We let you live, and stay free. We say nothing to anyone about you killing Nakagawa. You find out for us where Wong Mei-ling is, and everyone forgets this happened."

Another derisive laugh came from her. "Even if she is alive, I could not find out where she is. And if I could, what good would it do you? You could not free her from the *Juntong*."

She was right, but Doug couldn't bring himself to admit it out loud. His heart sank. Mei-ling was gone, and there was nothing they could do.

"What price do you want from the American spy for the information in this room?" Lucy asked, her voice level and cool, and Doug couldn't keep from smiling at her.

That's my girl.

They came to an arrangement.

While Lucy kept Lin-wen's gun pointed at her, Doug and Jonesy photographed all of the files Jonesy had pulled from the cabinets, which used up all of their film anyway. Doug promised a transfer of U.S. dollars to an account at the HSBC the next day, after he had delivered the film safely to the American embassy in Nanjing.

As a last precaution, Doug emptied the magazine of the Baby Browning into his hand, and shoved the bullets into his pocket before handing the empty pistol back to Lin-wen.

They slipped out the front door after the guards rounded the side of the house, and ran for the front gate.

Once they were safely on Broadway in front of the compound's wall, Doug turned to Jonesy.

"Lucy and I will go straight to the station, and get on the next train to Nanking. You see if you can locate anyone from Wong Mei-ling's cell. They'll be deeply hidden, if they're alive."

Jonesy gave him a boastful half-grin. "I have my ways."

Doug knew that was true. "Stay safe, and we'll meet you at the Cathay at noon on Thursday."

Jonesy touched two fingers to his brow in a sort of salute, and rushed off toward the Garden Bridge and downtown.

Doug took Lucy by the hand and hailed a motor cab in front of the Broadway Mansions Hotel. They scrambled into the back. "Train station, and hurry."

Hutson

34

Tuesday, September 29

"This is incredible, Bainbridge," Commander Shock told Doug the next morning. "Your observations of the Japanese marines will be invaluable. I'm not sure what we'd do with most of the rest of this, though. The communist files are interesting, but none of this is naval."

It was after five o'clock when Doug and Lucy arrived at the American embassy in Nanjing on Monday, and most of the staff had left. It took a little effort, but Doug was able to convince a Third Secretary to lock up the film and call Shock to arrange a meeting first thing in the morning.

The naval attaché wouldn't meet with an unauthorized civilian, so Doug had to leave Lucy in the lobby. She understood, but he knew she wasn't thrilled about it.

"If you shared the intel with the staff at the embassy, it might put State in our debt," Doug suggested. "And there's more where this came from, as long as my source continues to cooperate."

"You said it's a disgruntled wife," Shock said, looking doubtful. "Those can be fickle sources. Be very careful. You don't have diplomatic immunity, so if you get charged with espionage, we can't help you."

"I understand, sir."

"And keep in mind that she killed a Japanese spy. Who's to say she won't eventually try to do the same thing to an American spook?"

Lying awake much of the night, with Lucy asleep beside him in the hotel room they'd checked into as "Mr. and Mrs. Jones," Doug had come to grips with the reality that he was in fact now an American spook, like it or not.

And he was certain Jonesy would never let him live that down.

"I'll be careful, sir."

"Also, State's still squeamish about stealing other countries' secrets," Shock said with a condescending scowl. "But that's their problem, not ours."

"About the payment to my source…" Doug said, tentative.

"Yes—a thousand dollars. Seems pretty steep, but it might be worth it, once we've analyzed everything. And maybe we can get State to subsidize some of the cost, since most of this is going to be in their playing field."

"I promised her the transfer would be made today," Doug reminded his boss.

"I'll take care of it," Shock said. "We'll worry about the accounting later. But remember we still have to be mindful of the budget. The taxpayers are trusting us not to waste their hard-earned dollars, so I'm not authorizing any further expenditures until we've fully analyzed all of this intel and determined its value—either to us, or to State."

"Yes, sir. I understand."

"If either ONI or State authorizes another acquisition, I'll send you a telegram telling you to buy the picture. If I don't quote a price, it's the same."

"Thank you, sir."

Shock stood, and returned Doug's salute. "Good work, Bainbridge."

"Well?" Lucy whispered when he reached the lobby and she took his arm.

"They'll let me know soon if we're in business."

She nodded, but her silence as they walked out of the embassy seemed tense. He touched her hand. "Are you ok?"

"Yes—well, mostly. I'm afraid for Miss Wong. We'll probably never know what happened to her, but I think we both know it's not good."

He nodded in silent agreement. That undeniable truth had left him with an overriding sense of melancholy, sharing uneasy space next to his pleasure at presenting his boss with a treasure trove of secret Chinese intelligence.

He looked off at Nanjing's ancient and formidable walls—fifty feet high and forty feet thick—visible from any point in the city. "We have a few hours until the afternoon train," he said. "Care to do a little sight-seeing before we leave?"

Lucy's face brightened a bit. "It's my first time in Nanking. Mother and I never came here last summer. I would love to see Sun Yat-sen's tomb. And maybe the government buildings, if there's time."

"Dr. Sun's tomb it is," Doug said, giving her a smile in spite of the pervasive melancholy he couldn't quite shake. He steered them toward the Gate of Great Peace.

They arrived back in Shanghai at three o'clock after a two-hour train ride. "Can I put you in a cab by yourself?" Doug asked Lucy as they walked across the grand hall. "I have something I want to do, but I'll swing by your apartment before dinner."

"That's fine," she said, and stopped in the middle of the hall to touch his cheek and stare into his eyes for a few seconds. "I was afraid for you yesterday."

He gave her a cocky grin that he didn't quite feel. Then he laughed at himself and admitted, "Yeah, I was, too." He gave her a kiss, and led her out to the line of waiting motor cabs.

"Doug! I wasn't expecting you." The look on Kenny's face when he opened his office door made that obvious enough. "You haven't been in your office since you were released. I wondered if you might be avoiding the building."

He didn't say "avoiding me," but Doug imagined that's what he was thinking.

"No, I had something important I had to do." Doug stood awkwardly in the door for a moment before asking, "May I come in?"

Kenny blushed and stepped aside. "Yes, of course you can. I'm sorry—I don't know where my mind is. Do come in."

"Kenny, I've been a world-class ass the last couple of weeks, and I'm sorry," Doug said after Kenny closed the door.

Kenny looked embarrassed, and looked away. "Thank you for saying so. I appreciate and accept your apology."

Doug took a half-step to his right, putting himself in front of Kenny's gaze again. "You and Abbie are like family to me, and I don't know how I could have gotten through this last year without your friendship and support. You both mean the world to me, I want you to know that. I'm sorry I haven't shown it much lately."

"I understand," Kenny replied, barely more than a whisper.

Doug took a few seconds to search for adequate words to express what he wanted to say. "I'm not very close with my brother, you know. We don't write each other often, or say very much when we do. We haven't been close for years, and, well…"

Kenny's cheeks were crimson, but he looked Doug in the eye as if in anticipation of every word.

"I just—I love you, Kenny. Sometimes I wish you were my brother instead of Will."

Kenny blinked rapidly, his eyes getting wet, and he looked away and cleared his throat. "I don't have a brother, myself, only sisters—but I know how you feel. Thank you, Dougie."

Doug took two steps forward before he could change his mind, and put his arms around his tall friend for a moment. After a few seconds' hesitation, Kenny's arms encircled him, and he squeezed Doug tight.

Just when it began to feel embarrassing, Doug released his arms and took a step back. Kenny looked away and cleared his throat again.

"Dinner tonight?" Kenny asked, staring at his desk. "Table for four at Velardi's?"

Doug grinned. "That sounds swell. Seven-thirty, Lucy and I will meet you there."

He patted his friend on the back and let himself out.

Thursday, October 1

"I got an unexpected visit at home yesterday, before dawn," Jonesy whispered when Doug took the seat next to him at the bar in the Cathay two days later. "From Wu Shan and three of his goons."

Doug felt his heart skip a beat, but forced himself to remain calm. "Oh? Need I ask what they wanted? You look like you're in one piece, at least."

"In short, if I write anything about Ming Lin-wen killing Nakagawa, and framing Wong Mei-ling, they will kick me out of the country—*after* they rearrange my face." Jonesy took a long pull from the half-empty martini in front of him.

"I take it you're going into hiding soon?"

Jonesy snorted, and shook his head. "No, I'm killing the story. I'm not an idiot."

Doug was shocked. "I thought you were a journalistic warrior, speaking out against the powerful," he said. "Weren't you the one who said he used to defy threats from business owners and Pinkerton detectives, and exposed their heavy-handed violence against union strikers?"

"I was young and stupid then," Jonesy said, a wry half-smile briefly passing across his lips before turning serious again. "I've learned it's better to live and fight another day. Who knows? Maybe I'll write the story someday, when I'm safely back in the States."

"Does that mean you don't want to go with me the next time I go to Miss Ming's mansion to photograph Wu Shan's files?" Doug had received the telegram from Commander Shock that morning with the go-ahead to continue.

"I wouldn't go that far," Jonesy said with a chuckle. "Besides, I have a personal interest in finding out if the local *Juntong* have been tracking a certain Soviet GRU agent. You can translate for me."

Doug shook his head and sighed. "Do I want to know?"

"Absolutely not. Now tell me about Nanking."

Friday, October 2

"Hey, it's Doug and Lucy!"

Pete's excitement made Doug smile, as did the chorus of cheers from their friends. Pete came up and slapped him on the back, a touch too hard, but Doug didn't complain. "How the hell are you, Dougie? We haven't seen you in a couple of weeks. But I know there was a bit of excitement in your neck of the woods last week, so you're off the hook."

"Yes, that must have been terrifying!" Julia chimed in, touching the double-strand of pearls at her throat. "We even heard that you had been *arrested* for trying to kill a Japanese man. That must have been *awful* for you, Douglas."

The look in her eyes told Doug that she might have been genuinely concerned—but once she knew he was alright it was now something exciting to dish about.

"I won't want to repeat the experience, that's certain. But Kenny here got me cleared of the charges." He put his arm around his tall friend's shoulders.

"They were ridiculous charges," Kenny said with embarrassed modesty.

"We're all glad you're both safe," Betty said, taking Lucy's arm and patting her hand.

"Speaking of the man Doug was accused of trying to kill," George said in his rich baritone, which always got everyone's attention. "You might be interested to know that Takahiro Kawakami came out of his coma yesterday morning."

"That's wonderful news," Doug said, not sure if it was good news or not. "Is he out of the woods, then?"

"He's still in pretty serious condition, but not critical," George said. Betty beamed up at him proudly. Then George frowned before continuing, "But the strangest thing happened a few hours later. A Japanese doctor—who doesn't work at St. Luke's, I found out later— came and took over Mr. Kawakami's case. When I came back from my rounds, his bed was empty. The charge nurse said a group of Japanese orderlies took him away. She didn't recognize any of them. What do you make of that?"

"He must be someone important," Julia said, and took a sip of her champagne cocktail.

"Maybe a spy!" Abbie said, excited.

Kenny glanced at Doug before patting his wife's arm. "I think you've read too many Eric Ambler novels, dear."

Abbie laughed at herself. "Yes, probably."

Lucy flashed Doug a knowing look while everyone laughed, and slid her arm through his.

He loved that they shared the secret.

Hutson

EPILOGUE

Saturday, November 21, 1936
Wuzhou, Guangxi Province, southern China
11 PM

The Nationalist security agents wore no identifying uniform, but there was no mistaking who they were as they stalked up Taidong street toward the riverfront inn, and the crowds of late-night revelers fell silent and parted for them, avoiding eye contact.

They knew which room, and marched to it and pounded on the door. The sound of men's drunken voices singing a bawdy song stopped. A young woman answered a few second later, and the quick look that passed between her and Captain Chen said that she'd been expecting them.

She stepped aside.

Wang Yaqiao sat cross-legged on the floor between two men in army uniforms, all staring bleary-eyed at the five men in suits. Sudden recognition dawned as the men drew their guns.

Five shots were heard on the street. Police ran to the inn within minutes. They found an open door, and pushed through the gawkers to find the room empty—except for the body of Wang Yaqiao lying in a pool of blood.

END

Thank you for reading Assassin's Hood. If you enjoyed this book, please tell a friend, update your social media, and/or write a review on Amazon, Goodreads, or other forum.

Be sure to check out the next adventures of Doug, Lucy, Jonesy and their friends in **No Accidental Death**, book three of the Death in Shanghai series.

Questions or comments? Feel free to contact me at
www.garretthutson.com

Also by Garrett Hutson:

In A Safe Town

The Jade Dragon

No Accidental Death

Hidden Among Us

Spy Tango

The Swiss Conspiracy

Gray Paree

About the Author

Garrett Hutson writes upmarket mysteries and historical spy fiction. He lives in Indianapolis with his husband and their four dogs and two cats. He has one grown daughter. You may contact him at his website, www.garretthutson.com.

Afterword

This is a work of fiction, and the characters and events portrayed are fictitious, although I have alluded to some real historical events and persons.

When I have alluded to historical figures in the story—except as noted below—the real people alluded to are **not** portrayed as characters, and are, to the best of my ability, discussed by the characters in their correct historical context. Examples include President Franklin Roosevelt, Chiang Kai-shek, Dai Li, Wang Yaqiao, Jin Shixin, and the Japanese victims of Chinese assassins (Hideo Nakayama, Kosaku Kayao, Junzo Nakano, Niwajiro Yoshioka, Tomomitsu Taminato, Yoshitune Yawata, and Yoshimi Ideriha).

Thomas Macy Shock, who served as the U.S. Assistant Naval Attaché to China in 1936 and held the rank of Commander at that time, is the only historical figure who makes an actual appearance in this story. Everyone else is fictitious.

The clandestine tracking of Japanese naval maneuvers by Chinese agents working for a "retired" Marine officer, starting in September 1935, was a real operation, and it represented the first foray by the Office of Naval Intelligence into clandestine spycraft. The marine officer who ran the operation out of Shanghai was Major General William A. Worton, and he recounted his experiences in 1969 during an oral history interview with Benis M. Frank of the U.S. Marine Corps Historical Center. As portrayed in this book, his identity was a closely-kept secret, which is why Doug never learns his name during this story.

The August First Declaration was real. There is documentation that agents of the Chinese Communist Party were among the assassins who killed Japanese nationals in 1935 and 1936. There is also documented evidence that Wang Yaqiao himself was the assassin who killed Kosaku Kayao in Shanghai on July 10, 1936. I have used my imagination to describe the cooperation of the Chinese communists with Wang's Axe Gang, and I believe it's a plausible explanation.

The assassination of Haruto Nakagawa (or Nakagawa Haruto, as the Japanese would render it) is fictitious, as is the attack on Kawakami. Both Nakagawa and Kawakami are products of my imagination, and are not based on any real people.

As always, I have done my best to be as historically accurate as possible, except where noted above. Any errors are mine alone.

Acknowledgments

I started work on this story in October 2017. I wanted to write a sequel to *The Jade Dragon*, and I knew there was a lot more I wanted to do with those characters (especially Doug and Lucy). Then during research about the Japanese invasion in 1937, I stumbled across the series of assassinations of Japanese nationals in southern China in 1936—mostly in Shanghai—that formed the basis for this novel. Once I discovered that Japanese marines twice occupied parts of the International Settlement in Shanghai in response to attacks on Japanese navy sailors, I knew I had to put Doug into the middle of this. I couldn't wait until November and NaNoWriMo to get into it, so I started writing.

Many people contributed to the development of this book in ways big and small. As always, many thanks to my awesome partners in the IndyScribes critique group—Laura VanArendonk Baugh, Stephanie Cain, Stephanie Ferguson, Marcia Kelly, Peggy Larkin, Jim Meeks-Johnson, and Jim Thompson—who patiently read and critiqued many sections of the first draft, and provided excellent feedback. You all are the best!

I will always owe a debt of gratitude to the wonderful people at Midwest Writers Workshop for making me the writer that I am today. I eagerly await the return of MWW this summer, and I look forward to seeing old friends and making new ones.

My deepest thanks to Brenda Havens, Stephanie Cain, and Peggy Larking, who took the time to read the entire manuscript and provide valuable insights and feedback. You are all amazing, and you helped bring out the best in this story. It is definitely better for your comments. Steph, I have to repeat that your productivity as a writer amazes and inspires me.

Thanks to Steven Novak for another amazing cover.

Thank you to my long-time close friends, who have taught me the meaning of "found family" for twenty-plus years. You know who you are. That notion of "found family" is so important in my life, and I hope I've done justice to it in this story of Doug Bainbridge and his friends.

And lastly, most importantly, my eternal gratitude and devotion to my husband David Lee, for letting me live the crazy, frustrating, exhilarating, depressing, wonderful life of a writer without complaint, and always being supportive through all of its myriad ups and downs. I love you more every day, far more than you can know.

-Garrett B. Hutson, June 2019

www.ingramcontent.com/pod-product-compliance
Lightning Source LLC
Chambersburg PA
CBHW072008110726
47910CB00005B/1689